THE TRUTH ABOUT FAMILY

A PRIDE AND PREJUDICE VAGARY

LUCY MARIN

Quills & Quartos
PUBLISHING

Edited by Debbie Styne and Mary McLaughlin

Cover by Penny Dreadful Book Covers

ISBN 978-1-956613-55-1 (ebook) and 978-1-956613-56-8 (paperback)

The Truth About Family was written in the shadow of the COVID-19 pandemic, and I dedicate it to my human loves, B & A, and my furry loves, C & G, for making lockdowns and stay-at-home orders bearable.

ONE

Early 1811, London

Elizabeth Bennet had been in town three days when the moment she had most anticipated arrived. She was conversing with her dearest friend, Miss Rebecca Darcy, in the drawing room of the Curzon Street townhouse when three gentlemen entered.

Elizabeth's eyes were immediately drawn to Fitzwilliam Darcy. Keeping her welcoming smile merely friendly and disguising the wild joy she felt was challenging. Only a few months had passed since they were last together, but it might as well have been a decade as far as her heart was concerned. Darcy, six and twenty, tall and with a long, athletic build, dark hair, fine patrician features, and an excellent character, was Elizabeth's ideal of a gentleman.

Heat rose from her belly to her cheeks as she regarded Darcy, and she prayed her face would not colour and betray more than she wanted anyone, especially him, to see.

"You are well, I hope, Elizabeth?" he asked politely.

"Very well, now that you have returned my foster brothers to me. And you?"

When Darcy glanced at Colonel Fitzwilliam, she saw a flash of concern pass over his countenance. Fitzwilliam had served in the Peninsula, only returning to England recently. Viscount Bramwell, the colonel's brother, and Darcy had gone to meet him and escort him to town.

Elizabeth studied Fitzwilliam, noticing how wan he looked, and missed Darcy's mumbled response. All five of them got caught up in the general conversation, and he did not address her directly again for some time.

"How long will you stay in town?" he asked.

"I shall be here until Easter, after which I return to Romsley Hall." Of course, it was entirely possible Lord and Lady Romsley would receive an invitation to spend the holiday elsewhere and make other arrangements for her. She did not expect them to consult her about it first.

The viscount clapped his hands together, evidently overhearing. "That gives us almost three months. How shall we amuse ourselves? It is the first time we have all been in town since Elizabeth was fifteen, and we ought to make the most of it."

"Unfortunately, it must begin with dinner in Grosvenor Square this evening," Fitzwilliam said. "Mother wants everyone there, no doubt to make Lady Catherine's presence easier to tolerate. Have you seen her?"

His question was directed at Elizabeth, who shook her head. "I did know she was here, however. Your mother told us when we went shopping today."

Lady Romsley said her sister-in-law was not pleased to be abandoned while the countess went to look at fabrics and various accoutrements, but she refused to break the appointment. Elizabeth suspected if it had been just the two of them going on the excursion, Lady Romsley might have felt differently, but no right-thinking person would miss an opportunity to see Rebecca or her mother, Mrs Julia Darcy.

"She returns to Kent tomorrow, unless Lady Anne asks her to stay with you at Berkeley Square," Bramwell explained, referring to the Darcy townhouse.

Darcy scowled. "If she does, I shall seek a bed here, if my aunt and uncle will have me, or at an inn."

Elizabeth laughed. "A grown man forced from his home by two middle-aged ladies? What a terrible crime that would be!" Her tease brought a smile to his face, and she was satisfied. "Let us return to Bramwell's question. I would much rather think about all the fun we shall have than Lady Catherine de Bourgh."

⁓

Elizabeth had first met Darcy and the other members of his family when she was a child of five years old. She was sent to live at the Romsley family estate in Worcestershire with the dowager countess, Lady Romsley, Darcy's grandmother. That lady was also a childhood friend of Elizabeth's paternal grandmother, and the pair had arranged the scheme because Elizabeth's mother did not like her and was cruel in her rejection.

Elizabeth was supposed to remain with the dowager countess long enough for Mrs Bennet to successfully deliver the baby she was then carrying. Because Mr Bennet's estate was entailed, they were desperate for her to bear a son, and Mrs Bennet claimed Elizabeth's presence agitated her and was a risk to her health.

In her memory, Elizabeth could hear her grandmother and father saying, 'It is not forever. Less than a year, and you will be home again'. But Elizabeth never returned to Longbourn, and none of the Bennets ever visited her.

Although naturally frightened and confused at first, Elizabeth was not formed for unhappiness, and soon, in the way young children can, she became engrossed in what was immediately in front of her—her bright, fine room in the dower house, the Romsley estate, which offered great scope for exploration, lessons with her governess, and childish letters to and from Rebecca, whom she had met within a week of leaving Hertfordshire.

The introduction happened when the dowager countess and Elizabeth attended the annual gathering of the Fitzwilliam and Darcy families at Pemberley, located only fifty miles from Romsley Hall. Rebecca's father, Frederick, was brother to Darcy's father, Hugh. Darcy's mother, Lady Anne, was one of the dowager countess's three children, the others being the present earl and Lady Catherine de Bourgh, who lived in Kent.

The dowager countess was patient with Elizabeth, and she was embraced by both Mr Darcys and Mrs Darcy. Lord and Lady Romsley were amiable if aloof towards Elizabeth, but Lady Catherine had taken an instant dislike to her, and where she led, her younger sister followed. They disapproved of their mother taking in a child who was not related to them and from a family situation they found repugnant. It was enough that the Bennets were comparatively poor and so much their social inferiors, but when Mrs Bennet's connexions to trade were added to the mix, they saw no reason to like Elizabeth. If anything, they worried about her being in company with their vastly superior children, certain she would take advantage of her good fortune in living amongst them.

Elizabeth and Rebecca were instant friends, having discovered a shared love of exploring the natural world and reading. For the almost fifteen years since that first meeting, they had been as close as sisters. The only other young people in the family were Miss Anne de Bourgh, as unpleasant a girl as possible to imagine, the earl and countess's two sons, and Darcy—all of whom were considerably older than Elizabeth and Rebecca. Anne had no interest in the younger girls, and while the boys were kind, they were not suitable playmates.

Until Elizabeth was eighteen, she and Darcy had not spent

much time in each other's company. For many years, she only saw him when the extended family gathered in the summer or autumn, or for a few scattered days here and there. At those occasions, he was mostly occupied with Viscount Bramwell and Colonel Fitzwilliam and hardly seemed to notice her.

Bramwell and Fitzwilliam had taken a brotherly interest in her almost from the beginning, but especially when the dowager countess died, and after some discussion amongst the adults about what to do with Elizabeth, she had gone to live at Romsley Hall with the earl and countess. A decade later, she remained their ward.

Fitzwilliam, who had overheard some of the adults' conversation, told Elizabeth that Lady Catherine had argued she should be sent back to the Bennets, having 'relied on our charity long enough'. Darcy's father refused to permit it, saying the Bennets had shown no interest in her, and they had no reason to suppose Longbourn would be a healthful home for Elizabeth. Rebecca's mother and father wanted Elizabeth to live in town with them, but the country was deemed a more suitable situation for the ten year old.

"Uncle Darcy wants you to live at Pemberley," Fitzwilliam had told her, "but Lady Anne will not hear of it. I am sorry, Elizabeth, but Bramwell and I are glad you will stay with us."

Romsley Hall was a grand place to call home, and Elizabeth was grateful to the earl and countess. They, like the dowager countess before them, ensured she had everything she needed, from an excellent education to fine clothes. She even supposed they liked and cared for her, but she was an unexpected responsibility, and they had busy, active lives and little time or inclination to be parents to her.

As for the Bennets, she seldom thought about them and heard from them even less, exchanging perhaps a handful of letters a year with Mr Bennet or her elder sister, Jane. Upon occasion, Elizabeth dreamt of Longbourn and reacquainting herself with the Bennets, especially the four girls who were her sisters. Only her memories of Jane were strong. Mary and Catherine—Kitty—were babies when Elizabeth was sent away, and Lydia had not yet been born.

She did not know when, but she was convinced that one day she would see her true family and home again.

＊ ～～～ ＊

Preparing to enter the drawing room at the Romsleys' townhouse in Grosvenor Square later that day, Elizabeth dreaded seeing Lady Catherine. The woman had earned her distaste not only for her own mistreatment but also for her insistence that Darcy marry her daughter, a scheme Lady Anne fully endorsed. That Darcy had no intention of doing so had never been sufficient to stop his mother and aunt's persistent demands of him.

She heard Lady Catherine's strident tones through the door. "I cannot imagine why you still keep her. She is twenty years old, surely old enough to *finally* return to her people."

The countess replied, "She will remain in town until Easter, mostly with Mrs Darcy, so she and Miss Darcy can amuse themselves. The earl and I decided it would do her good to see more of society."

"This is not *her* society. You may have forgotten her origins, but *I* have not." Lady Catherine continued. "She must rejoice to have such a treat. What has she ever done to deserve it? I warn you, it will only make her think herself above her station. You were wrong to do it."

Elizabeth sighed. None of the sentiments were new to her, and she was mostly inured to the sting of them, but it disheartened her a little. She had hoped to escape Lady Catherine's notice for the evening, but she accepted it was too much good fortune for anyone to expect.

She pushed open the door and saw Lady Anne sitting beside her sister. Elizabeth recalled the first time they met. To five-year-old Elizabeth, she was the loveliest, most graceful woman ever, and Elizabeth was immediately drawn to her, but it was apparent she did not return the feelings. Even then, Lady Anne had ignored Elizabeth.

During a picnic, Rebecca collected a bouquet of wild-flowers for her mother, and Elizabeth followed suit with some for Lady Romsley, who had called her sweet, and Lady Anne, who stared at the collection of colourful summer blossoms before turning away. Only years later did Elizabeth learn that Lady Anne had recently suffered a grievous loss—a stillborn daughter. At the time, the rejection was painful for Elizabeth who had, after all, just been sent away from her home because her mother despised her.

There were moments, admittedly rare, when Elizabeth convinced herself Lady Anne felt some measure of affection for her. The earl and countess often sent her to Pemberley to keep Lady Anne company when her husband was away from home or when they were absent from Romsley Hall for a prolonged period and did not want her to be alone.

Of late, Elizabeth found it increasingly difficult to know what Lady Anne felt. Whenever they were together, the woman regarded her with an unreadable expression—apart from those times when her beauty was marred by scowls that left Elizabeth questioning if she had done something to offend her.

Elizabeth approached Lady Anne and curtseyed. Her eyes ran from Elizabeth's hair to the tips of her shoes and back again, and she answered Elizabeth's enquiry about her health with a curt nod before again turning to her sister.

Looking around the room, Elizabeth saw everyone she expected. Darcy stood behind the settee on which his mother and Lady Catherine sat, and he nodded when their eyes met. Lord Romsley stood with his sons in the corner. When her gaze settled on the colonel, he made a silly expression, just as he had done when she was a child, and he wanted to erase the sting of someone's slight towards her. She smiled in reply, and moved to join the three gentlemen to await the call into dinner. Bramwell gave her a quick kiss on the cheek then went to Rebecca, and the earl began a conversation with the elder Mr Darcy.

"We shall be a merry party this evening, do you not think?" There was a touch of bitterness in Fitzwilliam's tone she was not used to hearing. Before she could remark on it, he shook his head. "Pay no attention to me. Too much of my aunt's company has given me a headache."

"I am afraid you are hours away from any possible cure."

He gave her arm a quick squeeze. "It will be better now that you and the others are here." As though to force himself into good humour, he sniggered and indicated the remainder of their party. "Look at them. My brother is doing everything possible to show his intentions towards Rebecca. I would say it is mostly in defiance of Lady Catherine, who let us all know how little she likes the prospect of that possible, dare I say probable, match.

"I feel most sorry for Darcy. He and Lady Anne arrived an hour ago, and both she and Lady Catherine have hardly allowed him to say a word to anyone else. If he has to tolerate much more of it, I am afraid his hair will start to turn white from the strain of their company."

Dinner soon began, and during it, Lady Catherine's voice was most often heard, the earl or countess occasionally interceding to nudge her endless remarks and observations along a less tedious line. Sipping her wine and taking small bites of her food, which was all Elizabeth could manage under the circumstances, she held an inner debate on whether Rebecca's family—whom Lady Catherine pointedly ignored—were more fortunate or if *she* ought to feel grateful for each of the woman's scowls because at least it meant Lady Catherine recognised her existence. The only person to whom she showed any kindness was Lady Anne, though even with her sister, her manner was imperious. *Why,* Elizabeth wondered, *did she tolerate it?*

Lady Anne sat as she always did—her back straight and muscles seemingly so taut Elizabeth was certain she would hear one snap if Lady Anne moved even a fraction of an inch incorrectly. It did not matter with whom she was in company. The only time she appeared to be even slightly at ease was when she had her son by her side. Any sympathy Elizabeth might have extended to Lady Anne was dampened by the look of mistrust and anger she levelled at her, whose only crime— as far as she could tell—was sitting beside Darcy. Was she so jealous that he might talk to her for a minute or two? She could hardly suppose they were flirting with each other, let alone forming an attachment. Even the thought of it made Elizabeth blush, and she hastily took up her glass and used it to hide her face.

Elizabeth had a secret, one she had not even told Rebecca. She was deeply in love with Fitzwilliam Darcy and had been since she was eighteen. Despite fighting against it and attempting to convince herself it was simply infatuation, nothing she had considered and none of the separations they had faced had dampened her sentiments.

Her affection for him had grown during the months she spent at Pemberley after his father's death two years prior. She and Darcy walked and rode together, talked about the estate, their memories of his father, and all manner of subjects. He was considerate and intelligent, interesting and handsome—how could she not love him?

It was an impossible situation. He was destined for a very different sort of bride, and the family would never accept their union—even had he returned her affection, which he gave no indication of doing. If he did and proposed, she would accept him and hope for the best. What would she care for anyone's disapproval if she could be Mrs Darcy?

Midway through dinner, Darcy addressed her. "I was calculating, and we last saw each other almost five months ago."

Elizabeth nodded. "At Pemberley."

He smiled. "We were fortunate in the weather, except for one day. Do you remember that ride?"

She laughed. "I am unlikely to forget."

Darcy, Bramwell, and she were caught in a sudden downpour far from the house. Rebecca was not with them, not being much of a horsewoman. They were soaked and covered in mud when they reached the house. It had been oddly exhilarating.

"Tell me what you have been doing with yourself."

"What I always do. I am afraid age has not yet taught me to be lazy."

Elizabeth busied herself around Romsley Hall, taking on some of the duties for which Lady Romsley often did not have time, including settling squabbles amongst the servants, visiting tenants, involving herself in charitable works, to say nothing of walking and riding for exercise and playing the pianoforte, which was one of her favourite pastimes.

"We were fortunate with the weather in October and November, and I spent as much time as I could outside, which I suppose is not a surprise."

"My father always said you would *live* in the open air, if it were not impractical."

Elizabeth inclined her head in agreement. "I should say I have been improving my mind by extensive reading. That will give you a better impression of me." He chuckled at her teasing words, and she continued. "Last autumn, for some reason, I decided to reread all of Shakespeare's dramas. I forgot how many deaths there are in them!"

"You ought to alternate a tragedy with a comedy, at the very least."

"What a wise suggestion! I shall be sure to remember it. What has occupied your time?"

As he told her about being at Pemberley and visiting friends, Elizabeth sensed someone's eyes on her. A quick look at their company showed that Lady Catherine had joined her sister in glaring at her. Elizabeth turned away at once. Her appetite dissolved, and although she still listened to Darcy, she could no longer respond with the same enthusiasm.

When they were settled in the drawing room later that evening, Rebecca and Elizabeth entertained the company with music, playing duets at the pianoforte. Rebecca was a very good musician, but Elizabeth was acknowledged as the more accomplished, for she had a genuine feel for music and devoted more of her time to developing her skills. The dowager Lady Romsley had been a great lover of music and insisted Elizabeth begin lessons at the pianoforte and singing as soon as she came to live with her. It was an interest shared by Lady Anne, but not Lady Catherine who—according to the dowager countess—had given up lessons when her younger sister showed more aptitude for it. After the duets, Elizabeth continued to play and sing, while Rebecca turned the pages for her. Lady Catherine's voice filled the room, almost as though she hoped to drown out the sound of Elizabeth's mezzo-soprano.

"Anne is doing exceptionally well, as I was saying at dinner. Her health has improved greatly under Mr Patterson's care, just as I knew it would. You know how adept I am at determining the quality of a person, be they low born or high. 'Mr Patterson,' I said to him upon our first meeting, 'you are just what my dear daughter needs.' I suppose they," her voice grew deeper as she indicated Elizabeth and Rebecca, "are competent. My Anne would have been an exceptional performer, had her health allowed. It is regrettable Mr Patterson did not come to my knowledge sooner, but such is life. Anne has greater recommendations to her than being able to accurately press a few keys on a pianoforte. She is blossoming, as you will see when you and Darcy come to Rosings at Easter, Sister."

Elizabeth glanced at Darcy, who once again stood beside where his mother and aunt sat. Even at a distance, she saw his jaw tighten, his expression like stone. She could not understand why his mother, who she knew loved him, would continue to press him when he showed no interest in marrying his cousin. Elizabeth pushed aside the sudden emptiness she felt and returned to her song.

Once it was finished, she stood from the instrument. "I am afraid my throat is dry. I long for a cup of tea."

"I shall get you one," Fitzwilliam said, as he gestured for her and Rebecca to join him across the room. Darcy watched them, and a stab of sympathy pierced Elizabeth's heart. She smiled at him, for whatever comfort it provided.

I pray he does not succumb to his mother and aunt's demands and marry Anne de Bourgh.

He would never be happy with her as his wife. But, even if he did not marry Anne, he would select a lady such as her—

one of excellent birth and great fortune. As she sat, Elizabeth lowered her chin for a moment and pressed her eyes closed. She had seen the burdens Darcy carried since the early death of his father and was afraid the issue of his future wife was yet another one, if only because Lady Anne made it so. Elizabeth wished he could marry for affection alone. He deserved to have a lady by his side who would value him and help him experience all the joy that comes with life. Elizabeth believed she would be such a woman. She would do everything in her power to make him happy and be an excellent wife, mistress, and mother to his children.

With a surreptitious shake of her head, she set aside all thought of Fitzwilliam Darcy and his marriage prospects. What were they to her, after all? She had much better think about her future, and she resolved to do just that—after her winter of fun.

TWO

All of them, except Lady Anne, had been greatly relieved when Lady Catherine returned to Rosings. Darcy only wished he could avoid his aunt for the next year, if not longer, but his mother had arranged for them to go to Kent at Easter.

He was already dreading it. His mother and aunt would press him to offer for Anne, seemingly unwilling to accept that he was his own master and would not be forced into a marriage he did not want. He had told all three ladies the match would not happen, but they continued to act as though, if they only kept talking about it as a decided fact, he would eventually accede.

For the month after his return to town, Darcy hardly had an idle day, being greatly occupied with meetings regarding various investments and maintaining social connexions. He also spent time with his family, who celebrated Rebecca's birthday in early February. Two days later, Bramwell confided in Darcy and Fitzwilliam about a conversation he had with her father.

"He wanted to know my intentions," said Bramwell. "Most awkward interview of my life."

"You have not exactly made a secret of your affection for her these past two years," Fitzwilliam said.

The couple had grown closer when they were at Pemberley after Darcy's father's death. Lord Romsley sent Bramwell to help him as he sorted through everything that went along with a sudden death and change in master of a large estate. Uncle Darcy had come as well, bringing Rebecca with him, ostensibly to keep Lady Anne company, though Darcy suspected his concern was mostly for Elizabeth, who had remained at Pemberley several months to support his mother during her worst period of grief. She had helped him enormously too.

"He did not warn you off?" Darcy asked.

Bramwell shrugged, a light dusting of colour on his cheeks. "He accepts that I shall do what I can to convince her she prefers my company above all others but told me I shall have to wait a year until she is one-and-twenty before asking her to promise me anything." Looking first at his brother, then at Darcy, he continued. "I expect both of you to assist me. Devise excuses for us to be in company as much as possible."

It was no hardship for Darcy to be with his cousins or Elizabeth, and he prayed such company would restore Fitzwilliam's customary cheerful manner. Thus, he was happy to oblige Bramwell.

At the end of February, Darcy attended the theatre with his mother, his Darcy relations, and Elizabeth. He planned to offer Bramwell and Fitzwilliam a ride in his carriage, but Lady Anne asked that he not in the event she wished to leave early. The implication was that he would escort her home, leaving his cousins to amuse themselves without him. It was an odd request, but their conversation as they drove to the theatre offered a clue to his mother's motives.

"You are spending too much time with Elizabeth Bennet." Her mouth curled into a displeased pout.

"I do not take your meaning, madam." Darcy pulled at his gloves in lieu of looking at his mother, who sat across from him.

"It will give her ideas."

Darcy almost scoffed. "Elizabeth is a friend and closely

connected to our family. I enjoy her company, and I see no reason to neglect the fact I have known her since I was twelve years old. I can hardly avoid her, even if I wished to—which I do not."

Darcy may have known Elizabeth for most of his life, but he had only started to consider her a friend over the last two years. By then, she was eighteen, and Darcy had grown to appreciate how mature, kind, and interesting she had become.

"I do not like it," his mother said. "People like her will take advantage of people in our position, and if you do not exercise greater caution, she will take your friendship and try to make it into something more."

Darcy chose not to respond, and they spent the rest of the ride in silence.

<hr />

"Mr Darcy, how wonderful to meet you here so unexpectedly." The voice was carefully modulated, and the expression on the countenance of the woman who spoke sought to appear beguiling.

Inwardly, Darcy sighed before he greeted Charles Bingley, his two sisters, and brother-in-law who had just approached his party.

"I had no notion you would be at the theatre tonight! I suppose we did not talk about it when we met last week, did we?" Bingley grinned, and the annoyance Darcy felt when he acknowledged Miss Bingley eased.

Charles Bingley had been a friend for the better part of a decade, ever since he—several years Darcy's junior—had arrived at Eton, and Darcy mentored him. He had found he rather liked Bingley, despite his coming from a decidedly different family background. His father had been in trade until his son's birth.

Darcy met Mrs Hurst during her first Season and Miss Bingley when she was seventeen and entered society. In the three years since, Caroline Bingley made it abundantly clear she was interested in securing a wealthy, well-connected husband. Darcy was not interested in the role.

Darcy performed the necessary introductions between his family and the Bingley party. After the usual commonplaces were exchanged, Bingley addressed Elizabeth.

"Miss Bennet, how lovely to see you once again. Why, it must be above a year since we met."

"I believe so, sir. You and Mr Darcy came to Romsley Hall when you were travelling from Pemberley to…I cannot recall."

Bingley laughed. "Neither can I!"

At the signal to take their seats, Darcy felt compelled to invite the Bingleys and Hursts to sit in his box.

"It will be quite the crush," said Lady Anne.

His mother spoke with barely disguised disdain. She would never approve of people with ties to trade being amongst his acquaintance. That, Darcy expected, was at the root of her sentiments for Elizabeth.

"Oh, but Louisa and I are quite slim, as you can see, Lady Anne. You will not even notice we are there," Miss Bingley said. "Your earrings are exquisite. Are they a family heirloom?"

Bingley caught Darcy's eye and sent a silent apology for his sister's forward manner.

The box was crowded, but the number of people was not what vexed Darcy. Hurst was inoffensive and said little to call attention to himself, but Bingley's sisters were presumptuous. They clearly wished to demonstrate that there was greater intimacy between his family and them than existed. Were it not for Bingley, Darcy would not associate with either of them.

Fortunately, he was separated from the ladies—but unfortunately, he was perfectly positioned to see his mother's cold expression when she watched Elizabeth, as she did for a good portion of the performance. His only comfort was that she was not as bad as Lady Catherine. He would never understand their dislike for Elizabeth, who was an admirable person, truly a young lady anyone should be pleased to know. Despite how long she had been a part of the family, they refused to see her as anything other than the little girl his grandmother took in because of some sort of difficulty with her parents. Her mother was cruel to her and did not like how inquisitive she was, or some such nonsense.

He quietly chuckled remembering the first time his grandmother brought the little girl to Pemberley. She was keen to understand why leaves were never violet or blue. His father, excellent man that he was, patiently answered her questions. And Elizabeth had been fascinated by Thor, Darcy's big oaf of a Great Dane dog. Thor was twice her size, but revelled in the attention and was gentle with the little girl.

Even if my mother found it difficult to be around her then, it was so long ago, and Elizabeth is an adult now, and she is—

Darcy stopped himself mid-thought, straightened his spine, and forced his attention back to the stage.

Elizabeth liked Mr Bingley. With his wavy blond curls, which seemed to defy any attempt his valet made to arrange them in an orderly fashion, and an almost perpetual happy expression and desire to please, he reminded her of a puppy. It was a comparison she kept to herself, knowing few would understand she, who had always adored animals, meant it as a compliment.

As for his sisters, she was convinced they would never be friends. After the theatre, they attended a soirée to which the Bingleys and Hursts were invited. When Miss Bingley and Mrs Hurst sought her out, they apparently believed she was alone. In truth, Fitzwilliam was nearby, his back turned for a few minutes while he greeted an old schoolmate.

Miss Bingley said, "I could not place you at first. Eliza Bennet is a very…common name. You are the girl taken in by Mr Darcy's family."

"I am, and I prefer not to be called Eliza." Lady Catherine often used the nickname.

"You are not *actually* a member of the family?" Mrs Hurst said.

Fitzwilliam was suddenly by her side. "We very much think of her as one." His tone was harsher than was warranted, but his temper had been quick since his return from the Peninsula. "My brother and I view Elizabeth as a sister, and I assure you, our family could not do without her."

"Any true connexion is remote, is it not?" Miss Bingley presented Elizabeth with a smile she believed the woman meant to appear friendly but was little better than a smirk.

Fitzwilliam dipped his chin just enough to avoid being rude. "Mrs Hurst, Miss Bingley." With that, he took Elizabeth's elbow and guided her away.

"Thank you for coming to my rescue. Why do you suppose they have taken such an aversion to me? We have only just met!"

"Miss Bingley has made it plain she wants to be Mrs Darcy. Rather, she wishes to be mistress of Pemberley." Elizabeth turned her astonished eyes to him, and he nodded. "You are often in company with Darcy, and if they can think poorly of you, then you are not a rival for his affections."

Elizabeth laughed. The sound burst from her, drawing the attention of several people.

"Does the idea that you might be surprise you so much?"

Elizabeth hoped the candlelight was dim enough to hide her blush. "That anyone would believe it possible, yes."

He made a noise that was difficult to interpret—part speculation, part disbelief, with a touch of humour, if she was not mistaken.

"Let us not concern ourselves with them. Please, darling foster brother, find me a glass of lemonade. I am parched."

Later that evening, Elizabeth had a brief conversation with Darcy. They had hardly spoken all day, and without even asking if she enjoyed the theatre, he said, "Is my mother being disagreeable? To you, I mean."

"Nothing I cannot laugh about, which as you know, is how I prefer to deal with everything, good or bad. I shall never claim Lady Anne has embraced me as warmly as Mrs Darcy has, but it is not as though she treats me as dreadfully as Lady Catherine."

Darcy frowned, and she chuckled. Not for the world did she want to distress him or add gloom to the time they spent together. He liked her to be cheerful. She recalled him once saying as much, and there was little else she could give him. As well, he really should not need to ask. When had Lady Anne ever been truly kind to her?

* * *

Fitzwilliam's remark about Mrs Hurst and Miss Bingley possibly seeing her as competition for Darcy's affections remained with Elizabeth far longer than it should. Even a month later, something would happen to remind her of it—seeing the ladies, a conversation with Darcy, even Lady Anne staring at her when they were in company together was enough, although she did not understand why the last would have such an effect.

"It hardly matters," Elizabeth said to her reflection as she prepared for a ball. "In less than a fortnight, I depart for Worcestershire. I shall not see Darcy again until the late summer, and as for Mr Bingley's sisters, I happily anticipate not meeting them for many months longer than that."

The two months she was in town had been pleasurable. Beyond amusing herself with Rebecca, Bramwell, Fitzwilliam, and Darcy, she met many other young people and enjoyed conversations, card games, promenades, and dances with agreeable gentlemen. Her life would be simple if only she could cease to admire Darcy and attract a respectable man she would be willing to marry. It must be what the earl and countess wanted. Then she would no longer be their responsibility. Lady Catherine would rejoice to have her removed from the family at last, and whatever her opinion, Lady Anne concurred.

But no gentleman had caught Elizabeth's eye. She was at fault, not them. Until she could forget her attachment to Darcy, how could she feel enough for another man to want to be his wife? With the example of the love match between Rebecca and Bramwell always before her, it would take someone extraordinary to tempt her into marriage. She wanted a gentleman with whom she could share a connexion such as theirs. Bramwell would inherit an earldom and could look much higher, and his lack of concern about making a better match, his putting affection above any other consideration, was wonderful to Elizabeth.

Elizabeth busied herself by changing her necklace. Forcing

a chuckle, she murmured, "What a joke to imagine anyone believing Darcy would feel that way about me! I am fortunate he considers me a friend. I know he would never consider me as a possible marriage partner."

When she was at Pemberley the previous September, she had overheard him talking to Bramwell. It was before breakfast, and she was sitting on a bench in the gardens. She surmised that the gentlemen had been riding and were walking to the house. There had almost been an argument the night before when Lady Catherine pontificated on how the drawing room would be refurbished to accommodate her daughter's taste when she and Darcy were at last wed.

"I do not know what to say to make Lady Catherine and Anne—and my mother, for that matter—accept that I will not be badgered into marriage," Darcy had said. "I can think of a dozen ladies I would rather offer for, and I am not sufficiently tempted by any of *them*, let alone our cousin. I shall do what my father expected and choose a bride from a noble line, as he did, one who will bring both connexions and wealth to our union, but *never* Anne."

"Some ladies have a great deal more to offer than their family and dowry," Bramwell said.

"It is different for you," insisted Darcy. "You know your father and mother esteem and love Rebecca. It will be difficult enough to convince my mother to accept a lady other than Anne, and I shall never know what my father thinks of the choice I make. I shall have to comfort myself by choosing the sort of woman of whom I believe he would have approved."

Pulling herself from the recollection, Elizabeth said, "Besides, I would not want a woman such as Lady Anne as my mother-in-law. I want a home where I am loved and respected, embraced as a dear relation. If I cannot find that in marriage, I shall concoct a different future for myself."

THREE

L ater that evening, Elizabeth sat at the side of a brightly lit, elegantly decorated ballroom. The final set was about to begin, but she had declined a gentleman's invitation for it.

Darcy took the chair next to hers. "I beg of you, if any mamas or aunts or grandmothers or the like come to talk to me, say you cannot do without my company."

Elizabeth laughed. "Are you using me to escape the attentions of those who only wish to introduce you to their charming and eligible charges?"

"Teasing me is unkind." He groaned and tilted his head this way and that as though his muscles were sore. "I danced more than I like this evening."

"Four times?" Apart from her and Rebecca, she saw him with one woman she knew and one she did not. "Who was the lady you danced with after supper? Her hair was even darker than mine."

Without pause, he said, "Anna Maria Genova. Her father is an ambassador of some sort from Italy, and they are in town for a year or two. You would like her. She is very interesting. She and her mother might have left already, but another time, I shall introduce you."

His eyes searched the room. It was seldom Darcy spoke of any lady with such enthusiasm, and Elizabeth felt a brief stab of jealousy, which she pushed away as inappropriate and unfair to Miss Genova.

"I am always keen to meet new people."

He nodded absentmindedly and several breaths later said, "I would leave, but I came with your foster brothers, and they are both out there." His warm brown eyes indicated the lines of ladies and gentlemen waiting for the music to begin.

"You could make a permanent escape from such troublesome attentions if you succumbed to your mother and aunt's scheme."

He shot her a look, but his smile belied any true annoyance. "Say no more, Miss Bennet. I might be forced to tease you in return."

Again, she laughed. "How would you accomplish that? You are not known for your skill with banter."

Their eyes met, and he took a moment to consider his response. Elizabeth's heart began to beat faster, and her smile softened even as she told herself not to let her expression change.

"You danced with Mr Corcoran."

That gentleman was bottle-headed, and her set with him was the most tedious of the night.

Continuing to use a light, joking tone, she said, "We could both find safety from the perils of the marriage mart by uniting to each other."

Darcy guffawed. "Could you imagine?"

She could, which was her chief problem. Embarrassment made her ears burn. Despite the manner in which she had spoken, did he have to laugh quite so heartily? There was no denying it stung.

They watched the crowd. Before long, Elizabeth spotted Miss Bingley and Mrs Hurst, who appeared to be looking for someone.

She could not resist saying, "There are other ladies who would be pleased to rescue you."

What she expected him to say, she did not know, but the pair had been dismissive towards her whenever they met, and Elizabeth supposed she wanted Darcy to admit he did not like them. Better still would be if he condemned their behaviour towards her. If he did, it would restore a measure of her bruised ego.

After a soft snort, he said, "My mother would never accept Miss Bingley or one of her ilk as my wife. You know I value Bingley's friendship, but his family's ties to trade are too recent."

Surely, this was ample punishment for her imprudent comment, both of them. Worse than his words was the haughty tone with which he spoke. Darcy was one of the best men she knew, but when they were in town, it was evident how much he felt his position as a wealthy young gentleman from a noble line. When they were in the country, surrounded by family, he was more relaxed and did not seem to need to display such an awareness of his consequence. At times, Elizabeth thought it was possible the *country* Darcy could look at her as an eligible match, but the *town* Darcy never would.

Without meaning to speak, and certainly not wanting to defend Miss Bingley, Elizabeth heard herself saying, "She was raised a gentlewoman and has a fine fortune."

"You know very well my parents expect more from me." He tugged at his shirt cuffs. "Why are we talking about this? Perhaps we should talk about *your* marriage prospects next."

She gave an exaggerated shudder. "No, thank you. Let us settle on a suitably innocuous subject instead, such as the weather."

He offered her a quick smile, and they lapsed into silence.

～◦～

Sitting quietly with Elizabeth was one of the more enjoyable interludes of the evening, and Darcy was glad he had spotted her alone. He never would like balls, but his attendance at them was necessary. He was content to remain quiet and assumed she was, too, given how late it was.

Towards the end of the set, Elizabeth said, "I think Fitzwilliam's spirits are improving. I am returning to Romsley Hall soon, as you know. He has promised to come as soon as he can, but first he goes with you to Rosings. You will, I mean to say—"

"See his progress continues, despite the less-than-salubrious setting?" When she nodded, he sought to reassure her. "Do not worry about him. He will be well again with time."

"I shall try, but I can promise nothing."

Her cheeks were a lovely shade of pink, and she looked especially charming that evening. Besides her physical attractions, Elizabeth was an estimable woman, and her concern for Fitzwilliam exemplified her caring nature. He was surprised she did not have more suitors. But, when he thought about it, Darcy did not know many men worthy of her, and he would hate to see Elizabeth marry someone who would not appreciate her as she deserved.

The day before she and the Romsleys departed for Worcestershire, Elizabeth walked in the park with Darcy and Freya, his Great Dane. Bramwell and Rebecca were ahead of them.

Elizabeth's hand reached out to stroke the dog every so often. Darcy was never a loquacious man, and he had less to say for himself than usual. She did not mind. There was a gentle comfort in his presence. He exuded strength and stability, and she was in particular need of it.

Watching Rebecca and Bramwell, Elizabeth's heart ached at knowing she would soon have to say goodbye to her dearest friend. It did not matter that they would see each other again in five months and had faced longer separations in the past. For some reason, she had the sense that everything was changing. By the same time next year, Rebecca and Bramwell would likely be engaged, if not already married. Darcy would soon select a wife, and Fitzwilliam had his career.

And I have being useful to the countess and informing her and the earl of what is happening at Romsley when they are absent, as they so often are.

That might be at the root of her melancholia. After so much gaiety and being surrounded by people she loved, Elizabeth was returning to Worcestershire where she would be alone more than she liked. The idea of Darcy marrying was particularly worrisome. Nothing would ever be the same. A wife would not like him being her friend, and he would put distance between them.

Refusing to continue indulging in such reflections further, she smiled down into Freya's tawny face.

"I cannot believe how much she has grown since last autumn."

"It is hardly a surprise. She was only seven months old when you saw her at Pemberley."

"Perhaps not, but is it not required we remark on how babies are getting so big and strong, whether they are human, canine, feline, or any other species?"

Darcy chuckled. "You are more likely to notice if it is a dog or cat or horse."

She laughed. "Do you think so? Ought I to accuse you of calling me a misanthrope?"

"Not at all. You have always held an uncommon affection for animals. I do not say it is a bad thing."

"I leave you to imagine my relief that you do not think so poorly of me!"

Their eyes met, and they exchanged a smile. After stopping to greet acquaintances, they continued their stroll.

"Are you glad to be returning to Worcestershire?" Darcy asked.

"I am, but I also regret leaving town."

"I had much rather remain here than go to Kent."

Elizabeth slipped her hand around his arm and let it rest on the crook of his elbow. "Fitzwilliam will be there as company for you. I pray that makes your visit less difficult."

He grumbled but briefly pressed her hand. "It might, if I had any confidence my marriage to Anne would not be talked about as a fait accompli."

"Perhaps you need to reconsider how you tell your mother and aunt you will not marry Anne. What you are saying is evidently not enough."

"They are stubborn and do not want to hear it. Lord Romsley tells them, as did my father."

"But the earl is not you, and as much as I wish it otherwise, your father is no longer here to keep them in check. We young people know your opinion on the matter. I do not think your mother, aunt, and Anne are as convinced you hate the idea." There was a growing bubble of annoyance in her belly when it came to the topic of his and his cousin's possible union.

Darcy's response was kind but dismissive. "We are going our separate ways soon enough. I would rather enjoy our time together than talk about the matter further."

She agreed and left him to his thoughts. There was a family dinner at Curzon Street that evening, and she would make the effort to ensure they spoke about something amusing then. It would be a final pleasant memory from her time in town, something to carry with her until all of them were together again in September.

To begin repairing her spirits, Elizabeth reflected on how elated she was that she would not be required to go to Rosings. Remembering her two visits to Kent, she shuddered. The de Bourghs had acted as though she were invisible—when they were not treating her like the lowest of their servants. Anne de Bourgh despised Elizabeth as much as her mother. She shoved and pinched Elizabeth repeatedly when she thought no one was looking. The countess had been so displeased with how Lady Catherine and her daughter treated her, she vowed never to bring Elizabeth to Rosings again. Even Lady Anne appeared a little uneasy at such behaviour, but Elizabeth knew that might simply be what she wanted to believe.

With that, she patted Freya's head, smiled at Darcy, and gave her attention to the splendour of a fine spring day and the presence of a handsome gentleman by her side.

FOUR

Mid-August 1811

E lizabeth's fingers flew across the pianoforte's keys as she played a fugue by Bach. Her back was rounded, her eyes closed, her mind empty of everything but the music. As the tempo gained speed, so did her heart and breath until she completed the piece with two incongruous, discordant chords. Remaining where she was, she let the sudden silence wash over her.

The day was still young, and when she stood and took in her surroundings, the morning sunlight enhanced the elegance of Romsley Hall's large, fashionable drawing room. It was a space meant for a crowd, certainly more than a single occupant.

"Even I shall not be here to enjoy it soon enough," she murmured. "I cannot delay my departure much longer, but oh, I do not want—" She summoned her sense of duty. "Goodness, I am acting as though I am going to the gallows, not Pemberley."

As she quit the room, her thoughts drifted to Lady Romsley's latest note. It arrived several days prior to alert Elizabeth that she and the earl would not return to Worcestershire as originally arranged. They were visiting one of the earl's estates in Northumberland, and they were enjoying renewing acquaintances in the neighbourhood.

You will go to Pemberley. Lord Romsley has arranged it with Lady Anne. She is alone there, and you can be company for her and she for you. It would be better than remaining alone at Romsley. I am confident you will find a way to make yourself useful to her.

Elizabeth doubted Lady Anne wished for her company or assistance. Likely, the earl had told her to expect Elizabeth, rather than asking her if she wanted company, just as the countess had ordered Elizabeth to go.

Since receiving the letter, Elizabeth had debated whether she would prefer to stay at Romsley Hall or go to Pemberley. Here, she had tasks to attend to, but in the absence of the family, she could be lonely. She ate meals alone, went riding with only a groom for company, and walked the estate with a footman trailing silently behind her. Apart from Easter, the earl and countess had been in Worcestershire only for a fortnight at the beginning of July. The earl had estates to tour and important people with whom to confer, and they had friends they liked to visit. They had kindly taken in Elizabeth at the dowager countess's death, but it was too much to expect they would treat her as a daughter and bring her with them on their travels.

She was not entirely devoid of company, of course. One of her neighbours would sometimes volunteer to act as Elizabeth's chaperon, allowing her to attend various amusements in the neighbourhood. Elizabeth would have more freedom and someone to talk to if she had a companion, but Lady Romsley had rejected the notion of securing one for her.

Shortly before Elizabeth's eighteenth birthday, when her last governess left to get married, the countess said, "Companions are nasty creatures. Look at that Mrs Jenkinson of Anne's. You are such an industrious, independent young lady, Elizabeth. You would hate to have someone always hovering nearby."

Half an hour later, Elizabeth was in the carriage, watching the passing landscape. Her maid, Herriot, sat across from her, and the earl's local solicitor and his wife accompanied them to ensure their safety. She told herself to be pleased to go to Pemberley, which was a wonderful estate. In a month or thereabouts, everyone would be gathered there, and Darcy was expected even sooner, from what Rebecca wrote in her last letter. Elizabeth did not relish having only Lady Anne for company, especially after how peevish she had been in the winter, but once Darcy joined them...

Elizabeth would not voice it, even to herself, but there would be moments when she could pretend that was her life, that she lived at Pemberley as Darcy's wife. She would savour their time together, even if it were a dream. Doubtless, they would go riding, which brought to mind her mare. She tried to catch sight of the horse trotting beside the carriage. Nutmeg had been born at Pemberley, and the elder Mr Darcy had given her to Elizabeth for her sixteenth birthday. The spring before, Elizabeth had spent a month with him while Lady Anne was at Rosings Park. He had been a true friend to her, even from the day they first met. Her feelings about going there at present would be entirely different if he were still alive. As it was, Elizabeth doubted she would have an easy day until Darcy was there to alleviate the tension that would inevitably exist between her and his mother.

Darcy, along with Bramwell and Fitzwilliam, spent Sunday at Curzon Street. His aunt Darcy had invited him and his two cousins to take dinner with them. The only person they were missing was Elizabeth. Her laugh was infectious, and she completed their small fellowship of young people.

He watched, half-listening, as the others talked about a recent excursion to Kew Gardens. The silk wing chair in which he sat was comfortable, and his family occupied similar chairs and a sofa, all artfully arranged in the cosy drawing room. Darcy liked the house on Curzon Street, which was less needlessly fine than his town house in Berkeley Square.

"When do you go into Derbyshire?" his uncle asked.

Darcy shook off his reveries. "Tomorrow. I leave first thing. I am having some building done on the estate, and I want to ensure it and some other improvements are going well."

"You will have Elizabeth to keep you company and assist you, which you know she would be pleased to do." Fitzwilliam turned to his brother, and they sniggered.

Darcy would never understand their jokes. "What do you mean?"

Bramwell grinned. "Elizabeth will be at Pemberley by the time you arrive. My father's latest missive informed us he and Mother intend to go directly there from wherever they are."

"Thus, they decided to send Elizabeth to your mother," added Fitzwilliam.

"Are you not pleased?" Bramwell asked.

Darcy *was* glad, but he saw no reason to admit it. Instead, he addressed his aunt. "Do you still intend to quit town on Wednesday?"

His aunt gave him a fond look. "We do. It will give us almost three weeks to stop wherever we like and amuse ourselves."

"I am looking forward to it, but not quite so much as I am to being at Pemberley. It has always been one of my most favourite places." Rebecca's smile encompassed them all, lingering just a touch longer on Bramwell.

Uncle Darcy said, "If we had known Elizabeth would be

alone at Romsley Hall all these weeks, we could have arranged our journey differently and taken her with us."

"I do not like to think of it," said his aunt. "How can Elizabeth not feel lonely?"

Bramwell sought to reassure her, and likely Rebecca too. "She and Darcy will keep each other cheerful until we arrive. Then what fun we shall have."

"Just as we always do," Fitzwilliam said. "I am especially anticipating it, having been away last year."

It would be the first time they were all together in Derbyshire for three years. Two years ago, Darcy's father's recent death left his mother unwilling to entertain a houseful of guests, even one composed of family, and last year, Fitzwilliam was in the Peninsula. This year, they would be a merry party. Darcy would not let even Lady Catherine and Anne's presence ruin it.

<hr>

Lady Anne received her in a small drawing room and only nodded in response to Elizabeth's curtsey and enquiry about her health. Elizabeth's initial fascination with Lady Anne had abated with age and the woman's indifference to her, but she retained the vestiges of a desire to please the older woman. She supposed it was a response to her perpetual air of sadness and the tight, controlled way she held herself.

"You will want to change out of your travelling clothes," Lady Anne said, not quite meeting Elizabeth's eye.

"Shall I join you when—"

"That is not necessary. I have letters to write and shall see you at dinner."

Surprised at Lady Anne's manner, which was brusquer

than usual, Elizabeth could only say, "Very well," before going to her bedchamber to change.

Dinner was largely silent, and Lady Anne retired after drinking a cup of tea. With no reason to remain in the drawing room, Elizabeth went to her bedchamber to read.

⁕ ⸙ ⁕

The following day, a Sunday, began with attending church. Breakfast was again silent, but Elizabeth felt the weight of Lady Anne's gaze on her throughout, which left her struggling not to squirm. Since her hostess had no need for her after the meal, Elizabeth went for a walk. Her feet led her through the grove, along the stream, and, eventually, to Mr Darcy's final resting place. She placed a bouquet of wildflowers beside the headstone and whispered a prayer.

There was a wooden bench nearby, and Elizabeth took a rest. She removed her straw bonnet and used it to fan her face. The sky was cloudless, and the sun was strong. The only sound she heard was faint birdsong. The peaceful setting was a contrast to her sorrowful thoughts of Mr Darcy and his final days.

She had come to Pemberley a week before his death after an express from Lady Anne arrived at Romsley Hall, informing them he was gravely ill and begging Lord Romsley to come at once. The earl and countess were away visiting one of his political allies, leaving only Elizabeth to receive the summons. She would not let Lady Anne suffer alone and rushed to Pemberley, where she did what she could for her and Darcy, once he arrived from town.

I hope I provided you with some comfort. I believe I helped Darcy, but whether or not Lady Anne benefited from my presence at that awful time, I do not know.

At length, Elizabeth ambled back to the manor, stopping by the stables on the way to see that Nutmeg had settled in.

Stroking the horse's long brown nose, she said, "We shall go out tomorrow morning. What do you think of that, girl? You enjoy galloping across Pemberley as much as I do."

The ladies did not meet again until dinner, after which—in what was almost as much an order as a request—Lady Anne had Elizabeth play the pianoforte. She said nothing, but Elizabeth was aware of her stare as she sat at the instrument. She would give a great deal to know just once what the woman was thinking.

The clock chimed ten, and Lady Anne stood. "I shall retire."

Also rising, Elizabeth said, "I intend to ride before breakfast unless you need me?"

Again, Lady Anne studied her. This time, her expression was almost hesitant.

After a pause, Elizabeth surreptitiously sighed. "I wish you a good night, madam."

Lady Anne did not reply but turned and left the room.

Before Elizabeth was even out of bed the next day, a servant knocked at the door to her bedchamber. Herriot answered and repeated the message to her.

"Lady Anne says you are to dress and go to her immediately. She is waiting for you in the green drawing room."

Elizabeth leapt out of bed, alarmed by the unexpected summons and pulled at the ribbon securing her hair. "Quickly. Any gown will do."

Her heart racing, Elizabeth flew down the stairs a short

while later, praying it was not dreadful news but unable to imagine what else it could be.

Lady Anne, her complexion pale, was pacing when Elizabeth joined her. She held something in her hands, and Elizabeth was confused when she recognised her pelisse, bonnet, and reticule, which Lady Anne thrust at her.

"You are leaving. At once."

"Leaving? I-I do not understand." Her chest ached from the pounding of her heart.

"Yes, leaving. Make haste."

Lady Anne walked to the door. Dazed, Elizabeth trailed behind her, her steps faltering when they exited the house, and she saw a waiting carriage. The door was open, and one of the grooms stood beside it.

"You are going to Rosings Park."

"No!" Elizabeth gasped. "I will not!"

"Get in the carriage, Elizabeth." Never had Lady Anne's voice been so frigid. Never had she sounded so much like her elder sister.

"If you do not want me here, I will return to Romsley."

Lady Anne hissed, "You will do no such thing! You *will* go to Rosings. My sister awaits you, and my coachman will carry you nowhere else. I will not have you here. Never again."

It took a few minutes, but Elizabeth realised that unless she wanted to be physically thrown into the carriage or was prepared to walk back to Romsley Hall, there was no choice but to ascend the steps, particularly after a burly footman escorted a dazed, frightened-looking Herriot to the carriage. Pemberley's steward, Mr Holt, was already within.

"Lady Anne asked me to accompany you," he explained as the coach began to move. "It is just for a few weeks, Miss Bennet, until Lady Catherine and Miss de Bourgh come to Pemberley. Then you will be back with your friends."

Elizabeth forced her voice to be steady. "I see. Did Lady Anne say why her sister desires my presence?"

"She did not, and naturally, I did not enquire."

Sitting beside her, Herriot began to shake. Elizabeth worried the footman had treated her roughly, and she would ask later when they were alone. Elizabeth felt the sting of angry tears, but she would not give in with Mr Holt as a witness and when her maid needed her strength.

She took Herriot's hand. "It will all work out for the best. Never you mind."

FIVE

The distance to Kent felt twice as long as it was. Apprehension and fury at having only Mr Holt to protect her on such a long journey, one that involved several nights at coaching inns, made it impossible for Elizabeth to think clearly. She struggled to understand why Lady Anne had evicted her from Pemberley and sent her to a place she had never been welcome. There was no making sense of it, and she did not know what to expect when she arrived, but she was certain it would be unpleasant at best. She would never think of Lady Anne in kindly terms again—not after this.

Lady Catherine and Anne de Bourgh held twin expressions of satisfaction, even glee, mixed with disdain when they greeted her. After peering at her for a long moment, Lady Catherine sniffed loudly, her nose wrinkling.

"As much as I despise having one such as you in my house, it is as well you are here. As soon as my sister informed me that my brother insisted you go to Pemberley, I knew what we had to do. I ordered her to send you here. At last, I will relieve the family of its loathsome responsibility. It ought to have been done years ago."

Lady Catherine evidently expected Elizabeth to respond, and after a long pause, she did. "I do not understand why I am here, but if you require my assistance—"

"I require nothing of *you*, Eliza Bennet, other than you finally leaving my family alone. I know just what to do with you," Lady Catherine said. "It will all be settled before my daughter and I depart for Pemberley."

Alarm shot through Elizabeth. What exactly did Lady Catherine mean with her talk of dealing with her?

Lady Catherine continued. "I will no longer tolerate you interfering with my plans. I will see my daughter and nephew united in marriage before Yuletide. How you have tricked Darcy into liking you, I do not know—comparing you to Anne, how well you play and draw, how good you are on a horse and with the earl's dependents, how quick witted! As though *you* are somehow superior to *my* daughter, the grand-daughter of an earl!"

"I do not understand you," Elizabeth interjected.

An ugly expression covered the older woman's face, and she spat out the next words. "Distracting Darcy from his duty! Acting as his friend, flirting with him, and putting yourself forward! He does not need a female friend. He needs a *wife*, and it will never be you."

Elizabeth's blood turned to ice. "You are ridiculous, madam. If he wanted to marry Anne, my presence would not stop him. What gives you the right to decide—"

"Hold your tongue! I will not permit you to speak to me in such a manner. His mother and I agree *you* are a problem we will no longer tolerate. You are twenty years old—old enough to make your own way in the world. I shall secure a position for you. *That* will remove you from Darcy's sphere once and for all."

"You intend to force me into a life of service because Darcy is not acting in accordance with your wishes?" If Elizabeth were not so distressed, she might have found the situation comical.

Lady Catherine ignored her question and continued. "Your

room is next to Mrs Jenkinson. I advise you to observe her and understand the proper deportment of a companion. Though, with the education my mother wasted on you, a position as a governess might be better. Yes, wasted I say! The money she spent on you was the rightful property of my daughter or my nephews. Thank God her fortune devolved to my brother. Lady Anne ought not to have allowed her husband to leave you a farthing, let alone five thousand pounds. I did not permit Sir Lewis to continue the foolish scheme hatched after my mother's death, and I will ensure my brother does not, either. We owe you nothing!"

Elizabeth had been shocked to learn of Mr Darcy's bequest after his death. Bramwell had explained that at the same time the older generation agreed she would not return to Long-bourn, they decided to make provisions for Elizabeth's future. Each of the gentlemen set aside a sum of money to settle on her upon her marriage or at their deaths. It was generous, and she was gratified they thought well enough of her to do it.

"If you will excuse me, I wish to refresh myself after my unexpected travel."

Not caring that it was rude, Elizabeth walked away. A footman offered to show her to her bedchamber, and she followed him but had to stop before they reached it to lean against the wall and take several breaths to restore her strength. Feeling an urgent need to be alone, once in her room, she dismissed Herriot, who had been arranging Elizabeth's belongings and muttering over wrinkles, a result of her clothing being hastily packed. Elizabeth had been surprised to find that Lady Anne had sent everything with her from Pemberley if her stay at Rosings was to be short, rather than the six weeks or more she expected to stay in Derbyshire. After listening to Lady Catherine's plans for her—which she did not believe would come to pass—it made more sense. Only at this moment did Elizabeth recall Lady Anne's parting words that she would not have Elizabeth at Pemberley again.

Regarding her pale visage in the mirror, Elizabeth murmured, "I am being absurd. Lady Anne could not possibly have meant what she said, and Lady Catherine can do nothing to me without my permission. Force me into service? Never! She seeks to intimidate me, but she will find it is not so easy. In a fortnight or thereabouts, she and Anne will depart for Pemberley, and I *will* travel north with them."

After all, where else did she have to go?

At dinner, Elizabeth learnt that Mr Holt had been sent back to Derbyshire. While Elizabeth tried to eat, having consumed little over the last few days, Lady Catherine told her how she was expected to behave.

"You will do what Miss de Bourgh or I tell you to do. When we receive callers, you will absent yourself. I shall not have you putting yourself forward, demanding attention to which you have no right. You will visit no one. Fortunately, there are few unmarried men in the neighbourhood for you to *accidentally* encounter."

Elizabeth's brow furrowed as she tried to puzzle out her final statement. When Lady Catherine continued, Elizabeth had to swallow a laugh of incredulity at the woman's portrayal of her.

"I know your sort. You will attach yourself to the first eligible man just to secure your future. Grasping—that is what people like you are. I will hear no complaints from you. Is that clear?"

Not trusting herself to speak, Elizabeth nodded in agreement.

By the time they went into the drawing room, Elizabeth's head throbbed painfully, and she was so tired it was all she could do not to yawn incessantly. The tea tray was brought in, and Lady Catherine demanded Elizabeth prepare cups for her and Anne. She proceeded to criticise everything she did, but somehow Elizabeth held her tongue long enough to drink her tea. Lady Catherine spoke on and on, though what she said, Elizabeth would not have been able to repeat.

As soon as an opportunity arose, she stood. "I am fatigued after so much time in the carriage. I shall retire to—"

"You will not," Lady Catherine said. "I have not given my permission, and you will learn to think about the needs of your betters rather than your selfish wants. You will play." She nodded to indicate the pianoforte, placed in a far corner of the room. "Whether you are a companion or a governess, decent musical ability is expected."

Too tired to argue or to determine the best way to cope with her current situation, Elizabeth went to the instrument. She let her fingers do as they liked, and after several pieces she knew exceptionally well, she stood and faced the two ladies.

"Truly, I can do no more," she said, "not unless you care to see me fall asleep and use the pianoforte as a pillow."

Lady Catherine's vexation at Elizabeth's flippant tone was everything she expected, and while her hostess—if she could be considered such—was enumerating the many ways in which Elizabeth was lacking, she made her escape.

Darcy approached Pemberley, glad to be home. He had not been there in almost three months—not since the spring when he invited Bingley, his sisters, and brother-in-law to stay for a fortnight. They were on their way to London after visiting family in Yorkshire. Darcy had needed to be at his estate but did not want to be alone with his mother. He was displeased with her after their time in Kent at Easter and was afraid they would argue without someone else there.

Since his father's death, Darcy had not spent much time in Derbyshire. He would come for a few weeks or a month, then return to town or go to visit friends. While he would never openly admit it, it was because of his mother. She was demanding—it was time for him to get married, he was away from Pemberley too much, she did not like this friend or that, et cetera. It was easier to stay away, yet he did not like to, given his responsibility to the estate and its efficient operation.

Knowing he would have Elizabeth for company brought a smile to his face. They would enjoy the outdoors, and there would be interesting conversations about books and politics and any manner of other topics to help pass the time. He chuckled as he remembered everything they did the previous winter and how she revelled in it. She was still as curious and lively as she was as a child. It did her good to get away from Worcestershire now and again and see more people than those she regularly encountered in the country.

Once he arrived, he was confused not to see Elizabeth waiting with his mother. He greeted Lady Anne, and looked around the small drawing room, his eyebrows pulled together. There was no sign of Elizabeth, not even a book or shawl that might be hers, which was odd, even if she was presently seeing to some errand or taking a walk.

He said, "You have been keeping well, I trust."

"I am in perfect health. I hope your journey was not too tedious. Shall I ring for refreshments, or would you prefer to go to your apartment? Dinner is at six o'clock, but you might like something to eat before then. Food at even the best of inns cannot compare to that at Pemberley."

She was babbling, and he wondered why. "I require nothing, and I shall change out of my travelling clothes in a minute. Where is Elizabeth?"

Lady Anne sat on a bergère chair and began some piece of needlework. She did not look at him as she spoke. "Elizabeth? Why would you ask about her?"

There was a brief pause, and Darcy heard the hesitancy in his voice when he said, "The earl wrote Bramwell and Fitzwilliam that since he and the countess were not returning to Romsley Hall until after they were here next month, Elizabeth would join you."

His mother kept her eyes on her work. She made a small noise as though what he said was mildly interesting.

"You must have misunderstood, or my nephews did." When he did not respond, she continued. "I believe such a scheme was mentioned, but it came to nothing. My brother must have taken her with them, wherever they went."

Disappointment struck him like a blow to the stomach. He ought not mind, given how occupied he expected to be. As much as he was anticipating seeing Elizabeth, she would be at Pemberley in just a few weeks.

·⸺ ⟋⟋⟍ ⸺·

Over the next several days, Elizabeth discovered Lady Catherine meant exactly what she said when she arrived. She was largely confined to the house, though she escaped to take

a walk now and again. It meant having to tolerate being repri-
manded for going out without first ascertaining whether Lady
Catherine, Anne—whom she was expected to call Miss de
Bourgh, despite the practice of over a decade—or even Mrs
Jenkinson required anything. Lady Catherine refused to allow
Elizabeth to go to church with them.

What she *was* allowed to do was be useful. She assisted
Mrs Jenkinson in all the little tasks she did for Anne, played
and read aloud when Lady Catherine or Anne said she should,
and fetched shawls and other items as though she were a
servant. To Elizabeth's amusement, Mrs Jenkinson believed
Elizabeth was being trained as her replacement. The two
women got along better once Elizabeth assured her that she
had no intention of ever being Anne de Bourgh's companion
and would leave Rosings Park before the month was over.

Throughout each day and late into the night, Elizabeth
worried about what she should do. If Rebecca was in town,
she could seek shelter with her, but she was not. The only
resolution she came to was that Lady Catherine and Lady
Anne's despicable actions demonstrated it was time for her to
decide how to live her life. To stay amongst the family meant
risking further disappointment and abuse. The earl and
countess were partly to blame. They had so little interest in
her, it was no wonder Lord Romsley's sisters believed it was
time to send her on her way.

At the root of it, however, was Darcy. Her heart broke
even to think it, but it was the truth. His mother and aunt
evidently despised her and blamed her for his failure to marry
Anne simply because they were friends, and he liked her more
than he did his cousin. Had she not told him he needed to find
a way to make them understand a union with Anne would
never take place? If he had, she would not be in this position.

Staying would also mean subjecting herself to the torment

of watching him select his bride, which would be made worse by knowing he concerned himself only with superficial matters of birth and fortune. He had admitted as much during a conversation in town. If he was intent on marrying for love, surely his mother and aunt could not argue with his refusal to marry Anne. After all, one either loved someone or did not. It could not be willed to happen. But while Darcy remained determined to marry for status and wealth, Anne was a good choice.

Twice Elizabeth prepared her pen to write to Rebecca or Lady Romsley, and twice her attempts failed.

She stood at the window of her bedchamber. The silence felt oppressive, and she spoke her thoughts aloud. "What is so difficult about saying I am at Rosings Park? Rebecca certainly does not know, and surely Lady Romsley does not either. She made it plain years ago she did not like me to be here, and if her opinion had changed, she would have said something about it in her note when she told me I was to go to Pemberley."

※ ～ ※

Throughout Elizabeth's first days at Rosings Park, Lady Catherine continued to speak about her fine education and how she would use it to earn her keep.

"I shall find an appropriate position for you. You need a firm master and mistress who will teach you proper deportment. I would undertake the chore myself, but I have more important matters to which I must attend, and I shall not unnecessarily expose my daughter to your insolent manner."

I am perfectly willing not to expose myself to your daughter or suffer your disgusting, arrogant behaviour. You are free to send me back to Romsley Hall at any time.

Elizabeth's response was silent because she had learnt that unless she wanted to enter into a verbal battle with Lady Catherine, it was better to hold her tongue. As for Lady Catherine's talk of finding her a position, Elizabeth dismissed it out of hand. She could not be forced into employment, and although they had never discussed it, Lord and Lady Romsley had never indicated that was the future they envisioned for her.

Soon, Lady Catherine began to imply, even outright state, that the earl and countess were in perfect accord with her efforts. She said, "My brother and sister do not need the expense of you. Of what use are you to them?" Another time, she told Elizabeth, "They know I excel at placing young people into proper situations. Why do you think you are here?"

A secret fear that Lord and Lady Romsley wished to be rid of her, that they had long desired to be done with the responsibility of her care, plagued her waking hours. It made Elizabeth more determined to make her own arrangements for her life. She would be one-and-twenty in December, which she believed would give her more freedom, but she wondered what she should do in the meantime.

Unable to sleep one night, she clutched her pillow to herself and worried about her situation. She refused to be a burden to anyone ever again—not the earl and countess, not Bramwell after he inherited the Romsley estate, not Rebecca's parents, even though they might give her a home if she asked.

Her thoughts drifted back through the years to people she scarcely remembered, some of whom she knew existed even though she had never met them. Her true family. She had a father and mother and sisters, even aunts and uncles and cousins. Although they had not seen each other in fifteen years, they must be as curious about her as she was about them. *My mother found me irritating when I was a precocious child, but I am an adult now. We might reconcile.*

Elizabeth had always believed she would return to Longbourn one day, just as her father and grandmother had assured her she would. Perhaps the time was upon her.

SIX

A week after her arrival at Rosings, Elizabeth was called into the drawing room in the early afternoon. As she approached the door, she reminded herself to remain calm and polite. Lack of sleep and a poor appetite had made her more argumentative, and she had to be doubly cautious not to antagonise Lady Catherine, yet remain firm in the face of the woman's bullying.

Lady Catherine was not alone. Sitting beside her on a chair several inches lower than her own was a parson. The man was large and nervous looking, and as soon as he opened his mouth, it was clear he was very much Lady Catherine's minion. His name was Mr Collins, and he had recently been granted the Hunsford living.

"Mr Collins will counsel you on your Christian duty," Lady Catherine said. "Do not attempt to use your feminine arts and allurements on him. They will not work. I warned him about you."

"Whatever do you mean?" Elizabeth silently added, *you hateful harridan.* She remained standing, as Lady Catherine indicated she should. It was supposed to make her feel inferior, but instead, it gave her a sense of power since she could more easily walk away.

"I know your sort. You will seek to trap him, either by helping you gain access to my nephew or to convince Darcy not to marry Anne. Perhaps you may even goad him into offering for you. You will not be satisfied until you have destroyed my family, and I will not permit it. Mr Collins, tell her she is cruel and evil and must bow to the wishes of her betters."

Mr Collins nodded vigorously, his limp brown hair, which badly needed cutting, falling over his eyes. "Just so, Lady Catherine, just so." He contemplated Elizabeth for a long moment. "Miss Bennet did you say? It is a curious name."

Elizabeth rolled her eyes. "I believe it is not so uncommon. Surely you have heard it before."

Lady Catherine's lip curled. "None of your flippancy, Eliza Bennet!"

Mr Collins spoke only to his patroness. "I apologise, Lady Catherine. It did not strike me when you first mentioned *her* to me. You see, my cousin, the one whose estate I shall inherit, is named Bennet. It is only fifty miles from here, in Hertfordshire, as I believe I told you."

Lady Catherine waved his words away and opened her mouth to speak.

Before she did, Elizabeth heard her own voice. "What is it called?"

Lady Catherine and Mr Collins spoke at the same time. "What difference does it make to you?" she said while he said, "Longbourn. It is a small—"

Elizabeth's sudden laughter stopped him. Both of her companions stared at her. "The universe—or God if you prefer —is playing a cruel joke on all of us. Longbourn is the estate of my father, Mr Rupert Bennet. That means you, Mr Collins, are a distant—*very* distant—cousin of mine. Are you not diverted, Lady Catherine?"

As it happened, Lady Catherine was not amused. She hissed at Elizabeth to leave them, and Elizabeth was happy to obey.

Elizabeth managed to escape the house to go riding the next morning, hoping the exercise would help order her thoughts. Lady Catherine would leave for Pemberley soon, and Elizabeth still did not know what would happen to her.

Alone with her thoughts, Elizabeth contemplated her prospects. If she remained firm and polite, if she did not argue with Lady Catherine and did as she asked, she would surely bring Elizabeth with her when she and Anne went to Derbyshire. Once she saw them, Elizabeth would talk to the countess and earl and raise the notion of finding employment as a companion. She could not bear to be a governess. If, as Lady Catherine said, that truly was what they wanted, they would help her find a place with a family they all liked.

I will not remain where I am not wanted or needed. If they are opposed to me entering service, which is not a step I am keen to take if I can avoid it, I shall make some other sort of plan. I am resolved that I and I alone will decide what my life will be from now on. I will no longer allow others to make decisions for me, go where they say I must and when.

Walking towards the house after her ride, she saw Herriot pacing anxiously along the path between the stables and the manor.

"Oh, miss, Lady Catherine is looking for you. She has callers, and she said you are to join them at once, and you had best look respectable and demure."

Hiding her surprise, Elizabeth gave the maid's arm a comforting touch. She did not need to see Elizabeth's apprehension, clearly feeling enough of her own. Given what happened the last time she received a similar summons, Herriot's reaction was understandable.

"I had better change my gown, then. That will help with the respectable part, but I am afraid demure might be beyond me at the moment. Let us avoid detection and go to my chamber. Quickly."

What was most astonishing to Elizabeth when she entered the drawing room was not the fashionable young couple but Lady Catherine's attempt to appear as though she liked her. Anne sat near her mother, grinning as though she had been presented with her favourite cake—or as if Darcy finally gave into his mother's wish and proposed.

"Ah, Elizabeth. I trust you enjoyed your ride." Lady Catherine had not used her given name in years, unless it was said as a whole—Miss Elizabeth Bennet—and in the tone of a jeer.

"I did, thank you." Elizabeth trusted the callers would not hear the suspicion in her voice.

"Good. Mr and Mrs Livingstone, this is the young lady I told you about."

The Livingstones greeted her with a degree of eagerness Elizabeth could no more explain than she could Lady Catherine's manner.

"This is one of the families we discussed." Lady Catherine sent her a piercing stare, daring her to ask her meaning. Elizabeth held her tongue, and Lady Catherine continued. "They leave for India shortly and have four children."

"So we do," Mr Livingstone interjected. "Three boys, ages eight, six, and five, and a girl, who has lately turned three."

Lady Catherine said, "You will replace their governess."

"Our current girl does not wish to leave her family," Mrs Livingstone explained. "She told us only last week. Can you imagine? We were ever so relieved when my mother informed us that Lady Catherine knew a young woman with a fine education who would not object to spending three or four years abroad. Oh, I can tell just by the look of you this will work out perfectly!"

Elizabeth barely managed a polite smile. "I regret you have been misinformed. I am not seeking a position as a governess."

"But-but," Mr Livingstone stammered, his eyes darting between Lady Catherine and Elizabeth. His wife clutched his arm.

"Yes you are!" Lady Catherine glared at Elizabeth, all pretence of amiability gone. "It is my express desire, and I insist on being obeyed."

Elizabeth kept her voice as calm as possible. "Even if I agreed to take a position—which I have not—it will be one of *my* choosing. I will never be a governess and would never agree to travel to India, of all places, under the protection of people I do not know."

Mr Livingstone stood and pulled his wife up by her elbow. "I believe it is better if we go. I thank you for your time, Lady Catherine."

Lady Catherine did not look their way or give any indication she was aware of their departure. Elizabeth continued to meet her gaze, refusing to be intimidated.

"My family paid for your education, and we will direct how you use it!"

"*You* did not pay for it. Your mother did and later your brother. If he wishes me to return the great service he did me, he can tell me so himself."

Lady Catherine's voice rose in both volume and pitch with each succeeding exchange. "That money was rightly my daughter's or my nephews'."

"As you have said before. Just because you *wished* it so, does not *make* it so. What Lady Romsley did with her income was up to her."

"Let me make your situation perfectly clear, Eliza Bennet. You will *not* be returning north. You will no longer be tolerated as a dependent on my family. We have done enough for you—far more than you ever had a right to expect or deserve, as your disgraceful behaviour today proves. You have no choice in the matter."

"Yes, I do, and nothing you say will convince me to change my mind."

Lady Catherine jabbed a finger in Elizabeth's direction. "No one else in this family will deal with you as your stubbornness dictates, but I will not give way. I will recall the Livingstones. You will humbly beg their pardon and prepare to depart with them in two days' time."

Elizabeth regarded her reddened face and heaving chest. Anne cowered on the sofa, her expression dazed. Without saying another word, she left them, Lady Catherine's demands still ringing in her ears.

*   ⟶⟿⟿   *

As she dashed to her bedchamber, Elizabeth muttered, not caring if she was overheard, "I thank you for warning me I was about to be sent away against my will, Lady Catherine. I will not allow myself to be abused in such a fashion."

Once in her room, she immediately went to the small pine desk and pulled out a piece of paper and pen. It was only then she noticed Herriot's presence.

As she wrote, Elizabeth said, "Longbourn is not far." Turning to her maid, she asked, "Can you make your way to the village?" When Herriot nodded, Elizabeth continued. "I shall give you a note to send express, and you must secure us passage to Meryton in Hertfordshire for tomorrow."

"V-very well, Miss Bennet. Hertfordshire?"

"My father's estate is nearby. We will not remain at Rosings any longer than is absolutely necessary. Go collect your hat."

While Herriot did as bid, Elizabeth finished both the letter to Mr Bennet and a quick note to Rebecca.

I am going away. Trust me when I say it is for the best. I shall write again as soon as I am able. I need a period of reflection before I know what else to say. You may share this with the earl and countess if you wish, and your dear parents, who have always been so good to me. Tell Bramwell and Fitzwilliam I am well.

We shall see each other again, though at present I cannot say when. I shall send my direction soon and tell you the entire, absurd tale that has led me here. Pray do not despise me for how I have acted.

With a trembling hand, she wrote the address, knowing the missive would be waiting for Rebecca when she arrived at Pemberley.

⋅ ∽◦∾ ⋅

Lady Catherine had Mrs Jenkinson inform Elizabeth that she was confined to her bedchamber until she was prepared to accept her fate. Further, she was being denied dinner. One missed meal did not disturb Elizabeth, and early the next day, she and Herriot made their escape. The assistance of a kitchen girl whom Herriot had befriended because she reminded her of her younger sister had been secured. The child's family lived nearby, and for a handsome sum, one of the sons transported them and their belongings to the coaching inn in a cart.

Elizabeth had not expected the journey to Hertfordshire to be agreeable, but it was worse than she imagined. A large part of it was due to her agitation of spirit. The fortnight since leaving Romsley Hall had been daunting. Lady Anne's betrayal and Lady Catherine's abuse—abetted by her daughter—added to the vague disquiet Elizabeth had felt since the winter when she wondered about her place in the world and what she should do.

Perhaps Longbourn will be my home, she reflected again and again. *It ought to be. It is where my family resides.*

She had memories of living there and of the beautiful sunny day her father took her for a walk and told her she was being sent away. Previously, she loved exploring the grounds with him because he always answered her questions and never scolded her for asking, unlike Mrs Bennet who called her 'unnatural' for being curious. She could still hear Mrs Bennet saying, "When does she leave?" when told of the scheme, and recall sitting in the carriage with her grandmother, who chattered about the importance of Mrs Bennet giving birth to a healthy son. Elizabeth had cried and watched everything familiar to her fade away, certain she would never return. But now she was, and she tried to convince herself all would be well. Her parents would welcome her, and her sisters were surely as curious to know her as she was them.

It was a comfort to have Herriot with her, but Elizabeth did not expect her to stay. She had family in Worcestershire, including a brother employed by the earl and countess. While they were in the coach, Elizabeth said, "Once we reach Meryton, I shall arrange for you to return to Romsley Hall."

To her surprise, the maid shook her head. Her expression was unusually stern. "I cannot leave you, miss. I will do whatever work is needed, so long as I can stay with you."

Elizabeth agreed to say no more about it for the present.

She had some money of her own—what she saved from gifts and the generous allowance Lord Romsley gave her, to say nothing of the bequest from Hugh Darcy—and could pay Herriot's wages, if it came to that. However, what funds she had were her future security, and she would have to exercise caution with her expenditures. In addition, if she should become a companion, she would no longer be able to keep a maid.

When she arrived in Meryton, Elizabeth discovered Mr Bennet had sent his carriage to meet her. A tall, beautiful young lady who was vaguely familiar stood beside it.

Elizabeth went to her. "Jane?"

"Elizabeth?"

Elizabeth embraced her. "I did not expect anyone to meet me. I am very glad to see you."

"I hardly recognised you. You are…"

Elizabeth chuckled. "So grown up? We both are. Can you believe it has been fifteen years since I went away?"

"I suppose it has. Oh. Is that *your* maid?" Jane's eyes grew round as she watched Herriot approach, carrying Elizabeth's things.

Elizabeth glanced at Herriot, who, while clearly a servant, dressed like one who worked in an earl's household. She was struck by a sudden unease, which she soon dismissed as a product of fatigue and the strain of her time at Rosings Park. After all, Jane could not have expected her to travel alone, and as a young lady, it was not so strange she would have a lady's maid, was it? She had not considered it before, but she supposed that at a small estate such as Mr Bennet's, it was impossible for each daughter to have her own maid. Believing she sensed disapproval in Jane's manner, and desiring to be liked and accepted as one of the family, she made light of the situation. It might be necessary for Herriot to leave Elizabeth, regardless of either of their wishes. A day or two would surely determine the best course of action.

"I hope a place can be found for her at Longbourn. For-for a short while. Until she returns to Worcestershire."

As they were settling in for the drive, she heard Jane mutter, "Your own maid."

Certain she detected envy in her sister's voice, Elizabeth did not know what to say. After several awkward minutes, she began to speak about the journey, a topic which saw them all the way to Longbourn.

⁓

Longbourn looked much smaller than Elizabeth remembered. It did not disturb her, but that she immediately compared it to Romsley Hall did. Sternly, she reprimanded herself. She must not think of what she left behind but of the opportunity to know her true home and family again.

They went into what was evidently a family sitting room. The dimensions were good, but there was so much furniture in it, including two tables littered with all manner of items, that it felt far too small for the five people awaiting their arrival.

Jane announced, "Well, here she is."

Jane went to stand with Mr Bennet, leaving Elizabeth alone to face the staring eyes of her relations. She smiled, hoping her expression did not show how uneasy she felt. As her eyes took in each young lady, she tried to determine who was who. The one she thought was Mary had brown hair, while the other two were fair, like Jane. The prettier of the two whispered something to the other, and both giggled.

"It is very good to be here." Elizabeth curtseyed, not sure how to behave or what to say.

One of the girls embraced her, saying, "I am happy to meet

you. I am Kitty." As she stepped away from Elizabeth, she flushed bright pink.

"I am very glad to see you at last, Kitty. And Mary?" She looked towards the dark-haired young lady who nodded. "Which means you are Lydia."

Lydia pinched Kitty's arm causing her to flinch. "It is very strange to have you here. None of us thought we would ever see you."

"Lydia!" Jane hissed.

Mr Bennet, who had been studying Elizabeth with an intense curiosity, turned to his wife. "My dear, shall we invite Elizabeth to sit?"

Elizabeth had been reluctant to look at Mrs Bennet, but she promised herself not to think of the past. After all, Mrs Bennet had likely long ago forgotten her antipathy for her second daughter. Her eyes flickered to Mrs Bennet while also taking in the rest of the family and her setting. The room's disorder made her fingers itch to straighten the books or rearrange the cushions on the sofa.

Lydia pulled Kitty to the table they appeared to be using to trim bonnets, while Elizabeth took the brown armchair Mrs Bennet indicated. Mrs Bennet, Jane, and Mary sat on the sofa, and Mr Bennet went to a chair slightly apart from the rest of them, took a newspaper from the side table, and placed it on his lap as though prepared to open it at a moment's notice. His interest in her appeared at an end, for the present at least.

"What a fine lady you have become." Mrs Bennet dabbed at her nose with a lace handkerchief as she scrutinised Elizabeth's person. "Tell me, why are you come after all this time?"

Mr Bennet spoke before she could reply. "Now, now, my dear. Elizabeth will think you are not happy to see her." He looked ready to laugh, with one eyebrow quirked and the corners of his mouth twitching.

Mrs Bennet adjusted her shawl. "There is nothing curious about her being here, just that she has come."

Elizabeth attempted to make sense of Mrs Bennet's words but gave up and said, "I longed to see all of you."

Mrs Bennet shrugged. "Well, I dare say you will find our way of life very different from those people you were with. If you look to find us running off to town whenever we are bored, or getting up to intrigues as the *ton* does, you will be disappointed."

"Of-of course not."

"We prefer to seek our amusement by making sport of our neighbours," Mr Bennet explained.

"You will meet some of them in a few days," Jane said. "We are having an evening party."

"And we go to dinner at the Gouldings on Wednesday," Kitty added.

Before Elizabeth could make any response, Mrs Bennet announced it was time to prepare for dinner. Mary showed her to her room, and Elizabeth was relieved to have a few minutes to herself.

SEVEN

At the start of dinner, Mrs Bennet demanded, "You brought a lady's maid with you?"

Before Elizabeth could explain, Lydia said, "I wish I had my own maid. I would make her learn all the latest hairstyles and spend every day trimming my gowns. I would be the best dressed of all my sisters and have the most beaux."

Jane scowled, Mary sighed and drank her soup, and Kitty pouted.

"If you had your own maid, I dare say Kitty would expect one, and I could not bear to have even more females in the house." Mr Bennet winked at Elizabeth, who tried to laugh at his jest.

Mrs Bennet soothed Lydia. "I dare say you are already the most popular of your sisters. You are so pretty, not as beautiful as my dear Jane but almost, and so lively. Young men do like a lively girl, not one who is forever reading." She gave Mary a disapproving look.

"What sorts of books do you like, Mary?" asked Elizabeth. "Poetry, philosophy, novels?"

Mary straightened her spine and dabbed the corners of her mouth. "I am sure we do not read the same books and would not think the same thing about them if we did."

"But perhaps we do, and if we disagree on their meaning, it will make for good debate, do you not think?"

"You are a reader, are you?" Mr Bennet asked, not giving Mary time to respond.

Elizabeth said she was, and they spent several minutes discussing the books she had lately enjoyed. Mr Bennet's curiosity went no deeper than asking titles, but Elizabeth hoped it would lead to further conversation.

Mrs Bennet interjected. "I trust the guest room is good enough for you."

It was an odd question asked in a sneering tone, and Elizabeth was not certain about the right response. In truth, she found the room small and the furnishings well past their prime. Not for the world would she say such a thing aloud. "It is very cosy."

Jane stared at her, her cheeks pink.

"It is not the best guest room," Mrs Bennet said. "We have another. You may not think that is much to boast about, but no other family in the neighbourhood, not one with four children, has two guest rooms."

"Five." Mr Bennet chewed a piece of chicken and grinned at his wife, his eyebrows arched.

The realisation that he was waiting to see if she puzzled out his meaning shocked Elizabeth.

Mrs Bennet's voice was half an octave higher when she replied. "Five? Whatever are you talking about? There are two guest chambers, Mr Bennet."

"Children, my dear. We have five."

"Oh Mr Bennet, how you vex me!" the matron cried. A moment later, she returned to the subject. "I suppose Romsley Hall has any number of apartments."

"It is a large house."

Mrs Bennet huffed. "In *this* neighbourhood, only Netherfield Park has more than Longbourn, but it is vacant. Lady Lucas is quite envious of our guest rooms. I suppose you will meet her. She and Sir William are particular friends of ours."

Kitty said, "Do not forget Charlotte and Maria."

"I hardly could with you shouting at me. If only someone would let Netherfield. A family with two or three sons would do nicely."

"Why not daughters?" Mr Bennet held his glass to his lips, but Elizabeth could make out amusement in his eyes.

"You know I am thinking of our girls."

"Are they in need of playmates? Surely, if they are, daughters would serve the purpose much better than sons. I did think they were grown too old for such things, though some of them are silly enough to make me think they left the nursery too soon. I cannot speculate on Elizabeth's level of maturity. Yet."

When Elizabeth saw Jane watching her, she smiled. Jane looked away.

"*Husbands*, Mr Bennet. A rich family at Netherfield with two or three sons would be a fine thing for our girls."

Lydia said, "I say, that is a fine gown. Did you get it in London? Did they take you to town? Have you—"

"Perhaps you should let Elizabeth answer your questions instead of throwing more and more at her." Mary's voice was flat.

Lydia stuck her tongue out at Mary, and Mr Bennet shook his head but said nothing.

"Thank you, and no, I had it made in Worcestershire."

Kitty asked, "*Have* you been to town?"

Elizabeth nodded, and when pressed, admitted to several trips to London.

"They keep a house in town?" Mrs Bennet asked. "I suppose they are impoverished like so many of the nobility and could no longer afford you and your expensive wardrobe."

"Now, Mrs Bennet, let us be glad our second daughter has come to see us."

Elizabeth was grateful he spared her the need to respond. Hoping to forestall a return to the topic of Lord and Lady

Romsley, she asked Kitty to tell her about Charlotte and Maria Lucas.

* ⌀ *

After eating, Mr Bennet retreated to his book-room, where he was not to be disturbed. Mary read in the corner, sending occasional dour looks at her mother and sisters, before going to the drawing room to practice the pianoforte. Kitty and Lydia argued with each other or gossiped with their mother, and Jane sewed beside Mrs Bennet. Elizabeth tried to sit with Jane and Mrs Bennet but found it impossible to take part in the conversation. Mrs Bennet spoke about their friends, hardly pausing to breathe let alone allow Elizabeth to ask a question. Jane made the occasional sound of assent or curiosity. Kitty and Lydia called for Elizabeth to join them at the worktable and quizzed her about parties and gentlemen and her clothes. She sat with them for twenty minutes and found they spent as much time bickering about nonsensical things as they did listening to her. After Mary returned to the sitting room, Elizabeth attempted to engage her in a discussion of music.

"I suppose you had a master," Mary said.

"I did. You are the only one who plays?"

Mary nodded. "It behooves a young lady to find wholesome activities with which to occupy her time."

"Very true." After Mary confessed she had only sporadic access to a music teacher, Elizabeth offered to help her, should she wish. "We might play together. We could learn duets."

Mary did not embrace either idea, but neither did she dismiss them. Speaking to Mary about books was more difficult when she discovered her only literary interest was religious texts. It was an odd habit for one so young.

After two hours, Mrs Bennet retired to her apartment,

demanding Jane and Lydia attend her. Elizabeth took the opportunity to say good night.

As Herriot helped Elizabeth prepare for bed, the maid shared what she learnt from the Longbourn servants. The Bennets were said to be good people, although Mrs Bennet was prone to nervous complaints, the younger girls were too lively, and there was never enough money for what was wanted, including an additional maid to assist the daughters. Herriot was willing to help with the last.

Jane tapped at the door and opened it a crack. "May I come in?"

"Please do."

Elizabeth dismissed Herriot, and she and Jane sat on the bed that was covered in a faded yellow quilt.

Jane sighed and looked wistful. "This room has seen better days. I am sure you are used to much finer. Your clothes, your own maid… I suppose I should have expected it. You did live with an earl and countess."

"I am very comfortable here."

"I was thinking about when we were children. You were always so energetic."

"Not all my memories are strong, but I remember you and Mary and Kitty." And she remembered Mrs Bennet scolding her, telling her to act more like Jane.

"Mary and Kitty were babies then. You cannot know anything about them or Lydia. They are all out, you know, even though Lydia is not yet fifteen."

Elizabeth stood to find a shawl, even though she was not especially cold. It was an excuse to hide her shock.

Jane continued. "In some families, the younger sisters are

not out unless the older sisters are married. I wish Papa insisted on it. They are terribly embarrassing. I have tried to correct their manners, but alone, I have no influence on them. Are there many young men where you lived? The family you were with have sons, do they not? They must have their friends to stay. "

"Not really."

"No? What about relations?" Jane apparently did not remember what Elizabeth wrote to her about them any more than Mr Bennet recalled her telling him how much she enjoyed reading.

Elizabeth returned to the bed, a printed cotton wrap around her shoulders. Mrs Darcy had given it to her the previous year. Jane examined it, even reaching out to feel the soft fabric. "The earl has two sisters, and each has one child—a daughter and a son."

"A gentleman? Is he a particular friend of yours?"

Understanding she meant to imply something of a romantic nature, Elizabeth shook her head. Presently, she did not like to think about Darcy.

Jane sighed. "My mother's chief wish is to see us married." Her words slowed as she went on. "I feel I ought to caution you. Some of the young men here are not worth your attention—I shall point out which ones—and if you do see a gentleman you like, be very careful around my sisters. I love them dearly, of course, but Kitty and Lydia are outrageous flirts. Lydia would love nothing more than to marry before the rest of us. It hardly matters who the man is, as long as he is handsome. A handsome face is well and good, but a man must have enough money to support a wife and family. My mother has spoilt her. That is why she came out when Kitty did in the spring. Mama always talks about how good looking and lively Lydia is, but I am more beautiful. Everyone says so. Truly, you have yet to catch the attention of any eligible gentlemen?"

Elizabeth shook her head.

"That is a shame. There are more young ladies looking for husbands than there are single men in the neighbourhood. I would be happy to know a few more. One of our neighbours talked about a friend he expected to visit, but it was put off so long, by the time he came, he was already engaged. You know Longbourn is entailed?"

"Yes."

"As Mama says, one of us must marry very well. As I am the eldest and prettiest, it falls to me to secure the future welfare of my mother and sisters."

"Do you not want to marry for affection?" Elizabeth wondered if her memory of Jane as a sweet, caring girl was faulty, or if the years apart had changed her nature. Her focus on men and unkind remarks about Kitty and Lydia were distasteful.

Jane smiled; to Elizabeth it looked dismissive. "One must be practical. Charlotte, who is my dearest friend, says happiness in marriage is a matter of chance. I would prefer not to know a gentleman's defects, or to have him know mine, until after we are married."

It was impossible for Elizabeth to respond to such a speech. Mrs Bennet might not find Jane lively, but she was certainly loquacious.

A moment later, Jane asked, "My father was not certain. Have you returned for good, or is this just a visit?"

"I-I have no fixed plans." She had thought she might find a place for herself here, but already, doubt had crept into her mind.

Early the next morning, Elizabeth was walking down the stairs when she saw Mr Bennet and the housekeeper, Mrs Hill.

He said, "Good morning."

She replied in kind, and he invited her into his book-room. Elizabeth sat in a worn armchair, and he took a place behind his desk. A moment later, Mrs Hill bustled in with a cup of tea and a plate of biscuits for her. She was gone before Elizabeth could thank her.

"How was your first night in your ancestral home? Guest chamber satisfactory, despite not being lately and fashionably renovated? My wife, you see. She posited you, who have grown up in the splendour of an earl's abode, would look down upon our humble dwelling."

Before she answered, she tasted the tea, which was too weak and milky. "It is a charming room."

Mr Bennet laughed. "The Romsleys taught you fine manners to go with your fine feathers."

Elizabeth looked at her gown. There was nothing remarkable about it or the straw bonnet by her feet.

"As you see, the house is quiet in the hours before breakfast. The ladies are seldom about."

Elizabeth's eyebrows darted up and down. She could not imagine remaining in her bedchamber until the morning meal, which the Bennets took at nine o'clock.

"Perhaps someday you might entice them to follow your example. Tell me, how do you usually spend your time?"

The scent of the spice biscuits had enticed her, and she finished chewing a bite before responding. "I enjoy a number of activities, and there are many tasks I am used to undertaking. I help with the household budget, deal with the servants, visit tenants, and undertake charity work. When those do not occupy me, I read."

"You were becoming quite a good reader when you left."

She nodded and turned her eyes to the window. The sun was bright, and she planned to wander in the gardens for a while. "I also like to play the pianoforte, sometimes draw or paint, walk, ride—"

"You ride? Jane does, but the other girls had no interest in learning. You will find my stables are not as extensive as you are used to. When you go out, be careful lest you get lost. Take one of the girls with you. I recommend Jane or Mary, but not Kitty or Lydia. They are excessively silly and sure to try your nerves."

"I shall." She stood and said she would leave him to his reading.

"Before you go, we ought to discuss this business with your maid."

Elizabeth blushed, though she was not sure why. "If you are agreeable, Herriot will stay. I shall ensure her wage is paid myself. She would help my sisters' maid, Sarah." After less than a day at Longbourn, Elizabeth hated the idea of sending Herriot away, but she wondered if the maid's presence would cause discord. She hoped not.

He nodded indifferently and reached for a large tome. She left him to it.

⁂

With quick, firm steps, Elizabeth was outside and at the back of the house before she realised it. She wanted to explore the grounds, determined to love them as she did those at Romsley Hall, but, currently, she was too agitated to notice anything. Standing still, she closed her eyes and took several slow, deep breaths. When her heart stopped racing, she opened her eyes and continued her walk at a more sedate pace.

The conversation with Mr Bennet was irritating. It was as though he had forgotten everything she told him about her life in her letters. "And to say, 'when you left!' I did not leave. He sent me away, to live with strangers. I could forgive his language when referring to it, but dear God, the way he speaks about his family." She shook her head as she remembered dinner the previous night and the dismissive tone he used just minutes earlier. "If Kitty's and Lydia's behaviour is so distasteful, why do you not do something about it?"

She took another interval to calm her nerves and told herself she was simply unaccustomed to their ways. Before long, she would like being at Longbourn and consider it her home and the Bennets her family.

After spending an agreeable half an hour in the open air, she returned inside to prepare for breakfast and to assure Herriot she could stay.

EIGHT

At breakfast, Mr Bennet announced Herriot would remain at Longbourn. "Elizabeth cannot do without her, it seems."

Elizabeth gaped at him. When she averted her eyes, they fixed on Jane, who glared at her before schooling her features. Her voice was tight when she said, "You told me she was returning—"

Whatever else she meant to say was lost to Lydia and Kitty's complaints that it was unfair if Elizabeth had her own maid, while they had to share one.

Elizabeth said, "Herriot will assist Sarah, which will benefit all of you."

As the two youngest demanded Herriot perform all sorts of chores for them, Elizabeth vowed to ensure her maid was not overworked.

Mr Bennet retreated to his book-room as soon as he was finished eating.

Mrs Philips was to call that morning, and Mrs Bennet insisted her daughters remain inside to greet her properly.

Kitty protested. "But we see Aunt Philips at least thrice a week!"

"She wants to see Elizabeth anyway. Why do we need to be here?" Lydia said. "I want to go to Meryton."

Lydia agreed to delay her visit to the town once her mother promised her a few coins with which to purchase ribbons.

"But you must not tell your father. You know how he is about such things. He vexes me with his talk of economising!"

Elizabeth had long remembered her aunt as being a younger version of Mrs Bennet. Within two minutes of the woman's arrival, this impression was confirmed.

Mrs Philips sat beside her sister, stared at Elizabeth through narrowed eyes, then, in a voice that must have carried all the way to the kitchens, said, "Is she still as strange as she was before you sent her away?"

Elizabeth's neck and back muscles immediately tightened. Jane was sitting next to her, and Elizabeth was surprised and gratified when her sister took her hand. She wanted to be friends with Jane, but some of her behaviour left Elizabeth wary. They had been close as children, as much as possible given their youth, and Jane had cried bitter tears when Elizabeth went away. She hoped to find that girl again.

"I am very glad Elizabeth has come," said Jane. "Tell me, Aunt, did you happen to notice if there are new fabrics at the linen-drapers? I did not much care for the ones they had last week."

Mrs Philips remained two hours. Elizabeth could not always follow the conversation, and the ladies did little to include her in it. She struggled to keep a patient, polite countenance.

No sooner had Mrs Philips gone then Kitty and Lydia skipped out of the sitting room, giggling as they headed outside. Mary went to the pianoforte.

Mrs Bennet said, "Jane, come with me to my room. There is something I wish to discuss with you privately."

Jane offered Elizabeth a small smile as she stood and followed her mother.

"And that leaves me," Elizabeth murmured. She rubbed

her temples and debated what to do. She could go into the gardens, but Kitty and Lydia were there. Their loudness would turn her slight headache into a megrim. Dismissing a retreat to the guest room as cowardly, she went to find Mary, who was at the pianoforte.

Mary said little despite Elizabeth's attempts to draw her out. When Elizabeth suggested she would fetch her book and read while Mary played, as long as Mary did not object, she shrugged.

An hour later, she was startled from her half-sleep by the door opening. Jane whispered, "Would you like to take a walk with me?"

Elizabeth nodded, placed her book on the side table, and pushed herself out of the wing chair.

Jane was not a strong walker and felt the heat more than Elizabeth. After ten minutes, Jane directed their steps towards an iron bench situated beneath the boughs of an old chestnut tree.

"Mary is terribly fond of music," said Jane. "I cannot say she has much talent for it. I suppose you play."

Elizabeth said she did. "Old Lady Romsley considered it an essential part of my education."

"I see. My mother asked me a great many questions about you. She assumed I know more than I do because we wrote to each other."

The number had dwindled with time until, recently, they exchanged only one or two letters a year.

"Oh?"

Jane shrugged. "She wanted to know what you liked to do,

if you had many suitors or knew many eligible gentlemen. She seems to believe you are here because you were jilted."

Elizabeth laughed. "I have never been engaged or even close to engaged."

Jane said nothing for a moment, then asked, "What sort of gentleman do you want to marry? What would he be like, if you could choose?"

Elizabeth watched the breeze flow through the flowers across the stone path from them; it created a wave of vibrant colours. She could just make out Kitty's and Lydia's voices in the distance. "I suppose he would be hard-working—a gentleman would have investments and an estate to manage and dependents to care for—kind, fair, intelligent, well-read, interesting to speak to." Tall, with dark hair and eyes... *Enough! It was only ever a daydream, and one I despise. I will only think of Darcy as a friend henceforth—if I ever see him again. I will* never *be Mrs Darcy, I never want to be, because it would mean a closer connexion to his mother and aunt.*

"Rich?"

Elizabeth glanced at Jane. "I cannot deny wealth brings with it comforts and opportunities, but I would rather live with modest means and have a husband I truly respect and admire than be rich and have a husband I did not like."

Jane sighed and kicked at the stones.

Attempting to lighten the mood, Elizabeth said, "He must be handsome. I shall not marry an ugly man. Or one who likes beets. Vile things. And he must allow me to keep as many cats as I like."

Jane laughed. "Elizabeth, be serious!"

"Very well. I am a practical being, and I would not accept a man who could not afford to provide me with a comfortable life. Just as important, he must be a man I believe I can be happy with, even when we have only each other for company or are old." To have the security of her own home, she might have to give up her desire to marry for love.

Jane's eyes drifted towards the house, and Elizabeth wondered if she was thinking of Mr and Mrs Bennet's unhappy union. A moment later, seeking an easy subject, Elizabeth asked about the neighbourhood and how they amused themselves. Apart from the usual parties and the occasional excursions to nearby sights, Elizabeth discovered what most excited the Bennet girls were the assemblies held in Meryton.

"The next one will be in early October," Jane explained. "Papa does not go—he cannot abide such gatherings—but Mama will take us. She always hopes some new gentlemen will attend. We cannot risk not meeting them."

Elizabeth could not tell what Jane thought of the senti-ment, so she remained silent and counted yellow flowers until Jane was ready to continue their walk.

•──∞◦∞──•

On days the Bennets were entertaining, Mrs Bennet required her daughters to remain close at hand, apparently so they could listen to her fretting, make largely fruitless attempts to soothe her nerves, and run after Mrs Hill to remind her of what she already knew. Used to long walks or rides every day, and a large house to wander through when the weather was inclement, Elizabeth was restless. She longed for an interlude of quiet and a rational conversation.

After returning from visiting a tenant, Mr Bennet again sequestered himself in his book-room. When he had mentioned the errand at breakfast, Elizabeth asked to go with him.

He refused, saying, "We shall talk about crop yields and the like. Such things are of no interest to ladies."

As it happened, she *was* interested in these subjects, but he did not believe her. Deciding it was because she and the Bennets did not know each other well, she vowed to make the effort to improve the situation. Thus, she agreed to Kitty and Lydia's request to show them her wardrobe.

Kitty said, "We can help you decide on a gown for tonight."

"The right one to drive all the men wild. Jane will turn green with jealousy!" Lydia guffawed.

"I wish to make a good impression, nothing more."

Lydia rolled her eyes, and Kitty giggled.

Fortunately, all the clothes Elizabeth had brought to Pemberley were packed and sent with her to Rosings. She did not know what she would do if she remained at Longbourn beyond a month, yet, presently, she could not imagine being anywhere else. She no longer felt as though she had a place with the Fitzwilliam or Darcy families, which contributed to her determination to make the situation with the Bennets successful.

The girls exclaimed over Elizabeth's things, although Lydia pronounced several of the day dresses boring. After examining each item in her wardrobe, they began to argue over which gown Elizabeth should wear—a blue trimmed with gold and rose embroidery, or a Pomona-green dress decorated with crystal beads. Both were too fine for the occasion.

Jane entered the room, and Kitty and Lydia demanded she agree with their respective choices.

With a calmness Elizabeth envied, Jane sat on the bed. "Elizabeth can choose for herself what to wear. Come, girls, you have made a shambles of our sister's things. Put it all away."

Lydia snorted. "Oh Lord! Sister? Do you know, I quite forgot? It does not feel like—"

Jane cried, "Lydia!"

Kitty stared at her younger sister, mouth hanging open, a gown clutched in her hands. Bright pink spots appeared on Jane's face while Elizabeth felt hers drain of blood.

She stood, picked up a bonnet, and walked to the closet. "I am not surprised I seem like a stranger to you. You were not born until after I was gone."

Mrs Bennet's high-pitched voice flooded through the door. "Lydia! Kitty! Where are those girls?"

Jane's head jerked towards her two youngest sisters. "I forgot. My mother requires your attendance."

Lydia threw the green dress onto the bed and left the room. Kitty looked between the bundle of cloth in her hands, the door, the bed, and Jane. Jane stood, took the gown from her, and told her to go. Still standing at the closet, Elizabeth closed her eyes and let out a soft sigh.

"It looks like a windstorm struck your room." The following words were short and sharp. "I shall help you sort it out, unless you prefer to leave it to your maid."

Elizabeth turned to face her. "Herriot is helping Sarah prepare everyone's gowns for tonight."

Jane's mouth formed a silent 'oh'. She picked up the green gown and fingered the beads. Her features softened, and her expression was either one of longing or sadness. "I have never seen the like. Where did you get them?"

"They were a gift from Lady Romsley." Elizabeth's voice was unsteady with the mix of emotions thinking about the countess evoked, anger and rejection chief amongst them. Rightly or wrongly, a part of her blamed the countess and earl for not loving her and leaving her vulnerable to Lady Anne and Lady Catherine's abuse. But it was behind her now. Soon, she would be of age, and she would choose her own life. Never again would she let others decide where and how she would live, to shuffle her around like a poor, unwanted relation, as had been done since she was just five years old.

They worked in silence for a while before Jane asked what she would wear for her introduction to the neighbourhood. Elizabeth described a white gown with pink trim and returned the question. Elizabeth enquired into the shops in Meryton and expressed a desire to see the town.

⁕ ∽∞∼ ⁕

When she reflected on the party as she lay in bed that night, Elizabeth decided it was an interesting opportunity to study new characters and see how the Bennets interacted with those in their social sphere. Kitty and Lydia flirted with the young men, Mary said little to anyone, and Jane spent the evening in conversation with Charlotte Lucas. Mr Bennet seemed alternately pleased to talk to the other gentlemen and impatient for everyone to go home. Mrs Bennet gossiped with her sister and made loud proclamations on everything from the quality of fish available at the market to the latest fashion in sleeves and the marriage prospects of every single person in the neighbourhood.

There were moments Elizabeth wished herself far, far away but others when she quite enjoyed herself. Charlotte Lucas seemed amiable and sensible, and Elizabeth would not be sorry to know her better. Jane was in a happy mood and told Elizabeth, "I had so hoped you would like Charlotte. The three of us shall have such fun together." The young people spoke about amusements—walking parties and picnics and an excursion to show Elizabeth the ruins of an old church some ten miles away—which sounded promising.

One event left Elizabeth with mixed feelings. When the pianoforte was opened, Mary rushed to it, showing more enthusiasm than Elizabeth had yet seen from her. Alas, Mary was not a skilful player and had no feel for music. Elizabeth was embarrassed for her when, once she was finished her piece, Mr Bennet went to her and said, "Thank you, Mary. Perhaps now we should ask if any of our guests would care to play for us."

Mary all but stamped to the back of the room and sat as removed from the others as possible.

Several ladies entertained the party before Jane asked, "Elizabeth, will you not take a turn?"

Elizabeth was eager to do so and lost herself in the notes and the flow of a lively Mozart sonata.

When she was finished, one of the men exclaimed, "I say, Miss Elizabeth, you are awfully good," and asked if she sang.

Elizabeth played a Scottish melody she particularly liked and that suited her voice, after which she stood, having been taught not to play more than two pieces at a party. The first face she saw was Mary's. She looked as if someone had struck her, and Elizabeth's joy was gone in an instant. Inadvertently, unthinkingly, Elizabeth had injured her sister.

Mary said nothing for the remainder of the evening, going so far as to walk away from Elizabeth when she tried to speak to her.

Over the following ten days, Elizabeth grew more accustomed to life at Longbourn and the people she regularly encountered, such as the Philipses and Lucases. While familiarity did not breed contempt, neither did it breed love. She certainly liked some people, and felt compassion for them—such as Miss

Lucas, who at twenty-seven longed for a family of her own while recognising it was an unlikely prospect, or Mary, who was often overlooked by everyone. Even Mrs Bennet, married to a man who made sport of her at every turn—when he was not neglecting her—earned Elizabeth's sympathy.

On a few occasions, she spent perhaps ten minutes with Mr Bennet before breakfast, taking a cup of tea. The morning after a party at Mr and Mrs Philips' home, he asked, "What did you think of it? Your sisters were in fine form. Lydia was her usual self, but Jane—" He paused to chuckle. "Jane wanted to put her younger sister in her place, eh? Drawing young Mr Long's attention away from Lydia just to show she could. My goodness. I knew daughters would be expensive creatures, but I never realised they would be so diverting."

Elizabeth was speechless and glad to soon escape the room.

She also did her best to spend time with Mrs Bennet and the girls, hoping that by showing an interest in their opinions and activities, she would claim a place for herself in their lives. Mrs Bennet proved to be difficult. She regularly told her daughters what chores to do that day, be it visit a particular person, purchase something in Meryton, or cut fresh flowers for the drawing room. She never requested anything of Elizabeth and hardly ever addressed her directly.

Elizabeth routinely asked, "What shall I do? Sewing, or something in the garden, or—"

Mrs Bennet always replied, "I am sure you can occupy yourself."

Elizabeth also tried to talk to the woman, having observed enough to deduce which topics would best engage her. "I wondered if you would tell me more about the vicar and his family. You know so much about the neighbourhood, and I wish to familiarise myself with them too."

"I have no time for such things." Mrs Bennet kept her gaze averted. "Lydia, my sweet, I wish to speak to you."

When Elizabeth heard the topic was what Lydia would wear when they attended a card party the next day, she went to practise her music.

That evening, Jane said, "Mama, have you heard if the owners of Netherfield have had any luck securing a tenant?"

Elizabeth had learnt Netherfield Park was a large estate about three miles away whose elderly owners had removed to Bath the previous winter. She returned to her needlework as Mrs Bennet complained about it taking such a long time and reiterated her hope that whoever took the house would bring several single, rich gentlemen to the neighbourhood.

"You girls need husbands." Mrs Bennet's tone was almost scolding. "How you will find them, I have no notion. You are a good girl, Jane, so beautiful and gentle, which is what men look for in a wife. I know you will catch the attention of a very fine gentleman, if only we can meet one. Then I need not fear for the future."

Lydia announced, "I shall marry before any of my sisters. I am both beautiful *and* lively. What a great joke it would be if I really did!" When she laughed, so did Mrs Bennet.

"You very well might, dear girl. Your figure is better than Mary's or Kitty's. As for *her*, she is too skinny and always so serious, putting on airs as if she is better than us, talking about this and that. What man wants a wife like that? I cannot afford to keep her when your father dies." The 'her' was Elizabeth. Mrs Bennet seldom used her name.

Elizabeth was conscious that, unlike her sisters, she could afford to remain unwed. The five thousand pounds Hugh Darcy bequeathed her had grown since his death; she never touched the income from it and always saved part of her allowance. Proper or not, if she were careful with the money, she could find a little village and establish her own home. She imagined making friends and involving herself in the community. A cottage would do nicely for her, Herriot, and another servant or two. Wherever she ended up, Elizabeth vowed that no one would ever make her feel unwanted again.

NINE

Jane seemed like two different people to Elizabeth—one the dear friend she remembered from childhood, and the other who was too much a reflection of Mrs Bennet for Elizabeth's liking.

While they walked the grounds after breakfast one morning, Jane lamented the lack of potential marriage partners and spoke about going to stay with her aunt and uncle Gardiner in London. "Although I had no luck last year, perhaps this year would be different. I could return with them after they are here at Christmastide. I would rather marry a gentleman, but a wealthy man in trade would do. I am three-and-twenty and must marry soon. I could not bear it if Lydia marries before me, but she will do anything to ensure she does. You see how brazen she is. She will end up compromised or compromising someone before she is sixteen."

At other times, Jane was an excellent companion, and they shared stimulating conversations. They spent an agreeable morning in the still-room talking about novels and poetry and what it would be like to have the freedom men did. Jane longed to see more of the world. Elizabeth suggested several travel books she might enjoy and promised to lend her one she had in her possession. She had more, but they remained at Romsley Hall, and she did not have the heart to send for her things, even though she did not expect to ever go back. No doubt, she should write to Rebecca again or Lady Romsley, but Elizabeth had no idea what to say to anyone from her old life. At the same time, she could not believe the earl and countess remained ignorant of what transpired at Rosings. They must have deduced where she had sought refuge. If they wanted to know how she was, they could write to her. She was still overly angry and disappointed, and until her emotions were not so disordered, it was better for her to remain silent. She felt let down by Darcy and the Romsleys, even though it was Lady Anne and Lady Catherine who had injured her. The Bennets were another source of dissatisfaction. Elizabeth did not feel they welcomed her presence; her only comfort was that she had not been in Hertfordshire long, and the situation was bound to improve.

Elizabeth was crafting rose water while Jane prepared a peppermint ointment. Elizabeth was unfamiliar with such work, but Jane was willing to instruct her, and she found the exercise interesting.

Jane said, "I wish I could earn my own money, rather than have to marry it. To know I could support my mother and sisters upon my father's death through honest toil would be something. But I have not the education to be a governess, and I would hate to be a companion, always subject to another person's whims, while being paid next to nothing."

Worry marred Jane's features, but Elizabeth said nothing. She would not tell even Jane about her inheritance. If Jane was sometimes envious of a few gowns or because some man, even one she dismissed as a potential target of her matrimonial ambitions, spent an evening talking to Elizabeth, what would she say if she knew Elizabeth had over seven thousand pounds?

"One never can tell what the future holds. Perhaps a rich gentleman in want of a wife will take Netherfield, and you and he will fall madly in love."

They shared a laugh and continued their work.

By the time she had been at Longbourn a fortnight, Elizabeth was familiar enough with the neighbourhood to venture out on her own. Walking through the countryside provided a visual feast for her eyes and ears. She loved hearing the sounds of wildlife, seeing the rocks and plants and occasional signs of human activity. She was able to ride only once and missed the exercise.

When she first enquired, Mr Bennet made a quip about the inadequacy of Longbourn's stables, adding, "Perhaps we can prevail on the earl to supply you with a horse. I suppose you had one at Romsley Hall. What say you?"

He made comments such as this too frequently for Elizabeth's liking. She mentioned the chair in the guest room had a broken leg, and he said, "Shall we send to Romsley Hall for one? They have spares, I am sure, and much finer than I can supply." Jane asked Elizabeth if she wanted to go to Meryton, and Mr Bennet said, "Ah, but you must remember Elizabeth has shopped in London. She would not like what our insignificant village has to offer. Shall we ask the countess or one of her noble relations to send you a selection of goods from town?"

After that conversation, Elizabeth was certain to purchase a purple twill sarsnet suitable for a pelisse. She did not need it, but she would not let stand the notion she thought herself too good for the neighbourhood.

Mrs Bennet said, "A new pelisse? I hope you do not expect me to pay to have it made up."

"I assure you, I do not. I have a little money. The remainder of a gift."

Mrs Bennet sniffed. "It would look better on Jane or Lydia,

but if that is how you choose to dress yourself, it is nothing to me."

Jane said, "I think the colour will look charming on Elizabeth. With her dark hair, it suits her more than it would me."

Mrs Bennet grimaced and began a conversation with Lydia and Kitty.

Elizabeth was pleased with Jane's kind words of defence but knew not to expect such gestures. She assumed Jane would have said nothing, perhaps even agreed with her mother, had she not ordered a new gown. It was a lovely golden colour, and Jane intended to wear it at the assembly in October.

⸻ ◦~◦~◦ ⸻

Bramwell and Fitzwilliam arrived at Pemberley on the sixth of September, entering the drawing room like a sudden storm. They were laughing, and Fitzwilliam punched Bramwell's arm. Their dishevelled, dusty clothing was evidence they had ridden. Standing next to his mother, Darcy could sense her disapproval; she had firm notions about how a future earl should act, especially one who was eight-and-twenty. Sure enough, when Darcy glimpsed at her, her fine features were marred by a gentle scowl.

Bramwell cleared his throat and ran his hands down the front of his jacket. Fitzwilliam attempted to suppress his laughter.

"I beg your pardon, Lady Anne. How do you do?" Bramwell bowed.

"Lady Anne," Fitzwilliam said, "you are looking well."

He kissed her cheek, and Bramwell followed suit. One after the other, they slapped Darcy on the shoulder.

"We were racing," Fitzwilliam said, to which Bramwell added, "I won."

"Because you cheated."

Bramwell opened his mouth to respond, but then closed it and took in the room. "Where is my little sister?"

Darcy waited for his mother to respond, but when she remained silent, he did. "She has not been here. It seems your mother and father decided to take her with them. They did not write to tell you?"

Fitzwilliam's brow furrowed. "No, but I did not expect to hear from them, knowing we would meet here."

For some reason, this disturbed Darcy, and he again glanced at his mother. There had been a certain nervousness to her since his return, but he could find no reason for it. It was worse whenever he mentioned the family party.

They did not discuss Elizabeth further until later that evening. Lady Anne had retired, and the gentlemen were in the billiards room, playing a game. Darcy said he believed something was worrying his mother.

"I might be mistaken, but I am uneasy. I pray she is not ill. This business with Elizabeth is odd too. The earl says she is coming here, but she obviously has not, no one has received news about the altered arrangements, and—"

"Rebecca might have," Bramwell said. "Given the timing of my father's letter, anything Elizabeth wrote about it might not have reached her until after we all went our separate ways. She will be here soon enough and can tell us the latest news."

"Ought you to call her Rebecca?" Fitzwilliam asked.

Bramwell rolled his eyes. "I have called her Rebecca all her life, and I see no reason to stop. I remember to say 'Miss Darcy' in public, just as I call Elizabeth 'Miss Bennet,' which, you have to admit, is stupid since she is as close to a sister as you and I shall ever have."

"But not Darcy fortunately, eh?" Fitzwilliam sniggered, and Bramwell soon followed suit.

Darcy poked one then the other with his cue stick. He had no notion what Fitzwilliam was implying and did not care.

Fitzwilliam's levity changed to sympathy with a touch of seriousness. "Try not to worry, Darcy. In a few days, my parents will be here, Elizabeth with them, and soon Pemberley will be filled with your dear relations. We shall amuse ourselves for the rest of the month, and everything will be well. I am certain of it."

"As am I." Bramwell indicated the billiards table. "Whose turn is it?"

⁘ ⸰◞◦◟⸰ ⁘

The following Monday, his Darcy relations arrived. They were full of anecdotes about their trip, but to Darcy's chagrin, had no news of Elizabeth.

Rebecca said, "I received a letter from her the day before we left town. She said what you already know—Lord and Lady Romsley wanted her to come here. I am surprised I have not heard from her since. I assumed there would be at least one letter waiting for me during our holiday."

Addressing his aunt, Darcy asked, "You have not heard from the countess?"

Aunt Darcy shook her head. "We are about to spend three weeks together. Whatever she had to say to me, or me to her, could wait."

"Anne, you must have had a letter from your brother or sister about Elizabeth," Uncle Darcy said. "They would not arrange to send her to you, change their minds, and not inform you."

Her cheeks pinked, and Darcy studied her, expecting her to do just what she did—respond without really saying anything.

"We shall have the answers we desire when my sisters and brother arrive."

Sisters? Darcy wondered. What did Lady Catherine have to do with it?

The Romsleys were not expected until late on Wednesday or early Thursday, which made their arrival Tuesday unexpected. When Elizabeth was not with them, Darcy's stomach dropped to his feet. His eyes swept over his companions, and he saw perplexity and disquiet on every face except his mother's. She was biting her lower lip and her hands were tightly clasped together.

"Where is Elizabeth?" Lady Romsley enquired. "She is not ill, I hope?"

"I was about to ask you that, Mother," said Fitzwilliam, to which Bramwell added, "We expected her to be with you."

The earl regarded his sons, his eyes slightly narrowed, no doubt questioning if they were playing a trick on him as they had when they were adolescents. "Elizabeth ought to have been here for several weeks already."

Darcy's legs trembled. "She is not, sir. I arrived on the twenty-first, and my mother said your plans had altered."

As a collective, they all turned to Lady Anne. When she failed to speak, the earl said, "Anne, what do you know about this?"

When they came, the words burst from her mouth. "Oh, very well. She was here, but I sent her to Catherine."

"What?" exclaimed the earl, his question echoed by others.

"I wrote to tell her you were sending Elizabeth here, and… and…Catherine suggested I should."

"Why would Lady Catherine want her at Rosings?" Bramwell said. "She cannot abide Elizabeth's company."

Darcy stepped towards his mother, who seemed to shrink into her chair. "Why did you not tell me this before? You claimed no knowledge of her whereabouts. You could not have hoped to have hidden your actions forever."

His mother's lips parted, but for a long pause, the room was silent as everyone awaited her response. "Catherine was supposed to be here before my brother."

Darcy's blood heated. "She would explain your scheme and save you the bother of lying to us further?"

The earl stood beside him. "When are you going to stop hiding behind her skirts? You are not a child, cowed by your older sister any longer. I am seriously, seriously displeased."

From her position behind him, the countess said, "You had no right to do this, Anne. You know how I feel about Elizabeth going to Rosings."

Fitzwilliam muttered, "And how she feels about being there."

A sudden, dreadful thought occurred to Darcy. "Are you saying you sent her to Rosings on her own?"

Sounds of dismay filled the room.

"No, no, not on her own," his mother said, her voice weak. "Her maid was with her."

The earl, his voice like cold iron, said, "You sent her with only her maid on that long trip?"

Shaking her head repeatedly, his mother said, "Mr—" Her eyes grew wide, and she shot a look at Darcy.

"Go on," he said through clenched teeth.

When she did not immediately answer, Lord Romsley roared, "If you will not answer him, you *will* answer me! Who did you trick into helping with this scheme of yours and Catherine's? Was ever a man cursed with two such foolish sisters?"

Her voice was barely audible when she said, "Mr Holt."

"My steward?" Darcy gaped at his mother for a long moment; then, his head ready to burst, he strode out of the room to find Mr Holt, demand an explanation, and dismiss him.

If only he could do the same with his mother and Lady Catherine!

The wait for Lady Catherine's arrival the following day was endless. They could do nothing to make time move quicker and had no fresh information to talk over. Darcy's mother kept to her chamber, which amplified Lord Romsley's frustration, and he went to talk to her. The rest of the party was in the drawing room, trying to remain occupied and ease each other's anxiety. When the earl returned, his face was red, and his hands were in tight fists.

"She had nothing to say?" Darcy said.

His uncle shook his head.

Lady Romsley said, "I shall go talk to her. Perhaps she will be more open with another lady."

"I would not waste your breath." The earl sat beside Fitzwilliam. "She is determined to keep her own counsel for now. I will have a *very* serious conversation with my sisters once Catherine and the girls arrive. They will not like what I have to say."

Darcy paced, the murmuring of his guests too low for him to make out words. He stopped by a window and drummed his fingers on the glass. The day was clear with a smattering of clouds. Facing the assembled party, he said, "I am going for a ride. I cannot stay here without—" Silently, he completed the sentence, *berating my mother, possibly destroying our connexion forever.*

Fitzwilliam stood. "I shall go with you."

Darcy nodded, and when both of them looked in

Bramwell's direction, he glanced between them and Rebecca before shaking his head. Despite his distress, Darcy was gratified Bramwell's instinct was to comfort Rebecca, whose eyes were red and swollen. She had been nearly frantic since learning Elizabeth was not with Lord and Lady Romsley. Of them all, she best understood Elizabeth's feelings about Lady Catherine and his cousin Anne.

"Uncle?"

His aunt patted his hand. "You should join them. It would do you good."

Lord Romsley added, "I shall remain here lest Catherine surprise us and arrive ahead of time."

⁂

The three men took a long, hard ride. It succeeded in calming Darcy, if only marginally. He was worried about Elizabeth and furious his mother would send her somewhere she knew she would be disrespected, if not worse. He said countless prayers that Elizabeth was well and decided to talk to his aunts and uncles about Rebecca making a long visit to Romsley Hall, which would comfort Elizabeth after her present ordeal.

They were trotting to the stables when his uncle asked what happened when Darcy spoke to Mr Holt.

"He admitted to escorting Elizabeth and her maid to Kent. My mother asked him not to say anything about it to me. He did not know why."

Fitzwilliam asked, "What are you going to do?"

Darcy kept his gaze fixed ahead of him, attempting not to lose the iota of ease he had gained during the ride. "I dismissed him. I refuse to have someone here, especially in such an important position, who will listen to my mother more than they do me. Another man has been working with Holt, learning about estate management. I have asked him to take on the role. He lacks experience, but he is intelligent and diligent, and he is younger, which might be to his benefit."

"You have excellent instincts about people," his uncle Darcy said. "My brother always said so. He was the same way, as was my father. I am confident you made the right decision."

A fleeting smile of pleasure crossed Darcy's face, but the closer they came to the house, the more nervous he became. He knew it would continue until he saw Elizabeth.

TEN

As soon as they received word Lady Catherine's carriage had entered the estate, Fitzwilliam said, "I am going to greet them outside."

Bramwell leapt to his feet. "I shall join you."

Other voices followed, and in the end, they all stood in the courtyard, watching as the large travelling coach drew closer. Darcy had the impression the earl insisted Lady Anne accompany him, and she stood behind everyone else.

The vehicle slowed, then stopped, and at last, the steps were put down. Lady Catherine exited, followed by her daughter, Mrs Jenkinson, and…

No one.

Servants retrieved bags from inside the carriage, making the usual noises that accompanied their work. Lady Catherine's voice rose above it all as she told them what to do. For his part, Darcy stared at the unfolding scene, too stunned to know what to say.

"Inside. At once."

The fierceness of Lord Romsley's voice had everyone, apart from Darcy and Lady Catherine, immediately obeying. She took in her brother, her chin lifted, and eyes narrowed. When he repeated his demand, she sailed past them into the house appearing unconcerned. In the drawing room, the earl dismissed Mrs Jenkinson, only confronting Lady Catherine once she was gone.

"Where is she?"

Lady Catherine lowered herself onto a settee and feigned confusion.

"My ward!" He glanced at Lady Anne and demanded she sit beside her sister rather than remain hiding in the corner.

Slowly pulling off her gloves, Lady Catherine said, "I have got rid of her."

For an instant, Darcy was lightheaded. He almost fell to his knees.

"What the ████ does that mean?" the earl barked.

"I found a suitable position for her, something your wife should have done two or three years ago," Lady Catherine said.

In his sternest voice, Lord Romsley asked, "Where is she, Catherine? No more of your games."

Lady Catherine's eyes rested on Darcy. "I shall tell you once Darcy fulfils his duty to my daughter."

Uncle Darcy cried, "Are you attempting to bribe him, to force him to take a step he has *never* desired and my brother refused to sanction?"

Darcy snorted derisively. "I am even less inclined to have you as my mother-in-law—or Anne as my wife—than I was before."

Loud enough for everyone to hear, Bramwell said, "It is hard to believe that is possible."

Darcy threw up his hands in a wild gesture. "I would have agreed, yet here we are!"

At the same time, Lady Catherine said, "You will change your mind. I will have my way in this."

Lady Romsley's voice was thick. She was near to tears, if not actually crying. "Elizabeth is our child, not yours. You had no right to make such arrangements for her. Neither did you, Anne. What were you thinking, sending her to Kent when you knew Catherine would treat her ill? She came to Pemberley to keep you company."

Lady Anne said, "Why would I want to spend even an hour with her?"

At the same time, and at a louder volume, Lady Catherine spoke. "Anne wrote to tell me you insisted she have the girl here. *You* did not want her. Why should Anne? I told her to send her to me, and I would do what had to be done."

Darcy addressed his mother. "How could you? I did not think it possible you could be so hateful. I recall you were not welcoming to Elizabeth even when she first went to live with my grandmother."

"Or later." Uncle Darcy paced the area by the windows, a hand rubbing the back of his neck. "After the dowager's death, she told my brother she would never accept having a child 'like Elizabeth' living at Pemberley. I can only imagine what she meant by that."

The countess said, "We all understood it was too hard for you to see her when we first knew her. It was too soon after—"

His mother turned ashen. "Do not—"

Lady Romsley continued. "But to maintain such antipathy towards Elizabeth all these years, to place her in a situation where you knew she would be misused, is unconscionable." Looking at her husband, she said, "Where is Elizabeth? Oh dear God, why did we not take better care of her?" Mrs Darcy put her arm around the countess's shoulders.

Uncle Darcy stopped walking and faced his wife and daughter. "I should have insisted she come live with us."

"That is unimportant at the moment," the earl said. To Lady Catherine, he added, "What position did you force her into and with whom?"

"I assure you, she left of her own free will. It was days

ago, almost a fortnight. Her failure to contact you shows how fickle her affection is. Once I made it plain she would no longer be allowed to burden this family with her presence, she was done with you." She stood. "My daughter is fatigued. We shall go to our apartments and rest." Turning to Lady Anne, she continued. "You may send dinner to us there."

"You are not to leave this room until I am satisfied you have told me everything," said the earl.

"There is nothing more to say. She is gone forever, and it is for the best."

Uncle Darcy approached. "We need to know where to find Elizabeth. We will contact her, retrieve her at once."

Lord Romsley nodded, and Darcy was already considering how quickly he could prepare to go after her and which of the gentlemen would want to accompany him.

"You cannot." Silence fell at Lady Catherine's words. "By now, she is on her way to India. She is governess to a respectable family. It is good enough for one such as her."

A roar filled the room as everyone spoke at once. The countess's voice stood above the others.

"What of Herriot? She will provide us with more information if Catherine will not. Elizabeth would have told her everything. At the very least, we can learn the family's name."

"She is amply employed, and no, I shall not tell you where."

Never had Darcy been tempted to strike a woman, but Lady Catherine was testing his resolve.

Rebecca spoke for the first time. "I refuse to stay here with her." She pointed at Lady Catherine, and Aunt Darcy immediately echoed the sentiment.

The countess said, "We shall go to Romsley Hall. Oh my poor, poor Elizabeth."

Darcy kept his eyes fixed on Lady Catherine. "None of

you need leave, but *she* does. Get out. Leave Pemberley at once, and do not ever return."

His mother gasped. "You cannot do that. She is my sister!"

"This is *my* home. *I* am master here."

"Will you demand I leave next?"

"Do not tempt me, madam." He felt a hand on his arm; it was his uncle Darcy's, and it helped restore enough of his composure that he held his tongue.

The earl said, "If my niece agrees never to see her mother again, she can go to Romsley Hall for now. We shall make a more permanent arrangement for her later."

"How dare you!" Lady Catherine stepped towards her brother, who stood his ground.

"Leave, Catherine. Darcy does not want you here, and I will not have you at Romsley. You had best hope we find my ward well and soon."

Lady Catherine's gaze flew to her sister. "Anne—"

Darcy was slightly mollified to see that his mother kept her eyes averted. Lady Catherine turned purple. She spun on her heels and hastened out of the room followed by her daughter, who showed more vigour than she ever had before, calling, "Mama, Mama."

As soon as the door was closed behind the two women, Lady Anne held out a hand to Darcy and said his name. He moved away.

"Do not speak to me unless you are prepared to hear everything I am thinking at this moment or you can tell us something useful about Elizabeth."

"Go to your apartment, Anne," Lord Romsley ordered. "Leave us to decide how we will repair the immense amount of damage you have done."

Early one morning during the second week of September, Elizabeth finally decided to face the memory of Mr Bennet telling her she was leaving Longbourn. She walked through the park, past bushes and trees she hardly noticed, and went to the bench at which they had rested, staring at it for a long moment before sitting. Her feet touched the ground now, but that day she swung them back and forth, happy to be outside with her father.

She drifted back to that beautiful, shocking day.

"You are sending me away?"

"Grandmama has arranged this opportunity for you. Lady Romsley is a distant cousin, and she lives at a great estate, one much larger than Longbourn. This will be better for you, Elizabeth. It will be such an adventure."

Papa and Grandmama said she was very intelligent for such a young girl, but she did not understand. He no longer wanted her? Her chin began to quiver, and her voice was small when she begged, "Please, no. I do not want to go away. I want to stay at Longbourn with you and Jane and Mary and Kitty and the new kittens."

"You will be away from Mama for a time." Whispering, he added, "Which will be better for all of us. I hope."

Indifferent to the tears falling down her face, Elizabeth said, "This is because of Mama! I do not make her angry on purpose. It is hard to always have so many questions. I have to ask them."

Her father sighed and kissed the top of her head.

"You are sending me away because I was not born a boy and Mama hates me for it, even though it is not my fault. Now you do not want me either!" She stood and ran to the house.

Looking back on it, Elizabeth realised she had been too young to truly understand what was happening. To her, it seemed he agreed with his wife that their second daughter was troublesome, an inconvenience, an obstacle to what they most desired: a son to inherit the estate. Five-year-old Elizabeth could not imagine what it would feel like to leave the only home and people she had ever known and everyone she relied on to take care of her. She felt rejected by her father and grandmother, two people she thought truly loved her.

Away from Hertfordshire, her life had been good, on the whole, until August and her ill-fated sojourn to Pemberley. Currently, she was angry and bewildered and near desperate to believe she had been right to return to Longbourn.

She stayed at the bench for a long while. Her mind fell silent, and she saw and heard nothing, until the call of a bird of prey startled her out of her reverie. After a great breath in and out, she pushed herself off the bench and continued her walk.

Elizabeth went to her grandmother's grave two days later. She sat on the ground, unmindful of the dampness, and traced the lettering on the stone marker with her gloved finger.

She whispered, "Amabel Rupert Bennet, 1737-1797."

The last time Elizabeth saw her was during the carriage ride north to meet the dowager Lady Romsley. Her grandmother had promised to visit her in Worcestershire, but she was dead before she could make the journey.

"Did you believe you were doing what was best for me? Or was it what was best for Longbourn, a hope that, with me gone, Mrs Bennet's nerves would settle, and she would bear a boy?"

Sending her to live with strangers had been cruel. It had

been the easiest choice for them—rather than correct Mrs Bennet, they simply disposed of the thing that vexed the woman, regardless of whether her discontent was rational or of the damage it would do to an innocent child. Had they considered the consequences? The benefits of having grown up at Romsley Hall were obvious to Elizabeth whenever she was with her sisters; her education and understanding of the world were so much better. Then there was hearing the way Mr and Mrs Bennet spoke to each other. She could not imagine Lord Romsley making sly, sarcastic comments to his wife the way Mr Bennet did. How terrible to live with such parents all your life! However, being sent away had cost Elizabeth her family. Increasingly, it seemed unlikely that she and the Bennets would ever feel real affection for each other.

Darcy, too, had made the easiest choice in not being firmer with his aunt and mother about never marrying Anne de Bourgh, and the entire family had done what was simplest by moving her to Romsley Hall from the dower house when the old countess died. None of them ever considered what these decisions meant for her happiness and well-being. Would it have been so difficult to ask her what she wanted? Was that really such an outrageous notion? Though she recognised she was likely not being fair to them, at present, she could not fault herself for being selfish.

Elizabeth remained where she was until the vicar found her and asked if she required assistance. She told him she was praying, stood, brushed off her skirt, and returned to Longbourn and another evening with the Bennets.

⁕ ᗡᗯ ⁕

The day after Lady Catherine's expulsion, a note from Elizabeth arrived for Rebecca. The handwriting was nearly illegible, which they surmised had delayed its journey north. Darcy greeted its appearance with mixed feelings—relief, followed by renewed confusion and anxiety. It was brief and could easily be interpreted as confirming Lady Catherine's assertion that Elizabeth had left the country. Darcy read it a half a dozen times. She wrote of sending her direction when she could and them seeing each other again without offering even a vague suggestion of when that might be. It made Darcy want to break something. Of them all, he suspected Lady Romsley was the most severely affected. When she left her rooms to join them, she stared at people or walls or out of the window as though seeing nothing, and when she spoke it was to bemoan mistakes she had made regarding Elizabeth, whether they were real or ones she ascribed to herself in her misery.

At present, four days later, Darcy sat in his study, the chair pushed away from the broad oak desk, and gazed out of the window. The sky was overcast, but the rain from earlier in the day was gone. He wondered if the ground was dry enough to go riding. Likely, he should avoid it, if he was not prepared to be covered in mud. As soon as the thought started forming, he saw an image of Elizabeth, laughing, her clothes dirty after they raced across the park. It might have been from her visit to Pemberley last September or another occasion over the past several years when they, sometimes with Fitzwilliam or Bramwell, had thusly amused themselves.

Where was she? He tugged at his hair and attempted to tamp down the dread which brought acid to his throat.

His guests had departed the day before. His uncle Darcy was certain he would have more success making enquiries into Elizabeth's whereabouts from town, and the earl agreed. Fitzwilliam offered to go to Rosings Park to discreetly talk to Lady Catherine's servants, hoping one amongst them would have more information about the people with whom Elizabeth had left or even which route they took, and Bramwell went with him. They would also try to discover Herriot's direction. Not only might she help them find Elizabeth, she needed to be assured she was welcome to return to Romsley Hall.

If, as Lady Catherine said, Elizabeth was on a ship to India, it would be difficult to communicate with her, but perhaps something stopped her from travelling with those people. They had no evidence she had left the country, but equally no evidence she did not. If she remained in England, why had she not written to Rebecca or the countess and requested their assistance? A small voice in the recesses of his mind whispered, *Or mine. I would do anything just to know she is safe and well.*

He wanted to remove to town, but he had just installed a new steward at Pemberley, Mr Potter, and ought not to leave until he was confident the man was comfortable with his duties and competent in executing them. His original intention had been to remain in the country at least until mid-November to oversee several building projects taking place on the estate and in the neighbourhood.

Darcy grumbled and ran his hands through his hair, his agitation making him want to tear it from his scalp. How he hated being there and having to see his mother every day! He wanted to put as many miles between them as possible, and seeking solace, he told himself that perhaps by the end of the month, he would be able to leave Pemberley. Mr Potter was doing well, and Darcy could always return if necessary; however, if he remained, he truly believed he would end up hating his mother.

There was a soft knock at the door, followed immediately by the entrance of Lady Anne. With each step towards him she took, Darcy clenched his jaw tighter and tighter. She perched on the edge of the armchair across from him.

"I asked Mrs Reynolds to bring us tea," she said. "It is mid-afternoon, and you have been working all morning. You can spare the time to take refreshments with me, I trust."

Darcy looked beyond her shoulder and briefly considered leaving the room without answering. He had said as little as possible to her since the day her scheme with Lady Catherine came to light. Since the departure of his relations, she kept badgering him to spend time with her, as though nothing amiss had occurred. As he often did when confronted with a quandary, he considered what his father would want him to do. Hugh Darcy would remind him that she was his mother, no matter how vile her actions, and he owed her a measure of his respect.

"You are mistaken, madam. I have no wish to chat amicably with you while sipping tea and nibbling cake."

She made an exasperated noise, and after a short pause, said, "Have you discovered anything new about Elizabeth's whereabouts?"

"Do not pretend you care for Elizabeth and her well-being. This is what you wanted, after all. She is gone."

"Darcy—"

He did not remain long enough to hear what else she had to say.

ELEVEN

Mrs Bennet was in high spirits as they left church that Sunday. She and Mr Bennet led the way for the short walk home, and as she took her husband's arm, said, "Mr Bennet, there is the most delightful news!"

"Your nerves have spontaneously and permanently healed themselves?"

Elizabeth filled her lungs with the cool air and slowly released it as she forced her jaw to relax. How could a gentleman speak to his wife in such a fashion, especially where people might overhear? She was no longer surprised at Kitty and Lydia's absurd behaviour with such an example.

"Netherfield Park is let at last!" Mrs Bennet announced. "What do you think of that?"

"It was bound to happen sooner or later."

"The new tenant is a rich, young, single gentleman from the north. Is that not a fine thing for our girls?"

"I do not see how." Mr Bennet glanced over his shoulder and winked at Jane and Elizabeth.

Mrs Bennet talked about this mystery man marrying one of their daughters, "and very likely Jane, for she is the eldest and most beautiful." She insisted Mr Bennet visit him as soon as possible, especially before Sir William could, for the Lucases were desperate to marry off Charlotte.

Elizabeth's thoughts wandered. The description fit Darcy well, but it was ridiculous to suppose it might be him. He had

Pemberley and no reason to come to Hertfordshire, even if he had deduced she had returned to Longbourn. Why would he seek her out, given her note to Rebecca had made it clear she did not wish to see any of them?

Most especially, Elizabeth did not want to see Darcy. She could not help feeling that *he* was the reason his mother and aunt had treated her so shamefully. Lady Catherine had admitted as much. What made the whole affair especially egregious was knowing their scheming was pointless. Darcy had never felt for her what she once did for him. Even if he learnt to love her in the future, she would not have him, which ought to be some comfort to the ladies.

If she did see him, Elizabeth wondered whether she would want to embrace Darcy or yell at him. It was far better for all their sakes that they remain separated for the present.

* ⎯ ⸜◝⌣◞⸝ ⎯ *

The neighbourhood buzzed with excitement about the new master of Netherfield. Each titbit of information about him spread like wildfire from house to house and was dissected at every social gathering. His name was announced as Mr Bentley, and it was not until the man was installed at Netherfield and Mr Bennet, after enduring an excessive amount of teasing from his wife and four of his daughters, called on him that the mistake was discovered. The Bennets gathered in the small sitting room while he reported on his meeting.

"I do not know where the confusion began, but he assures me he has never been called Bentley."

"Then what is his name?" Mrs Bennet demanded.

"Is he handsome, Papa? What does he look like?" Lydia enquired while Kitty asked for a description of his clothing.

Mr Bennet's expression showed disdain. "I shall not

comment on his appearance except to say I believe all of you, save perhaps Elizabeth, will fall madly in love with him, whether or not he deserves such a treat. No doubt, that will encourage him to leave Netherfield before the month is out. He comes from the north—Yorkshire, I believe—and his name is Bingley."

Elizabeth heard no more. A roar filled her head, blocking the sound of her companions as the ladies continued to tease Mr Bennet for more information about their new neighbour. How they would stare if they knew *she* could tell them a great deal about the gentleman! Oh why, she wondered, did the new tenant have to be someone she knew—worse, a friend of Darcy's!

Standing, she said, "If you will excuse me for a few minutes."

Without waiting for a response, Elizabeth went to the guest room, seeking solitude to make sense of this turn of events and decide on her best course of action. From her seat at the window, she gazed at the gardens, her eyes wandering to the countryside beyond.

There was no chance she could avoid Mr Bingley. She dismissed her initial notion of asking him not to tell Darcy he had seen her. It would be unfair to ask him to lie for her, and she would simply explain her presence as paying a visit to the Bennets. There was nothing suspicious about that.

She sighed. The assembly was in a week, and she supposed it was time, past time likely, to write to Rebecca and confess where she had sought refuge.

"I *ought* to have written her already. I am a terrible friend, but she will forgive me once she knows everything. I would have thought someone might have guessed where I was and understood my desire not to see any of them. Still, I am surprised the earl and countess did not send an agent to make certain I was well. I suppose it only demonstrates how little they care." She pinched her arm in punishment for the bitter, unfair thoughts. While the Romsleys might not have embraced her as a daughter, they always took their responsibility to her seriously.

Her brow furrowed, and Elizabeth wondered whether it was possible they believed she was elsewhere. If that were the case, they would soon discover the truth.

She was certain Lady Catherine and Lady Anne had devised some tale that did not make them appear to be nasty, hateful people. Her only comfort was knowing Darcy was not with Mr Bingley. He would be occupied all autumn at Pemberley.

There were weeks, possibly months, before she would see him. She would put them to good use to restore her spirit and regain her inner fortitude, lest she be tempted to cling to whatever friendliness he offered her and make more of it than it warranted. To do otherwise would only lead to further heartache.

⚬───⌘───⚬

Darcy was astonished how quickly what he expected to be a pleasant sojourn at his estate had gone wrong. Once his family had finally begun to arrive, it was like a series of bombs exploded one after the other until everything around him was in ruins.

Elizabeth was missing, and the person best able to tell them about what had happened to her refused to do so. The near panic and desolation he felt—fear for Elizabeth's safety and the shame and anger at his mother's role in the appalling affair—would not abate until he knew Elizabeth's whereabouts and he saw with his own eyes that she was well. His mother's continued refusal to admit she was wrong to send Elizabeth to Rosings—and to lie about it afterwards—infuriated him.

Could Elizabeth truly be on her way to India? Darcy did not know what he would do if she had left England. They had been unable to trace her movements or even discover what happened to her maid. Somehow he, his uncles and his cousins had all failed to ask the right person the right questions.

It was a relief to quit Pemberley, and he was ensconced in Berkeley Square by early October. Thoughts of Elizabeth troubled him endlessly. There was no particular reason *not* to think of her, yet spending as much time as he did dwelling on her situation left him oddly confused and as a consequence, restless and with a short temper. Although he would not admit it openly, Darcy spent time devising a way to allow him to go to India to retrieve her, deciding it might be difficult for anyone else to undertake such a trip. If she truly had left England, it was essential she return home as soon as possible.

The day after his arrival in town, he received a letter from his mother which began,

> *I cannot be happy with how at odds we remain. I acted as I believed best for all of us.*

Darcy scoffed and took a sip of wine. Lady Anne could not possibly think it was best for Elizabeth. *She* was the only one who mattered in this circumstance.

He was in his study, sitting behind the desk that had been used by the master for three or four generations. It looked and felt solid and dependable, and at times, Darcy doubted whether he was worthy of it. That he had no notion of his mother's disdain for Elizabeth was a symptom of his weakness.

I expect you here in December. We shall have a quiet Christmas together. In January, I shall return to town with you for several months. Perhaps your disappointment will have faded by then, and you will allow me to guide you as you do your duty and seek an appropriate wife. I am confident you will discover my opinion is invaluable.

Darcy tossed the paper onto the desk. At seven-and-twenty, he was prepared to be a husband and father, should the right lady come along, but his mother was the last person from whom he would ask advice. He intended to choose his own wife. Whoever she was, she must be capable of fulfilling the duties of a mistress, someone with whom he liked spending time in conversation, and with whom it would be a pleasure to walk or ride the grounds of Pemberley. She must be caring, an essential quality in one who would be the mother of his children. Finally, she must have excellent connexions and a substantial dowry. His father had married an earl's daughter. Darcy's children deserve the same advantage, and he had every right to expect it. He knew his value on the marriage mart.

He sighed, looked at the ruby-coloured liquid in his glass, and struggled to set aside his anxiety about Elizabeth so that he could attend to his letters. He failed.

⁕

Fitzwilliam and Bramwell called the next day, and naturally, they talked about Elizabeth. Unfortunately, his cousins' excursion to Kent had yielded no clues to follow.

Bramwell said, "We talked to the new parson our darling aunt installed at Hunsford. He is so absurd, I believe I would rather have a conversation with Lady Catherine than him."

"The few servants at Rosings who would talk to us had nothing helpful to say," Fitzwilliam added. "We went to every coaching inn within fifteen miles. At one, we heard about a family with small children travelling at about the date we calculate Elizabeth left Kent. A man we spoke to recalled seeing a young lady with them, but he could offer no description and had no notion where they were going or the family's name."

Although Darcy had heard most of this news before via letters, he was bitterly disappointed. "I questioned my mother several times, but she claims she did not know what Lady Catherine had planned and can tell us nothing."

Fitzwilliam leant over the table, choosing pieces from the substantial tray of pie, cake, and fruit. "Do you believe her?"

Darcy shrugged. "She wrote to Lady Catherine. I did not see that letter, but my mother showed me the response. Lady Catherine refuses to tell her anything more unless I apologise for my treatment of her and marry Anne. She vowed that only *after* we were wed would she disclose everything she knows."

His cousins spent a minute cursing their aunt. When Fitzwilliam showed signs of growing agitation, Bramwell grabbed a piece of cake from his hands.

"Why did you do that? There is enough for you on the plate."

Darcy sat back, sipped his wine, and waited for them to finish their tussle. It was their way, and Bramwell teasing his brother in that manner was an effective method to ease the tension. By the late spring, Fitzwilliam had lost the brittleness he carried with him upon his return from the Continent. With Elizabeth missing, it had returned, along with a deep anger that worried Darcy and Bramwell, even though they understood it.

Once they were settled in their chairs, Darcy said, "I could bear my mother's company no longer. She attempts to pretend nothing of note has happened. She is confident Elizabeth is well, and Rebecca or Lady Romsley will receive a letter from her any day full of happy news about the adventure she is having." He made a noise indicating disgust. "I know my father would want me to forgive her, but…"

"That is presently impossible," Bramwell finished. "Tell us, Darcy, when we discover the wretched place where Elizabeth can be found, someone will have to go to her and escort her home. Have you decided it must be you?"

Darcy started, feeling as though he had missed an important piece of understanding. His cousins studied him, their eyes seeming to search for something as they awaited his answer. He wanted to kick them and demand they stop acting like idiots.

⌇ ∿∿ ⌇

Two days before the assembly, Elizabeth spent the hours from the end of breakfast until dinner carefully penning a letter to Rebecca. It took many tries before she was satisfied.

I pray you can forgive me for not writing sooner, dearest Rebecca. I have been in a great agitation of spirits and unequal to the task, despite it being one I have performed countless times since we first met.

As the direction suggests, I am at Mr Bennet's estate. At first, I supposed you had guessed where I went after Kent, but of late, I am not certain. I do not know how Lady Catherine explained my absence or how Lady Anne accounted for my not being where you had every right to expect to find me. Has Lady Anne told you how she forced me into the carriage and ordered the coachman to take me nowhere but Rosings and that the only protection I had was Mr Holt, a man I hardly knew?

You can imagine my distress. I was and remain angry, and I admit to you alone—deeply wounded. The less said about the nine days I was at Rosings the better. Lady Catherine and her daughter were as ever, and not an hour passed without one of them assuring me of my insignificance.

When I learnt Lady Catherine was attempting to send me to India as the governess to a family I had never met before, I knew I had to act. Herriot and I made our escape. Longbourn is only fifty miles from Hunsford. Even if I felt secure going so far as Worcestershire on my own, I was not sure what I would find once there. As for Derbyshire, Lady Anne vowed she would never have me at Pemberley again, and I do not doubt her.

As you are aware, I always believed I would return to Longbourn one day. Therefore, I seized the opportunity to come here. You and I have discussed my confused sentiments about the Bennets. It is time to set the past to rest. I can only accomplish that by being here and becoming familiar with Mr and Mrs Bennet and my sisters. I do not say it is easy to return after so long an absence, but in time, I shall be happy I came.

For the present, I shall remain in Hertfordshire. I must reconcile certain feelings, and there are several people I cannot tolerate the notion of seeing. I beg that no one seeks me out. I do not know exactly what my future will be, but I shall forever be your devoted friend.

Elizabeth

She stared at the words, an uncommon sense of uncertainty gnawing at her. Being at Longbourn was not easy, yet she could not imagine returning to her old life. At the same time, she did not want to alienate the people she loved—Rebecca, who had been a true and dear friend since they were five years old, most of all.

"It is the best I can do." Elizabeth hastily sealed the letter. "There will be other occasions for more explanation, and I shall trust her to understand how difficult the last two months have been. Rebecca will write to me, and I shall not hesitate to respond. It is not as though I have to see any of them just yet. I am not prepared to do so, and I do not know when I shall be."

TWELVE

Darcy and Fitzwilliam were talking in a small drawing room when the butler announced the arrival of Mr Bingley. The day was overcast, leaving the room dim.

Bingley grinned as he entered and took a seat, waving off Darcy's offer of refreshments. "I have news," he announced. "I hardly believe I have finally done it. I suppose it is not so unusual for a man my age. I am only three-and—"

Fitzwilliam barked, "Bingley, stop babbling!" and brushed crumbs from his meal off his coat.

Bingley looked between his companions and started again. "I found an estate to lease. I would have asked your opinion," he told Darcy, "but you were not in town when I heard about the opportunity. I drove there one morning, looked it over, and decided right there and then it was exactly what I was looking for in an estate."

"Congratulations!" Fitzwilliam said. "We—by which I mean my cousin—shall make a gentleman of you yet."

Bingley looked sheepish. "Caroline and Louisa ought to be pleased, but until they see the place, who is to say? It is in Hertfordshire."

A spark of a notion popped into Darcy's mind. "Where in Hertfordshire?"

"Near a town called Meryton. There is not much of note about it, but it is pleasant. The estate is called Netherfield Park."

Darcy turned to Fitzwilliam, who returned his gaze. Elizabeth's father's estate was in Hertfordshire, and by the way his cousin had started, the name was familiar to him too.

"Have you met any of your neighbours?" Fitzwilliam all but demanded.

"A few of the local gentlemen called on me. I was only there for a few days, making sure everything was in order. I go back next week. Caroline will keep house for me, of course, and Louisa and Hurst will join us. You are both welcome to come too."

"I am not at liberty to accept," Fitzwilliam said, "but, Darcy, you should go."

"I certainly will."

Bingley left a short while later. Darcy *might* have rushed him out the door, but if he did, he trusted his friend had not noticed or would think nothing of it.

Fitzwilliam and he stared at each other for a long moment before his cousin said, "Longbourn is near Meryton, is it not? Are you thinking what I am?"

"Why the ▓▓▓ did no one write to Mr Bennet to see if he has heard from Elizabeth? She would not leave for who knows where and for who knows how long without informing someone from that family. How stupid of me! I shall talk to Mr Bennet as soon as possible.

"I cannot think well of the man. What sort of person sends away one of his children and neglects them for years? Yet, I do not wish to alarm him by writing to say we do not know where to find Elizabeth. I pray he can tell me more."

Fitzwilliam began to pace. "I wish I could go with you, but there is no way I can, and Bramwell remains out of town."

"Let us go inform my mother and father about this turn of events. After that, we shall see the Darcys. I do not know about you, but I feel this is *important*. Nothing else we have done has helped at all, but talking to the Bennets will. I just know it."

⁑ ꞁᷤꝏᷤᷡ ⁂

At breakfast the day of the assembly, Mrs Bennet was excited to the point of agitation. "Mr Bingley is sure to ask at least some of you to dance."

Lydia, always one to want to garner attention, said, "I shall only dance with him if he is handsome."

"He is rich," Mrs Bennet said sharply. "Nothing else signifies."

"Indeed," Mr Bennet muttered behind his newspaper. He lowered it only when his wife addressed him.

"You must escort us," she said.

"Why must I, my dear? I can think of nothing I would like less."

"To promote the interests of your daughters! A single, wealthy gentleman has taken Netherfield, and I mean for him to marry one of my girls."

He rolled his eyes. He did it so often Elizabeth had begun to wonder whether they would become stuck looking upwards or if the muscles would weaken until he could no longer control their motion at all?

His face again hidden by the paper, he said, "You are more than capable of throwing them at him and advertising their best attributes. They are all silly, ill-informed creatures. If he is foolish enough to offer for one of them, he may come see me."

Mrs Bennet protested, but he would not be moved.

After breakfast, Elizabeth was called on to critique each girl's outfit for the evening. Knowing that her superior under-standing of fashion was the only reason they found her valuable left a sour taste in her mouth. To the Bennets, even though she was flesh and blood, she was not part of their family. It had grown without her, and they had fifteen years of memories of which she had no part. She was a curiosity, someone who ought to fit in like a missing piece of a puzzle, but one whose edges were not quite right.

She should not decide there was no place for her, Elizabeth told herself, not after so short an interval. Surely, if she showed her sisters kindness and patience, in time, they would embrace her.

Contrary to that wish, she was afraid that once they discovered she knew Mr Bingley, they would be unhappy with her, but given how much of a fuss Mrs Bennet and the girls were making over him, Elizabeth had been reluctant to admit they were acquainted. She did not like being deceitful, but she would say she assumed it was a different gentleman because such coincidences were unlikely.

Jane was anxious that Mr Bingley would like her new gown and asked Elizabeth's opinion.

"You will look charming," Elizabeth assured her. "Herriot will dress your hair using the red flowers. The effect will be striking."

Mary asked Elizabeth about the fit of her best gown and which colour sash she should choose. "I do not care what Mr Bingley or any other gentleman thinks of me. However, my mother will tease me if she believes I have not put enough effort into looking my best, such as it is."

Kitty and Lydia pestered her with requests to borrow this or that from her. Elizabeth did her best to ignore how Lydia stamped her foot when she refused to give her one of her dresses to remake to fit her.

"It is very selfish of you," Lydia said. "You have nicer things than any of us, and you refuse to share them. The gentlemen will still like me better. I dare say I shall forgive you, but only because it is the Christian thing to do."

The girls had once again taken out almost every piece of clothing, bauble, and ribbon and left disarray in their wake. As she worked to tidy the room, she reflected that it was just as well she wrote Rebecca. She would need Lady Romsley to send more of her things since it was autumn, and the weather was becoming cooler. While she had supplemented her wardrobe with a few pieces, such as the new pelisse, she did not wish to spend too much of her money, not knowing where she would go once she left Longbourn.

⁕ ⌇ ⌇ ⁕

When the assembly room began to buzz with people whispering, Elizabeth steeled herself to see Mr Bingley and his family and to face the confusion and likely contempt of the Bennets. She looked towards the entrance, seeking the gentleman. Any hope she had that it was a different Mr Bingley was soon lost. He stood, taking in the room, the Hursts and Miss Bingley to his right, and to his left—

Darcy!

Elizabeth's knees buckled. She wanted both to hide and to rush forward and throw herself into his arms. The two of them had only embraced once—after his father's death. He squeezed her arm now and again and twice kissed her cheek on special occasions, but they seldom touched each other unless it was for the commonplace reasons. Presently, she could imagine nothing more magnificent than to feel his strong body holding her, and after all the turmoil of the last weeks, to rest in the comfort of his arms.

Then a surge of anger shot through her. She knew she

ought not to blame him for her current predicament—his mother and aunt were at fault—but she did.

Lydia cooed. "Ooh, who is that gentleman? He is awfully handsome and so tall."

While the Bennets speculated on Darcy's identity, his eyes settled on Elizabeth. Even from a distance, she was certain she observed shock on his countenance, although it was quickly erased. When he began to walk towards them, the Bingleys and Hursts followed him.

"They are coming," Mrs Bennet hissed. "Girls, smile!"

Mr Bingley called, "Miss Bennet, what an incredible surprise! Darcy, you did not tell me—"

"Do you know him?"

Elizabeth assumed she was the intended recipient of Kitty's question. Darcy stared, almost glared at her. She found it difficult to avert her gaze but managed to force her eyes towards the other newcomers.

"M-Mr Bingley, I did not expect it to be you when I heard the name of our new neighbour. I have come to stay with my —the Bennets for a time. How do you do?" She repeated the question to his sisters and brother-in-law before facing Darcy and curtseying.

The resulting commotion was hardly astonishing, but in light of where they were, she explained her connexion to the Netherfield party quickly and made the introductions. Louisa Hurst managed a brief smile and a few mumbled words. Caroline Bingley gave her a curt nod and studied the room, her lips curled in displeasure. Mr Hurst scratched the back of his head, looking bored and disinterested. Mr Bingley's eyes repeatedly turned to Jane, who accepted the attention by acting shy and smiling as though embarrassed while repeatedly peeking at him through lowered lashes.

Just as Mrs Bennet was asking the gentlemen's opinions of dancing, the signal for the first set was given.

Mr Bingley spoke first. "Miss Elizabeth, will you do me the honour of dancing with me?"

"I would be delighted." She avoided seeing Darcy and tried to ignore Jane and Mrs Bennet's scowls. After all, she was not to blame for Mr Bingley asking her to dance rather than Jane.

"I trust you will dance the second with me." Darcy's deep voice caused Elizabeth's cheeks to heat. Although he did not say her name, there was no doubt whom he meant. She nodded her consent.

Before escorting Elizabeth to the lines of dancers, Mr Bingley secured Jane's hand for the following set.

While moving through the patterns, Elizabeth did her utmost to chat amicably with Mr Bingley, lest he wonder at her discomfort. Darcy's odd behaviour after seeing her, which others must have noticed, would raise enough questions.

"I have never been so taken aback in my life!" Mr Bingley grinned and returned the many welcoming smiles the other dancers offered him. "How could I possibly guess the estate I let was so close to your family's?"

He repeated himself many times before the set was out, and each time he referred to the Bennets as her family, Elizabeth became more irritated. While he was not incorrect, to her shame, she did not *feel* as though they were.

Better were the times he asked her about the neighbourhood. Sharing her recently acquired knowledge was easy enough, and during the interval, she introduced him to several people, doing her best to avoid Darcy as long as possible.

When he approached them, Mr Bingley excused himself to find Jane. Elizabeth could have told him exactly where to locate her. Jane had been observing them closely since the set ended, her expression suggesting she was far from pleased.

⁓

Even had his life depended on it, Darcy did not believe he could put together a coherent thought. He had only been so stupefied twice before—when his father died and when he learnt what his mother and aunt had done to Elizabeth. His only expectation of the assembly, apart from ennui and vexation, was an introduction to Mr Bennet who, it transpired, was not even in attendance. Seeing Elizabeth across the shabby room almost made him forget himself, and it took until part way through the first set for him to feel his composure was slightly restored.

It did not help that Mrs Hurst and Miss Bingley refused to leave his side once Hurst took himself off to the card room. Darcy spent the interlude ignoring the ladies and watching Elizabeth. When he heard a shrill voice mention 'Mr Bingley's rich friend,' he sought the source only to discover it was Mrs Bennet. She gesticulated wildly, pointing at Bingley and mentioning her eldest daughter. Curious about the other girls, Darcy searched the space until he spied one of them sitting by the side of the room, her face pinched as though she smelt something foul. The two youngest were making spectacles of themselves, laughing loudly and flirting with any man unfortunate enough to be in close proximity to them. Miss Bennet was standing with a young couple.

As his shock receded, Darcy was angry he had not considered Elizabeth might actually be in Hertfordshire, regardless of every reason he had to believe she had left England. It was not as though Lady Catherine and his mother were incapable of lying if it suited their purpose. Some of his irritation was directed at Elizabeth, whether or not she deserved it.

Standing across from her, he loosened his jaw enough to say, "You are here."

With a nonchalance that made him want to roar, she said, "Evidently."

Darcy scrutinised her. She did not look well, and he added another target of his fury—the Bennets for not taking better care of her. How could Elizabeth remain in such an unhealthy setting? *Why* did she? His mood was not helped by having to dance—an activity he despised—to secure a few minutes of relative privacy with her. There was so much he wanted to ask her.

"I trust Lady Anne was well when you last saw her," Elizabeth said.

"I suppose. *You* are not, however." She was thin. The added prominence of her cheekbones showed it.

"I am quite well."

"No, you are not. Are you getting enough exercise? Your colour is good, but—"

"Stop," she hissed. "Pray remember, your words might be overheard. How are the earl and countess, and Bramwell and—"

He could not prevent sarcasm entering his voice. "Remarkably happy, considering everything. Why are—"

Elizabeth shook her head. "I can imagine what you want to ask me, but do not do it here. You need to smile and look pleased before people start gossiping about us."

The dance separated them, and Mrs Bennet's voice disrupted his reflections.

"How well Jane and Mr Bingley look together! I suppose he felt he had to dance with *that girl* for the first, since he knew her previously. The sly, hateful creature said nothing

about it! He has four or five thousand a year, you know! Mr
Bingley was taken with Jane at once, just as I knew he
would be."

"Naturally," Mrs Philips said. "She *is* the most beautiful
girl in the county and has the sweetest disposition."

Elizabeth's eyes dimmed. "That is Mrs Philips, Mrs
Bennet's sister."

Darcy wished he could alleviate her evident embarrassment. The Bennets were clearly vulgar, objectionable people,
and sensible as she was, Elizabeth no doubt regretted seeking
shelter with them. She would agree to depart as soon as it
could be arranged.

When he could speak only for her ears, he said, "When
and where can we meet?"

"Tomorrow morning before the breakfast hour. There is a
path along the stream that runs between Longbourn and
Netherfield."

Darcy gave a curt nod. Tomorrow, they would talk freely,
and she *would* answer his questions.

⁕ ⎯ ᔕᕷᔕ ⎯ ⁕

The Bennet ladies began to question Elizabeth about Mr
Bingley, his family, and Mr Darcy as soon as they were in the
carriage for the ride back to Longbourn. She had no desire to
discuss anything having to do with the assembly and wished
she could be alone. The Bennets' behaviour had mortified her
more than once from the moment they saw Mr Bingley to the
time they wished him good night. Mrs Bennet had seized the
opportunity to assure him of Jane's good nature and her
certainty that his 'dear sisters' would enjoy knowing her better.
Poor Mr Bingley had looked unsure how to answer, and Eliza-

beth had avoided looking at Mrs Hurst and Miss Bingley who must have delighted in the absurdity.

Jane asked, "Why did you never tell us you knew him?"

"I did not suppose it was the same Mr Bingley."

Mrs Bennet made a noise of disbelief. "Very likely you hoped to keep him for yourself."

Elizabeth was glad for the darkness, which kept her from seeing Mrs Bennet's expression or that of the girls who sounded angry and suspicious. She was assailed with questions about when they first met, how many times they had been in company together, his family, his likes and dislikes, and too many more to possibly answer, especially since the ladies spoke at once and hardly paused to let her respond.

Jane leant across the seats to grasp her arm. "Mr Bingley *is* single? There is no lady in town or elsewhere with whom he has an understanding?"

"Not to my knowledge."

"Jane, my dearest girl, this is wonderful news! He was very taken with you. I saw it immediately. How could he not be?" Mrs Bennet said. "What about Mr Darcy? Is he also single? Well, girl, is he?"

Elizabeth bit her tongue to prevent the retort that first came to mind. "Yes."

"He is the most disagreeable man ever," Lydia said. "He gave me *such* a look just because I was having fun and am not afraid to show it."

"Does Mr Bingley have any brothers? Will his other friends come to stay?" asked Kitty.

"He has no brothers, and I cannot say if he will invite any friends to Netherfield, let alone who they might be."

Bile climbed up her throat as she listened to Mrs Bennet talk about how they would go about securing Mr Bingley for

Jane and how overjoyed she would be the day her daughter became the mistress of Netherfield Park.

"Everyone will envy me, especially Lady Lucas. I shall speak to your father about buying you new gowns, Jane. We must ensure you look your best whenever he sees you."

Mr Bennet was awake and in the drawing room when they arrived at Longbourn. Elizabeth assumed he was curious about the assembly, despite what he said to the contrary. He expressed interest in Elizabeth's acquaintance with Mr Bingley, his family, and Mr Darcy.

"How exciting. You must be glad to see friends again, eh, Elizabeth?"

"It was unexpected, but that does not mean it was unpleasant."

"Mr Bingley was charming!" Mrs Bennet walked around the room, waving her handkerchief. "He is everything a young man ought to be, and he will do nicely for Jane. That other man though, Mr Darcy—"

"Is horrible," Lydia said. "He did not even dance!"

Kitty said, "Except with Elizabeth, Mrs Hurst, and Miss Bingley."

Mary joined her mother and younger sisters in glaring at Elizabeth as though she were to blame. "I am not responsible for his choices in partners." What she wanted to say was that any man of sense would stay far away from such silly girls.

Mr Bennet did not show the same restraint. "Mr Darcy displayed remarkable intelligence. Why anyone dances, I do not know, but if one is going to engage in the exercise, they ought to avoid standing up with girls whose heads are full of nothing but fluff."

"Oh Mr Bennet!" his wife cried, as Kitty squeaked in protest.

"It matters not to me," Lydia said. "*I* danced every set."

Mrs Bennet sat beside Jane. "Mr Bingley asked Jane twice. He did not dance more than once with any other lady, but then, none of them have her beauty."

Elizabeth was thoroughly tired of hearing about Jane's looks and sweet nature. Even if it were true, repeating it over and over again was tiresome. Jane's sly smile as she watched Elizabeth did nothing to improve her mood.

Jane twisted a curl around her finger. "I enjoyed meeting Mr Bingley's sisters. I noticed you did not spend much time with them. You said you are not friends."

"We have little in common." The ladies had decided she was an inferior being and treated her accordingly. Seeing them with Jane, Elizabeth sensed their friendliness was intended to demonstrate how much they preferred her sister to her. In the morning, she would find a way to caution Jane about them.

When Mrs Bennet whispered to Jane, her voice carried across the room, the matron's talents not extending to discretion. "She is jealous because Mr Bingley and his sisters like you more than they do her. Watch her, Jane."

No one, not even Mr Bennet, defended Elizabeth, but she had not expected anything different.

Mrs Bennet continued. "Mr Darcy might be disagreeable, but he is rich and must be in want of a wife. What do you know of him? What kind of ladies does he favour?"

Every set of feminine eyes was locked on Elizabeth, even Mary's. Mr Bennet chuckled. She considered mentioning Lady Anne's determination to see her son married to his cousin, but she did not wish to inadvertently create rumours about Darcy.

Instead, she said, "I would be very surprised if he married a lady without a large dowry and excellent connexions. It was what he was taught to do."

"What about Mr Bingley?" asked Jane.

Mrs Bennet patted Jane's cheek, "Nothing will stop him from marrying you."

Mr Bennet said, "Do not be so hasty, my dear. I rather hope Elizabeth has similarly discouraging words about him. Take heart if she does. Not even she can be right all the time."

Elizabeth's nails dug into her palms. "I do not seek to be discouraging, only honest. I do not know Mr Bingley's views on marriage. His elder sister married to improve the family's social standing, and Miss Bingley intends to do the same. I have long supposed he would too."

"Mrs Hurst and Miss Bingley were amiable," Jane said. "I cannot believe they give as much credence to connexions and fortune as your words suggest. They would wish their brother to select a lady he likes."

"I hope they do put affection and compatibility above other considerations."

When Mr and Mrs Bennet began to quarrel about the necessity of purchasing new clothes for Jane, Elizabeth quietly slipped out of the room.

THIRTEEN

Darcy surveyed the countryside as he rode to his meeting with Elizabeth the next morning. It was pleasant, he supposed, but if the prior night was indicative of the society here, he would just as soon depart that very day. The only reason to remain was to be near Elizabeth, and *that* would not be an issue for long.

No sooner had he stepped into the carriage the previous night than Mrs Hurst and Miss Bingley began to share their opinions on the evening, none of them good. Bingley was his usual enthusiastic, optimistic self, and claimed everything and everyone was delightful. Darcy wished his friend would be a little more discerning. Bingley never saw a fault in anyone or anything, and that tendency would surely lead him into trouble.

When he was not studying Elizabeth at the assembly, Darcy watched his friend. It was evident he enjoyed the company of Miss Bennet. Whether she deserved the attention remained to be seen, but from what Darcy saw, she did not. None of the Bennets, other than Elizabeth, were worthy of his notice.

His Great Dane gave a loud bark and raced off, leaving Darcy to call after her and urge on his horse, Barbary. Just past some hedges, he saw Elizabeth crouched down, a smile on her face, scratching Freya's ears and patting her side. The way the morning light reflected off her skin and hair was enchanting.

As he dismounted, keeping the reins in his hand, she stood.

After they regarded each other for a fraction of a second, Darcy found his arms around Elizabeth and hers around him. He had not intended to embrace her, but it felt both right and necessary. She soon stepped away and returned to petting Freya.

"It is a lovely morning, is it not?" She glanced at him as she spoke.

He was in no mood for chit-chat. "Is this where you have been the whole time?"

She took a deep breath before responding. "Where did you think I was?"

He wanted to grab her by the shoulders and make her look at him. "Lady Catherine told us you had taken a position as governess and were on your way to India. India! Nothing we discovered told us differently. Despite every effort my uncles, Fitzwilliam, Bramwell, and I took, we could find no information on the family we supposed had hired you, no hint as to the direction you travelled, *nothing*! How were we—"

Before he could go on, she said, "I assumed at least one of you would guess I had come to Longbourn since it is so close to Rosings. If you did not think I was here, why did you come? Was it just because Mr Bingley invited you to his new estate?"

"I did *not* expect to see you. I wanted to talk to Mr Bennet and discover if you had written to him. How could you not tell anyone where you were? Do you not understand how frantic we have been?"

"I wrote to Rebecca."

"The short missive she received at Pemberley that told us absolutely nothing?"

Elizabeth's cheeks coloured. "I wrote her again three days ago. She knows exactly where I am by now and will have told your aunts and uncles."

"Three days?" Darcy slammed his teeth together, struggling not to lose his temper. "Is Herriot with you?"

"Yes."

"That is a relief. Lady Catherine said she had a new position but would not tell us where." He did not want to admit that the vile woman had attempted to bribe them, saying she would only tell them where Elizabeth and her maid were after he married his cousin Anne.

"We will go to Longbourn. You can tell her to pack your things, and we will leave for town this morning."

Elizabeth looked incredulous. "I beg your pardon? I am not going anywhere."

"You cannot want to stay here! You should be at home—"

"Where exactly would that be?"

He gaped at the question, confused by her meaning. "With my aunt and uncle."

She shook her head dismissively. "I lived in *their* home. That did not make it *my* home."

"How can you say that? The earl and countess have been distressed, my aunt distraught, not knowing where you were or if you were even safe."

Her expression darkened, and she averted her gaze. Although she muttered, he heard her say, "I doubt it."

"You are being unfair," Darcy insisted.

"Unfair? What about any of this is fair to me?" Elizabeth struck her chest with a fist. "Was it fair when they told me to go to Pemberley, even though they must know your mother has never liked me or desired my company? Was what your mother and aunt did to me fair? Do you know what Lady Catherine told me? It was because of *you*, because you are my friend, and they do not like it. I distract you from doing your duty, they despise me because—*apparently*—you praise me but say nothing complimentary about Anne."

He kicked a rock, turned his back to her, and went to watch the stream for a short while before he said something he would regret. Darcy wanted to scream, but the true targets of his fury were not there. Over the years, he had many reasons to condemn his mother and aunt, but that they had used *him* to abuse Elizabeth was the most unforgivable.

The silence between them lasted for what felt like ten minutes but was likely not even one. The only sounds in the clearing were from the flowing water and Elizabeth's soft murmurings to his dog and horse. When she spoke to him, her voice calm but firm, he turned to face her.

"Darcy, I have no intention of leaving at present. This is an opportunity to know the Bennets, and I…require a period to restore my spirits after what happened."

A sense of sadness settled on him. After her disclosure, he did not have the strength to argue with her further that morning. He knew at once that he would remain at Netherfield to observe her and, in the coming days, convince her to return to Lord and Lady Romsley.

"Why did you not ride here? You might have shown me the best paths between the two estates. Bingley would like to know."

Elizabeth shrugged offhandedly. "Only Mr Bennet keeps a riding horse. The others in Longbourn's stable must serve several purposes." He was not aware of his expression changing, but it must have, because she rested her hands on her hips and fixed her eyes on his. "It is not so uncommon. The Bennets have more than most people here."

"I realise that." He raised a hand in supplication.

"Do you? Their income is perhaps one-fifth your own, but far more people are in their position than in yours. Do not forget that *this* is who I truly am. I come from a family of modest means, where the daughters have no dowries, poor prospects, and connexions to trade. If you did not already know me, the Bennets and I are the sorts of people with whom you would never wish to associate. Well, now you have the opportunity to rectify the error that began with my being sent to live with your grandmother!"

She spun on her heels and stalked away, leaving him vexed and confounded.

⁂

If she could have, Elizabeth would have avoided breaking her fast with the Bennets. She had not known what to expect from her meeting with Darcy, but it had been both pleasurable and painful. The way he had held her was…words could not describe it.

Staring at herself in the mirror as she prepared for the morning meal, she murmured, "I wanted to stay in his arms forever, which is a dangerous sentiment. Never have I felt so safe and peaceful, even though it lasted but a moment."

In the aftermath, she was peevish, especially when he treated it as a given that she would leave and return to her old life.

"Go back to people who are responsible for my present circumstances?"

A sad laugh escaped her lips. Mr and Mrs Bennet bore some of the blame, too, for having banished her from her rightful home and family when she was a child.

"There is nothing I can do about it now," she insisted to her reflection. "I shall remain where I am at present. I have not given up hope that I can establish a closer connexion to the Bennets—Jane at least. The fact that Darcy and I argued only convinces me I am not prepared to see Lord and Lady

Romsley or anyone else. We might quarrel, and who is to say where that would leave us?"

She recalled the daydream she had before going to Pemberley of spending the coming weeks imagining she was Darcy's wife. The very thought of what her life would be like if they had married and Lady Anne was her mother-in-law left her nauseous. It would be nothing but distress and acrimony.

"I admit I was happy to see him. It is only natural. But any tender feelings I had for him are at an end. To cling to them is to do myself a grave disservice."

Conversation at breakfast centred on Mr Bingley. Elizabeth only half-listened because when she paid attention to it, it disturbed what little peace of mind she retained. After one meeting, Mrs Bennet was already talking about Jane having captured Mr Bingley. Fortunately, they appeared content to neglect Darcy. His lack of friendliness had done him—and her—a good turn.

Part way through the meal, Mr Bennet made a show of announcing that, for the first time, Elizabeth had received mail.

"Two letters from London." With a flourish, he passed them to her. Likely, his manner was meant to embarrass her, amuse himself, or both. Her temper flared, and she bit her tongue. A quick glance at the handwriting showed her who had sent them. It was as she expected.

Mrs Bennet demanded, "Who would write to her?"

When everyone looked her way, it felt as though worms were crawling down her back. "They are from Lady Romsley and Miss Rebecca Darcy."

Jane, in a high tone, said, "You have never spoken of Miss Darcy before."

Elizabeth stopped the sigh that was her immediate response and explained how she knew Rebecca.

"I suppose she is very elegant," said Jane.

"She is very kind," Elizabeth replied. Never had Rebecca's generosity of spirit been more in evidence than during the months they were together at Pemberley after Hugh Darcy's death. She had shown endless patience with Lady Anne while also grieving her beloved uncle and doing what she could for Darcy and Elizabeth. Bramwell had come for six weeks at the same time, and watching the romance between him and Rebecca develop had been amusing and heart-warming at such a dark time. That was also when Elizabeth fell in love with Darcy.

As soon as possible, she went to the guest room, threw herself on the bed, and tore open the letter from the countess.

My darling Elizabeth,

The earl and I are more relieved than you can possibly know to learn you are safe and well. We feared the worst, especially when the boys failed to find any trace of you. We had no notion how ill Anne would treat you when we decided you should go to Pemberley. It is, regrettably, easier to believe it of Catherine, but I thought Anne had more sense than to send you to Kent, especially knowing Lord Romsley and I would not like it. I do not believe I have ever seen my husband so angry as he has been with his sisters since their despicable actions came to light. I am very sorry we did not keep you with us.

Oh my dearest girl, I believe there is a great deal we must say to each other, but I shall wait until we are together and you are prepared to have that conversation. Please believe that you are very dear to me and to the earl.

THE TRUTH ABOUT FAMILY

Mr Darcy has shared your letter to his daughter with us. I would much rather you were with us in town or at Romsley Hall, but he has convinced us you should be allowed to remain where you are since it is what you wish. I will only agree if you write to me at least once a week. I understand Rebecca will invite you to stay at Curzon Street after they return from seeing Mrs Darcy's family in Dorset, and you are, of course, free to accept. You are to inform me at once should you wish to leave Hertfordshire before then or should you need anything at all. I shall arrange for more of your clothes to be sent to you.

Lord Romsley sends his sincerest regards and affections, as do I.

Yours &c.,
  Lady Romsley

The countess's words were warmer than Elizabeth expected, and she had included a substantial sum of money, more than Elizabeth could possibly need or spend while in Hertfordshire. She almost believed Lady Romsley was frightened by what happened and not knowing Elizabeth's whereabouts.

Elizabeth was still shocked that the family had believed her bound for India. Had she known, would she have written sooner? She was not certain. Anticipating Rebecca's letter would offer greater explanation, she turned to it next.

Dearest, dearest Elizabeth,

Words cannot describe how happy I was to receive your letter! We had no notion where you were and our anxiety has been unbearable. Lady Catherine led us to believe you had taken the position you wrote about. She assured us you had already left for India, and no matter how much Lord Romsley demanded she tell him the name of your employers or where Herriot was so she could be questioned, she would not. I should start by telling you what happened at Pemberley.

Rebecca wrote about Lady Anne first claiming Elizabeth had not been at the estate, later admitting to having sent her to Rosings Park, and the argument that arose when Lady Catherine and Anne de Bourgh arrived without her.

I do not know who was more furious—Papa, the earl, or Darcy. My cousin says he feels particularly responsible, given his mother's involvement in the scheme. I suspect Darcy regrets not questioning her further and discovering her lies sooner. Before he left town in August, Bramwell and Fitzwilliam told him he would find you at Pemberley.

Darcy demanded Lady Catherine depart at once. My parents and I remained several days, until the gentlemen decided it might be easier to trace your movements from town. Papa went to carry news of your well-being and location to Lord and Lady Romsley.

By now you might have seen Darcy. He was to go to Mr Bingley's new estate, which Bramwell tells me is in the same neighbourhood as Longbourn. I shall overlook the coincidence of you finally writing and Darcy being there and instead believe you always intended to tell me where you were.

As much as I long to go to you or have you here with me, I reluctantly accept your desire to be with the Bennets for now. If any good has come out of this, it is that you have the opportunity to know your parents and sisters. I am tempted to tease you by saying 'your other sisters,' for you know I have considered you my sister since the day we met.

I insist you promise to come to us this winter—if not before then, should you tire of being at Longbourn. Mama and Papa begged me to remind you that you always have a home with them, as you will with me, wherever I live in the years ahead.

Mama and I leave to stay with her sister and brother-in-law next week. I like visiting Dorset, and with Papa departing for Wales a day or two before we travel south—you recall he is accompanying the travelling judges—it is preferable to staying in London. Regardless, we are determined to bring you to us, or collect you and return to town at once, should you even hint you wish to leave Longbourn.

I beg you to write to me again soon. Tell me what it is like to be at your old home again. Is Jane as you remember? What of your younger sisters? I pray you have found four dear friends in them. Assure me you are well, but if you are not, do not hide it from me. I can do nothing for you if you do. Always remember you are loved by me, Mama and Papa, and many others.

Rebecca

Elizabeth buried her face in her pillow and released her

sorrow and regret for the life she had left behind in a torrent of tears.

⚬ ⤳⟋⟍⤳ ⚬

Throughout the day, Longbourn was visited by a steady stream of callers. Everyone wanted to ask Elizabeth about Mr Bingley. She was also asked about Darcy, but his aloof manner at the assembly had made him far less interesting than the affable young tenant of Netherfield Park. Elizabeth did her best to say as little as possible, if only to avoid falling into the trap of gossiping about someone she considered a friend. It was difficult to be easy when it was evident the attention she received irritated Mrs Bennet and Jane.

At dinner that night, Mr Bennet said, "Well, Elizabeth, I dare say you have not been so popular since your return. Are you enjoying your success?" He cocked one eyebrow, and a corner of his mouth was raised.

Yes, I am very fortunate to be the object of your amusement. Lucky, lucky me! she thought. Aloud, she said, "If I can ease Mr Bingley's way as he joins the neighbourhood, I shall be happy to do so." Seeing Jane's eyes fixed on her, her mouth a firm, straight line, Elizabeth added, "I shall soon return to my previous obscurity. My knowledge of the gentleman is limited, as you know."

That night, Jane came to the guest room and repeated the same questions about Mr Bingley that Elizabeth had already answered several times.

"Is there nothing more you can tell me about him?" Jane asked.

"I regret there is not."

Jane scowled and studied the painting of an unknown Bennet ancestor that hung over the bed. After an interval, she looked at Elizabeth, her features and voice now inviting confidences. "Elizabeth, tell me truly, do you *like* Mr Bingley? If you do, I shall think of him no more."

"I do like him but as a friend only." Elizabeth twisted the ties of her robe in her fingers. "Jane, you have just met him. You danced with him twice. You can hardly know whether *you* like him or not."

Jane shrugged, stood, and said good night.

FOURTEEN

In the week after the assembly, the Bennets saw the Netherfield party twice. Elizabeth went through such a range of emotions during that time, she hardly knew what to think. Her anger at Darcy for his role in what Lady Anne and Lady Catherine did, unintentional as it was, made her want to refuse to see him and demand he leave Hertford-shire. But Elizabeth was weak, and his presence, especially since he said nothing about August or her returning to the earl and countess, was a comfort.

Her harsher sentiments dissipated, and she remembered that whatever else she had once felt, Darcy was her friend, and she absolutely needed a friend at present. Naturally, she expected he had written his uncles and cousins. She wished to know what he told them and at the same time was glad she did not.

Forced indoors from a walk in the gardens by the rain that had started to fall, Elizabeth found Jane waiting for her.

"Look what just arrived!" Jane shook a sheet of paper under Elizabeth's nose.

Elizabeth cautiously took it from her and discovered it was an invitation for them to spend the morning at Netherfield Park with Mrs Hurst and Miss Bingley.

Jane spoke quickly and began to pull Elizabeth towards the stairs. "Does it not show how much they like me? What should I wear? Mr Bingley must be there. Where could he go in the rain? Help me select a gown. I have already spoken to my father about using the carriage."

There were few ways to pass a rainy day that Elizabeth anticipated less than in company with Mrs Hurst and Miss Bingley, but as it happened, spending it at Longbourn was one of them. Accordingly, Elizabeth put on a yellow gown adorned with stitched autumn flowers and leaves that she deemed appropriate and prepared to accompany her elder sister to Netherfield. Privately, she dared the ladies to find fault with her dress. Lady Romsley had selected the fabric, and while Mr Bingley's sisters might criticise Elizabeth's tastes, they would never knowingly say a bad word about a countess.

Mrs Bennet issued instructions to Jane as they walked to the carriage. "Take every opportunity to speak to Mr Bingley. Remember to smile and push your shoulders back. It shows off your figure to best advantage." She tittered. "If they press you to stay to dinner, as they likely will, accept at once. Oh, if only it would storm! Then they would *have* to ask you to stay for dinner and very likely for the night."

Elizabeth adjusted her hat as a way to hide her face and the expression of disgust she could not prevent at hearing the matron's machinations.

Jane and Elizabeth did not speak during the drive. At Netherfield, they were shown into a drawing room. Elizabeth had never been to the estate before and took in the surroundings with interest. The chief colour was ivory, from the walls to the sofas and chairs, with only a few portraits and other furnishings to add contrast. It created a rather washed out, empty effect.

"My dear Miss Bennet," Miss Bingley called. "We are so glad to see you. Sit here beside Louisa and me." She dipped her chin at Elizabeth.

Mrs Hurst's greeting was only slightly warmer. Sensing

she was not wanted, Elizabeth chose a chair a little apart from them. A number of books were set on the table beside it; the bindings showed they were Darcy's. Elizabeth selected one at random—*Richard III*—and settled in to read.

Over the next two hours, she made good progress with the play and overheard snippets of the ladies' conversation. Miss Bingley and Mrs Hurst asked about the Bennet family and, if they did not already know, learnt that Longbourn was entailed to a distant, estranged cousin and Mrs Bennet's brothers were in trade.

Elizabeth had a private moment of amusement when she recalled meeting the heir, although the memory of Lady Catherine's sycophantic parson was unpalatable. She had not told any of the Bennets about meeting Mr Collins.

Elizabeth glanced up in time to see Miss Bingley's expression as she looked at her sister. The woman's brow was arched, and her lips were pinched as she shook her head back and forth. Jane was turned to Mrs Hurst and did not see it.

When the ladies were served a light repast, Mr Bingley and Darcy entered the room to join them.

"Mr Darcy, I despaired of seeing you at all this morning," Miss Bingley cooed as she stood, went to his side, and linked her arm with his.

Darcy's eyes met Elizabeth's for an instant before looking at his hostess. "Your brother and I had accounts to go through, as he informed you last night."

"I shall reward you for finishing with a piece of spice cake. I know how you favour it."

"We are not done. A cup of tea would be quite enough for me."

"Nonsense! Come, see everything I ordered. There must be something I can tempt you with." Miss Bingley giggled and pulled him to a table where platters of fruit, cake, bread, cold meats, and cheeses were arranged.

Mr Bingley immediately took a seat next to Jane, and after exchanging greetings with her, addressed Elizabeth. "You are well this morning?"

"I am, thank you. I can see you are, despite the weather."

He laughed. "Even though it is raining, I may ride out. Darcy is keeping my nose to the grindstone. He is right to do it, as much as I would rather be amusing myself. I never realised how much work was involved in managing an estate. He knows just what to do and is so good at it that it makes me feel incompetent!"

Elizabeth chuckled.

"Oh Mr Bingley, do not say such a thing!" Jane's tone was disturbingly close to the one Miss Bingley used when she spoke to Darcy. "I am sure you do yourself a discredit. I have never met a wiser gentleman, I am sure."

A light blush coloured his cheeks. "That is very kind of you, but I have no head for figures. I had much rather be riding or shooting or fishing."

He looked between the two of them, which Elizabeth could see Jane did not like. If only she could convince Jane that she was not her rival, they might get along better.

"Your sisters tell me you travel to Yorkshire to see your family every year," Jane said. "Will you tell me about it? I have heard Yorkshire described as the most beautiful county in England."

Mrs Hurst remained in her seat until Miss Bingley and Darcy approached the sofa, having made their selections. The woman then rose to prepare herself a plate.

Mr Bingley leapt to his feet. "How rude I am being. Miss Bennet, Miss Elizabeth, please do let me assist you."

Jane held out a hand for him to help her stand.

Darcy announced, "There is no need, as far as Elizabeth is concerned. I have fixed a plate for her. As I told your sister, I am not hungry." He nodded to Miss Bingley, ignored her subtle hints he should join her on the sofa, and walked towards Elizabeth.

Holding a half-filled plate, Mrs Hurst stared at Elizabeth in surprise while Miss Bingley glared at her, angry red spots on her face. Elizabeth chose to ignore them.

"Thank you, sir. That was kind," said Elizabeth.

Darcy took the chair next to her and in a low voice said, "I did not bring you any cake. It is better than any other variety I have had at Netherfield, but it is still terrible."

Her lips twitched in amusement as she regarded him. "You are in a fine mood."

Darcy ran a hand over his forehead. "I spent the morning with Bingley, trying to explain the intricacies of certain estate expenses while Hurst sat in the corner snoring. We left him there. I would rather still be in the study, but Bingley insisted we take refreshments with you."

Elizabeth's hand paused as she raised a piece of cheese to her mouth. "It is lovely to see you again too."

He met her eye for a moment before grunting. "My apologies." He lowered his voice again. "I am very glad to see you. Miss Bingley grows tiresome, and I would rather not be in company with her more than I must. I suppose she has neglected you since you arrived?"

Elizabeth nodded and tried to decide what to eat next. She was frequently so tense while sitting at the table with the Bennets that she could not eat, but she had no such hesitancy with Darcy beside her, despite the current state of their friendship.

She had decided there was no purpose to being angry with him. Darcy never meant to injure her, even though he had by never viewing her as more than a friend and not standing up to his mother and aunt. Blaming him for any of it was irrational and kept her from taking comfort in having someone familiar in the neighbourhood. It helped that he had stayed quiet about her supposed-disappearance and returning to the earl and countess.

"Earlier, the ladies discussed not inviting you, no doubt meaning it as an insult. Bingley insisted they ask both of you or neither. How could such an agreeable person have such disagreeable sisters?"

"It is one of the great mysteries of life." She contemplated her plate and selected a piece of apple. "Do not feel obliged to speak to me. You have a brief reprieve before you must play teacher again. I am content to read."

He asked which book she had chosen, and they spoke about the play. When Mr Bingley was finished his repast, Darcy stood and suggested they return to the study.

To Elizabeth, he said, "I had some books sent from town for you. New volumes I thought you would enjoy and might not see for several months otherwise. I shall have them placed in your carriage."

His thoughtfulness brought a smile to her face. "Thank you."

"If there is anything else you require or would like, you need only tell me. I believe we dine together in a day or two."

"I believe you are correct."

"Perhaps the weather will improve before then, and you will be able to walk in the mornings. I assume you have not the last few days."

"I hope so, and you assume correctly."

After Darcy wished Jane a good day, and Mr Bingley said he hoped to see the Bennets very soon, the ladies were left to themselves once again.

While Miss Bingley and Mrs Hurst told Jane about attending St James's, Elizabeth opened her volume. Although she stared at the page, it was several minutes before she began to read. Her thoughts were too full of Darcy.

―――― ⌒⌒ ――――

In the carriage on the way back to Longbourn, Jane spoke about how pleasurable she had found the morning. "I would have liked to stay to dinner. I could see Miss Bingley wanted to ask me, but there was no excuse to offer an invitation, and I did not bring a proper gown. They always dress for dinner, even when it is just the family. Mrs Hurst told me it is customary amongst the finest families. I suppose the people you lived with do." Jane was oddly reluctant to name the earl and countess.

"They do."

It was a moment before Jane spoke again. "Mrs Hurst and Miss Bingley are the most affable ladies I have ever met. I do not know why you felt you had to caution me about them. *You* may not have made a good impression on them, but they like *me*. They see their brother's interest in me and approve. Perhaps you have not been friends because they did not think you would suit him."

Elizabeth almost stopped the carriage to get down and return to Longbourn on foot. She turned her head to the side to look out of the window.

They did not talk again, and Elizabeth spent the remainder of the short journey wondering whether she stood any chance of establishing a close connexion to Jane, and if it was too much to ask to want to feel settled. Having even one true friend at Longbourn would help.

At dinner, Mrs Bennet insisted on hearing every detail of

Jane's morning. After listening to what the ladies talked about, what Miss Bingley served, and what Jane said to Mr Bingley and he to her, Mrs Bennet said, "What a great thing it will be when you marry him! My daughter, mistress of Netherfield. He has five thousand a year. Five thousand! We need never worry about money again. You must secure him as quickly as possible. When will you next see him?"

"At the Longs for dinner the day after tomorrow," Kitty answered.

Jane and Mrs Bennet stared at the girl until she mumbled something and returned to her dinner.

Mr Bennet said, "Another time, Kitty, you will have your share of the conversation. For now, let us partake in the great diversion your mother and sister are unwittingly offering us."

Elizabeth quietly placed her fork and knife on the table.

"What shall I wear, Mama?" asked Jane.

"The rose—or perhaps the orange with the net. Oh, if only *that girl* was closer to your size, you could wear her blue gown. It would look much finer on you than it does her!"

'That girl' was an increasingly annoyed Elizabeth. They discussed trapping a gentleman she had known three or four years, and she was supposed to help them? She would not allow them to injure Mr Bingley. If Jane honestly grew to care for him, Elizabeth would do nothing, but if Jane simply wished to marry him because he was rich, she would have no choice but to intervene. It would make her relationship with the Bennets more fractious, which she regretted, but she saw no other option.

⸻

The following morning was fair, and Darcy slipped out of the house early to avoid Bingley. He went for a ride, hoping to meet Elizabeth. The day was cool, but not cold, and the air was crisp and refreshing—just the sort of day to attract her.

He saw her close to where they had talked the morning after the assembly. She was gazing up at a tree, perhaps taking in the beauty of the bare branches in their varying shades of brown and grey against the brilliant azure sky. He only had eyes for her and did not know when he would have spoken had not Freya barked and loped up to her, demanding to be pet. As Elizabeth played with Freya, she offered Barbary a carrot.

Darcy said, "You will spoil them."

Elizabeth shrugged and ran her hand along Barbary's nose.

"I had Nutmeg, which I still say is a stupid name for a horse, brought to Netherfield. She arrived yesterday, after your departure." Nutmeg was the horse his father gave Elizabeth for her sixteenth birthday.

Her eyes flew to him, and her cheeks flushed. "What am I supposed to do with her?"

"You said there was no horse for you here, and you missed riding."

Elizabeth huffed and shook her head. "I cannot keep her at Longbourn. The expense—"

"The earl will pay, or I shall take—"

"No! I am not his responsibility, and I am certainly not yours."

Darcy was shocked by her words. It was not so much as they pertained to him, though he was slightly offended since he only meant to do her a kindness, but regarding the earl, he could not have understood her correctly.

"You do not consider my uncle responsible for your care? You have lived with him and my aunt since you were ten years old." Elizabeth would not look at him. "You have nothing to say to that?"

Her jaw set, she locked her eyes on his. "Why did I live with them, Darcy?" When he shook his head, confused, she continued. "Because no one knew what to do with me after your grandmother died. I was never supposed to stay away from Longbourn for so long. It was to be six months or a year, just long enough for Mrs Bennet to be safely delivered of her child." She lifted her hands in a gesture of resignation. "Yet no one came to get me, and no one sent me back. I know there was a debate about returning me to the Bennets. Fitzwilliam told me years ago. Your mother and Lady Catherine were in favour of it, and at last, a decade later, they succeeded."

"Elizabeth, you are —"

"Save your breath. I am glad I came. I ought to have insisted on it years ago."

Darcy wanted to roar. How could she be happy to be here? The Bennets were, at best, ill-behaved, and it was painfully easy to see signs of distress in Elizabeth's countenance. While still lovely, she had lost weight and looked as though she was not sleeping well. Wanting to avoid arguing with her, he took a handful of steps away, once again watching the stream as he had done during their last private interlude. When he was calm, Darcy turned to her.

"I shall say nothing more about it today. As for your horse, she will stay at Netherfield, and you can go there when you want to ride her."

Elizabeth blinked several times in rapid succession, and her voice was thick. "Do you have any idea of the position in which you have placed me? How am I supposed to explain that I have my own horse at Netherfield? You have no..."

When she failed to continue, Darcy said, "Finish what you were going to say."

"You have no idea how little they would like it." She

changed the pitch of her voice. "Oh, Elizabeth has her own horse, whereas we do not."

"Frankly, I do not care what they think."

"How arrogant of you! They are my sisters."

His expression showed the scorn he felt. The Bennets were *not* her family in any meaningful sense. "I am thinking of your health. You need the exercise. Go ride like the ████ across the countryside. It might help you think rationally again."

Elizabeth straightened her spine and tipped her chin upwards. "What is that supposed to mean?"

"I knew they were not treating you as they ought. Why do you tolerate it? As for your implication that the earl and countess, to say nothing of other members of our family, see you only as an obligation, it is unfair and unkind, and the Elizabeth Bennet I know is neither of those things."

Averting her gaze, she said, "You do not understand."

"Then tell me," he begged, stepping towards her. He almost took her hand, but apprehension stopped him, although he could not say what frightened him.

She shook her head.

"If you will not or cannot explain it to me, write to Rebecca, or Lady Romsley, or Aunt Darcy."

After a pause, she said, "My situation is not as bleak as I suspect you fear. I *want* to remain here."

There was a lengthy pause before he gave her a brief smile. "I do not believe you, but I do not want to argue with you. Shall I tell you about the letters I received from my uncles, Lady Romsley, and your foster brothers?" He deliberately referred to his cousins in that manner to remind her they were her true family.

All of them had many questions regarding Elizabeth's welfare and his impression of the Bennets. He was not entirely honest about his ill-opinion of them, in part because he knew

Elizabeth would not like him to say they were detestable and in part to avoid causing too much anxiety, especially in his aunt. He was most open with Bramwell and Fitzwilliam. All of them urged him to remain in Hertfordshire as long as possible, since Elizabeth tolerated his presence.

"No, thank you. I trust you are not exaggerating or speculating on anything that will only distress them or cause them to come here."

"Your reluctance to see them baffles me," Darcy admitted.

Again, she took her time before responding. "I know, but please respect my decision. I am not hiding or-or saying I will never go back, and I write to Rebecca and Lady Romsley regularly."

"The countess mentioned you may go to Rebecca again this winter, once she and her parents are returned from Dorset. Will you?"

"Probably." She adjusted her hat. "I ought to return to Longbourn. I shall be late for breakfast if I do not hurry."

In an instant, she was gone.

FIFTEEN

Having overcome the barrier of sending the initial letter to Rebecca, the two resumed their habit of frequent correspondence. Elizabeth also wrote to Lady Romsley, if only to prevent her from growing over-anxious and coming to Longbourn to see her. She could not imagine a meeting between the Romsleys and Bennets ending in anything other than the earl and countess insisting she remove with them at once. Elizabeth gingerly told Rebecca of the difficulty she faced in establishing a connexion to the Bennets, and Rebecca replied.

I do not think you at all unnatural for saying they did not immediately feel like your family. How could it be any different, given the long separation between you?

"How, indeed," Elizabeth murmured as she read the letter for a third time. She had expected it to be an easy matter to think of Jane, Mary, Kitty, and Lydia as sisters and for them to view her as such. "I expected too much. I *wanted* too much after what happened this summer."

Another part of Rebecca's letter was worthy of repeated study.

Bramwell and Fitzwilliam are in town again. They are over-joyed to know you are safe, and they admitted to being tempted to ride to Hertfordshire to see you. Lord Romsley told them they must respect your wishes, so I believe you do not need to worry about unexpected visitors. Darcy wrote to Papa and Lord Romsley, and I do not think either of them were entirely satisfied with his report. In short, my dearest friend, he expressed concern regarding your well-being, especially your spirits, which he believes are depressed. How could they not be, after what those horrible women did to you in August? I pray having someone you know so well as you do Darcy nearby for these next weeks will help.

I saw Lady Romsley yesterday. Whenever we meet, she questions me closely about your letters, my opinion on your mood, &c., and Lord Romsley and Papa speak about you often. I know you have felt they do not care for you as much as you would like. Recent events have shaken them, and I believe they recognise your true worth and the depth of their affection for you at last. I understand your reasons for wanting to remain at Longbourn for the present. I am trying to, I should say, but I am a selfish creature, and I long for your assurances that you will come to town once my parents and I return from Dorset. You will find the situation with the earl and countess improved.

Elizabeth ran her hand over the soft leather cover of a volume of verse. It was one of the books Darcy gave her. His attentiveness to her, to wanting to ensure she was as comfortable as possible at Longbourn verged on too much. Setting the book on the side table, she told herself to do something other than remain alone, thinking about Darcy and how much she missed her old life and the people in it, and debating whether she trusted Rebecca's word about Lord and Lady Romsley.

While appreciating the earl's present insistence that everyone abide by her wishes, she worried it would not last. If she returned to town or Worcestershire, would he and the countess again begin to order her life for her, take away her ability to choose? Beyond that reason to remain where she was, a part of her refused to give up on the possibility of the Bennets becoming her family. It felt vitally important to know that at least some of them cared for her, although she could not really articulate why other than feeling her place in the Fitzwilliam and Darcy families was insecure.

Elizabeth put Rebecca's letter in her pocket, curling her fingers around it. It comforted her to have it close by as she went about her day.

⌁

Several days later, Elizabeth saw Darcy at an evening party. As they had when they were at the Longs earlier in the week, they did not speak much. Unlike that occasion, this time Mr Bennet attended, and Elizabeth observed the two men spend some minutes in conversation. It made her nervous, and when an opportunity arose for her to speak to Darcy privately, she asked him about it.

"I know you called on Mr Bennet when you first arrived in the neighbourhood. You cannot have that much to say to him."

He regarded her, his deep, dark eyes penetrating, for long enough that her mouth grew dry with nervousness.

"Meet me tomorrow, and I shall tell you about it."

Elizabeth agreed, and while the sky was still dusky, she set out from Longbourn the next morning. This time, their paths crossed closer to Netherfield.

Without even words of greeting, Darcy said, "I almost

brought Nutmeg with me. Why have you not been to ride her yet?"

"Good morning, Darcy. You are well, I trust?"

He kept a steady gaze on her and waited for her to answer his question. She did not know what to say. The previous afternoon, after listening to Mrs Bennet and Jane again discuss Mr Bingley and how wonderful it would be when Jane was his wife, Elizabeth had almost gone to Netherfield. She stopped herself when she realised what she most wanted was to ride all the way to London and pretend she had never been in Hertfordshire.

"I hope you do not intend to be stubborn and refuse to ride her simply because you disapprove of my arrangements," he said when she, too, remained silent.

"You mean because you were high-handed? No, I will not. I simply have not found the time. What did you and Mr Bennet talk about?"

"Why have you not told him the reason you are here? He was not even certain where you were when you informed him to expect you the following day."

"Are we going to spend the morning exchanging questions?"

"I shall stop if you will."

Tilting her head to the side, she watched him, her brow arched in a manner that demanded he provide her with answers first.

"I did not tell him what happened, if that is what you want to know. I have not told you, and I should have, but, Elizabeth, I cannot apologise enough for what my mother—"

"You did not have a hand in it, and I expect no apology from you."

"But what Lady Catherine said to you about me, our friendship—"

"I would rather not talk about it."

Darcy clenched his jaw and paused before continuing. "Mr Bennet's manner is disengaged. Is he always like he was last evening?"

Elizabeth shrugged. She had all but given up hope that the man she remembered from her childhood still existed within the current Mr Bennet.

"How long do you intend to remain here? At present, Uncle Darcy believes they will return from Dorset before the end of the year, but that is still over a month away. Why not go to the countess for now?" Although Elizabeth shook her head, Darcy persisted. "You can remove to Curzon Street as soon as Rebecca and her parents are in town again."

They were quiet for an interval, the only sounds those of his horse snuffling and Freya, who sat by Elizabeth's feet, gnawing on a stick.

When she decided Darcy would not speak until she did, Elizabeth said, "I am not prepared to do that. Unless something here changes, I prefer to wait until I can go to Rebecca directly. If nothing else, I am secure from unpleasant encounters with Lady Catherine there, given how much she hates Mr Darcy."

He did not look satisfied, but chose not to pursue the subject—at least immediately. "And Mr Bennet?"

She sighed. "At first, I did not tell him because none of them asked, not even him, and I had no wish to recall my time in Kent. They still have not enquired, and I do not see any purpose in making the disclosure. What difference would it make? Do you imagine it would alter how they see me if they knew your mother and aunt attempted to force me into becoming a governess and sailing to India?" Even she heard the bitterness in her voice, but when he said her name, Elizabeth waved her hand impatiently, suggesting she had nothing further to say on the subject.

"Business calls me to town for a week or perhaps two. I must make arrangements for some land I want to buy, and I might, at last, have a strong candidate for the Kympton living."

"Oh. You are coming back?" She almost collapsed with relief when Darcy nodded.

"Bingley has decided to give a ball at the end of November, and I promised I would attend. Do not tell anyone about it yet. They will announce it soon." When she nodded, he went on. "Bingley extended an invitation to your foster brothers. You know they wish to see you."

The mere thought of being with Bramwell and Fitzwilliam again made her feel lighter than she had in some time. "If they are at liberty, I would not object to their coming—as long as you make it clear I do not wish the entire family to follow them."

The only other person she felt capable of seeing was Rebecca. If any of the older generation came to Hertfordshire, even Mr and Mrs Darcy, Elizabeth believed she would immediately have to seek shelter somewhere far away where they would not find her until she wished it.

"I may not be able to remain long after the ball."

"I understand. In truth, you have been here longer than I expected."

"How can I want to leave when you will not?"

Elizabeth's mind screamed that Darcy did not mean it the way it sounded.

He continued. "I would not, if I could attend to my duties from here. I left Pemberley sooner than I intended this autumn, and as much as my new steward is competent, some of the older tenants are making his job difficult, likely because of his young age. I should return before there is much snow to ensure everything is prepared for the winter—the rebuilding complete, ample supplies of grain stored, and the like."

"You have a new steward?"

"Do you truly believe I would continue to employ Mr Holt when he played any part in forcing you to go to Rosings or when he failed to tell me about it for weeks afterwards?"

Darcy was a good friend, she decided, and Elizabeth would appreciate him for that without allowing other feelings, which she had worked so hard to suppress, to reassert themselves.

When he placed his hat on his head, she knew it was time to part. Elizabeth gave Freya and Barbary kisses on their noses. Darcy gently squeezed her arm, they said their adieus, and went their separate ways.

Jane and Mr Bingley met several times over the next week. Watching her sister with Mr Bingley, Elizabeth experienced an uneasy sensation in her stomach. Whether they were at the Gouldings' home for dinner, the Philipses' for an evening party, or in Longbourn's drawing room, Jane did everything she could to engage Mr Bingley and was not pleased when he paid attention to other young ladies. Yet, Elizabeth detected no sign that Jane truly esteemed him. She did not know what to do about it and was comforted by the knowledge that the couple had not known each other long. He would not be so foolish as to propose marriage on so short an acquaintance.

In the second week of November, Lydia's birthday was celebrated with great fanfare, and two pieces of news spread through the neighbourhood, causing much excitement. The first was that a regiment of the militia was to make their winter quarters in Meryton. The second was that the Bingleys would host a ball.

Mrs Bennet welcomed both. "All those officers," she said at dinner. "I do like to see a fine-looking gentleman in a uniform."

"Will we see them often, do you think, Mama?" Kitty asked.

"I dare say we shall."

Lydia laughed. "They will like me most of all, for what could be more welcome after doing whatever it is the militia does all day than a girl such as me to keep them company? Jane, you can have Mr Bingley. I want an officer!"

"Mr Bingley never wanted you, so you cannot give him to me," Jane hissed.

"Girls, girls! There will be enough gentlemen for all of you," Mrs Bennet exclaimed. "Oh, I do hope one or two of them will be rich enough to make good husbands!"

Lydia laughed again. "I shall find out who is. I might still be married before Jane."

Elizabeth saw Jane's nostrils flare.

"Oh, for the day you are all married, and I am free from such nonsense!" Mr Bennet complained.

For a minute or two, the only sound in the room was that of knives and forks scraping across plates. Lydia, Kitty, and Mrs Bennet chattered during the rest of the meal, and Jane joined them in speculating on the possibility of there being eligible officers. Elizabeth did her best not to hear any of it and wished Mr Bennet was more inclined to talk about books or the news with her. Wanting to avoid hearing the subject of the militia discussed all evening, Elizabeth excused herself for the night after drinking a cup of tea, saying she had a headache.

As she left the sitting room, Mrs Bennet said, "That girl does get a lot of headaches."

Mary said, "Perhaps the air in Hertfordshire does not agree with her."

Elizabeth thought, *No, I do not think it does.*

SIXTEEN

Life at Longbourn continued as usual over the next week. Elizabeth missed Darcy and came to appreciate how much his presence made being in Hertfordshire tolerable. She wondered whether she should leave with him after Mr Bingley's ball or with Bramwell and Fitzwilliam if they attended. Was it only stubbornness keeping her there? The answer was elusive, but whether she removed with her friends at the end of November or waited for Rebecca to be in town, Elizabeth would not remain in the neighbourhood much longer and increasingly found she did not regret it.

Colonel Forster, who was in charge of the local militia, and several of his officers dined at Longbourn along with Mr and Mrs Philips. Elizabeth spoke to several of the gentlemen and enjoyed their brief conversations, which were the bright spots of the evening. For the party, Kitty and Lydia lowered the necks of their gowns, and Elizabeth was mortified as she saw them leaning forward or bouncing up and down in animation while officers watched their bosoms. Lydia again and again touched one man's hand or playfully slapped another man's arm. Kitty watched and copied what her younger sister did. Mrs Bennet and Mrs Philips encouraged them and spent their time gossiping about their neighbours, not minding that other people overheard, including those who were little better than strangers to them.

Jane was another source of discomfort. As soon as Colonel Forster arrived, she did everything she could to show she desired his company. Mr Bingley was apparently forgotten, at least for the moment. Jane's interest in the colonel ended before the meal, and in the drawing room, she approached Elizabeth.

"Did you know Colonel Forster goes into Sussex in a few days for his wedding?" Disappointment briefly marred Jane's countenance. "I do not believe any of the officers are eligible matches, however much Lydia and Kitty flirt with them. They are shameless, are they not?"

With that, she left Elizabeth and went to Mrs Bennet and Mrs Philips. Elizabeth remained with Mary, though they did not speak. When Mrs Bennet suggested music, Mary shot a warning look at Elizabeth before going to the pianoforte. Despite all her practise, she did not perform well. When she sang, Lydia and Kitty giggled, and Elizabeth saw several of the young men exchange grimaces.

After two pieces, Mr Bennet asked Elizabeth in an overly loud voice if she would take a turn. "Delight us with what you learnt from the Romsleys."

Elizabeth declined. She felt no need to exhibit, especially after such an introduction, even had Mary not been glaring at her.

<hr />

Jane knocked on Elizabeth's door soon after the family retired for the night. She sat on the chair while Elizabeth was on the bed, her back against the headboard, running her hands over the blankets. The wool was slightly abrasive, which suited Elizabeth. It would be odd, discordant to find softness here.

"I did not realise Mr Darcy was going away," Jane said. "Will he return for the ball?"

"He said he would." She hesitated before continuing. "Did you enjoy tonight?"

Elizabeth longed for the contemplative Jane who dreamt of seeing the world more than she did securing a rich husband. With Mrs Bennet telling her she must marry Mr Bingley at every turn, it was not surprising that making a brilliant match was utmost in her mind.

Jane shrugged and examined the items on the table: a letter from Rebecca, Elizabeth's silver hairbrush, and a few deep-hued ribbons destined to be trim for a bonnet.

"The officers are good company. It is a shame none of them can afford a wife. Mary played remarkably ill."

"Kitty and Lydia seemed well-amused."

Jane gave a snort of laughter and looked at her. "It was just what I expected from them. I told you when you came that Lydia would do whatever she can for attention. If she can convince one of the officers to marry her, she will, if only to laugh at me."

Elizabeth sat forward, resting her elbows on her knees. "Do you not think Mr or Mrs Bennet—" Jane was already shaking her head, and Elizabeth did not finish her question.

"My mother sees nothing wrong with their behaviour, and my father cannot be troubled to check them. You will grow accustomed to it, Elizabeth, *if* you stay." She stood and pulled her shawl closer around her arms. "Good night."

After Jane had shut the door behind her, Elizabeth blew out the candle. While she agreed with Jane about Mrs Bennet, she was determined to talk to Mr Bennet. She retained memories of him as a caring father, and that man would want his daughters to be respected, not laughed at as ridiculous flirts.

A voice in her head whispered, *Yet, he sent you away.*

Another voice responded as she drifted off to sleep. *Was that not a blessing in disguise?*

Elizabeth approached Mr Bennet the next morning. Their conversation was brief and fruitless.

"They are too young and silly for anyone to take seriously," he said. "No, Elizabeth, I shall hear no more of this nonsense. Besides, girls are a mother's purview. Talk to Mrs Bennet if you are so concerned." With that, he waved her out of his book-room.

Two days later, Kitty and Lydia returned from a walk in Meryton and reported they had met several new officers. Elizabeth was at the pianoforte, but Jane called her to sit with the other ladies and take refreshments.

"One of them just joined the militia today," said Kitty.

Lydia giggled. "He is the handsomest man I ever saw and very agreeable. His name is—oh Lord, I have forgot already."

Mrs Bennet questioned them about the new officers, and Elizabeth let her thoughts drift to the music she had been playing, which had a soothing effect on her mood.

Mrs Bennet saying the words 'Netherfield' and 'ball' recalled Elizabeth's attention. "Jane, you must have a new gown."

Kitty huffed and stamped her foot.

"But, Mama, Jane just had a new one!" Lydia protested.

Mrs Bennet's voice went up in pitch. "Well, I would buy you all new clothes, but your father will not stand the expense. I had to tease him a great deal before he agreed to one. The rest of you will have to make do with your best gowns. We shall dress them up a bit, but Jane must have something Mr

Bingley has not seen. It is essential your sister look her best. The ball is in her honour, you know."

Mary spoke up. "I have not heard that said."

"Oh, be quiet!" hissed Mrs Bennet, the sound so harsh, Elizabeth's ears ached. "One does not always need to say these things for them to be understood. The ball *is* in Jane's honour, and a proposal cannot be far behind. He might even ask that evening. Once Jane is Mrs Bingley, she will buy you all new things, take you to town, and introduce you to other rich gentlemen. So, you see, Lydia my sweet, buying Jane a gown for the ball is best for you too."

***

In Meryton the next morning, Elizabeth met Lydia's new favourite. While Mrs Bennet took Jane to look for fabric and Mary went to the circulating library, Kitty and Lydia insisted Elizabeth accompany them to several shops, no doubt hoping she would purchase them gifts.

As they walked between the bakers and haberdasher's, Kitty gave a great cry, grabbed Lydia's arm, and pointed down the street to three soldiers.

"It must be them. I do not see the red-headed one, but there is the new officer."

The girls quickened their pace and waved to the gentlemen, Lydia imploring Elizabeth to hurry. Hoping she might succeed in keeping the girls from shaming the entire family, Elizabeth followed.

Lydia began to make introductions. "You remember Denny and Sanderson, and this is—"

Blood roared through Elizabeth's ears, drowning out Lydia's words. Standing in front of her was George Wickham, wearing a red coat, a smirk, and one cocked eyebrow. In an instant, she was thrown back to the last time she saw him, the spring she was fifteen.

Elizabeth had spent a month at Pemberley, keeping Uncle Darcy company while his wife and son were at Rosings. They had returned the day before.

During a long ramble, as she approached a copse, she heard a young woman's giggle and a man's deep voice. Looking to see who it was, she found herself staring at George Wickham and Molly, one of the maids. When she realised the sort of encounter she had interrupted, Elizabeth began running back to the house, Wickham calling her name as he pursued her. He soon had her arm in his grip.

"Let go of me!" she cried.

"Now, now, little one. Just what do you think you saw?"

At the smoothness of his voice, Elizabeth's foot itched to kick him. The way he looked at her made her feel as though ants were running up and down her limbs. It was hardly the first time he had evoked such a reaction. Every one of their infrequent meetings since she was nine or ten years old had left her feeling nauseous and dirty.

"I know exactly what I saw. Let me go!" She gasped at the pain in her shoulder as she tried to free herself.

"Not until you promise to keep your mouth shut, dear, sweet, innocent Elizabeth."

She stamped on his foot with all her might. He gasped and tightened his hold on her arm.

"I would not want Mr Darcy finding out about this…interlude. He wants me to marry you. Did you know? Oh, what fun we shall have." Wickham's eyes fell to her bosom. "I look forward to taming that spirit of yours."

Elizabeth made a fist and slammed it into his stomach. He dropped her arm, bent over, and grunted. Immediately, she resumed her flight.

Elizabeth encountered Darcy before she reached the house. He questioned her, evidently seeing her distress, but young as she was, she was too embarrassed to tell him about the encounter with Wickham. He must have said something to his father, however, because the next day, Hugh Darcy, his manner sympathetic and gentle, asked her about her history with the man. He promised she would never have to see him again, and Wickham was gone from Pemberley before the day was done.

— ⁓ —

"Elizabeth Bennet. What a coincidence," Wickham said.

Kitty gaped at her, and Lydia asked, "You know each other?"

Her mouth so dry it made speech difficult, Elizabeth said, "Kitty, Lydia, we must join Mrs Bennet and Jane at the linen-drapers. If you will excuse us." She nodded at the gentlemen, but before she could walk away, her sisters' protests stopped her.

Speaking at the same time, Lydia said, "No, we must not," while Kitty insisted, "We have another quarter of an hour."

Wickham grinned, his gaze fixed on Elizabeth. "That will give us time to renew our acquaintance—will it not, Elizabeth?"

"I do not give you leave to call me—"

"But I always did."

Elizabeth balled her hands into fists. "Long ago when I was a child. I am not a child any longer, and you will address me properly."

"How do you know each other?" Lydia interjected.

"My father was steward at Pemberley. I met your sister when she was sent to live with the dowager Lady Romsley." Wickham winked at the two girls and added, "We are quite old friends, you see."

Lydia clapped her hands in delight. "That makes you—oh, I do not know—a friend of the family?"

"You must tell us what she was like." Kitty stepped towards him.

"And I shall," he promised. "I am sure you will excuse me for taking a few minutes to speak to your sister. We have not seen each other in years."

The girls were happy to accommodate any wish of his and went to flirt with the other officers.

"You have lost none of your false charm, I see," Elizabeth said.

"How you wound me. I am simply a poor—and I do mean poor, thanks to you and that infernal arse Darcy—"

"I will not tolerate any—"

"Now, now, little Elizabeth. We were always such good friends. We should have been more."

A loud laugh from one of the girls drew their attention.

"Such lively young things. Just the sort to tempt me," Wickham whispered. He then ran his eyes along Elizabeth's body. "You are the one I most regret, and I am very, *very* glad to have this opportunity to see you again. Tell me, dear little Elizabeth, do you still take long, solitary walks? Perhaps we shall meet one morning and…have a private conversation. I would so like to know what you told the old man to make him send me away with nothing."

Elizabeth put distance between them. "Stay away from me, and stay away from my sisters." Raising her voice, she continued. "Kitty, Lydia, I insist we go. Now! We have taken up enough of the gentlemen's time."

Kitty readily obeyed, but Elizabeth had to grab Lydia's arm to make her heed the order. She said nothing while they remained in Meryton or during the carriage ride back to Longbourn. Her distress must have been visible because Jane asked if she were ill.

"N-no. I own, I—"

"Have another headache? I am surprised you do not consult a physician," Mrs Bennet said.

Perhaps she did use the excuse too often, but the woman's voice and company was exceedingly irritating. "I did not sleep well last night and am fatigued."

"Is that why you looked so unhappy to see Mr Wickham?" asked Kitty.

"I think she was in love with him, but he did not return her feelings. She is heartbroken." Lydia laughed merrily at her joke.

"I am happy to report I have better sense than to admire such a man, and I recommend you follow my lead."

Lydia rolled her eyes. "I shall make him fall madly in love with me. How envious everyone will be!"

"But does he have any money?" Mrs Bennet enquired. "You cannot marry a poor man."

Lydia shrugged, and as she and Kitty talked about the officers, Elizabeth closed her eyes and rested her head against the back of the seat.

As soon as they reached Longbourn, Elizabeth sought out Mr Bennet in his book-room. "I must talk to you, sir."

Mr Bennet closed his book and gestured for her to take a seat. "What has you so agitated?"

She told him about the meeting with George Wickham. "Despite having every advantage given to him by the late Mr Darcy, he is undisciplined and unprincipled. He should not be trusted near any young lady. Kitty and

Lydia are delighted with him, and no good can come of it."

Mr Bennet appeared unconcerned. "If he is so despicable, your sisters will soon discover it for themselves. They are silly girls, but they are not lost to all decency. Let them learn they are mistaken about his character for themselves. It would do them good."

Elizabeth stared at him for a long moment. Keeping her voice as calm as she could, she said, "They will find themselves in trouble without realising it is happening. They are not only silly, they are ignorant and reckless. I believe Lydia would do just about anything, regardless of propriety, to prove she is the favoured sister."

"No man of sense would pay them the least bit of attention except to laugh at them. They have no money, no connexions that would tempt a gentleman."

"Men such as Wickham are not only interested in money or connexions."

Mr Bennet stood. "That is quite enough. You ought not to speak of such things. I have no doubt I shall meet this Wickham myself before too long, and *I* will decide what is best for my daughters."

Elizabeth recognised the dismissal in his actions. She climbed to her feet, nodded, and left the room.

In the guest room, she punched a pillow until her agitation lessened.

SEVENTEEN

With George Wickham in the neighbourhood, Elizabeth no longer felt secure walking alone and confined herself to the gardens closest to the house, checking the distance to the door every minute. It was so cold, she expected snow to fall from the clouds that hung low in the sky. She found a large stick and absently swung it at a rock beside the path.

If Darcy was still at Netherfield, perhaps he could convince Mr Bennet to act. It was more than a week since his departure, and Elizabeth began to worry that he would not return, despite his promise to Mr Bingley. She clung to the notion of seeing him again and prayed Bramwell and Fitzwilliam would come too. How she would like to see them, if only for five minutes!

She found a stone several inches in diameter, held the stick in both hands as though playing cricket, and hit it as hard as she could before continuing to walk. Berating herself for wanting the gentlemen to solve her problems, she took long, quick strides. Mr Bennet's attitude was frustrating and infuriating. Would not any caring, responsible father take seriously the type of warning she had given him? Elizabeth rested against a tree and slid to the ground, her knees bent, one hand still clutching the stick.

Of all the places Wickham might show himself, why did it have to be Meryton?

She dropped her forehead to her knees and allowed herself

a brief interlude to rally her spirits. Standing, she brushed off her gown, straightened her velvet hat, and took a deep breath. She resolved not to let the likes of Wickham frighten her or make her miserable ever again. If Mr Bennet would not listen to her, he would surely listen to Darcy. Until then, she would do whatever she must to protect those foolish, thoughtless girls from themselves and their parents' neglect.

In the few days that followed, Elizabeth saw Wickham twice, once when he and other officers called at Longbourn, and once at an evening party. Kitty and Lydia were as intemperate as always, and Elizabeth had the additional strain of observing Jane with Mr Bingley. She longed to see some sign that there was more to Jane's attention to him than a desire to make an advantageous marriage. While acknowledging she did not know Jane well enough to be certain, she could see no proof that her heart had been touched.

The only good thing that came out of the evening was learning the officers would all be occupied two mornings hence. Elizabeth was determined to seize the opportunity to go for a long, much needed ride.

⚬⚬⚬

Worry about Elizabeth gnawed at Darcy during his time in town. Bingley was a poor correspondent, and Darcy did not even have mention of her in letters from his friend to assure him she was well. Not that he would have believed it. She could not be happy at Longbourn.

After describing everything he witnessed in Hertfordshire and each of his conversations with her to Bramwell and Fitzwilliam, they agreed with him that it did not sound like a healthful situation. Fortunately, his cousins were able to arrange matters to join him on his return to Netherfield, but none of them knew what to do about Elizabeth's refusal to return to her proper home with the Romsleys.

"Mr Darcy, how glad I am to see you again!" Miss Bingley said when he joined the family in the drawing room. She sat with Mrs Hurst on a long sofa. Hurst occupied a chair in the corner, his head propped on one hand, looking bored.

Darcy nodded and murmured a few polite words. "My cousins will be down shortly."

Miss Bingley patted the empty space beside her, but Darcy chose an armchair across from her.

The lady frowned, and said, "Louisa and I have been desperate. The company here is even worse than I had supposed."

Mrs Hurst agreed. "Charles insisted we attend an evening party at the Philipses the other day. You remember them, do you not?"

"I had a grand time," Bingley exclaimed. "If you would but exert—"

"You enjoyed yourself because you spent the evening tethered to Jane Bennet." Mrs Hurst sounded as though she were scolding a child.

Miss Bingley's voice was low and full of disdain. "The Bennets. Mr Darcy, I know you agree that family is simply—"

Darcy would hear no more. "I will remind you that one Bennet has long been associated with *my* family."

"And I shall not hear a word against Miss Elizabeth," Bingley added. "I consider her a friend, even if you two do not." Bingley turned to Darcy. "She was here yesterday morning."

Miss Bingley made a noise of disgust. "She arrived unconscionably early to go riding, without invitation or even asking permission, as rude as *that* would have been."

Bingley replied, "You did not even see her, so let me hear

none of your complaints. She comes to ride her horse, and *I* told her she was welcome at any time. You only know she was here because you heard me discussing it with the footman."

Miss Bingley's upper lip curled, and she looked at the mantle clock. "Every last one of them will be here in two hours. My brother insisted we invite them to dinner."

A surge of pleasure shot through Darcy. He, Bramwell, and Fitzwilliam had decided to go to Longbourn the next day to see Elizabeth, but this was better.

His cousins entered the room, and after greeting the Bingleys and Hursts, Fitzwilliam asked, "Who is coming to dinner?"

"I have invited the Bennets," Bingley said.

"Excellent! I am looking forward to seeing Elizabeth again."

Fitzwilliam sounded nonchalant, which was exactly what the three of them had decided was necessary. They did not want the Bingleys and Hursts to realise there was anything remarkable about Elizabeth spending the autumn at Longbourn.

Bramwell fell into a chair, and Miss Bingley eyed him suspiciously. Darcy sensed she did not like him, but she would not risk offending the heir to the Romsley earldom.

She proved him wrong by saying, "It is not just Eliza who is coming."

Darcy said, "She does not like being called Eliza."

"As she has told you several times," Bramwell added.

"But you like Miss Bennet," Bingley insisted. "You made a point of befriending her."

"Charles, Miss Bennet is a lovely creature, but she is poor, and her family is dreadful," Mrs Hurst said, still sounding like a governess reprimanding her charge. "We may like her, but…" She shook her head.

Bingley flushed. Bramwell and Fitzwilliam exchanged looks, their eyebrows arched in identical fashion.

Bingley began to pace. "I, for one, am not ashamed to know any of the Bennets. Their circumstances mean nothing to me. And we should not forget that Miss Elizabeth is Lord Romsley's ward."

Miss Bingley ignored him. "Mr Darcy, you must convince Charles not to pay so much attention to Jane Bennet. You understand how these insignificant country societies work. A woman such as Mrs Bennet will take a few dances as an offer of marriage."

"I was not aware you had so much experience with country life," Fitzwilliam said. The Bingleys were city-folk, both in London and Yorkshire.

"Or marriage proposals," Bramwell murmured low enough one could pretend not to have heard, but the pallor of Miss Bingley's visage suggested she had.

There was silence in the room for a long moment before Fitzwilliam spoke. "So, how are the arrangements for the ball coming along?"

—◦—✦—◦—

As soon as Elizabeth entered the drawing room, Darcy's blood heated. She looked worse than he remembered—pale, thin, her stance too rigid, and her demeanour that of suppressed anger. Other than the usual pleasantries, he was unable to speak to her before dinner because Mrs Bennet demanded his attention. Her youngest daughter, wearing a gown that pushed the boundaries of propriety, was beside her, and Miss Catherine stood behind.

"We are very glad you have returned, Mr Darcy. Lydia was just saying the neighbourhood was poorer for your absence."

She giggled as though she had made a joke, but her not-very-subtle reference to his wealth was vulgar, not amusing.

"With the militia here, we have been very busy," Miss Catherine said.

Miss Lydia asked, "Why does your cousin not wear his uniform? I think a man is nothing without a red coat."

Mrs Bennet tilted her head in Darcy's direction and winked at her daughter before again addressing him. "Next to my dear Jane, Lydia is my most beautiful daughter. And such a vivacious girl! She would do well in any society. As much as I would miss her, I know I must be prepared to share her with the world."

"Oh Lord," Miss Lydia muttered, and Miss Catherine snorted.

Darcy bowed and went to Fitzwilliam.

"What was that about?" his cousin asked.

Darcy fought to keep a sneer from forming. "I believe Mrs Bennet was suggesting Miss Lydia would make me a good wife." When Fitzwilliam sniggered, Darcy asked, "How do you think Elizabeth looks?"

Fitzwilliam's countenance sobered. "Not good. I tried to talk to her, but I could not get her alone."

"One of us must sit beside her at dinner and discover what is wrong."

He should not have underestimated Miss Bingley, who just happened to be at Darcy's elbow when they were called to go through to the dining room. She instantly took his arm while Mrs Hurst did the same to Bramwell.

"Charles, you will escort Mrs Bennet, will you not? Oh, and Colonel Fitzwilliam, do please see Miss Bennet to the table," Miss Bingley called.

Even though it was not the fashion, Miss Bingley had place cards arranged. Darcy was between Miss Bingley and

Mrs Hurst, and their end of the table also housed his cousins. Since Elizabeth was at the other end, Darcy entertained the notion that Miss Bingley was purposely trying to make him despise her.

The meal was too long, and during the separation of the sexes, Darcy could only think about joining the ladies and demanding Elizabeth tell him what ailed her.

"So, you are come back, Mr Darcy," Mr Bennet said while the other men discussed local sport.

"As you see."

"I would have thought a man with such a great estate would need to spend more time at it."

Darcy remained silent.

"Have you brought any other gifts for Elizabeth? Perhaps it is your cousins' turn to do so. A footman, perhaps, or a pianoforte if the one at Longbourn is not to her liking." He scowled before adding, "I know about the horse."

Darcy wondered at his antagonism. The man sent his daughter to live with the dowager countess, had never visited her or sent for her to visit Longbourn, and seemed to resent that the life she had lived was materially richer than the one he could provide for his wife and other daughters. He should rejoice to have this time with Elizabeth. If Darcy had his way, it would soon be at an end.

"Did she tell you?" Darcy asked. "If she did, I imagine she also mentioned she did not know I had her mare brought to Hertfordshire. Elizabeth expressed concern about the burden it would place on your stables, thus I asked Bingley to keep Nutmeg here. Riding is good for Elizabeth, and she likes the exercise."

Mr Bennet's lips twisted in displeasure, and he left to refill his glass.

When they finally went into the drawing room, Darcy

discovered Bingley's sisters sitting on a sofa with Miss Bennet between them. The three were engaged in a lively conversation. Elizabeth was on a settee near the sofa, Miss Mary beside her, neither of them talking. The other Bennets sat together in a corner. Miss Bingley stood and approached the men, not noticing or caring that Miss Bennet was in the middle of a speech. Bingley slipped into the seat his sister had just vacated.

Bramwell stepped towards her. "Miss Bingley, I must beg you for a cup of tea. Tell me, do you favour Ceylon tea? Or perhaps Assam? I had the most delectable blend…"

Darcy heard no more because Fitzwilliam pulled him aside and whispered, "He planned to intercede if anyone kept us from talking to Elizabeth."

Elizabeth glanced up at their approach, and Darcy jerked his head to indicate she should join them by the pianoforte, where they would have more privacy.

When she reached them, she asked, "What, pray tell, is Bramwell talking to Caroline Bingley about? I do not believe he has paused long enough to breathe since you entered the room."

Fitzwilliam shrugged. "You know if he did not distract her, she would have occupied Darcy's attention all evening, and we wanted to talk to you."

"You are not well," Darcy stated.

Fitzwilliam slapped his arm. "Why do you not just tell her she looks terrible, since you appear to want to insult her?"

Elizabeth looked between the two of them and sighed. "And to think I was anticipating seeing you again."

Fitzwilliam grinned. "Of course you were. God, it has been too long, but I shall not reprimand you for scaring us all half to death. I shall leave that to Bramwell. Truly, sister dearest, are you ill?"

Elizabeth looked over her shoulder at the assembled party. "I cannot talk about it here, but there is something I must tell you."

Mrs Bennet's voice filled the space. "Miss Bingley, this is a very pretty room. Such fine furnishings. The chairs alone must have cost a great deal—and the drapery! My girls and I were wondering where you found them?"

"Excellent question. I, too, am curious. Shall we, Miss Bingley?" Bramwell held out an arm, indicating they should join Mrs Bennet.

"You owe him for that," Elizabeth said. "Miss Bingley *and* Mrs Bennet, Kitty, and Lydia."

Darcy cared nothing for Bramwell's present suffering. There *was* something distressing Elizabeth, and he burned to know what it was.

"Tomorrow morning by the stream?"

Elizabeth nodded, and a moment later, a servant entered with the tea service.

When Miss Bingley suggested music, Elizabeth was relieved for the diversion. She found the haste with which Miss Bingley sat at the instrument amusing. She had looked— almost snarled— at her and Mary. Elizabeth was not certain which of them she wished to discourage from playing, but she expected it was both because it would take attention away from her. Next, Mrs Hurst played a piece by Chopin. Miss Bingley then had no choice but to ask if any of the other ladies would take a turn.

Mary immediately stood and went to the pianoforte without saying a word. She selected her music, which Elizabeth knew she brought from Longbourn and placed by the instrument in preparation for this moment. Mary entertained the company with a ponderous concerto Elizabeth had tried to dissuade her from learning. Even in competent hands, it was not one to enliven a room full of people.

As soon as she was finished, Mr Bennet said, "Thank you, Mary. Let us not strain your fingers any further this evening."

Miss Bingley and Mrs Hurst looked at each other and, as one, covered their mouths with their hands, which only partly concealed their sniggers. Mary stood with great dignity, straightened her sheets of music, and returned to the settee.

"Elizabeth," Bramwell called from across the room where he stood with Fitzwilliam, "you must play for us next."

Elizabeth tried to demur, but they insisted, and Darcy stepped to her side and held out a hand to help her stand. By the time she reached the pianoforte, Fitzwilliam had chosen a piece from the available music, and Bramwell stood ready to turn the pages for her. All three gentlemen remained close by. The selection was a lively piece by Clementi she had learnt several years earlier. After the first half a page, Elizabeth closed her eyes and played from memory, feeling the rise and fall of the phrases. Her anxiety faded.

When she was finished, Fitzwilliam said, "Now you must sing. I will not hear a refusal." He went so far as to cover his ears with his hands. "What was that song you played for us in the spring?"

Bramwell said, "When we were at Romsley Hall."

"I recall playing many."

The brothers looked at each other and began to hum. Elizabeth nodded, played a few notes, and when they said it was the right one, sang the Irish air. There was some polite applause after she finished, and Bramwell and Fitzwilliam offered her exaggerated thanks. With reluctance, Elizabeth closed the instrument and stood.

Fitzwilliam laughed. "Do you remember the time Darcy and my aunt and uncle were at Romsley?"

Darcy gave a bark of laughter. "The rain. Five days inside!"

Bramwell said, "Elizabeth played for us. Kept us amused for hours."

Elizabeth laughed. It had been four years prior, but she still remembered that fortnight fondly. "My poor fingers! I could hardly move them."

"And you could hardly talk from all the singing you did," Bramwell said.

"Which was your purpose in encouraging me, was it not?" She lowered her voice. "'Oh Elizabeth, just one more song.'"

Fitzwilliam said, "It is not our fault you play and sing so beautifully."

They were laughing at a shared remembrance, Elizabeth experiencing a moment of almost pure happiness for the first time in months, when she glimpsed such a look of hurt and anger on Mary's face that her laugh caught in her throat.

"That was delightful, Miss Elizabeth," Mr Bingley said as Darcy led her to a chair. "The colonel has the right of it." Turning to Jane, he continued. "Do you not think your sister's playing is wonderful?"

Jane shot Elizabeth a cold look before smiling at Mr Bingley. "Yes, of course. But then, I do not have your experience hearing the finest performances. If you say she is good, then it must be so."

Miss Bingley, now sitting next to Jane, arranged her skirt. "Really, Charles, have a care to what you say. You would not wish to encourage Miss Eliza to think too highly of herself."

Darcy tensed beside her. Before he or one of her foster brothers said something in her defence, she smiled at Miss Bingley.

"Elizabeth. You forget I do not like to be called Eliza. I understand. You have met so many new people since coming into the neighbourhood. It can be quite challenging to remember everyone's name."

"So much so she forgets what Darcy told her this very afternoon," Fitzwilliam muttered.

Miss Bingley's cheeks coloured, and her lips formed a tight line.

Mrs Hurst said, "Miss Elizabeth, you must be pleased to be in your rightful place—I mean to say home—again. How delightful to know all your sisters and neighbours. It is quite the change from Worcestershire, but I am certain you feel easier here."

The comment was like a slap to the face. Elizabeth knew she was paying for correcting Miss Bingley and for garnering praise when neither she nor Miss Bingley had received any.

"They are very fortunate to have this chance to know her," Fitzwilliam said.

Elizabeth could have kissed him and Bramwell when he added, "Would you not agree, Mr Bennet? Miss Bennet?"

Jane offered a faint smile and nod while Mr Bennet said, "As you say."

EIGHTEEN

Once they were settled in the carriage for the drive to Longbourn, Mrs Bennet praised Jane for spending so much time with Mr Bingley.

"He was captivated, and his sisters are so fond of you. If only *Eliza* knew how to keep a civil tongue. You hear me, girl, I will not have you ruin Jane's chances with Mr Bingley by your rudeness to his sisters."

Knowing it would be futile to say anything in her defence, Elizabeth ignored her. She closed her eyes and rested her head against the seat as Mrs Bennet encouraged Jane to tell her everything Mr Bingley said.

When they reached Longbourn, Elizabeth said good night and went upstairs. She did not realise Jane followed her until she turned to close the door to the guest room and saw her. Jane sat on the side of the bed while Elizabeth went to the table and removed her jewellery.

"You do play and sing very well. Far better than Mary," Jane said. "Tonight was a great success, do you not think?"

Elizabeth murmured something she trusted would be taken as agreement.

"Mr Bingley spoke to me more than he did anyone else. He was *so* attentive! You saw that, did you not?"

Elizabeth ran her fingers along the smooth chain of the necklace she had just placed on the table before turning to face Jane.

"Do you like him? Admire him? I have heard what Mrs Bennet says to you, and it all seems so...rushed."

Jane dismissed this with a snap of her hand and stood. "Mr Bingley is a fine gentleman, and I would be silly not to encourage him. He is perfectly amiable and very respectable. He likes me. I told you when you first came that one of us must make a good marriage, and I *am* the eldest."

"But, Jane, do you—"

"You might think that since you have been in the world and I have not, it should be you, but Mr Bingley did not want you, even though you have known him longer."

"That is not fair." Elizabeth climbed to her feet to avoid looking up at Jane. "I never as much as hinted I was interested in Mr Bingley in that way."

"Mr Bingley likes me," Jane repeated. "Why should I not marry him when it would bring so many advantages to my family?"

"What about affection?" Elizabeth insisted. "Are you in love with him?"

Jane pressed her lips closed, and her eyes flickered this way and that. After a moment of silence, she walked out of the room.

·— ᴄᴏᴏᴏ —·

Elizabeth missed her long morning walks and was certain it was impacting her health and mood. As soon as she encountered the gentlemen, Fitzwilliam nearly pushed the last particle of air out of her lungs by hugging her so tightly, and Bramwell's embrace was hardly less powerful.

"Tell us what is wrong. It is clear there is something troubling you," Bramwell said.

"I shall, if you give me a chance." She pulled at the

ribbons of her bonnet and took it off. The sun was feeble, and it was cold enough to see her breath. "The militia has set up a winter camp in Meryton."

"I know." Darcy gestured for her to go on.

"I was—oh, I might as well just say it. George Wickham has joined it."

Elizabeth told them about meeting him. Bramwell and Fitzwilliam cursed, and Darcy's expression turned to stone.

"Kitty and Lydia were immediately enamoured with him. You know what he is like. In the space of a week, he called at Longbourn, we met him at the Philipses, and Kitty and Lydia saw him at least once in Meryton when I was not with them."

Fitzwilliam asked, "Did you tell Mr Bennet he is not to be trusted?"

"I said everything I could think to say, except to tell him about—" Realising she almost disclosed more than she wanted, Elizabeth closed her mouth and hoped they had not noticed.

"Tell him about what?" Bramwell asked with deceptive calm.

All three gentlemen stared at her, awaiting her answer. Elizabeth looked down and kicked at the dead leaves. "It is not important."

Darcy spoke, his voice low and controlled. "Did he do more to you than I know? It was that day I saw you walking, just before I told my father everything I knew about Wickham. Father would never tell me what you told him, though I know it affected him deeply."

Elizabeth pressed her eyes closed to avoid seeing their stern expressions, fury creeping into their eyes. "It was nothing, not-not compared to what he did to those who believed his lies."

"Let us judge the nothingness of it," Bramwell said.

"I do not see any purpose in telling you."

"Well, I do," Fitzwilliam argued.

Darcy raised his voice to be heard over his cousins. "Very well. If you do not wish to talk about the past—at this time— tell us what happened when you saw him last. What did he say to you? What did Mr Bennet do when you warned him?"

"Mr Bennet believes Kitty and Lydia's ages and lack of fortune mean Wickham will have no interest in them even *if* he is as terrible as I suggested. He has not changed, though. I know he has not, and that is what I find so alarming. Wickham as much as told me he would…amuse himself with them, and they are exactly the type of girl he likes." She felt the toast she ate before leaving the house threaten to come up.

Teeth gritted, Fitzwilliam said, "Did he touch you? Last week, five years ago, or at any other time?"

Elizabeth ran a hand across her forehead. Sensing they would not be satisfied until she explained what had happened between her and Wickham, she admitted he had made her uneasy since she was a young girl.

"It started when I was perhaps nine or ten."

"Nine?" Bramwell's voice was appalled and, as she expected, enraged.

Elizabeth's gaze went from him to Fitzwilliam who looked pale and furious. "Around that age. He would say inappropriate things about-about my person, and the way he looked at me made me…" Her voice trailed off.

Darcy said, "Tell us about that morning when you were fifteen."

Knowing there was no escape, she did.

"I will kill him." Fitzwilliam's words were a statement.

"*This* is why I did not want to tell you!" Elizabeth punched his shoulder. "You will not fight him, Thomas Hugh Fitzwilliam.

When I saw that—him again, I was reminded of how I felt in the past, and I am frustrated Mr Bennet would not listen to me. You have seen enough of Mrs Bennet to know she will not check her daughters. Indeed, she sees nothing wrong with how they behave. One or both of the girls will find themselves in a great deal of trouble without even realising they are in danger."

"I am less concerned about them than I am about you," Darcy said.

For some reason, his words made her want to cry, and Elizabeth wished she could fall into his arms and rest against him. Instead, she moved away, stopping beside Bramwell.

"I am worried for Kitty and Lydia and every other young girl in the neighbourhood who does not see Wickham for what he is. They see only a handsome face and charming manners, and I can do nothing about it. No one here knows me. They do not care about my opinion."

Bramwell draped an arm across her shoulders and led her to a fallen tree where they sat down. It was the most at peace she felt in weeks, apart from the brief moment Darcy had embraced her the morning after the assembly. With Fitzwilliam and Darcy standing across from them, they devised a plan of action. Fitzwilliam would talk to Colonel Forster about his new lieutenant while Darcy spoke to Mr Bennet. All three of them would warn the local shopkeepers that Wickham had a habit of leaving debt behind him.

When Bramwell wanted to talk about why she was at Longbourn, Elizabeth realised how late it was becoming and insisted she needed to return before she was missed.

The following morning, Elizabeth entered the house, having taken a walk in the gardens. The day was cold and overcast, and the air felt heavy with moisture.

"Elizabeth."

The sound of her name caused her to start. Mr Bennet gestured to her, and she followed him into his book-room.

"Sit by the fire. You look cold." Mr Bennet went to his customary place behind the desk and observed her. His fingers were steepled in front of his face, obscuring most of his expression. "I had an interesting visit from Mr Darcy yesterday afternoon."

Clasping her hands together, Elizabeth waited to hear what he had to say.

"It appears I underestimated the danger posed by Mr Wickham or so he assured me. Did you know he would warn me about the man?"

Elizabeth nodded. When Mr Bennet regarded her with an arched brow, she said, "Once he, the viscount, and the colonel learnt he was in the neighbourhood, it was inevitable they would act."

"Hmm. He was quite forceful in his manner, insisting Wickham should not be allowed near any young lady, but especially that *you* should never have to meet the man. I believe he used words such as 'unthinkable' and 'unconscionable,' even 'not to be borne' when he spoke about you so much as having to set eyes on Wickham. You have quite the champion."

How could she possibly respond to such a statement? Should she grin and rejoice in what it said about Darcy's affection for her or wish one of her foster brothers had spoken to Mr Bennet instead, lest Darcy's actions lead her to recall how she had once been in love with him?

Mr Bennet continued. "The impression Mr Darcy gave

was that you had...*particular dealings* with Lieutenant Wickham." Speaking more gently than she was used to hearing him, Mr Bennet said, "Your friend assured me that, to the best of his knowledge, Wickham did not physically harm you."

"He did not." She was embarrassed Darcy told him so much, but if it helped to make Mr Bennet take the threat Wickham posed seriously, she would not object.

Mr Bennet frowned. "That is something, I suppose. The conversation made me realise how little I know about your life. I should have tried harder to visit you or found a way to have you come to Longbourn upon occasion. I do not like to travel, I admit, and..." He gave a half-hearted shrug. "Your grandmother's death, and your mother—we had hopes for a son after Lydia, but she lost the babe and suffered for it. I could not leave Longbourn then, as much as I might have wished to, and even had the Romsleys offered to bring you here, it would not have been wise. You were very young, but I assume you remember what your mother was like towards you."

Elizabeth nodded.

"Your absence helped, but for years, whenever she was unhappy, she would disparage you, say she was glad you were gone. Time went by so quickly. I suppose not seeing you became a habit, and habits are difficult to change."

He regarded her for a long moment. "Now, here you are. There is a reason you chose to come, or rather, to leave the earl and countess. I do not expect you to tell me, but should you wish to..."

Elizabeth said nothing. His words did not encourage her to share her secrets with him, especially weeks after her return.

"Well, off with you," he said in his usual dismissive tone. "It is almost time for breakfast."

It rained all day, and Elizabeth spent several hours at the pianoforte. She hoped to see her foster brothers but was not entirely disappointed that the weather kept them from calling. If they had questions after seeing how the Bennets behaved at Netherfield Park, they would likely pack her trunks for her and toss her into a carriage if they witnessed life at Longbourn.

The weather cleared just long enough for Mrs Philips to call. Elizabeth did not see her since she was reading in the guest room at the time. However, she heard about the news she brought at dinner: George Wickham was gone.

Kitty said, "Colonel Fitzwilliam called on Colonel Forster yesterday, and Mr Wickham was sent to a regiment somewhere far away."

"It is not fair." Lydia huffed and pouted.

"My aunt said he already owed the shopkeepers in Meryton a great deal of money. Mr Wickham has only been here a fortnight. How could it be possible?" asked Kitty.

"It is very easy for men like him," Elizabeth muttered.

"Oh, who cares about your opinion?" Lydia cried. "Mr Wickham is gone, and it is all that awful Colonel Fitzwilliam's fault!"

Mrs Bennet patted Lydia's hand and pushed a plate of turnips, one of Lydia's favourites, towards her.

"Now, now, my sweet girl, he may be disagreeable, and it is a terrible shame that someone as pleasant and handsome as Mr Wickham has gone, but Colonel Fitzwilliam is an earl's son. Oh, but Mr Wickham was so taken with you, and you did so enjoy his company. It is very hard."

Lydia pointed a finger at Elizabeth. "You had something to do with it!"

Mr Bennet chuckled. Mrs Bennet stared at Elizabeth and demanded, "Did you? You made no secret of not liking him."

"Because he did not like you. He liked me." Lydia's voice rose into a whine.

Elizabeth turned to Mr Bennet hoping he would say something either to defend her or quiet Lydia. He cocked an eyebrow at her and sipped his wine. Elizabeth regarded Jane, who seemed interested in her response, then down the table, past Mary, whose expression was cool, to Mrs Bennet, Kitty, and Lydia.

"I have good reason for my feelings. Colonel Fitzwilliam, Viscount Bramwell, and Mr Darcy all dislike him, and none of them would speak ill of another person unless they deserved it. Does it not tell you something that Wickham had already amassed enough debt in Meryton for it to be noteworthy? Mr Hugh Darcy disavowed him after supporting him for years and years, which shows—"

Lydia threw her fork onto the table and, by the way the dishes rattled, stamped her foot rather heavily. "What do I care about Mr Hugh Darcy? If he is half as disagreeable as his son—"

Elizabeth was on the point of replying, but Mr Bennet stopped her.

"Save your breath to cool your porridge—or your mutton." He dipped his chin towards her plate. "Lydia will not admit the justice of anything you say, and I have heard enough of the matter. Lydia, you will either remain silent or go to your bedchamber."

NINETEEN

The next several days were marked by heavy rain. Being confined to the house left Elizabeth feeling oppressed. Knowing her friends were a mere three miles away and the weather prevented them from meeting made bearing the Bennets' company all the more difficult. Fortunately, by the afternoon of the twenty-fifth, the weather cleared. Outside, servants began to tidy the disarray created by the prolonged spell of bad weather. Inside, the ladies began to make their final preparations for the grand event. Charlotte Lucas called to talk over the gossip about Wickham, and as she was leaving, Bramwell and Fitzwilliam arrived. Regardless of her worries about them coming to Longbourn, Elizabeth was delighted to see them.

Mrs Bennet arranged the seating to her liking, ensuring Jane and Lydia were as close to the gentlemen as possible. Kitty was permitted to be nearby, but the matron pointedly overlooked Mary and Elizabeth's presence.

"Let me see if I understand correctly," Mrs Bennet said. "You are the only children of the earl and countess of Romsley. It was your grandmother, your father's mother, that took the girl?"

Bramwell's tone was curt. "Yes. Elizabeth lived with our grandmother until her death, at which time she removed to our home to reside with us. "

"You have no sisters or other brothers?" Mrs Bennet pressed. "It is just the two of you?"

Fitzwilliam caught Elizabeth's eye. She wished she could explain that Mrs Bennet was likely calculating how the family's fortune would be divided upon the earl's death. With only two sons, it was likely Fitzwilliam would receive something substantial—by the Bennets' standard—despite not inheriting the title, and there were fewer dependents drawing on the estate. When Fitzwilliam glanced Lydia's way and sent Elizabeth another questioning expression, she surreptitiously looked upwards. Lydia was pointedly ignoring him, occasionally shooting dark looks his way.

Bramwell continued. "And, of course, Elizabeth, our foster sister."

Elizabeth appreciated his attempt to make it clear that he—and by extension Fitzwilliam and his parents—considered her part of their family, but he would have to be far less subtle if he expected Mrs Bennet to understand.

Mrs Bennet's features briefly pinched in displeasure before she once again donned a smile that was supposed to be charming but was clearly false.

"Neither of you are married? Your mother and father must be eager to see you settled, you especially, Lord Bramwell. A gentleman in your position, at your time of life, must be in want of a wife."

Fitzwilliam interjected before Bramwell responded, apparently aware there was a certain way the viscount's eyes narrowed when he was about to say something cutting.

"I wonder, Mrs Bennet, if my brother and I might take Elizabeth for a turn in your gardens? I have heard them spoken of as the finest in the neighbourhood, and we have not seen her nearly enough since the spring."

Bramwell stood. "Excellent notion. We—um, have a message to impart from our father. You understand." He stepped towards Elizabeth and held out his hand, his fingers twitching impatiently.

Once out of doors, Elizabeth led them away from the view of anyone watching from the drawing room windows.

Fitzwilliam took it upon himself to break the silence. "I am not convinced the Bennets treat you as they should. Darcy does not have a high opinion of them, and after the other evening and that—" he jerked a thumb over his shoulder indicating the house and shook his head as though in disbelief. "Does Mrs Bennet always act as though you are not there?"

"She clearly does not love you as you deserve," Bramwell said.

Elizabeth did not know how to respond and held her tongue.

"Elizabeth, you must be honest with us about your situation," Fitzwilliam said, his tone firm.

"Please stop," Elizabeth interjected. "I have never claimed that my time here is wonderful and delightful and full of joy— not to Darcy or in my letters to Rebecca and the countess."

"Then why do you insist on staying?" Bramwell said. "Bingley's blasted ball is tomorrow, and since we said we would attend, we must."

"But after that, you can come home with us. Mother and Father are at the town house," Fitzwilliam added.

Elizabeth shook her head. "I know you believe that would be better for me, but I do not agree. I wish you and Darcy would stop trying to convince me to leave before I am ready."

Fitzwilliam said, "Perhaps if you told us directly what happened with Lady Anne and Lady Catherine it would help us understand why it took you so long to write to Rebecca— let alone the rest of us—and why you are staying here."

How could she explain that she did not feel as though the earl and countess's homes were hers and that she could not bear the idea of seeing them unless she knew she had somewhere to retreat to for safety? How could she tell them that she did not yet feel capable of withstanding Lord and Lady Romsley's indifference and was afraid she would either argue with them or experience even greater sorrow than she did currently? She could not even imagine what she would do if she had to see Lady Catherine or Lady Anne. With Rebecca away, there would be no easy escape from the Grosvenor Square town house, especially because she doubted she would ever return to Longbourn again. It was better to stay where she was for a few weeks longer.

"Tell us," Bramwell urged.

"Will you please accept that I am acting in the manner I believe is best for me at present? I have not been here long, not when you consider how many years I was away. I have an opportunity, perhaps the only one I shall ever have, to know the Bennets, to establish friendships with the girls. I am not yet ready to say the task is futile."

That was partly true, at least in relation to Jane, but when Bramwell scoffed, Elizabeth continued with more vehemence than she otherwise might have exhibited. "Do you or do you not have something to tell me from the earl?"

Bramwell pressed his lips together and stared at her, his demeanour evidence of his displeasure.

Fitzwilliam sighed heavily. "Father sent this." He dug in his pocket and extracted a wad of bills.

"I do not require any additional funds. The countess has sent me enough, more than I could possibly use in Hertfordshire."

"He anticipated you might not remove with us, since we must depart the morning after next, and wanted you to have enough to hire a proper conveyance, should you need to make a hasty escape from this…place," Bramwell explained.

"The message," Fitzwilliam said, "is that you should send an express to Grosvenor Square the moment you decide you are ready to return home. One of us will come get you immediately or arrange for your safe passage. Mother and Father plan to go to see friends for a week or two before returning to Romsley Hall for Yuletide unless you agree to leave with us on the twenty-seventh. Bramwell and I do not go to Worcestershire for at least another three or four weeks, but I cannot promise we shall be in town all that time. If you find you cannot or do not want to wait for us to escort you, you are to use these funds to hire a carriage. Father also wanted to ensure you had enough money to pay Herriot's wages."

"You might as well take it, Elizabeth. We will not leave until you do."

"Oh, very well." She stuffed the money into the pocket of her gown.

Fitzwilliam said, "I would stay, but I must return to my duties."

"And I shall murder Miss Bingley if I have to share a roof with her much longer!"

Elizabeth managed to laugh. She kissed Bramwell's cheek. "Thank you for tolerating her for my sake. I know you only came to see me."

Fitzwilliam insisted he deserved a kiss too. "You know we would do anything for you, darling little sister."

Tears filled her eyes but not enough to fall down her cheeks. "We shall not be separated much longer." She glanced towards the house. "I should return, but you need not."

Bramwell enunciated each word carefully. "Thank you."

They arranged for Elizabeth to dance the second set with Bramwell and the supper set with Fitzwilliam before they departed.

While Mrs Bennet and the girls fretted over whether they would be able to get the right shoe roses to match their gowns, Elizabeth sat in the guest room re-reading Rebecca's letters. All along, she saw Elizabeth's time in Hertfordshire as a visit, as did others in the Darcy and Fitzwilliam clans, almost as though they knew Elizabeth would not find a home with the Bennets, despite them being her true family. There was no denying they were correct. Elizabeth anticipated seeing Rebecca and spending the winter at Curzon Street, but she could not settle on what she would do afterwards.

Elizabeth pulled the shawl she wore closer around her shoulders. Having given up her love for Darcy, if she could find another worthy gentleman, she would be very happy to be a wife and mother, thus securing a home of her own. She doubted such a future was before her, however.

Elizabeth was thus occupied when Mrs Bennet, trailed by Jane, entered the bedchamber without the courtesy of a knock at the door. Mrs Bennet went directly to the dressing table.

"She will have something you can wear. Perhaps a hair ornament. You must look like the sort of lady a gentleman like Mr Bingley would marry."

As Mrs Bennet reached for a small rosewood jewellery box, Jane said, "Mama, those are Elizabeth's things. We should—"

"Nonsense! It is the least she can do." Mrs Bennet held the box in her hands.

Elizabeth remained sitting on the bed, her back against the headboard. Jane looked embarrassed and slightly nervous.

"It is now six weeks since Mr Bingley met you. Many a couple have been betrothed after less time than that," Mrs

Bennet said. "We must encourage him to come to the point. Your new gown is lovely. With the right jewellery—"

"Let me talk to Elizabeth about it." Jane gently tugged the box out of Mrs Bennet's hands.

"You must look perfect. Mr Bingley *must* make you an offer before some other girl steals him away or that girl—" She pointed at Elizabeth.

"I shall ask her." It took a while longer, but Jane managed to steer Mrs Bennet into the corridor.

Elizabeth prayed Jane would speak against Mrs Bennet's mercenary intentions, but she did not expect it.

An uncomfortable pause preceded Jane's words. "I know you do not like Miss Bingley, but tomorrow is very important to me. I do not want anything to spoil it. Please, will you try to get along with her?"

Elizabeth delayed responding until she dampened the ball of fire in her belly. "Tell me, Jane, have you asked Miss Bingley to refrain from insulting *me*?"

The sisters stared at each other until they heard Mrs Bennet calling for Jane. Her sister set the jewellery box on the table and left the room.

Elizabeth braved the remaining mud and went for a long walk the following morning. The sky was free of clouds, and the sun was as bright and warm as it could be at the end of November. She kept to those paths that were the driest, which meant she did not take the route along which she usually met Darcy. Nevertheless, after twenty minutes, she heard the sound of hooves, and from around the bend, she saw him astride Barbary. Her heart stuttered at how handsome and noble he was. Freya ran beside them and immediately approached Elizabeth for pets, which Elizabeth was happy to deliver, if only because it gave her an excuse not to look at Darcy.

"She will ruin your dress," Darcy remarked.

"It is dark and will hide the mud." Elizabeth felt freer and more light-hearted crouched down on the path with a muddy dog licking her face than she ever did in the dry, warm rooms of Longbourn.

He dismounted. "I was not sure you would walk, given the recent rain."

"After several days indoors, I was not going to let a little dirt stop me."

"Little?" He looked at his boots, the hem of Elizabeth's dress, Barbary's legs, and Freya, all of which were splattered with mud. Elizabeth shrugged, and they laughed.

He asked after the Bennets, and she asked after everyone at Netherfield.

"Being confined with the Hursts and Miss Bingley has been…unpleasant."

Elizabeth chuckled. "Bramwell and Fitzwilliam gave me that impression when I saw them yesterday."

He rolled his eyes. "Bramwell has done nothing to hide his dislike of Miss Bingley. To be honest, I do not believe she understands half the slights he aims at her. It is her own fault. She will not desist in provoking him."

"You mean she continues to insult me?" She spoke as though it mattered not, which considering she had no warm feelings for Miss Bingley was true.

After studying her for a moment, Darcy nodded. "She makes disparaging remarks about people with connexions to trade who seek to improve their social position through marriage. Bramwell, naturally, let her know none of us have forgotten who her father was."

Elizabeth laughed. "I would not have minded being there when he did."

The soft smile he gave her made it impossible to look away, even when she felt her cheeks warm under the steadiness of his gaze.

"Will you dance the first with me?" Darcy asked.

She curtseyed. "How very kind of you, sir. It would be my honour."

His expression sobered. "Your brothers return to town tomorrow, and I must depart soon too. I am for Derbyshire. You should leave with them or me."

Elizabeth shook her head and turned away.

"You cannot remain here. Everything I have seen and heard tells me it is impossible. Bramwell and Fitzwilliam agree."

"Enough, Darcy!"

"You cannot be happy here."

Her chest rose and fell quickly, her breath audible as she exhaled through her nose. She felt the sting of tears in her eyes. For some inexplicable reason, Elizabeth could not keep her feelings to herself.

"Happy? No. I thought I was coming home to my family. After what happened with your mother and aunt, I prayed I was, but I am no more wanted here than I was at Rosings or Pemberley or Romsley Hall. Why should I be? They do not know me. After fifteen years, a few letters now and again are all that bind us."

Darcy stepped towards her. "Then leave. Come back to town with us. You are wrong to say you are unwanted elsewhere."

"I have ample reason for my feelings, or have you forgotten what happened—"

"But Lord and Lady Romsley—"

"I do not want to hear it. I cannot…not yet. How many times must I tell you?"

Darcy ran a gloved hand over his mouth. "Rebecca and my aunt and uncle do not return to town until the end of next month, and who is to say it will not be postponed? I cannot bear leaving you behind."

"Yet, here I shall remain. Wickham is gone, thanks to you, and nothing here can harm me." When he made to speak, Elizabeth shook her head. "I have nothing more to say about this matter. I shall see you at the ball."

Elizabeth began her walk back to Longbourn, a heavy cloud hanging over her. Having confirmation of Darcy's impending departure left her bereft. She would be alone again, and it would be worse than even her loneliest times at Romsley Hall, because here she was surrounded by people she doubted would ever care about her. She had been reluctant to admit it, still did not want to, but how long could she hide the truth from herself?

<hr />

Elizabeth remained apart from the family as much as possible that afternoon, but she could not avoid them in the carriage. The three miles to Netherfield were very long, between Mrs Bennet's instructions to Jane on how to make Mr Bingley propose before the final set and Kitty and Lydia's plotting how to best enjoy their evening. The youngest girls were determined to make Fitzwilliam fall madly in love with them then break his heart to punish him for his role in Wickham being assigned to a distant regiment.

The ball was as mortifying as Elizabeth feared it would be. Lydia and Kitty did everything they could to make spectacles of themselves. Apart from the few times she was asked to

dance, Mary sat primly with the matrons, looking disapprov-
ingly at the crowd of guests. Jane remained as close to Mr
Bingley or his sisters as possible. Mr Bingley asked her to
dance twice, which Mrs Bennet crowed about to her neighbours. During supper, she announced to them—at sufficient
volume for all to hear—that soon her daughter would be
mistress at Netherfield, and Jane would ensure her sisters met
Mr Bingley's rich, single friends frequently.

There were moments of pleasure, such as her dances with
her foster brothers and Darcy. During those interludes, Elizabeth was able to immerse herself in the music, the movements,
and the conversations. It took a few moments for her and
Darcy to dispel the awkwardness arising from their exchange
that morning, but as he seemed to wish to forget it, she was
happy to do so as well. Neither he nor Fitzwilliam raised the
idea of her returning to London. The closest any of them came
to the subject was when Bramwell made her absolutely,
unequivocally promise to go to Curzon Street as soon as
Rebecca and her parents were in town.

Before the end of the evening, she, Fitzwilliam, and
Bramwell found a private moment to say goodbye.

TWENTY

Having told Elizabeth he had to leave Netherfield
soon after the ball, Darcy was glad their paths met
on the twenty-eighth. He delayed his departure as
long as possible to give her an opportunity to change her mind
about going with him, despite her insistence she would remain
until she could remove to Curzon Street.

Darcy found Elizabeth slowly strolling near the creek,
hands clasped behind her back. Something was evidently
worrying her, and she did not realise he was there until Freya
ran up to her. Elizabeth managed a small smile for the dog and
fed Barbary an apple, but her greeting of him was indifferent.

"How are you this morning? I trust everyone at Longbourn
is well after the ball," he said.

Elizabeth nodded and suggested they continue along the
path. A glimmer of humour appeared in her expression, which
Darcy was glad to see.

"Miss Bingley is to be congratulated. The Bennets were
full of praise for her efforts, which I know will bring her great
satisfaction. The opinion of such people, her nearest neighbours, the family of her new, dear friend, et cetera, is so very
important to her."

They walked in silence for a while. He considered how
best to broach the subject of her travelling at least as far as
London with him, but before he knew what to say, Elizabeth
spoke.

"I have not known what to do, but I like and respect Mr

Bingley too much to stand by while he might unknowingly enter into an unequal marriage. You must have seen how much he likes Jane's company."

He nodded and watched her as much as the path as they continued to stroll. He had also heard Mrs Bennet speculating on Miss Bennet and Bingley possibly making a match of it, though his attention was all for Elizabeth.

"Jane welcomes his interest, but I regret I cannot say for certain if she has genuine feelings for him. Oh, I feel as though I am betraying her, but I see no other choice. She speaks about her desire to secure a wealthy husband, and Mrs Bennet encourages her, as does Miss Lucas. Neither Mrs Bennet nor Miss Lucas believe affection is an important consideration, but I am less certain about Jane. There have been occasions where she hints she disagrees with her mother and friend and when she says or does something that makes me believe she might care for Mr Bingley."

"I see."

"There are other reasons Mr Bingley might want to hesitate before he entangles himself with the Bennets. You know their circumstances—the estate is entailed, and Jane and the others have no fortunes—and you have seen how they behave. That alone should not make Mr Bingley decide against Jane if he loves her and she loves him, but…"

"But you suspect she would accept him only because he is rich."

Elizabeth nodded. "Mrs Bennet anticipates him proposing very soon—indeed, they were disappointed he did not make her an offer at the ball—but I wish you would tell him to take more time. I shall endeavour to discover Jane's sentiments."

He agreed and, in a few minutes, informed her he was departing the next day. Bingley was going with him, intending to return in a few days. "Will you please come with me? I will take you to my aunt and uncle, or we could go to Pemberley if you do not wish to go home immediately. You have always liked being there." She gaped at him and made a noise of astonishment. "I am certain my mother regrets what she did, and I promise not to leave you alone with her. You are not happy here. You admitted it yourself." He sounded as though he was pleading with her, which he hated, but not nearly as much as he did his anger at her stubbornness. As upsetting as August had been, three months had passed since then.

"I am not happy here, but I doubt I could explain to you why I will not return to the Romsleys and certainly not to your mother."

"Try, I beg of you."

She averted her gaze, and seeing her distress made Darcy want to tear at his hair. He did not want to injure her, he wanted to help her, but she was not letting him. *If she would only admit she is being irrational, she would tell her maid to pack her things, and we could both forget we ever heard of a place called Meryton!*

After what felt like an hour, she said, "If you do not like what I say, pray recall you asked me to tell you. For years, I have understood myself to be a responsibility to your family. Your grandmother was kind to me, but she left me to nurses and governesses more often than not, as did Lord and Lady Romsley once I went to live with them.

"I understand. I had no right to expect more from them, and truly, they gave me a great deal in return, especially a fine education, which I value more than I can say. Yet, I feel my entire life has been marked by people making decisions for me without ever asking what I wanted or what would make me most happy. Last summer, they decided I would go to Pemberley, even though your mother has never wanted my company, Lady Anne decided I would go to Rosings, and Lady

Catherine decided I would simply go away. I am tired of having so little say in where and how I live and feeling... unwanted." She paused briefly before continuing. "For some reason, when I first met your mother, I especially wanted *her* to like me."

"But she did not." Shame burnt through Darcy, though he was not to blame.

She shook her head. "On reflection—and I have thought about this a great deal—what she did to me last summer is not shocking. Nevertheless, what happened left me...bruised and unsettled and with a great many matters to think over and resolve *by myself*. Chief amongst these is that I am determined to decide *for myself* what I want to do. I am not satisfied letting others continue to direct my life. You would not be. Why should I?"

Darcy did not understand. She had been hurt, likely more than he had appreciated, but where better to heal than amongst those who most cared for her? Her next words caused every thought to flee from his mind.

"Although I know Lady Catherine was acting out of unwarranted intolerance towards me, I cannot say she was entirely incorrect about my need for employment. I must do something other than depend on the earl and countess to support me. I am considering seeking a position as a companion. If I can find a lady who required someone for *that* position and did not mean to treat me like a slave, I would save my salary and add to my fortune. In time, I would feel secure enough and be of sufficient age to find a quiet corner of the country and make a home for myself."

"You cannot be serious!" The loudness and harshness of his tone caused her to start and Freya to bark.

"I assure you I am."

Darcy began to pace if only to avoid taking Elizabeth by

the shoulders and shaking her. "Absolutely not! The earl would never allow it. Neither will I or-or Bramwell or Fitzwilliam."

"If I decide it is the most appropriate course of action for me, what could you do? I am almost one-and-twenty, and I am responsible for my own life. I will live it in a manner I know will constitute my happiness." She paused before almost blurting, "I want a *home*, Darcy, a place I belong, where I have chosen to be and I am wanted, not where I have been imposed on others. I will do whatever I must to find one for myself, even if it means living on my own in some little village where people gossip about me and the impropriety of my situation."

He stopped pacing and held out a hand to her but, as much as he wanted them, no words came.

"I have not decided what I will do, and I promise I shall not simply disappear or take any irrevocable steps without discussing it with Mr and Mrs Darcy, whose opinion I trust, if not Lord and Lady Romsley. Please say nothing about it now. After a period of reflection, you might find you understand. I ought to return to Longbourn. It must be almost time for breakfast."

He looked into the distance, seeing a plume of smoke rising from some remote house. "You *will* go to Rebecca as soon as they return to town?"

"For a time, yes."

He regarded her for a long moment. A stab of disappointment and sadness shot through him.

"Safe travels, Darcy." She lightly touched his arm before walking away.

He almost reached for her, to stop her, but did not.

How did I come to say so much? Elizabeth wondered. It had started when she attempted to explain why she was not prepared to leave Hertfordshire. Her distraction almost caused her to trip over a small rock. Keeping watch on the path, she muttered, "In truth, I am very willing to say goodbye to Longbourn and Meryton and the Bennets. There is no place for me here. I cannot believe Darcy suggested I go to Pemberley! He must be mad. The possibility of seeing Lady Anne—or, God forbid, Lady Catherine—is one of the chief reasons I will remain exactly where I am."

She had not forgotten Lady Catherine's unexpected appearance at Grosvenor Square in January. If the woman learnt Elizabeth was in town, would she make her way there again and cause further mayhem? Would the rest of the family overlook her behaviour to avoid a breach that would cause gossip? Lady Catherine was, after all, a true relation. Elizabeth was not.

As to telling Darcy about her notion of being a companion, what had she wanted him to say? "Did I expect him to somehow save me from such a future as he rescued me from Wickham's presence in the neighbourhood? If I did, then I am the one who is mad."

She let out an exasperated breath. "Well, I did what I set out to do by asking him to talk to Mr Bingley. Once he returns from town, he can take the next weeks, or even months, to know Jane better and reflect on what he wants for his future life. I hope Jane will do the same."

***

Mr Bingley did not return to Netherfield.

Four days after the ball, Jane received a note from Miss Bingley. Elizabeth was at the pianoforte, studying new music by Beethoven that the countess had recently sent her, when she heard Mrs Bennet cry out. Upon going to see what had happened, she discovered Jane sitting on the settee and the other girls scattered around the room. Mrs Bennet paced and waved a sheet a paper. When she saw Elizabeth, she stormed up to her, causing Elizabeth to stumble backwards.

"I know you had a hand in it! Unnatural girl! You frightened him away just to spite me and because you are jealous of Jane." With that, she dropped onto the nearest chair and began to wail.

"I do not understand," said Elizabeth.

Mary stood, extracted the paper from her mother's hand, and gave it to Elizabeth before returning to her seat.

The note read:

Dear Jane,

My brother decided to remain in town, and Louisa, Hurst, and I shall join him. I knew how it would be once he was reminded of the superior society and variety of activities available to him there. We shall not quit London again until we go to Yorkshire next summer. Along the way, we shall tour available estates. We are agreed it would be wise to purchase one in the north. We have so many friends in Derbyshire and neighbouring counties, and it would be closer to what family we have beyond each other.

Hertfordshire has been an interesting diversion. I wish to thank you for making our stay here agreeable.

Yours &c.,
Miss C. Bingley

Elizabeth ran a hand over her mouth. She did not know if

what she disclosed to Darcy had anything to do with Mr Bingley's decision to abandon Netherfield, but if it had, she was sorry for it. It was not her intention he take such a drastic step. She supposed Mr Bingley's sisters were so busy slighting her, they had failed to grasp how close Jane and their brother were becoming until they heard Mrs Bennet speak about them marrying at the ball.

"What did you say to him?" Mrs Bennet's face was blotched, and she was visibly furious.

Elizabeth refused to be intimidated. "I do not know the basis for your accusations against me, madam, but I have not spoken to Mr Bingley since we met the other night."

"You were rude. You did it purposely to ruin Jane's chances with him. Hateful girl! Oh, why did you come back? We got along very well without you, and if you had just stayed away, Jane would be engaged!"

Lydia gave a snort of laughter, and Elizabeth's anger and pain turned her insides to ice. Shaking her head, she walked towards the door, refusing to stay and be abused. Why had she ever thought Mrs Bennet could be a mother to her? The impossibility of it was evident within a week of her arrival. Then, however, she had been too angry about what had happened and desperate to find a place in the world.

"Where do you think you are going?" called Mrs Bennet, but Elizabeth ignored her.

In the corridor, Elizabeth spied Mr Bennet standing by the door to his book-room. He gestured for her to join him. Although reluctant, she did.

"What is all the fuss about?" He returned to the armchair behind his desk and waved her into a seat. After she explained, he said, "Am I to understand she blames you for the Bingleys' departure?"

Elizabeth nodded. When he chuckled, she almost

screamed. Fear of sounding like Mrs Bennet kept her silent.

"What nonsense! If Mr Bingley is old enough to lease an estate and be the subject of your mother and sister's matrimonial machinations, he is old enough to decide where to spend his time. It is not to be at Netherfield, it appears, though are we to trust his sister's account? What say you, Elizabeth?"

"You may have the right of it."

Mr Bennet yawned, patting his mouth as he did. "Well, do not mind whatever my wife said to you. This will blow over in a day or two."

Elizabeth kept her eyes on the window and dreamt of walking away. She should have left with Bramwell and Fitzwilliam, but it was too late for regrets. A few more weeks at Longbourn would not be so bad, she hoped.

"I was surprised your friends left the neighbourhood without speaking to me about you returning to town or Worcestershire. You have been here three months, which I would have thought longer than you could tolerate. I did not see the viscount or colonel after the ball, but when Mr Darcy called the other day, I expected him to mention it. Yet, he stayed only long enough to make his adieus."

A sour taste filled her mouth, and Elizabeth fixed her eyes on him. "Are you asking me to leave?"

He studied her for a moment, his fingers tapping the table-top. "No, not if you wish to remain."

"Then for the present, I shall. I anticipate seeing the Gardiners. I have a vague memory or two of Mr Gardiner, and Mrs Gardiner is spoken of in such agreeable terms that I long to meet her." She stood. "If you will excuse me?"

Mr Bennet continued to watch her for a moment. He sighed, frowned, and said, "Off with you. I do not recommend returning to the ladies. Take dinner in your room if you like. A well-timed headache might be in order."

TWENTY ONE

Darcy spent a few days in London before going to Pemberley. His final conversation with Elizabeth rankled and seeing his mother before his temper cooled would be unwise. Elizabeth was dispirited, her health suffered, she was talking about hiring herself out as a companion of all things, and it was partly because of his mother. The very notion of anyone using her the way his aunt and cousin did Mrs Jenkinson was infuriating. He growled and threw the last of a large glass of wine down his throat.

Why, he wondered, could not his mother have embraced Elizabeth, and how could she retain such antipathy towards her for so many years?

While it was true Lady Anne was proud of her heritage, she was too sensible to let Elizabeth's parentage have such an effect on her opinion when Elizabeth had been amongst them for so long. If his mother had allowed herself to love Elizabeth, they would not be in this dreadful situation.

Darcy poured another glass of wine and took a sip. He had drunk the first glass quickly and would take more time with this one, lest he overindulge.

Fitzwilliam and Bramwell had come to dinner at his house in Berkeley Square the day after his arrival. Soon they, too, would be leaving town, Fitzwilliam to Shropshire on an assignment from his general, and Bramwell on a vague errand suspiciously close to where his aunt Darcy's sister lived. After they ate, the cousins sat in the drawing room drinking port and brandy and talking about all manner of things.

"I tried to get Elizabeth to leave again. If she did not want to remain alone in town, I told her she could return to Pemberley with me. She has always liked being there. She refused, even though she admits not being happy in Hertford-shire. I cannot believe she is so stubborn."

He sat low in a chintz armchair, his cousins across from him on a striped sofa. They stared at him, wearing matching puzzled expressions.

Bramwell asked, "You suggested she go to *Pemberley*? Without an army to protect her from Lady Anne?"

"I would be there!"

Bramwell gave him a disgusted look.

Fitzwilliam said, "Elizabeth would never agree to go to Pemberley. Frankly, I am surprised she went there alone last summer."

"I doubt Mother and Father presented it as a choice."

Fitzwilliam agreed. "Darcy, you realise your mother has not been kind to her, even before conspiring with Lady Catherine to send her away."

"Rebecca has told me tales that, I admit, make it difficult for me to think well of Lady Anne," Bramwell said. "I am sorry to say it, but…"

Darcy grunted. "Then what do we do?"

"I do not know there is anything we *can* do," Bramwell said. "Once Rebecca and her parents are in town, Elizabeth will go to them. From the sounds of it, she might not like to live at Romsley Hall again, unless my parents can convince her they care for her."

Fitzwilliam tapped his chin as if the notion had just occurred to him, but it seemed somehow false. "Do you know, what Elizabeth really needs is a husband. If she were properly settled with an honourable man who would always protect her from the evil harridans of the world, give her the love and respect she deserves—"

Darcy said, "What the ████ are you going on about?"

Watching him, Bramwell said, "Elizabeth needs a husband. Why do *you* not marry her?" He then snorted and fell into a raucous laugh. Fitzwilliam immediately joined him.

Darcy stared at them, his upper lip curling in disgust at their behaviour.

Still laughing between words, Bramwell said, "The look on your face! We do think you should marry her, but my poor little sister—Lady Anne would be her mother-in-law!" He wiped a tear from his face.

Clearly, they were more inebriated than Darcy suspected. "Marrying Elizabeth is out of the question. You know what my father expected of me."

Doing a remarkably poor imitation of him, Fitzwilliam repeated his words. Bramwell laughed so hard he fell off the sofa, while Fitzwilliam clutched his stomach as he guffawed.

Darcy observed them for a moment, collected the decanters, and gave them to the footman who opened the door when he kicked it.

"We shall not need these again."

In the middle of December, Elizabeth received a letter from Rebecca, announcing they would leave Dorset after Twelfth Night and could now fix a date for Elizabeth to join her and her parents in London.

As much as I have enjoyed seeing my relations again, I wish our visit had not been extended so you and I could see each other sooner. Your letters are becoming less cheerful, and from what Darcy wrote to Papa and what little Bramwell told us when he was in the neighbourhood, I am anxious for you, as are my parents. If we had realised you were so unhappy, we would have had you join us here. I am still tempted to demand you do. You must not hesitate to write to me if remaining there another few weeks is distasteful! Papa will leave immediately to escort you here, or we shall simply return to town early, despite the entreaties to stay for Yuletide.

If you are content to remain at Longbourn, Papa will send the carriage for you on the fourteenth.

I can hear you saying it is unnecessary, but you know none of us are easy having you travel even an hour by any other means. I do not believe my parents have yet recovered from you going all the way from Kent to Meryton on public conveyance with only Herriot accompanying you.

In less than a month she would leave Longbourn, likely forever. The thought ought to make her sad, but all Elizabeth felt was relief. Any concern about returning to her old life was drowned by the certainty that she needed to be amongst people she knew liked her. That would surely help her overcome the anger and injury caused by the events of the previous summer, to say nothing of her ill-advised *tendre* for Darcy and the disinterest and occasional hostility she faced in Hertfordshire. It was a point she ought to have considered weeks ago.

The situation had worsened since her foster brothers and

Darcy left the neighbourhood. Once it was certain Mr Bingley had left Netherfield Park with no plans to return, Mrs Bennet and the Miss Bennets all but stopped speaking to her, except to blame Elizabeth for his departure.

Elizabeth decided to wait before telling the Bennets of her decision to leave Longbourn, not that she supposed they would care.

At breakfast the following day, Mrs Bennet said to Jane, "Miss Bingley wrote that they would be in London all winter, did she not?"

"Yes, Mama."

"You must go to town. I could not live with myself if we did nothing, and the next thing we hear is that Mr Bingley is engaged or even married." Her voice dropped, although her whisper was almost as loud as her usual voice. "Those London ladies will do anything to catch a man."

It was the most absurd thing Elizabeth had heard in a week, and she almost laughed aloud.

Mrs Bennet continued. "The Gardiners are bound to ask you to return with them, and you will accept. When you call on Miss Bingley, Mr Bingley will see you, and before you know it, he will offer for you. It would be better if I could go with you, to help you along, but I am needed here. The militia remains in Meryton until the spring. I still hope more marriageable officers, ones who would do for Kitty and Lydia, will join them. Then I must see if there is anything I can do for Mary."

Jane methodically took bites of food or sips of tea. Elizabeth could not tell what she thought of Mrs Bennet's plan.

"We shall go into Meryton today and order your clothes, Jane," Mrs Bennet announced.

"I beg your pardon?" Mr Bennet lowered his paper just

enough to look at his wife. "There is no more money for finery. I acceded to your requests this autumn, and you promised me a son-in-law. Yet, no gentleman came to take any of these girls away."

"But Mr Bennet…London! Jane must—"

"Jane will have to make do with what she has."

"I shall, Papa," Jane hastened to say.

As Mrs Bennet protested, Mr Bennet patted Jane's hand.

"You are a good girl, Jane, and if I can be excused for sounding too much like your mother or Mrs Philips, I know you would have caught Mr Bingley if you could. Let us have no more talk. This has gone on long enough." Mr Bennet waved a hand to indicate the dishes on the table. "Eat so we can all get on with our day."

<hr />

When he could justify no further delay, Darcy went to Pemberley. There was a thin layer of snow on the ground, and the estate was particularly picturesque as he approached. He was reminded of his last arrival and anticipating the pleasure of spending time with Elizabeth and later his cousins as they amused themselves in the late summer weather.

In the final minutes before the coach reached the house, Darcy's mind took him back to the evening with Bramwell and Fitzwilliam. Never had he seen them act so nonsensically. He had loathed seeing Elizabeth in Meryton as much as they did, but suggesting *he* should marry her was unthinkable.

Beyond his reasons to look elsewhere for a bride, Elizabeth would never accept him. She would want to love her husband, and as much as they were friends, there had never been anything romantic between them. To be sure, Pemberley would be fortunate to have such a mistress, but Lady Anne would never give her blessing and neither would his father. It was something Darcy could not overlook. It was his duty to bring to his estate a bride with a large dowry and excellent connexions. One day, he would meet a lady who had both and for whom he could share a deep affection.

Entering the house, the butler informed him Lady Anne was waiting for him in the green sitting room. Darcy went to her, hoping to say a brief greeting before escaping to his apartment until dinner.

"You look well," his mother said.

He inclined his head.

"Are you not going to enquire about *my* health? We have not seen each other in above two months."

Darcy looked into a corner of the room and counted to twenty before meeting her eye briefly. "How do you do, madam?"

Lady Anne's chin fell to her chest for a breath or two. She sat, but Darcy remained on his feet.

"Were you in town?" she asked.

"For a week, I was. Before that, as I wrote, I was at Bingley's estate."

A flash of disapproval crossed her countenance, and Darcy's hands curled into fists. She had always hated his friendship with Bingley because his father once was a tradesman.

"Elizabeth was there. Longbourn, Mr Bennet's estate, is the closest neighbour to Bingley's new home."

He had not told her, and as far as he knew, his aunts and uncles presently wrote to her infrequently or not at all, such was their anger. Because he studied her response, Darcy witnessed multiple emotions cross her countenance, each appearing and disappearing too quickly to identify. He believed he saw curiosity, fear, and perhaps dawning under-standing. It was the first that convinced him that part of his mother, perhaps just the tiniest speck, regretted colluding with Lady Catherine against Elizabeth. If he could only nurture that emotion into something more, convince her to reconcile with Elizabeth and make amends, how much easier his life would be!

He wanted his mother to ask about his cold manner simply to have a reason to tell her it was because Elizabeth was miserable, but she remained silent.

Keeping his eyes fixed on her, he said, "Are you not even going to ask about Elizabeth's health or if she finds being there agreeable? Would you be glad or distressed if I told you she does not?"

When, after a pause, Lady Anne still did not speak, Darcy left her.

On the twenty-third of December as the family was finishing breakfast, Mrs Hill told Elizabeth several packages had arrived for her, and she would find them in the sitting room. Elizabeth thanked her but wished she had shown more circum-spection.

Kitty and Lydia rushed down the corridor to investigate, trailed by everyone else.

"Look how many there are!" Lydia cried, taking up a small box. "Open it. I want to see."

Mr Bennet was at Elizabeth's elbow. "I recommend you get to it. There will be no slipping away with your bounty now."

She felt the weight of six pairs of eyes on her as she sat next to the table where the packages had been arranged.

Mrs Bennet waved a finger at the small pile. "Well, girl, what is all this?"

Resentment roiled in her stomach, and Elizabeth looked between Mr and Mrs Bennet. "I imagine they are birthday gifts from my friends."

Mrs Bennet looked disapproving, even irritated, as though Elizabeth had no right to have a birthday, but chagrin darkened Mr Bennet's countenance before he once again adopted his usual air of disaffection.

"Your birthday?" Kitty said while Lydia asked, "Oh lord, is it? How old are you?"

"I am one-and-twenty." This was not where she would have chosen to celebrate her coming of age, and for what felt like the thousandth time, she regretted not leaving with her foster brothers or joining Rebecca and her parents in Dorset.

Elizabeth opened the parcels as quickly as possible, intending to enjoy the notes that accompanied them in private. The gifts were all thoughtful, and the drawing of the jewellery the countess and earl would give to her when they were together showed it to be extravagant. She ignored the exclamations and demands from the Bennets that she must share the candies sent by Bramwell and Fitzwilliam.

There was one parcel she avoided as long as possible because it was from Lady Anne. Carefully unwrapping it as though it might contain something lethal, Elizabeth discovered a bracelet instead. The silver and gemstone creation was delicate and evoked bright summer flowers.

Elizabeth ran a trembling finger across the smooth surface. There was no note, and had it not been for the writing on the paper, she would not have known who it was from. Why would Lady Anne send her such a thing? Was it meant as an apology? Did she do it to satisfy Darcy?

Elizabeth could not bear to be with the Bennets any longer. Gathering her presents and letters, she said, "If you will excuse me, I shall put these upstairs," and left the room.

Mr and Mrs Gardiner arrived the next day and would stay a week. He was an intelligent, fashionable gentleman who had prospered in his profession, and his wife was genial and sensible. Their four children were delightful, and Elizabeth liked them. There was little opportunity for private conversation with the couple, unfortunately, until the day before their departure, when Elizabeth found herself alone with Mrs Gardiner. She was surprised when the lady admitted to once having lived in Lambton.

"I calculated that I removed to town less than a year before you went to live in Worcestershire. I know you spent time at Pemberley and must be familiar with Lambton."

"I am. It is a charming village."

They spoke about Derbyshire for over an hour, which Elizabeth found remarkably agreeable.

"If I might be serious for a minute." Mrs Gardiner took hold of her hand, and Elizabeth's good cheer evaporated. "I know why you were sent away as a child, and your uncle and I see that time has not made Mrs Bennet kinder towards you. We cannot imagine you are happy at Longbourn. Would you like to talk about it? I shall understand if you say no. We hardly know each other."

"After so long a separation, they and I are not used to each other and…"

"Your sisters and mother see you lived a very different sort of life and are sometimes jealous?"

Elizabeth said nothing.

Mrs Gardiner squeezed her hand. "Your uncle and I want you to know you may stay with us whenever you like—immediately, if you so wish—or you may simply write a letter or arrive at our door."

Elizabeth blinked away the sudden wetness in her eyes. It was a most generous offer. "I have not told them, but in a fortnight, I am going to stay with my dearest friend, Rebecca Darcy."

"I am glad to hear it, but it does not change what I said. You may find you cannot or do not wish to stay with friends forever, Elizabeth. You have family who would welcome you."

The words lifted Elizabeth's spirits. She thanked Mrs Gardiner and promised to write to her and call when she was in town.

As much as Elizabeth was satisfied with her visit with the Gardiners, Jane and Mrs Bennet were not, since the couple left without inviting Jane to go with them.

Ten days later, Elizabeth told Mr Bennet of her plans.

He regarded her for a long moment looking almost sad. "I cannot say I am surprised. When do you go, and do I need to make any arrangements for you?"

"Next week, and no, thank you. Rebecca's father will send his carriage for me."

He made a noise of understanding and frowned. "It is good you came, Elizabeth. I wish—well, I suppose the least said the better at this point. Do write to me, and let me know how you get on."

She would have liked to hear what he was going to say, particularly if it was an expression of sorrow at having abandoned her and for doing so little to ensure she felt at home upon her return. In the end, it did not truly matter.

At dinner, she announced to the others that she was leaving in a few days. The responses from the ladies were what she expected, and since she was prepared, their lack of distress at her departure and their envy that she would spend the winter in town did not touch her.

TWENTY TWO

"I am so glad you are finally here!" Rebecca exclaimed. "I shall not let you leave again."

Elizabeth laughed and looked over her shoulder at her friend from where she stood at the dressing table, arranging her newly unpacked things. Rebecca reclined on a cosy velvet chaise longue. Bright fresh flowers and plants gave life to the room, and Elizabeth sniffed a rose before joining her friend.

"You will have to, once a certain event takes place." She waggled her eyebrows, and Rebecca laughed.

"We shall see. I might contrive to keep you with me even then. After all, I have no sister but you, and it is common for a newly married lady to have another woman with her."

Leaving Longbourn was like ridding herself of a great weight. Elizabeth hoped—believed—she made the best possible choice in returning to her old life, but only time would tell. She had not left the Bennets behind entirely, however. Jane would be in town in a day or two.

Just after New Year's, Jane wrote the Gardiners to ask if she might stay with them. Elizabeth supposed she did it at Mrs Bennet's direction. Before Elizabeth's departure from Long- bourn, Jane had found her alone.

"I hope to see you in town. Away from…" Jane's eyes slid to the closed door, then to Elizabeth's surprise, she embraced her. "I shall miss you. I know it has not always seemed like it, but I am glad you came." Releasing Elizabeth, Jane had left the room before she could respond.

It was moments like those that made it impossible for her to forget Jane was her sister, not just someone who happened to share her surname. Separating from Jane forever would have been much easier if she had never seen any kindness in her.

Rebecca's voice pulled Elizabeth back to the present. "I must be serious for a moment. I *am* glad you are here. You know Mama and Papa are too."

"That was evident."

Mr Frederick Darcy had come to Longbourn to escort her to town himself. He spent a quarter of an hour sitting rigidly in the drawing room, saying as little as possible to Mr and Mrs Bennet and nothing at all to the Miss Bennets. Once at Curzon Street, Mrs Darcy had embraced her, refusing to release her for a long while.

"We were so worried about you. Frantic, really, until I received your letter."

Her chin lowered, and Elizabeth nodded. "I am sorry it took me so long to write. I just…" She shrugged.

Resting her head on Elizabeth's shoulder, Rebecca said, "I can only imagine how terrible it was. Do you want to tell me about it? You need not today, if you would rather not."

Elizabeth took a slow, deep breath. "It was so odd being there, seeing these young women I know are my sisters, but I never felt as though they were. I longed to have a connexion to them, especially to Jane because I have memories of her from when we were little girls, but no matter how hard I tried, I did not." She gazed at Rebecca. "Saying this is awful, but I began to realise I was fortunate that Mr Bennet sent me away. I had so many more advantages than the Miss Bennets did, especially in that I was surrounded by good people who treat each other with respect. I cannot possibly describe what the atmosphere is like at Longbourn."

"You are here now and need never go back."

Elizabeth pressed her eyes closed. "I spent hours trying to imagine what I would be like had I not gone to the dowager. I might be just like them. I tried to reassure myself I would improve, if shown a better way. One of the reasons I remained there so long was because I kept praying Jane at least would take something good from my presence."

"You never would have been like them, regardless of Mr and Mrs Bennet's behaviour. You would have seen how wrong it was and done what you knew was right, no matter how much it displeased them."

"I hope I would have." Elizabeth squeezed Rebecca's hand. "Enough about Longbourn."

"Papa will attempt to hide it from you, but he is still furious with both Lady Anne and Lady Catherine."

"How they acted was despicable, not only towards me but for what it meant to all of you. The episode has made me realise I must decide what I want for my future. I cannot continue to ask Lord and Lady Romsley to give me a home. They do not need or want the responsibility of an unmarried young woman."

"You could live with Mama and Papa, and you would always have a place with me. Especially once…"

A spark of good humour resulted in a chuckle and fond smile. "Especially once you and Bramwell marry."

Rebecca lightly tapped her arm. "Do not tease me, not now. You are feeling distressed still, which is perfectly reasonable after all you have endured. A few weeks with those who love and appreciate you, and you will be more yourself. You will not feel so restless then."

When Elizabeth only offered an indifferent nod in response, Rebecca continued. "Reconciling with Lady Catherine is impossible, but for Darcy's sake, Papa is determined to be civil to Lady Anne. She is his sister-in-law, and I know he and my cousin consider what Uncle Darcy would have wanted them to do. This is all with the understanding she remains apart from Lady Catherine, no longer badgers Darcy about marrying Anne de Bourgh, and is not cruel to you."

"I never expected anyone, let alone Darcy, to disavow Lady Anne."

"He apparently feels she is sorry for what happened, even though she will not admit it. They arrived in town a few days ago. Mama and I went to call on her." Hesitantly, Rebecca added, "I have the impression she hopes you call."

Elizabeth was astonished. Might she want to apologise? It would gain her favour with Darcy, amongst others. The birthday gift Lady Anne sent gave credence to the notion she was remorseful.

"I suppose I could see her. I told you about the bracelet, and if she does want to make amends or show she will treat me with politeness, then I ought to give her the opportunity—for everyone else's sake, more than my own."

Rebecca looked dubious. "I do not know if it is wise, but I understand. Shall I go with you?"

"I think it is best if I do this alone. Lady Anne is proud, and if she *does* want to apologise, she is more likely to do it when no one else can witness it. And, if she attempts to abuse me, I want her to see that she cannot intimidate me. I will not meekly climb into a carriage again, so to speak."

They debated the need for the call and the timing of it for a short while before Rebecca changed the subject, claiming a desire to speak of more amusing things.

"Is there anything in particular you wish to do now that you are here? Beyond the usual, I mean."

"Shopping. I feel in need of some pretty new things, and I read about a new exhibit. It sounds very interesting. I cannot recall the details, but I shall find the notice. What have you planned for us?"

The two friends continued to chat about dinners, friends, and warehouses until dinner time.

Bramwell and Fitzwilliam called the next day. The first thing they did upon entering the drawing room was hug Elizabeth, which was awkward as they fought over who had the most right to embrace her first and for how long. Bramwell gave her a loud kiss on one cheek, and Fitzwilliam repeated the action on the other.

"I am glad you are finally away from Longbourn," said Fitzwilliam.

Bramwell held her by the shoulders and stared into her eyes. "We will have no more talk of you living apart from us. What nonsense! As your eldest brother, I insist on being obeyed in this matter."

Elizabeth donned her best sceptical expression. It made Fitzwilliam laugh.

Settling into the room that Elizabeth always considered exceptionally cheerful, Rebecca and Bramwell occupied a settee, while Elizabeth and Fitzwilliam chose to sit at a little distance to give the couple privacy.

"It *is* good to see you here," Fitzwilliam insisted. "Neither of us liked Meryton. The neighbourhood was not offensive, but being at Netherfield Park…" He groaned. "Those women! They never had a kind word to say about any young lady."

"Especially me." Elizabeth chuckled. "You need not try to hide it. They did seem fond of Jane, but I do not trust them."

"Good! They were *not* complimentary to Miss Bennet in her absence."

Surely, Jane would discover the duplicitous nature of Miss Bingley and Mrs Hurst if she attempted to renew their friendship. Elizabeth worried for her, and at the same time, she thought it would do Jane good.

Fitzwilliam continued to speak. "My cousin bore the brunt of their bad behaviour."

"Have you seen Darcy?"

"Before he went to Pemberley, I did. He stopped by town for a few days after leaving Hertfordshire. Did you know?"

Elizabeth shook her head and wondered why humour tugged at the corners of Fitzwilliam's mouth.

"We met for a few minutes the day before yesterday. He was occupied with meetings related to investments or land purchases or something of the sort. You know I have no head for such things."

"No *interest* in such things, you mean!"

"True enough. Mother and Father will be here shortly. They are anxious to see you, but Father has a cold, which delayed their departure. I expect you will hear from her today or tomorrow."

In her most recent letter, Lady Romsley wrote that she and the earl intended to be in town in advance of Elizabeth's arrival. When they were not, Elizabeth supposed something amusing or interesting had occurred, and they decided a few extra days apart would not matter. She was rather glad their absence was unavoidable.

"I pray he has recovered or soon will."

"If his illness were serious, we would have heard," Fitzwilliam said. "Let us talk about a more pleasant topic.

Bramwell and I have devised all sorts of schemes to occupy our time in the coming weeks and erase the events of the summer and autumn from our memories."

As he spoke about parties and excursions, Elizabeth's eyes drifted to Rebecca and Bramwell. She was struck by how much in love they appeared. Their connexion had deepened a great deal since the last time she saw them together in April.

While she would gain her own home and family if she were to marry, how could she accept anything less than they had? Elizabeth wanted to marry for love, a man who would be her dearest friend as well as husband.

She forced her reflections aside, and she and Fitzwilliam chatted amiably until refreshments were served.

⁓

Two days later, Elizabeth went to Berkeley Square, having sent a letter informing Lady Anne she would call. Rebecca again offered to go with her, but Elizabeth declined.

"If she truly did not know her sister intended to force me onto a ship headed to India, perhaps she is mortified. If Lady Anne wishes, I am willing to begin anew. Not as friends, that is impossible, but as adults who can be polite to each other when we are in company."

Herriot accompanied Elizabeth and chatted animatedly in the carriage, showing Elizabeth how glad the maid was to be in London again.

The butler showed her to the drawing room. Elizabeth stood as still as a tree on a wind-free day as Lady Anne, sitting primly on the edge of a bergère chair, raked her eyes up and down her person. Elizabeth had chosen a crimson day dress with a muted leaf pattern because it added colour to her cheeks. There was nothing she could do to mask how thin she had become. Lady Anne scowled and pinched her lips, but Elizabeth did not know if she was distressed by the changes she saw in her, disapproved of her clothing, or even that she had come.

They sat at a shiny cherrywood table, and Lady Anne poured tea for them. There was shortbread, which Elizabeth favoured, and she nibbled on a piece. It was difficult to eat anything when she felt so awkward. She guarded each word and observed each of Lady Anne's movements, listening carefully to what she said, almost as though she would sense danger coming and be able to avoid it.

They spoke about their trips to town and exchanged news about mutual acquaintances. What Lady Anne did not say seemed louder than what she did—she failed to mention the last time they met, gave no indication Elizabeth was only in Hertfordshire because of the scheme she and Lady Catherine devised, and offered no apology.

Lady Anne pushed the plate of biscuits towards her. "Have another one."

Elizabeth had just managed to finish the first piece but could not refuse, especially when Lady Anne all but nudged the plate into her hand. Under Lady Anne's watchful eye, Elizabeth did as directed and took a bite. Forcing her lips not to twitch in a brief burst of merriment, she thought, *If I did not know better, I would suspect they were poisoned.*

They were silent for a long moment before Lady Anne looked at her locket watch and frowned. She straightened her spine and lifted her chin. When she spoke, her voice was steady and low.

"It was kind of Mrs Darcy to invite you to stay, but once I learnt you were in Hertfordshire, I expected you to realise it was where you belonged. You should be with *your* family."

The biscuit landed on the table with a dull thud as it fell

out of Elizabeth's hand. Heat flooded her cheeks, and bile burned the back of her throat. She stood and moved towards the door, refusing to stay and be abused.

Lady Anne blocked her way. Her words were almost urgent when she said, "It is time for my son to marry, and your presence, staying with his relations, prevents him from selecting an appropriate bride, one with connexions to match his own and a fortune that will enrich him. He should have married Anne, but thanks to you, that will never happen. With you always hovering around him, what chance is there he will select a proper—"

"What does my being in town have to do with his—"

"You know exactly what I mean, Elizabeth Bennet! No matter how much you may wish for the position, you will *never* be mistress of Pemberley. He will remember the duty he owes to his name."

Elizabeth's eyes grew round, and a bark of astonishment escaped her lips. Even if Lady Anne suspected she had once been in love with Darcy, she could not possibly imagine he would ever regard her in *that* way? Both ladies were startled by the door opening.

In walked Darcy. Lady Anne turned bright pink and gaped at him.

"Elizabeth, I did not know you were calling this morning. If I had, I would have been here to greet you."

"Well, you have seen me." She curtseyed, though it was shallow. "I must go. You know where to find me."

Lady Anne cried, "How dare you try to entice him, encourage him to forget his responsibilities, what he is owed. *You* are not good enough for—"

"Mother!" exclaimed Darcy.

A glimpse in Lady Anne's direction made it evident she

wished she had not spoken. A hand covered her mouth, and her eyes were locked on her son.

Elizabeth quickly left the house and raced down the stairs.

TWENTY THREE

Darcy could not believe what he witnessed between his mother and Elizabeth. Thank goodness he had returned earlier than expected, or he might have never known. Common sense suggested he calm himself before talking to Lady Anne, but her words demanded an immediate response. Elizabeth had been hurt enough already, and he felt stupid to have believed his mother regretted her part in Lady Catherine's scheme.

"What possessed you to say such a thing? Elizabeth is my friend and part of this family!"

His mother averted her eyes and hesitated before saying, "She is not. She is a *Bennet*, not a Fitzwilliam or Darcy or de Bourgh."

Darcy threw up his hands and paced as he attempted to discover what had passed between the ladies. His mother offered few details.

"Your grandmother took in the girl as a kindness. It was supposed to be a temporary situation. She remained entirely too long. She is a distraction."

"I am almost afraid to ask what you mean by that, yet I must."

She paused, and Darcy was on the verge of insisting she answer when she blurted out, "A pretty young lady, always there when you are with your cousins is a distraction. You should be taking a wife—an *appropriate* wife—one who will bring honour to this family."

Darcy glared at her. "If you so much as dare to mention Anne—"

"You may be angry with Catherine, and I know it has hardened your resolve against my niece, but she would have been the most suitable bride for you. Aside from her excellent breeding and fortune, we know she is trustworthy. *She* is not mercenary. People like Elizabeth Bennet—"

"Do not finish that sentence, madam. What has she ever done to earn your hatred? You, who have known her since she was five years old, know better than to suggest Elizabeth is anything other than honest and caring." He longed to throw one of the detestable Chinese figurines in the room against the wall. "Tell me, *why* do you dislike her? I know you lost a child not long before Grandmother brought Elizabeth north. Did you reject her because she was alive and your daughter was dead? It was unkind and unfair of you then. It is even more so now, so many years later, when you still treat her with hostility."

"One has nothing to do with the other!" Her chin quivered, and for a moment, she refused to look at him. "I accept you want nothing to do with Catherine, and her method may have been extreme, but her motives were sound."

"*Her* motives? *You* were very much part of that disgusting scheme, and if you believe your niece was not cruel to Elizabeth when she was at Rosings, it is because you are deliberately clinging to your obstinate prejudice against a young lady whose character is infinitely more admirable than Anne's."

"That is a terrible thing to say about your own cousin! You ought to be ashamed of yourself. Even if Anne is a bit…harsh, away from Catherine, she would improve."

Darcy sniggered. "Would she become more like you, a lesser Lady Catherine?" His mother's face drained of colour. "If you do not correct yourself, madam, your intolerance, your mean-spiritedness will become fixed as the essential aspects of your character. They might already be, but I pray they are not, because once they are, I promise you, our connexion will be at an end."

She paled.

"You have one last chance to show you will—at a minimum—treat Elizabeth respectfully. If you do not, you will leave my home." Darcy turned his back to her and strode out of the house.

⌇⌇

Elizabeth sat in the carriage, her fingers drumming on her knee, avoiding Herriot's curious gaze. She was angry, mostly at Lady Anne, but partly at herself. It had been the height of foolishness to think the woman wanted to make amends.

The drive felt three times longer than her earlier one to Berkeley Square. Rebecca was out when she arrived, which was just as well. Elizabeth went to her room, threw herself on the bed, buried her face in the pillow, and cried. There were several muffled screams, too, before she felt properly in control of her emotions. As she dabbed at her face with a wet cloth, there was a knock at the door, and Rebecca entered.

"Oh Elizabeth!" Rebecca took the cloth and wiped Elizabeth's cheeks.

"It is anger and frustration that has caused this, not injury."

"Even so, I am very sorry your visit with Lady Anne was so wretched."

Rebecca ordered tea, and they sat together on the chaise longue. Elizabeth clutched a rose-pink pillow to her chest and told Rebecca what happened.

"I feel stupid for expecting more, especially when the only reason I did was because she sent me a pretty birthday gift." She gave an incredulous laugh. "Well, I have the comfort of knowing I acted in the best interest of others. If she and I could reconcile enough to avoid discord within the family, so much the better. But now, if there is ill-will between her and Darcy or anyone else, it has nothing to do with me."

"Very true. It is difficult to think well of her, and once the earl hears of this—"

"I do not intend to tell him or anyone else."

"Darcy will. At the very least, he will tell Bramwell and Fitzwilliam, and you know they will tell their parents."

Elizabeth stared at the ceiling. "I wish they would not."

"You should not shield Lady Anne from the consequences of her actions. If people are vexed with her, she has only herself to blame."

"I know you are right, yet I hate that all of this trouble is because of me. It is," she insisted when Rebecca opened her mouth, likely to protest. "I had hoped we could be civil to each other when circumstance forced us into company. Perhaps it is still possible."

A maid delivered their tea. After sipping the warm, sweet liquid, Elizabeth continued. "I wish I could understand why she despises me. Arrogance and pride are at the root of her hatred, I suppose, and some belief I have too high an opinion of myself for someone with my background. I cannot believe she had the audacity to suggest *I* want to trick Darcy into thinking he has tender feelings for me."

Rebecca scowled. "Now that he is almost eight-and-twenty, she has to confront the truth he will never marry Anne. You are here, the two of you are friends, so she seeks to blame you. It is easier than thinking ill of her niece. If Lady Anne truly respected her son, she would let him decide when and whom to marry."

Elizabeth drained her cup and placed it on the side table. "I wish everyone had as simple a time in this game of marriage as you and Bramwell have."

"We are fortunate. Lord and Lady Romsley care more for his happiness than they do of him choosing someone of high standing and fortune. And you should not refer to marriage as a game," Rebecca said with mock solemnity.

"Yes, Mama."

The ladies sat side by side, their legs stretched out on the chaise, their arms linked.

"What troubles you, Elizabeth? I can see something does, and I suspect it goes beyond your encounter with Lady Anne. Are you worried about your marriage prospects?"

Elizabeth shook her head. "I *was* thinking of how people choose spouses but not for myself. I wrote to you about Mr Bingley's admiration for Jane, but I do not comprehend her feelings for him. Indeed, the longer I was at Longbourn, the more confused I became.

"Mrs Bennet's motive in promoting the match is purely mercenary. Jane told me several times that she must marry well. It is her responsibility to her mother and sisters since they will have little when Mr Bennet dies. At times, she seemed to embrace Mrs Bennet's thinking, yet at others, I believed she hoped for more. The one time I dared to enquire, Jane could not say she loved or even esteemed Mr Bingley."

"Esteem is important, but do all ladies love their husbands?" Rebecca asked. "Do all men love their wives? Is love a necessary ingredient for a happy union?"

Elizabeth tried to make a joke of it. "Such thought-provoking questions."

"Be serious. I know my parents married for love, but Lord and Lady Romsley did not, yet they are a devoted couple and grew to love each other dearly."

Elizabeth bit her lip and played with a pillow until Rebecca took it from her and put it on the floor.

"Jane will be in London soon. I know she comes in hopes of seeing Mr Bingley, and I know once she discovers Miss Bingley and Mrs Hurst do not consider her a friend, she will ask me to assist her."

"Do you believe she would treat Mr Bingley ill, or would she be good to him, whatever her reasons for wanting the match? If she is simply avaricious and will not be kind, then certainly do nothing. But if she would be a good wife, regardless of the depth of her affection..." She shrugged, suggesting with a gesture such a circumstance would make a difference. "Now, enough about Jane and Mr Bingley. Let us return to the subject of *your* marriage."

"No!" Elizabeth cried in mock horror. "Let us please, I beg of you, discuss something more interesting. What shall we do to occupy ourselves tomorrow?"

The housekeeper informed Darcy that his aunt was not at home and showed him into the drawing room to await Rebecca and Elizabeth. For the few minutes he was alone, he sat, then stood and looked out the window, then sat again. He would not be easy until he saw Elizabeth was well. He had taken a long walk before making his way to Curzon Street. It had done little to ease his disquiet.

When the ladies appeared, Darcy's gaze immediately fell on Elizabeth's swollen eyes. A surge of fury hit him because his mother had made her cry, likely not for the first time.

"On behalf of my mother, I apologise, Elizabeth."

When she gave him a look of disbelief, he gritted his teeth

and admitted Lady Anne had not asked him to apologise for her.

"I am sorry you were received so uncharitably. Although I do not know what was said before I entered the room, my...*conversation* with my mother was enough to convince me it was horrible." Carefully watching her, he added, "Will you tell me? I surmise you have confided in Rebecca already."

Elizabeth's cheeks darkened, and she clasped Rebecca's hand. Darcy's temper threatened to boil over as she explained that Lady Anne implied she wanted to secure her future by marrying him.

"It is absurd," said Elizabeth. "As though you would ever —as though *I* would ever!" She pulled her hand from Rebecca's and went to examine one of the numerous plants his aunt liked to have around her. "God knows how often Lady Anne and Lady Catherine have talked about the disgrace of my poor connexions. You are Fitzwilliam Darcy of Pemberley and need a lady of fortune and birth to match your own." She turned to him. "You cannot tell me you have not thought the same."

Darcy looked at Rebecca to see whether she would defend him, but her expression was as challenging as Elizabeth's. The truth was, he could not deny it. It was what he had been taught by his parents for as long as he could remember.

"Why are we speaking of this? Your well-being is the essential point. You were, once again, abused at my mother's hands. Why did you never tell me how horrible she was to you? I asked you last winter if she was being kind, and you had nothing ill to say. I am left to discover the depths of her antagonism by her actions and accidentally overhearing how she speaks to you."

"What could you have done?"

"I do not know because I was never given the chance to

find out!" Darcy spoke more roughly than he wanted. Elizabeth did not deserve his anger.

She stood tall and faced him. "Do you truly believe anything you said to her or Lady Catherine would have made a difference? Your efforts to make them understand you did not favour a match with Anne were ineffective. Perhaps I did not think it worth the bother of asking you to try to change their opinion of me."

There was a moment of silence, and Elizabeth seemed to regret her biting words, but Darcy knew if he had been more forceful with his aunt and mother about that matter, perhaps they would not currently be in this distressing situation.

Elizabeth's bearing softened. "I am sorry for speaking so harshly, Darcy. We are both agitated, and it serves no purpose to discuss your mother further. Let us speak of something else. Tell me, how is Nutmeg faring?" She took a seat, and Rebecca joined her on the sofa.

Darcy huffed in surprise at her change of topic and dropped into a chair across from them. "Your horse has settled into the stables at Pemberley. She returned there with my horses, and I decided she may as well remain until you are at Romsley Hall again."

He did not miss the brief expression of doubt that passed over her countenance. Once she saw the earl and countess, he was confident all would be well, and she would accept that her home was with them.

Seeking equanimity, he shook his head. "The Moores are hosting a ball next week. Will you be attending?"

Rebecca answered. "We are. Bramwell and Fitzwilliam will be there too."

"Then I shall also go." To Elizabeth, Darcy said, "Will you dance the first with me?" He was taken aback when she shook her head.

"Fitzwilliam already asked me."

He scowled but did not question his irritation. "The second?"

"Bramwell."

"The supper dance then." A muscle near his eye began to twitch. He took it to be a sign of exasperation.

Elizabeth hesitated. "Will your mother be there?"

He clenched his teeth for a moment before asking, "Does it matter? I wish to dance with you because I enjoy it. I think you would say the same. I do not intend to let her...opinions change my behaviour when there is nothing inappropriate about it. I have told her she has one final opportunity to prove she can behave in an acceptable manner—should you be gracious enough to agree. If she will not, I shall consult with the earl about where to send her. I will not allow her to remain with me." He likely should have told Elizabeth that earlier, but their conversation had not progressed as he had expected.

Elizabeth nodded, a bit tentatively perhaps, but there was resolve in her eyes. He admired her fortitude and goodness. It was more than his mother and, by association, he deserved.

Returning to her previous question, he said, "No, I do not believe she will attend."

At length, Elizabeth said, "Thank you. It would be my pleasure to dance the supper set with you."

Rebecca grinned at him, and Darcy felt his cheeks warm. After securing a set with his cousin, he suggested they attend the theatre soon. Elizabeth and Rebecca looked at each other, then nodded.

"I shall talk to Fitzwilliam and Bramwell and make the necessary arrangements," Darcy announced before standing and taking his leave. He felt a sudden need to be alone.

Darcy had the oddest sensation as he left the house. He could not name it, but it was as though there were a heaviness in his mind. He walked back to Berkeley Square, seeing and hearing only through a fog, his feet moving of their own accord.

Arriving home, he told his butler, "I am not to be disturbed."

With that, he climbed the stairs to his apartment. His valet fussed over him, stating he was certain Darcy had taken a chill. In a quarter of an hour, Darcy was sitting in front of a fire, his feet on a footstool, wearing a dressing gown, and with a tray of tea, bread, and cheese beside him. A book lay on his lap, but he could not settle his mind enough to read. His thoughts were too full of Elizabeth.

She had looked better than she had in Hertfordshire. Not even a week being amongst people who loved her as she deserved had made a noticeable difference. Seeing her again where she belonged made him...*satisfied*. That word did not quite fit, but there was something right about it, as though with her in town, his family was complete.

He watched the flames of the fire, and his thoughts drifted to the past. Elizabeth had grown into a lovely young lady. He had first noticed the change in her after his father's death. Lord and Lady Romsley thought she might be company for his mother, to help her cope with her grief. Yet, Darcy believed he was the one who most benefitted from Elizabeth's stay at Pemberley. Her friendly face, quiet company as they walked the grounds or went riding, and willingness to engage him in conversation about subjects other than his father—books and travel and politics—all of it made the days easier.

Her greatest service to him, one Darcy had never disclosed

to anyone, was when she listened to his fears about being able to fulfil his new duties. Elizabeth had known what to say and told him his father had ensured he was well-prepared for the role he would assume at his death. She said she had every confidence in him, and it had given him the strength to carry on.

He recalled his mother disparaging Elizabeth over the years. Again and again she would say, 'She is nothing to us,' but it never occurred to him that she would say something similar directly to Elizabeth.

In December, when his mother discovered he had arranged for Nutmeg to be brought to Netherfield, she expressed her disapproval, citing the expense, and 'the sort of message it imparts'. But she was also full of questions about Elizabeth's welfare.

Darcy could not believe she disliked Elizabeth as much as she said. Doubtless his mother was under Lady Catherine's influence, but there must have been something else making her act the way she had. If he could discover what it was, they could see an end to this strife.

He stood and poked the fire, sending sparks flying. Watching as they danced and faded, he vowed that he would never end his friendship with Elizabeth because of his mother's prejudice against her. He liked and respected Elizabeth too much and always looked forward to seeing her. Why would he not? She had many traits he greatly admired, being intelligent, caring, loyal, industrious—

And her eyes, so fine and expressive. The way they shine when she laughs.

Warmth suffused his body, and his stomach fluttered. Where, he wondered, had *that* come from?

Darcy closed his eyes for a minute but opened them when he realised all he could see were images of Elizabeth. Looking particularly lovely in her rose gown at the Netherfield ball. Wearing a broad grin, her hair dishevelled as she sat atop her horse after a hard gallop. Her eyes flashing as they debated the merits of a government proposal. A gentle smile as she played with his dog or watched the antics of squirrels and rabbits when they were walking together.

How it felt when I held her in my arms when we met in Meryton.

Elizabeth was part of his family, as he had told his mother. A part of his life.

A part of my heart.

"Oh, dear God, I am in love with her!"

TWENTY FOUR

Darcy remained in his rooms the entire day, even refusing to dine with his mother. He needed time to think. Half an hour taught him there was no point arguing with himself. Somehow, so gradually he did not notice it happening, he had fallen in love with Elizabeth Bennet.

Darcy knew Fitzwilliam and Bramwell would delight in ridiculing him about it. One way or another, they knew he was in love with their foster sister. They had seen that his feelings were deepening, even though he did not. Could his mother have noticed as well?

The following morning, he went to Grosvenor Square to see his cousins. He found them in a small drawing room and dropped into the place next to Fitzwilliam on a sofa, leaving Bramwell in a wing chair across from them. The brothers spoke together for a while before Fitzwilliam kicked his foot.

"What is wrong with you?"

Darcy was slouched low in his seat and played with his watch. "I saw Elizabeth yesterday." He told them what he had overheard between her and his mother, his argument with Lady Anne, and going to call on Elizabeth and Rebecca. "I wanted to assure myself she was well."

Bramwell said, "And this has you so glum because…?"

Darcy dropped the watch, sighed, and looked at his cousins. "I was thinking about what my mother said, and Elizabeth, and I-I realised I never realised how—that I—"

Fitzwilliam said the words Darcy could not. "Elizabeth is

the perfect woman for you, and you are madly in love with her?"

Bramwell chuckled, and Fitzwilliam grinned. To his brother, the viscount said, "Not really that much of a surprise, is it?"

Fitzwilliam replied, "It is what we deduced, oh, in March?"

"But the signs were there much earlier. At least the past two years."

Darcy growled, sending the pair into whoops of laughter.

"What the ▇▇▇ do I do?"

It took a few minutes and several mouthfuls of wine for them to calm down. Fitzwilliam decided he was hungry, and called for 'a bit of something, whatever is easiest'.

A few minutes later, the butler delivered a platter laden with food. Darcy picked at it, but Fitzwilliam ate as though it was his first meal in a week.

"Do you think she does not return your affection?" Bramwell asked.

Darcy covered his face with a hand. The conversation was bordering on humiliating, but he needed advice and support. "If I thought she did, I would not be here. I would be talking to her. She said my mother's anxiety about us marrying was ridiculous. Does that sound promising to you?"

Bramwell grimaced, while Fitzwilliam popped a grape into his mouth and shook his head. As he chewed, he said, "You are going to have to woo her."

Darcy groaned.

Bramwell slapped his arm. "It will not be that bad."

"You might even enjoy it," Fitzwilliam added.

"And we shall enjoy watching you at it."

The brothers looked at each other and guffawed. Darcy let

them have their fun for a moment, then demanded they be serious.

Bramwell said, "Show her how you feel. Talk to her, make her see her happiness and comfort are important to you. This is Elizabeth. She will be wooed by the intellect, not flattery and baubles."

"A little bauble now and again cannot hurt," said Fitzwilliam.

"I think you mean a book."

"Or a pet. She likes animals." Darcy murmured the words, not intending to be overheard, but his cousins agreed.

"Cats," Bramwell suggested. "We gave her one once, and she loved the little thing."

The brothers spent a few minutes debating ways Darcy could convince Elizabeth she wanted a life with him, and as he listened, his confidence grew—until he remembered Lady Anne.

"My mother will never accept Elizabeth as my wife."

Bramwell said, "With the greatest respect, and no real wish to compare Lady Anne to Lady Catherine—"

"She is your mother, and not as dreadful as our aunt, although it is hard not to notice *some* resemblance," Fitzwilliam said.

"Oh, the times I have thanked God my father was more like Grandmama *not* Grandfather!" Bramwell made an exaggerated shudder, and all three gentlemen grimaced as they remembered old Lord Romsley, who made Lady Catherine seem compassionate and charming by comparison.

Fitzwilliam resumed the argument he and his brother appeared to have rehearsed. "Lady Anne is not as severe as Lady Catherine. When she sees you are happy, she will be happy."

"It will just take some time." Bramwell gave him a reassuring grin.

Darcy asked, "Do you think so?"

They both nodded, and through a mouthful of pie, Fitzwilliam said, "The true difficulty may be convincing Elizabeth to accept Lady Anne."

"Fortunately, our darling sister is a generous, sympathetic soul. I think she will, once Darcy makes her fall in love with him."

"What about the rest of the family? *Not* the de Bourghs." Darcy's voice dropped in disgust. "I know what they will think."

Bramwell made a gagging sound, and Fitzwilliam said, "Mr and Mrs Darcy will be thrilled, and Mother and Father love Elizabeth dearly."

"And do not forget your father adored her," Bramwell added. "He would have been pleased." Darcy's scepticism must have shown, because Bramwell continued. "If he were here now and saw you and Elizabeth together and knew you loved her, he would approve. I shall tell Rebecca. She would gladly help with—"

"No!" Darcy exclaimed. "She would tell Elizabeth, and I shall not have her feeling she must accept my attentions because it would make other people happy."

"He is right," Fitzwilliam said to his brother. "You are not obligated to share everyone's secrets with her."

"Just you," Bramwell replied.

Fitzwilliam grinned. "Well, yes. If you start keeping things from me, I shall have to beat you."

"As though you would win." Bramwell smirked. "You never have. Remember—"

"Oh, be quiet," Darcy muttered.

Five days after seeing Lady Anne, Elizabeth called on the Gardiners and Jane. Knowing she would return to Curzon Street meant she could approach the visit with equanimity. Perhaps she would be pleasantly surprised to find that Jane, away from the Bennets, was more like she wanted her to be. There was something inside Elizabeth that longed to have a connexion to even one Bennet. She did not understand why it was currently important to her, but it was.

Mr and Mrs Gardiner's home was lovely. Although modest compared to what Elizabeth was used to, it was well-proportioned and very neat. There were flower boxes in the windows, and she could imagine them filled with colourful blossoms in the warmer seasons. The room in which they sat was prettily furnished.

After a few minutes of conversation, Jane announced, "I called on Miss Bingley and Mrs Hurst the day after I arrived." Bright pink spots appeared in both of her cheeks, and she studied her hands.

Catching Elizabeth's eye, Mrs Gardiner frowned and shook her head.

"Mrs Hurst remained only long enough to greet me, and Miss Bingley was not in good spirits."

"She has yet to return the call," Mrs Gardiner said.

Jane shot her an angry look, almost as though warning her not to say more. "She is very busy. The morning I called, Miss Bingley had only a few minutes to spare."

Elizabeth wanted to roll her eyes. "Has she written?" When Jane failed to reply, she continued. "As I told you last autumn, they are not kind or genuine women. What you and Mrs Gardiner say is no surprise to me."

"You cannot accept—"

Elizabeth interrupted. "Please do not say I am jealous because they like you and not me. I have no need for such fair-weather friends."

When Jane huffed, Mrs Gardiner patted her hand and smiled at Elizabeth. Elizabeth did not know the lady well enough to be able to tell if it was meant to be reassuring or encouraging.

"With all respect to my aunt, Gracechurch Street is not fashionable enough for Miss Bingley. She will not want to continue the connexion if she is aware of your interest in her brother, which you hardly disguised. Consider, Jane, if she truly wished for your friendship, she would have invited you to call again."

"Have you seen Mr Bingley?" There was a new eagerness in Jane's expression.

"Our paths have yet to cross."

Jane leant towards her. "When you do, will you tell him I am in town? Perhaps if you are going to a party where he will be, I could—"

Mrs Gardiner stopped her. "Elizabeth cannot do that. Remember, she is Mrs and Miss Darcy's guest. One of those ladies would have to request any invitation be extended to you, and you have not met them."

A maid came to tell Mrs Gardiner she was needed in the nursery. She excused herself and left the sisters alone. Jane stood and went to stand by the fire.

Her back still to Elizabeth, she said, "Will you tell him?"

Recalling her conversation with Rebecca, she agreed but added, "Mr Bingley is my friend, and I wish to see him happy in his marriage."

"You do not think he would be happy with me?" She did not sound accusatory, though her voice was a little hoarse.

"I think he would be bitterly disappointed if he suspected his wife did not care for him the way he did for her, if he felt he was accepted only because he is rich."

Jane's shoulders sank. "I would wish to marry for affection, but I cannot forget my duty." She resumed her place across from Elizabeth. "It is different for you. You did not grow up at Longbourn. You do not understand what it is like."

Seeing the tears in Jane's eyes, Elizabeth sensed herself being torn in two directions—one wanting to walk away forever and the other wanting to help someone she ought to hold in the deepest affection.

"If Mr Bingley expresses an interest in seeing you, I shall give him your direction. Please take the time to know him and understand your feelings. Do not act only to please other people. Do not let duty make you miserable."

A tear trickled down each cheek, and Jane bit her lips together. She embraced Elizabeth, who closed her eyes and hoped she had done the right thing.

<hr />

"You are here early," Elizabeth said to Darcy when they encountered each other soon after she arrived at Mr and Mrs Moore's ball that evening.

"Am I?"

"I have known you a very long time, and I know you do not like crowded parties. You avoid them, and when you cannot, you always arrive late and leave early. How do you account for your odd behaviour, sir?"

"I knew you and my family would be here." He smiled and added, "I have not seen your gown before. You look lovely."

Elizabeth laughed to cover her discomfort at the unexpected compliment. The dress was plum coloured with beading along the neck, hem, and sleeves.

"Have you become an expert on fashion?"

"Good lord, no!" He chuckled. "What have you been doing since I saw you last?"

She talked about calls and shopping and mentioned going to Gracechurch Street, which erased his smile.

"I assure you the Gardiners are not like the Bennets." Since he still looked uncertain, Elizabeth confided, "It makes me feel better to know I have some relations for whom I need not blush. Despite Mr Gardiner's profession, he is quite genteel. I think even you would like them, if you allowed yourself."

"If I allowed myself?" His tone expressed puzzlement.

"You are all that is good, but..." Elizabeth hesitated before continuing. "But you are Mr Fitzwilliam Darcy of Pemberley. While you might consult people like Mr Gardiner on business, you are not accustomed to meeting them as social acquaintances."

He straightened his shoulders. "Are you saying I am arrogant?"

She cocked an eyebrow, and they stared at each other for a moment. They were interrupted by Mrs Darcy, who said her husband saw a family friend they should greet.

As they began to follow the others, Darcy leant towards her and whispered, "If you like the Gardiners, I would be pleased to meet them. I trust your judgment completely."

Her cheeks heated, and Elizabeth stepped away from him, linking her arm with Fitzwilliam's, as they crossed the room.

It was not that she was unused to Darcy saying kind things to her, Elizabeth reflected as she and Fitzwilliam moved through the first set, but there was something else about his manner that seemed slightly altered or more attentive that evening. Likely, he felt responsible for how his mother had treated her, and she wished he did not. Fitzwilliam would hardly talk about anything other than his cousin—how Darcy had arranged for Nutmeg to be brought to Netherfield, his concern for her health and happiness, and his anger with Lady Anne.

"They have hardly spoken since you called on her," Fitzwilliam said.

"I do not want him to be at odds with his mother on my account!"

Fitzwilliam shrugged. "You cannot ask Darcy to deny how he feels."

Elizabeth did not know what he meant, and when next she was able, she asked him.

He grinned at her. "You are an intelligent lady. You will figure it out."

This pattern continued when she danced with Bramwell. He, too, mentioned how disgusted Darcy was with his mother.

"We saw him the next day, you know. Never seen him in quite such a state." Bramwell guffawed. "And I have seen him when—"

"I do not need to know." Elizabeth had heard enough about their exploits over the years.

Bramwell laughed. "Ah, dearest, sweetest—" She rolled her eyes, and he grinned. "Very well, I shall not tease you."

They danced in silence for a while, each smiling or nodding when they saw someone they knew.

"He is a good man," Bramwell said. "Very loyal to those he cares about. He would do anything for them. Do you agree?"

The dance separated them, giving Elizabeth an excuse not to respond. She caught sight of Darcy standing with his uncle and an older man she did not know. Her eyes lingered on him as long as possible before the sweep of the movement forced her to turn away.

It was during her next dance that Elizabeth saw Mr Bingley farther down the line, standing opposite a lovely lady whose fair looks reminded her of Jane. They smiled at each other, and when she was standing with acquaintances during the next intermission, he sought her out.

After exchanging the usual pleasantries, she said, "I saw Jane just this afternoon."

Mr Bingley said nothing for a moment. His eyes, although on her, seemed to take in nothing. "Miss Bennet?"

As she suspected, Miss Bingley and Mrs Hurst kept news of Jane's call from their brother. "She is staying with her aunt. Did your sisters not tell you they saw her? They hardly had time to greet Jane, from the sounds of it, and she is disappointed she has not seen or heard from them since. Not yet." She kept her tone light-hearted.

Mr Bingley's face went red, and he began to stammer an apology.

Elizabeth rested her hand on his arm. "Come, Mr Bingley. *You* have nothing to apologise for, and *I* am owed no such words."

Mr Bingley briefly covered her hand with his. "To show such a lack of civility! Was Miss Bennet offended?"

Elizabeth shook her head and glanced around, hoping someone would save her from the rest of the conversation. She was conscious of having separated Jane and Mr Bingley, although it was done inadvertently. Her intention was only that he would not rush into proposing, not that he abandon her.

"It is possible I might have Jane with me upon occasion—

for the day or if the Darcys and I attend some event or another. I do not know if you would like to renew your acquaintance with her, but away from the...distractions of Hertfordshire, you would have the freedom to know each other better."

The spark in his eyes confirmed her suspicion that he truly cared for Jane. "I will not deny I found Miss Bennet to be everything charming. Do you think she might return my—"

"I do not know, but it is possible." The conversation was making her want to claim a sudden need to flee.

Mr Bingley slowly nodded and smiled. "I would like to see her. If nothing else, Miss Bennet should know not all Bingleys are inexcusably rude."

"No one who has the privilege of knowing you would ever call *you* rude!" With that, Elizabeth excused herself and sought Mrs Darcy.

⚬⚬⚬

The first part of the ball passed quickly for Elizabeth. She renewed her acquaintance with several people she had met the previous winter and danced every set. Despite this, she was impatient for the supper set, when she would dance with Darcy. There was no reason for it, other than she always enjoy those times they stood up together. Even though he said he did not like to dance, she was certain he found it pleasurable at times. Convinced though she was that she had never flirted with him or encouraged him to develop a romantic interest in her, Elizabeth wondered if seeing them together had been enough to make Lady Anne conclude she wanted something more than friendship from him. There was no other explanation for her overt hostility.

Throughout the set, Darcy watched her closely, making a slow heat creep up her chest. To distract them both, she reminded him of his promise to make arrangements for them to go to the theatre. He assured her he had not forgotten.

"Have you invited Mr Bingley to accompany us?" Elizabeth asked.

"Yes. I am afraid his family will join us as well. Bingley said his sisters spoke of wanting to see the performance, and I felt compelled to include them. I know they are not friends of yours."

"I am too used to them to be bothered by their behaviour. Would you consider extending the invitation to Jane, as long as your aunt and uncle agree?" Elizabeth then told him about her conversation with Mr Bingley.

The dance ended, and they joined the throng headed into supper. "What of your concerns regarding Miss Bennet's motives?"

"She told me she wishes to marry for affection, and I believe her. Away from Longbourn, they have an opportunity to decide if they would be happy together." Seeing disapproval on his face, Elizabeth added, "I know it would not be an advantageous match for him, and his sisters would not like it, but if they love each other and believe they would have a good life, is that not more important than any difference in their social standing and fortune?"

Their progress through the room was slowed almost to a halt as they approached the door, and Darcy studied her. His gaze was intense and made her head swim.

At last, he said, "It is everything."

TWENTY FIVE

Darcy had proposed the theatre because he knew Rebecca and Elizabeth would enjoy it. The addition of his aunt and uncle was required to provide proper chaperons, and since he loved them, he had not minded at all. That modest party had grown far larger, and he had only himself to blame. If he knew asking Bingley would mean inviting his family, he would have held his tongue. When Elizabeth enquired about Jane Bennet being one of their numbers, he did not dream of saying no, especially once she spoke about the importance of love and happiness in choosing one's spouse. Lastly, his mother insisted she would go with them.

"You ought to have talked to me about the scheme as soon as you thought of it," his mother had said to him when she learnt of it. "What will people think to see your aunt and uncle as hosts instead of me?"

"Most will assume they arranged it because they enjoy the theatre and know Rebecca and Elizabeth do as well. I did not ask you because you would have sought a way to exclude Elizabeth and Bingley. Do you deny it?"

His mother's complexion became mottled, and her voice was tremulous. "I would not, not…her. I accept she will remain in town, and we are likely to meet, and I shall—"

"Treat her with the respect she deserves, or you will return to Pemberley. The *dower* house at Pemberley will be suitable until your brother and I decide on a more permanent home for you, one that is far from her *and me*."

Darcy had ignored how narrow-minded his mother had become, particularly since his father's death. Rather than address it and her attempts to order his life, he had avoided her, not unlike what Elizabeth had accused him of doing. No longer! He would not allow Lady Anne to be the impediment to his future happiness.

A picture of Elizabeth as she had looked at the ball came to mind, and anger faded into excitement. He would see her in just a few hours. Having accepted he was in love with her, the sensation of it being *right* settled over him. Elizabeth was the perfect woman for him, truly everything he had ever dreamt of, and he only prayed she would come to feel the same way about him. The reality that he would ask her to accept Lady Anne, her tormentor, as a mother-in-law perturbed him, but he would deal with it when the time came.

Once at the theatre, his mother nodded in response to Elizabeth's curtsey. Darcy thought the gesture was barely polite, but Elizabeth did not seem distressed, so he said nothing. His aunt and uncle engaged his mother in conversation and went so far as to seat her between them, pretending not to understand when she indicated she wanted to sit with him. In Darcy's opinion, she should be relieved they spoke to her at all, given her past behaviour.

Despite Miss Bingley's attempt to gain a place beside him, he avoided both her and her sister and, along with Bramwell, Rebecca, and Elizabeth, took the final row of chairs. Once, he had to kick the back of Hurst's chair to stop the man from snoring. With Miss Bennet sitting beside Bingley, Darcy was positioned to observe her on those brief occasions when he was not engaged with the action on stage or exchanging whispers with Elizabeth.

Jane Bennet was nothing to Elizabeth. The fact she would have accepted Bingley without understanding her own feelings told him everything he needed to know about her, without even taking into account her manner towards Elizabeth.

When the performance ended, his mother announced her desire to return home. "You will excuse me from partaking of supper," she said to Aunt Darcy. "My son will escort me."

Darcy was on the point of refusing when Fitzwilliam spoke.

"I shall escort you, Lady Anne. Tonight was Darcy's scheme. He should remain with the guests. I shall join them once I have seen you to Berkeley Square."

Lady Anne opened her mouth as though to protest, but before she could, Miss Bingley's voice filled the box.

"Oh Mr Darcy, you must ride with us. There is something—"

One sharp look at Bingley had his friend saying, "We do not have room for him. We shall go as we came, unless Miss Bennet would—"

"No, Charles, Miss Bennet would be crushed between us. She should stay with her sister," said Miss Bingley.

Darcy remained silent, although he wanted to point out how illogical she sounded.

Uncle Darcy intervened. "Let us go with whom we came, apart from the colonel taking my sister-in-law home. Darcy, you can bear Bramwell company. After you, Anne."

"I find I am not so tired," she said. "Darcy and I shall ride together."

He fought the urge to pinch the bridge of his nose. A hoard of hammer-wielding ████ had taken up residence in his skull, and Darcy expected their torture would get worse during the upcoming carriage trip.

After arriving at Curzon Street, Elizabeth took Jane to her room to refresh herself before the remainder of their party joined them for supper.

"The play was amusing, was it not?" asked Elizabeth, lacking anything else to say to alleviate the awkwardness she felt.

"Yes. Thank you for including me." Jane perched on the edge of the chaise longue and clasped her hands in her lap. "Mrs Hurst and Miss Bingley hardly spoke to me and said nothing about failing to return my call. You were right about them."

Elizabeth made a noncommittal noise. As much as she enjoyed the performance and Darcy's company, the night was not a success. The presence of certain ladies made that impossible, as far as she was concerned.

"If you are ready, we should go down."

Jane's expression remained downcast until they entered the drawing room. There, she donned a broad grin and waited for Mr Bingley to join her. Elizabeth left them to whatever they were doing. When Lady Anne and Darcy were announced five minutes later, his countenance was stormy and hers stony. Fitzwilliam grunted in disgust and went to his cousin, while the elder Mr Darcy escorted his sister-in-law to a chair.

Miss Bingley called, "There you are, Mr Darcy. My sister and I quite despaired of you ever arriving."

"You must help us understand the history of the play," Mrs Hurst added.

Darcy stared at them, looked at Mr Bingley, who was occupied with Jane, and said, "You will excuse me. Your brother can answer your questions about—"

"Darcy!" Lady Anne beckoned him to her side, momentarily dismissing her brother-in-law.

Her features taut, Aunt Darcy walked towards the door. "Now that we are all here, let us go into supper."

The food was excellent, but the collection of people was too mismatched to make the meal agreeable. Most difficult for Elizabeth to tolerate was the weight of Lady Anne's eyes on her. The few times Elizabeth peeked at her, the woman's expression was a mix of wariness and disquiet. After supper, Lady Anne insisted on leaving as soon as she had finished a cup of tea and an iced cake.

Bidding Elizabeth good night before he left with her, Darcy whispered, "I am sorry my mother's presence robbed the evening of its gaiety. I shall see you soon. Perhaps the day after tomorrow."

Elizabeth nodded, and he was gone. She, too, regretted how disagreeable the outing had become and blamed herself in part for it because she had asked to have Jane included. She wondered if it were wrong to wish Jane, Lady Anne, and Mr Bingley's sisters far away. Then, after four dismal months at Longbourn, she could laugh and amuse herself with her friends with nothing to disturb her equanimity.

Before Jane returned to Gracechurch Street, she embraced Elizabeth. "Thank you so much for inviting me. I am left with a great deal to consider." Her eyes widened. "Oh, not about Mr Bingley! He is everything a young man should be, and I hope to see him again."

The following day, Jane sent a note to Mrs Darcy to thank her and a brief letter to Elizabeth, who asked Rebecca's opinion of one passage.

I believe Mr Bingley still likes me. Would it be wrong to hope for more if his family disapproves? You are wiser in these matters than I.

"What should I say to her?"

The ladies sat in the drawing room taking comfort in the warmth of the sunlight and the fire in the large hearth.

Rebecca tapped her chin with a finger. "Hmm. That Miss Bingley and Mrs Hurst are horrible creatures, two-faced and—"

Elizabeth laughed. "I told Jane not to trust them, and apparently, she now agrees. The question is, should Jane encourage Mr Bingley, knowing his closest family does not approve of her?"

"If his sisters were good, sensible, kind, et cetera, I would advise her to consider their objections, but they are not. I say she should not care what they think, because they do not have their brother's best interests at heart.

"Darcy is in a similar position with his mother. Lady Anne may have given up her dream of him marrying Anne de Bourgh, but she will see every other lady as an inferior choice, no matter how admirable they are."

Elizabeth remained silent, and Rebecca continued. "It would be Mr Bingley's job to protect Miss Bennet and ensure his sisters know he would not tolerate their slights or insults. A lady in such a situation must be prepared to guard her feelings and not become miserable. She should not imagine she can win over people who stubbornly cling to their prejudices. I do not say their opinions might not change, particularly if they see their brother is happy, but it would be foolish to go into this expecting it to happen."

"That is good advice. Fortunately, you need not worry about your reception from the Fitzwilliams. They adore you.

As they should." She gave her a teasing grin. "It is just days until your birthday."

Rebecca's cheeks soon matched her pink gown. "Goodness, I feel like a rabbit waiting to be pounced on by a fox as soon as I am one-and-twenty."

"No doubt Bramwell *would* like to pounce on you."

They laughed, and Rebecca said, "I told him not to propose the minute I am twenty-one. I want it to be something of a surprise. What about you, Elizabeth? If the right man asked, would you accept an offer?"

"I am afraid I am very particular. For a gentleman to gain my affection and approval he must be intelligent, responsible, allow me to keep cats, and understand I shall never be content simply shopping or planning dinner parties."

"If you add rich and handsome, I might suggest Darcy."

Elizabeth let out a bark of laughter. "Lady Anne would not welcome me as a daughter-in-law, and I could never have her as a mother-in-law." She thanked God she had kept her past love for Darcy secret, even from Rebecca.

"Elizabeth, did you never think that Darcy *cares* for you?"

"Not in the way you are implying."

Rebecca's voice was as gentle as a caress. "I think he does. I say this both because of what I have witnessed lately and something Bramwell said."

"Bramwell?"

The way Rebecca lifted her shoulders was almost apologetic.

Elizabeth shook her head. "You are both mistaken. First, Darcy would not marry someone like me. Second, I would not have him. I will only accept a man with whom I share a love like you and Bramwell do. Please, Rebecca, let us speak of something else. *Anything* else."

Rebecca agreed, and they talked about a new work of

poetry they were reading, but it was not so easy for Elizabeth to dismiss the conversation from her thoughts.

Darcy was true to his word and called the next day. His cousins were with him, but they elected to sit with Rebecca, leaving Elizabeth and Darcy to themselves. They spoke about their evening at the theatre and inconsequential matters for a few minutes before he stood and excused himself.

"I just remembered something. I shall return in a moment."

When Darcy re-entered the room, he handed Elizabeth a slim volume. "I saw it the other day. It is about flowering plants in the Highlands. I knew you would like it."

"Thank you." Elizabeth sounded hesitant and wondered at herself. Darcy had presented her with books in the past, but his demeanour was unusual, and she offered him a strained smile, wondering when talking to him had become awkward. *Oh bother! It is because of what Rebecca said yesterday and Lady Anne's accusations.*

"I shall enjoy reading it." She looked at a few of the pages. "Did your mother enjoy the play?"

"I suppose. We rarely talk."

"Because of me."

"Because of *her*." He ran a hand across his eyes. "I find it difficult to forgive her, likely because, as much as she attempted to be polite the other evening, she has not apologised for her behaviour, and I fear she does not feel any true remorse."

"That is regrettable. Perhaps once the earl is in town and talks to her, it will have an effect. Lady Anne listens to him."

"Fitzwilliam says his parents will be here tomorrow, now

that Lord Romsley has been deemed healthy enough to travel. They will be glad to see you."

A cold had prevented the earl and countess from returning to town from Worcestershire earlier in the year. Nervous about the upcoming meeting, Elizabeth elected to change the subject.

"Do you think it will remain this cold much longer? I long to walk in the park, but your uncle has asked us not to until it is warmer."

Darcy watched her silently, and she began to squirm. Mercifully, Fitzwilliam joined them, and the three spoke of indifferent matters until it was time for the gentlemen to depart.

Elizabeth dined at home that evening, and the conversation amongst her and the Darcys evolved into one about female education, particularly the question of ladies undertaking advanced studies.

Elizabeth said, "I would have embraced the opportunity to study at a university."

Mr Darcy chuckled. "I believe you would have got more out of it than many a young man."

"I think one day ladies will be allowed at universities." Rebecca turned to Elizabeth. "While *we* might not be allowed such an education, our granddaughters or great-granddaughters will be welcome there."

"Ah, for such a just society!" Mrs Darcy said.

As her companions continued to talk, Elizabeth contemplated Jane and the discussion they had one morning in the still-room at Longbourn. Marriage offered ladies their best security, particularly if they did not have position and a fortune of their own, but she had not often considered what that meant for gently bred women like the Miss Bennets.

Elizabeth could support herself, and she had connexions

who could help her find a respectable position if it became necessary. With the bequest from Hugh Darcy, she need never worry about the future, provided she was careful with her modest fortune. She could even have one or two of the Bennets stay with her, provided they lived modestly, but apart from Jane, she struggled to feel even an iota of duty to any of them. It was a failing and one she knew she should overcome. They *were* her relations.

Yet, looking around the table, Elizabeth knew that Rebecca's family was more her family than the Bennets, despite there being no blood connexion between them. The reason why was simple: the decision made long ago by Mr Bennet, her grandmother, and the dowager Lady Romsley to remove her from Longbourn.

Who knew familial bonds were such fragile things?

TWENTY SIX

L ate the following afternoon, Lord and Lady Romsley
arrived in town and sent word to Curzon Street,
begging Elizabeth to join them at once. The earl and
countess were in a small family sitting room, and despite
being told again and again that they had longed to see her,
Elizabeth was surprised when Lady Romsley threw herself
into her arms and embraced her tightly.

"Oh my dear girl! Let me look at you." The countess held
her by the shoulders as her eyes took in Elizabeth's features.
"You are too thin and pale. I will never forgive—"

"Now, now, my dear, you will do Elizabeth an injury if
you keep on this way." The earl stood beside them, and as the
countess loosened her grip, he gave Elizabeth's cheek a kiss
and gentle caress. "Shall we sit?"

How much half of this overt affection would have meant to
her when she was a child! They had never been cold or uncar-
ing, just occupied with their own lives, and Elizabeth vowed
to remember that.

Sitting beside her, the countess clasped her hand. The earl
took the chair to Elizabeth's other side and seemed to scruti-
nise her even more than Lady Romsley.

"We ought not to have let you stay in Hertfordshire so
long," the countess said.

"It was what she wanted, and we agreed she had the right
to decide. By the time Fitzwilliam told us he did not think it
suited her, it was already Christmastide."

"I am sorry he said anything to alarm you." She asked after the earl's health, but he dismissed the question with a gesture.

"My wife made too much of a simple cold."

"If I did, then so did your physician." To Elizabeth, Lady Romsley continued. "We did not like to stay away, knowing you were in town, but we were advised not to risk travelling so far in the winter until he was fully recovered."

"I understand."

There must have been something in her tone because the couple exchanged a look that seemed significant.

Lord Romsley patted her hand. "I fear you are too good at understanding, my dear girl, and you excuse people who do not deserve it."

Heat shot up her chest and into her cheeks. Before she could stammer a response, Lady Romsley spoke.

"We have talked about this a great deal since September. You cannot imagine our relief when we learnt you were in Hertfordshire and not aboard a ship destined for India. We should not have left you alone so much or sent you to Anne just to alleviate our guilt about you being on your own at Romsley Hall."

The earl's voice was deep and sombre. "Nothing excuses my sisters, but at the very least, we should have asked you if you liked going to Pemberley. I knew Anne would never outright seek your companionship, but she did enquire, now and again, what you would do while we were away, and she never refused when we mentioned you staying with her."

"I always supposed Anne was lonely, given how little time Darcy spends in Derbyshire. Since you were by your-self at Romsley Hall and the journey from there to Pemberley is an easy one, it made sense for you to go to her."

"If you had asked, I would have agreed to go." If for no other reason than because she knew she would see Darcy.

Again, the couple shared a look before the countess spoke. "We truly were very frightened when Catherine arrived at Pemberley and said she sent you off to be a governess."

The earl stood so quickly the chair rocked and almost fell to its side. He walked to the fireplace, keeping his back to them.

Lady Romsley continued. "It made us realise we have not been attentive enough. It was one thing when you were younger and still had a governess, though even then we should have done better, but these last few years…"

Although previously resolved not to speak her thoughts, Elizabeth found herself saying, "It was very good of you to give me a home after the dowager died. You never asked for the responsibility of my care, and I have no right to expect—"

An exasperated noise came from the earl's direction, and Lady Romsley said, "Elizabeth, you had *every* right to expect our affection and our time, certainly more of it than you received. For two or three years before my mother-in-law's death, the earl and I talked about being at greater liberty to do as we liked with the boys soon entering Cambridge. We failed to alter our plans despite *willingly* becoming your guardians."

Mostly to soothe the countess's agitation, Elizabeth said, "I always knew you cared for me. Your lives are busy ones, and I was sufficiently occupied. There is no need to concern yourself with my welfare now."

For the third time, the couple regarded each other for a long, heavy few seconds. Lord Romsley cleared his throat and returned to the chair.

"Perhaps Elizabeth is correct. At present, we should simply appreciate being together again."

The countess nodded and offered Elizabeth a smile that

still seemed regretful. "Will you come home, or do you prefer to remain with Rebecca?"

"Unless you object, I shall stay at Curzon Street."

With evident reluctance, they agreed. "You are one-and-twenty and a sensible young woman. We have already agreed that you have a right to make such decisions for yourself," the earl said. "Indeed, we ought to have consulted you about your wishes more these last few years."

It was so similar to what she had been thinking that Elizabeth wondered if Darcy, either directly or through one of her foster brothers, had told them she felt that way.

The couple then questioned Elizabeth about her time at Longbourn. She said as much as she was comfortable sharing, and after taking dinner with them—and wishing in vain for Bramwell or Fitzwilliam to join them to alleviate the awkwardness—Elizabeth left Grosvenor Square with a promise to see them again soon.

In the carriage, she allowed she was not as angry as she expected to be. At last truly believing everyone who had told her how deeply affected her guardians were by the events of the previous summer, she wondered if she had been as unfair to them as Darcy claimed during their first conversation in Hertfordshire. Perhaps this would be an opportunity for them to establish a better understanding of each other—for them to see her as an adult and her to view them as the people who, flawed as they were, wanted to be her parents, unlike those to whom she had been born.

⁂

Rebecca hoped to treat her birthday as nothing noteworthy. However, the day was filled with good cheer and surprises, starting with the delivery of an enormous bouquet of flowers from Bramwell. He was at the house for breakfast before being chased away by Mrs Darcy, who arranged a surprise luncheon for Rebecca and her friends. Elizabeth was amused by her companion at the table, a young lady who introduced herself as Cyndy Henry.

"It is such a ridiculous name, is it not?" Miss Henry said. "My mother adores flowers and named me Hyacinth, which I detest, so I tell everyone I am called Cyndy." She giggled before continuing. "This is such fun. I am all anticipation for when a certain happy event takes place." Miss Henry nodded towards Rebecca. "She will make a fine viscountess. I knew they were going to make a match years ago. I know they are not yet *actually* engaged, but we all know it will happen very soon. I have a knack for seeing when a young lady and man are particularly well suited. Indeed, Miss Bennet, I know just the gentleman for *you*. Shall I name him?"

Elizabeth laughed uneasily. "No, pray do not."

"Very well, but I shall say he is someone you know *quite well* already, and you will be the envy of every single lady under the age of forty—and some of the married ones too! Be bold, Miss Bennet, and claim your happiness!"

Elizabeth had no notion who Miss Henry had in mind, let alone what she meant about claiming her happiness, and decided not to speculate. Instead, she gave her attention to the party.

That evening, the entire family gathered at Curzon Street for dinner to celebrate Rebecca's birthday. Over the past week, Elizabeth had spent part of each day with the earl and countess, and she was lighter and happier for it, which was an unexpected outcome. Not only did she embrace Rebecca and her parents as her true family, but increasingly, she felt the same way about the Romsleys. Bramwell and Fitzwilliam had long been the brothers of her heart. Regardless of what happened in the future, whether she married or not, she was increasingly confident she would always have a home with people who loved her and whom she loved.

Elizabeth sat between Fitzwilliam and Darcy. She laughed until her cheeks hurt and ate so much good food that the meal had likely made her regain most of the weight she lost at Longbourn.

After dinner as they sat in the drawing room, Rebecca was given gifts to mark the occasion. Elizabeth's present was a framed drawing she had done of the two of them as girls, sitting beneath an old walnut tree during one of their summer stays at Pemberley.

"Oh, I love it!" Rebecca cried. "Those were such happy days."

Darcy said, "I hope we shall have many more in the future."

Elizabeth felt more than one set of eyes on her but refused to let troublesome memories dampen her mood.

Fitzwilliam made a speculative noise. "I seem to remember two little girls who were forever getting up to mischief."

Elizabeth laughed. "*You* were the mischief maker, Fitzwilliam, not us."

He returned her laughter and waggled a finger at her, but before he could speak, his mother cautioned him.

"It would not do to insult any young lady, especially a foster sister."

Pleasure and affection coursed through Elizabeth. Neither Romsley had ever referred to her in such terms. Turning back to Rebecca, Elizabeth glimpsed Lady Anne. Her lips were pinched, and she looked as stiff as a tree. The woman had been quiet all evening, likely in part because her brother refused to speak to her. Lady Anne's silence was better than voicing her disapproval, but it left a dark cloud over the gathering, as though a storm were about to erupt, but everyone stubbornly refused to acknowledge it. Elizabeth knew she was not to blame for Lady Anne never liking her, nevertheless she worried about the discord and what it would mean to her loved ones.

The drawing was passed for everyone to see. When it was Lady Anne's turn, she stared at it long enough to make the atmosphere uncomfortable before mumbling, "Very nice," and handing it to Bramwell.

Rebecca and Elizabeth played several duets for the company, after which Elizabeth remained at the instrument for a while longer.

When Darcy came to turn pages for her, she told him not to sit down. "Everyone is already watching your mother to make sure she does not say or do anything to mar Rebecca's birthday. Do not provoke her by remaining by my side."

"I shall take over." Fitzwilliam clapped a surprised Darcy on the shoulder.

Elizabeth gave Darcy a pointed look that sent him back to his chair. "This past week or more, he seems to want to injure his mother, and he is using *me* to do it. Why?" she asked Fitzwilliam.

"I hate to disagree with you, but I recommend you rethink how you interpret his actions. You will sort it out, Elizabeth. Now, are you going to play or not?"

She nodded, pushed all thought of Lady Anne and Darcy out of her mind, and lost herself in the music.

⁂

"Are you making any progress with our lovely Elizabeth?" Fitzwilliam walked past him and dropped onto a leather armchair next to his brother. The three were at Grosvenor Square one evening after attending a tedious card party.

Darcy kept his gaze on Fitzwilliam for several seconds before turning to Bramwell. "When are you going to propose to my cousin?"

Bramwell waggled a finger at him. "No changing the subject. We want to know about you and Elizabeth." He nodded at the glass of port in Darcy's hand. "Finish your drink. It will loosen your tongue."

"How can we help you if you do not tell us?" Fitzwilliam asked.

Darcy closed his eyes and dropped his head to the low back of the chair.

"That bad? How is that possible? Elizabeth has been in good spirits when I have seen her lately," said Bramwell. "She was here yesterday with my mother and looks fully recovered after her harrowing ordeal last summer."

"Ready to go forth and embrace a happy future as a worthy man's wife."

"Since we need to be in a position to beat her husband senseless if he does not treat her as she deserves, we need you to get on with it and convince her to marry you."

Darcy stared at the ceiling and decided to disregard most of what his cousins said. "It is good to hear Elizabeth laugh again. I should not have left her in Meryton."

Fitzwilliam dismissed this. "If Bramwell and I could have convinced her to leave, we would have taken her with us. She decided to remain, for reasons of her own, and that was that. Elizabeth is stubborn. We like that about her."

His brother agreed. "She will need to be strong-willed to survive having a hostile mother-in-law."

Fitzwilliam gulped down the last of his drink. "So, are you or are you not making progress with her?" Darcy shrugged, and the colonel continued. "It has become our mission to see you and Elizabeth united in wedded bliss."

"It would make everyone happy," added Bramwell, "save our aunts and Cousin Anne. Though, honestly, do we know that Anne even thinks?"

Fitzwilliam tapped his jaw. "Good point. Lady Catherine tells her what her opinion should be, and that is the end of it."

Darcy begged, "Good God, will you not stop?"

Fitzwilliam and Bramwell laughed, and Fitzwilliam said, "We have several suggestions."

"I do not want—"

Bramwell said, "Yes, but we intend to tell you. You have three tasks.

"First, you must make Elizabeth see what her life would be like. She adores Pemberley and being able to give it to her as her home will mean more to her than connexions or fortune or jewels and all that sort of thing.

"Second, you must make her see you as more than the boy she has known since she was five years old. You must make her fall in love with you, at least enough to accept you."

Darcy grumbled, "I am not a boy, and of course I must make her fall in love with me. I am not stupid!"

Fitzwilliam completed the list. "Finally, you must convince her you will protect her from your mother."

Darcy stilled. The last challenge would not be easy. Very likely, Elizabeth did not think of him any differently than she had two or three years ago, unless her view of him had worsened. After all, it was his mother who had treated her wretchedly again and again, while he stood by and ignored it. "Let us talk about something else."

His cousins sniggered, and Bramwell said, "We are not yet certain how you will accomplish the last."

Fitzwilliam continued. "But here are our suggestions for numbers one and two."

Darcy stretched his long legs out in front of him and crossed his ankles. Nothing would stop them, so he thought he might as well make himself comfortable.

TWENTY SEVEN

A t the end of the month, Bramwell proposed to
Rebecca and was accepted. Lord and Lady Romsley
held an impromptu family dinner to celebrate the
news. Thanks to Lady Anne's delay while preparing for the
evening, she and Darcy were the last to arrive. They were
speaking more than they had recently, and as long as she was
polite to Elizabeth, Darcy would allow his anger to ebb away
and hope it would help him gain his mother's acceptance for
his choice of marriage partner.

They joined the others in the drawing room and offered
their congratulations to Rebecca and Bramwell, who sat beside
each other on a brocade sofa.

Elizabeth was lovelier than ever in a lilac gown that Darcy
did not remember seeing before. The colour made her hair
particularly luxuriant, and he longed to touch it.

"You look lovely tonight, Elizabeth."

"That is kind of you. I am very happy for Rebecca and
Bramwell, which no doubt adds to my good looks." In a
teasing tone, she added, "If you say you find today's news
anything other than joyous, I shall be very disappointed."

"I would not dare."

Once his mother offered her felicitations to the engaged
couple, Elizabeth dropped into a curtsey. "How do you do,
Lady Anne?"

Darcy watched as his mother's eyes flickered across Elizabeth before she nodded an acknowledgement. Elizabeth

caught his eye, gave an almost imperceptible shake of her head, and glimpsed towards Rebecca and Bramwell. Darcy clenched his teeth, took his mother's elbow, and led her to Lord Romsley.

At dinner, it was announced that the couple would marry in London at the end of May or in early June. As they and their parents discussed arrangements for a few minutes, Darcy kept his eyes on Elizabeth, sitting across from him, and dreamt of them soon reaching an understanding and another dinner at which the topic would be *their* wedding. When Rebecca mentioned Pemberley, it caught his attention.

The countess said, "I shall forgive you preferring Pemberley to Romsley Hall, because you are more familiar with it. Elizabeth and I shall just have to teach you to love our home, will we not?"

"We might have to settle for Rebecca deciding both estates are equally splendid." Elizabeth's smile appeared genuine, and Darcy was glad to see her reconciled to the earl and countess and the idea of Romsley Hall being her home—currently, at least.

Afterwards, Darcy could not account for what came out of his mouth next. "We should plan to spend Easter in Derbyshire. All of us."

Next to him, his mother started, and everyone looked his way. Alarm flashed across Elizabeth's countenance, but she quickly schooled her features. Darcy thought it might actually be good for her. It would remind Elizabeth what she liked about the estate and help banish the terrible memories. Importantly, it would remind her how happy she would be with the life he would give her.

Rebecca asked, "Are you in earnest?"

"Why not? Unless there is a particular reason anyone needs to be in town, we might stay three weeks or a month."

Elizabeth remained silent, and Darcy's heart raced as he watched her, afraid he had been callous, and she would think less of him.

Bramwell said, "If no one else will ask, I will. Elizabeth, your opinion matters most of all. I am sure I do not need to say why. What do you think?"

"If you do not like it, we will not go," Mrs Darcy said.

"You need never step foot in the county again, if Anne and Catherine have ruined it for you." The earl scowled at his sister, who paled.

"But," Fitzwilliam drew out the word, "going back might be just what Elizabeth and the rest of us need. We shall make new, happier memories and push the nasty ones aside."

Darcy leapt on the notion. "Exactly. That was my thought."

Rebecca said, "Elizabeth?"

"Whatever everyone decides, I am agreeable."

After some debate, they decided to depart London in the third week of March. Before then, the Romsleys would host a ball to share their joy at their son's engagement.

Darcy was almost gleeful at the thought of having Elizabeth at Pemberley again and spent the rest of the meal imagining what it would be like.

* * *

Elizabeth had been torn when the scheme of going to Derbyshire was raised. It would be difficult to confront her final awful minutes there, but what was the alternative? She could refuse to return, which would only distress her loved ones, and she did not want that. A part of her delighted in the idea of being at Pemberley, and images of where she would walk or ride and memories of the wonderful days she spent there in the past danced through her mind, each one making her want to have her bags packed that very minute.

But then there was Lady Anne to consider. If she was full of sour looks every time she saw Elizabeth, if Darcy and the earl's ongoing acrimony remained evident—the two gentlemen were the most prone to show their displeasure, though they were not the only ones to feel it—it would make everyone ill at ease and ruin what should be a wonderful interlude in the country.

She said as much to Rebecca two days later as they sat together, adding, "I could remain in town while you go. Mrs Gardiner invited me to stay whenever I like."

Rebecca sat beside Elizabeth and took her hand. "Do you not want to go? Will it be too difficult?"

"Who is to say whether it will be more pleasure or pain?"

"What does your heart say?"

"That as amiable as they are, I would prefer to be with all of you than stay with the Gardiners." She liked the couple and appreciated how welcoming they were, but Elizabeth had accepted that the Fitzwilliams and Darcys were her true family.

A thread, albeit a thin one, still pulled her to some of her blood relations, though. Perhaps the Gardiners and maybe Jane were best considered good friends or distant connexions. If she could settle on how she viewed them, it would bring her peace of mind.

"Good. I would not go without you, and I am looking forward to being in the country for a few weeks. Let my cousin worry about his mother. Even better, leave her to Lord Romsley."

Elizabeth acquiesced.

When Darcy called the next morning, Rebecca went to a

mahogany table across the room to write a letter, allowing him and Elizabeth to sit together in relative privacy.

"Are you looking forward to being at Pemberley again?" he asked.

Elizabeth regarded him with a cocked eyebrow.

"Are you still unsure? You know you will be well protected. I will not permit anyone to treat you with less than the respect you deserve. My mother would not dare with my aunts and uncles nearby."

There was something in his intensity she found unsettling, and she chuckled to dispel the awkwardness. "I hope not. I do not want our time there marred by conflict. I have promised Rebecca I shall be one of the party, and there is nothing more to be said other than that I shall endeavour to enjoy myself."

Darcy dipped his chin in agreement. "We shall speak of something else then. I heard about a lecture and exhibit of artefacts from South America. Would you like to attend, or will you and Rebecca be too busy shopping for the Romsleys' ball?"

Elizabeth laughed. "That does sound like me, does it not? Foregoing an opportunity to learn something new in favour of selecting fabric and lace. We do plan to find new gowns for the occasion, but we are clever enough to manage both."

Darcy observed her through narrowed eyes until she asked what he was doing.

"I was trying to decide what colour I hope you select."

"Fitzwilliam Darcy, I do not believe you have ever noticed the colour of one of my gowns in your life!"

He huffed. "That is not true."

"Name two that are not white," she challenged.

"You have one in Pomona green, which you wore to the assembly in Hertfordshire, and a light purple lace one you wore the other evening. I have seen the green before but not the purple."

Elizabeth blushed. If she did not know better, she would say he was flirting with her. A year ago, she would have savoured such moments, but *that* was all behind her now. What a fuss there would be if they actually announced a desire to marry! It was simply not worth the conflict it would create, not when everything had finally become as calm as she believed it ever would be, given Lady Anne's sentiments towards her.

"I stand corrected. Do you have any advice to offer regarding what I purchase?"

He studied her for a long moment. "Something gold."

A sudden urge to order a gold dress made her want to leap to her feet, and Elizabeth silently berated herself in the severest manner for acting like a schoolgirl suffering through an infatuation.

"I shall keep that in mind." Desperate for a topic that would stop her from inadvertently flirting with him, she said, "I had another note from Jane. It appears Mr Bingley is a regular visitor at the Gardiners'. I shall have to call again before we go into Derbyshire."

In the letter, Jane had written that Mrs Bennet was pressing her to make Mr Bingley propose, but Jane seemed content not to make any hasty decisions. She had not directly asked Elizabeth for advice, for which she was thankful. In truth, she hardly thought about Jane and Mr Bingley, and it was only a note from Mrs Gardiner that made her think about going to call.

She proceeded to tell him what Jane wrote and prayed for Rebecca to join them. Fortunately, Bramwell arrived not five minutes later, putting an end to Elizabeth's tête-à-tête with Darcy.

The next morning Darcy shuffled through the letters the butler had given him. One was from Rosings and addressed to his mother. In silence, he passed it across the breakfast table to her.

She looked to see who it was from, then met his eyes. "I-I wrote to tell my sister about Rebecca and Bramwell's engagement. That is all."

He grunted, and for an interval, the only sounds were those of his fork and knife scraping across his plate as Darcy steadily ate his meal. He glanced at his mother to find her hand was curled around the sheet of paper, her countenance pale and empty.

Apprehension passed through him. "What does Lady Catherine write?"

His mother's hand jerked, and she dropped the letter. It fell to her plate, and she brushed it aside. "You know your aunt does not like Bramwell's choice."

"That is nonsensical. Rebecca is a Darcy and my cousin."

"Bramwell is heir to an earldom. He could do better than a barrister's daughter."

He took a few breaths to cool his temper. "They love each other and have for years. That must count for something."

Lady Anne said nothing and picked up a piece of toast.

With little expectation of changing his mother's beliefs, he said, "When there is fortune enough, other matters, those of affection, can be given their due. Neither Bramwell nor I need concern ourselves with money."

Nothing more was said for several minutes, then his mother surprised him by saying, "Elizabeth looks better than when she first came to town. Was she ill?"

There was a forced casualness in her tone, and Darcy tried not to sound as hesitant as he felt. "Unfortunately, the reasons she was removed from Longbourn as a child remain unchanged. Spending so long with the Bennets was not good for her, especially when she was already distressed. To make matters worse, George Wickham joined the militia that is stationed nearby." She stared at him, her visage growing even paler. "Did Father ever tell you why he sent him away?"

"I heard stories about him, but your father never believed them. You told him, gave him proof Wickham was not... honourable." Her hand began to tremble. "Are you saying— did he do something to Elizabeth when she was at Pemberley? She was just a child!"

Darcy could not deny his mother looked genuinely alarmed. "Elizabeth says he never physically injured her, but he was...disgusting. Threatening."

Her breathing was heavy, and her body shook. She stood and bolted from the room, leaving him confused and frustrated. Darcy considered following her but decided against it. Time alone to contemplate why she was so distressed at the notion of Elizabeth being injured might do her good. If he went to her and insisted her behaviour meant she cared for Elizabeth, Lady Anne might feel compelled to dismiss it as arising from another cause altogether. No doubt, they would then argue, and that would not help his cause of having Lady Anne accept Elizabeth as a daughter-in-law at all.

 ⁕ ᘓᘐᘏᘓ ⁕

In early March, Elizabeth was at the house at Grosvenor Square, enjoying refreshments and chatting with Lady Romsley while Bramwell, Rebecca, and Mrs Darcy sat across the room from them.

"Take a piece of cake, darling. I had Cook make it specially for you. You are still too thin." The countess pushed a plate towards Elizabeth, much in the same way Lady Anne had thrust shortbread at her in January.

Elizabeth took a small bite. "I assure you, I am perfectly well."

"I hope you are." The countess covered one of Elizabeth's hands with her own. "Are you certain you wish to go to Pemberley? It is not too late to change your mind. The earl and I could make an excuse, take the blame on ourselves. The others could go, and we would say you are staying behind to assist me."

She seemed so earnest that Elizabeth offered her a warm smile. "I shall not lie and say it will be easy, but as Fitzwilliam said, it is an opportunity to make new memories and erase the unpleasant ones."

"I am afraid it will take more than one visit to do that, for me at least." The countess sipped her tea then continued. "After the wedding, I hope you will remove to this house, come back to Lord Romsley and me. We intend to remain in town until the end of June, after which we shall spend the summer in Worcestershire. The Darcys will visit, as I suppose you know."

"I do, and if you wish it, I will naturally return here. Mrs Darcy has been kind to have me stay for so long."

Elizabeth was satisfied with the decision. While she could not say she was entirely confident her life would not slowly slip back into what it was before, she was hopeful that would not be the case, especially if she remembered to speak up about her wishes.

Lady Romsley rapped her knuckles. "If you continue to speak nonsense, I shall never believe you are well. Mr and Mrs Darcy would be happy to keep you until you marry. They wanted you to live with them after my mother-in-law's death. Did you know?"

Elizabeth nodded.

"Was it Fitzwilliam who told you?" When Elizabeth again nodded, Lady Romsley shook her head, a fond expression on her countenance. "My son is terrible at keeping secrets. I suppose he learnt *some* discretion with age but not enough. Speaking of Fitzwilliam, he told me something about you I have been hesitant to mention."

Elizabeth's mouth went dry.

"He said you have an absurd notion to hire yourself out as a companion. You must take that idea out of your head at once, Elizabeth. If you are not content at Romsley Hall, we shall discuss what would make you happier. We could travel. You would like that, I know. While you remain unmarried, I promise to do everything possible to ensure your happiness. Not that I expect you will long be single, as lovely and admirable as you are.

"After the wedding, we can see about finding a husband for you, *if* you feel prepared to take such a step. I think about my nephew too. Fitzwilliam—it is *always* Fitzwilliam, is it not —he says Darcy is ready to settle down. Even though my sister-in-law will think only of rank and fortune, Darcy requires something more from his bride."

Elizabeth made a noise that was meant to sound indifferent and fixed her eyes on the wall behind her companion. She *had* given up the idea of seeking employment. It was clear no one wanted that for her, though, if she remained unmarried, she would have to find something to do with her life.

"I would like to travel," she found herself saying. "Perhaps when the earl must visit one of his estates or if there is some-where you thought of going, I could accompany you. It would be exciting to have such experiences, spend part of my time in new places and amongst new people—while not being separated for too long from those I most value."

No doubt, it was what she needed to feel more settled, and in time, she would be ready to accept a gentleman into the part of her heart Darcy had once occupied.

It was a lovely day for early March, and Elizabeth was enjoying a walk in the park with Darcy, his aunt Darcy, and Rebecca. The two ladies were a little behind them, and Freya walked beside Elizabeth. There was a chill in the air, but she found it refreshing, rather than uncomfortable. The sky was clear and every now and again, Elizabeth lifted her chin to it and relished the sensation of the sun on her face.

They were discussing people she knew in the neighbourhood around Pemberley and the possibility of seeing them at Easter. Darcy told her how Mrs Reynolds, the housekeeper, was preparing for their arrival, and painted a picture of them having a grand time full of engaging conversations, laughter over games, partaking in invigorating activities in the open air, and the like. It left Elizabeth with an ache in her chest, and she wondered why Darcy was insisting she would find their visit remarkable. Likely, it was simply because he was a good man and cared about her feelings.

Since he found her in Hertfordshire, and especially since January, Darcy had been so considerate—chivalrous really. It was almost too much, and while a part of her liked it very much, the other part hoped he would soon stop trying to make amends for the injury his mother and aunt had done her. To distract herself, she studied the elm trees to see which ones had the most evident buds forming, but that soon led to wondering what signs of spring she might see in Derbyshire.

Elizabeth could imagine the smell of earth still damp from the recently melted snow, a fragrance much sweeter and richer than what surrounded her currently. There might be lambs, their tiny newborn bodies nestled close to their mothers, their bleats ringing across the fields.

During her wool-gathering, she did not see Mr Bingley approach, and she dropped into a quick curtsey as he was straightening from his bow. He asked if he might join them for a short while and indicated he wished to speak to Elizabeth.

The party walked on, Darcy joining his aunt and Rebecca.

It took little time for Mr Bingley's purpose to become clear. He wanted to know if she would have Jane with her again soon.

"I see her at Gracechurch Street. The Gardiners are very kind…"

"But visiting elsewhere now and again would be pleasant."

Mr Bingley was obviously relieved Elizabeth understood. "I would have my sisters ask her to stay with them or to go with us to a concert or something like that, but, well…"

The reason hardly needed to be said. Elizabeth knew they hated Jane. "I shall talk to Rebecca and see if we can arrange something."

He expressed his gratitude and left them. Darcy asked about the conversation, and when Elizabeth told him, he scowled and asked her opinion of the request. In truth, it had not occurred to her to refuse. She had no great desire to see Jane or be further involved in her relationship with Mr Bingley, but it was too late now. She had committed herself.

She shrugged and felt Freya's head hit her hand, demanding a pet. Elizabeth looked down into the brindle face. "You are a spoilt girl."

Turning to Darcy, she found he wore an amused, fond expression, which she assumed was for his dog. He had several Great Danes over the years, including one named Thor, when she first met him. He had always preferred Norse names for his dogs, despite knowing Great Danes were from Germany. The summer she was eight, she was at Pemberley with the dowager countess when he learnt Thor had died. To make him feel better, Elizabeth spent an hour telling him silly stories. It was possibly the first time they had talked alone. They hardly said two words to each other for the remainder of the visit because the rest of the family arrived the following day, and she was occupied with Rebecca.

"Do not plan something simply because Bingley asked you to do it. If you will find Miss Bennet's company disagreeable, that is enough reason to decline," Darcy said.

Elizabeth's eyes fell to Freya, allowing her to hide an unexpected smile of pleasure. He was trying to protect her again. One day, she prayed, she would find a gentleman to rival him—one with whom she could share love and a happy future.

TWENTY EIGHT

With Mrs Darcy's permission, Elizabeth asked Jane to spend a day with her and Rebecca and attend a party at Curzon Street the same evening. Mr Bingley was invited, but his family was not. The young ladies had a pleasant time shopping, although Elizabeth, recalling the moments of Jane's jealousy when they were in Hertfordshire, was wary about making many purchases.

Jane came into Elizabeth's room once she was dressed for the evening. Elizabeth dismissed Herriot and remained at the table, putting on her jewellery.

"I like staying with my aunt and uncle," Jane said. "Even with four small children, their home is more orderly than Longbourn. Am I terrible for thinking that way? I never have before."

"Not if that is how you truly feel."

"I believe it is because I now see it through your eyes. I wish you had never gone to live in Worcestershire. You have so much sense and resolve, more than I do, and perhaps I would not have been swayed by my mother's view so much."

"Or perhaps I would have been too miserable to be a friend to you or anyone else."

Jane furrowed her brow and gazed at Elizabeth for a moment. "I suppose you feel it was good you left."

Irritation shot through her. She did not *leave*. She was banished. "I do when I remember the pain of hearing Mrs Bennet and Mrs Philips say cruel things to and about me. The dowager was benevolent, as were—*are*—the rest of the family."

"And they are rich. You would not have such fine things or friends had you remained at Longbourn. My parents assume the dowager settled money on you. I do not want to know. If I did and my mother asked, I would tell her."

Elizabeth turned to face Jane. "The greatest gift they gave me was the ability to become who I am. I was not stifled." Not prepared to continue with the subject, she said, "Tell me, what do you think of Mr Bingley now?"

Jane blushed. "I like him very much. He is so amiable, and he is patient with me. I find being with him immensely agreeable. Do you think he is very much attached to Netherfield?"

"I could not say. Why do you ask?"

Jane stood and ambled around the room. "If we were to marry, it would be better if we did not remain so close to Longbourn." She huffed and turned to face Elizabeth. "*You* escaped. I would like to go as well, but—unlike you—I know I have a responsibility to my mother and sisters. I do not know what to do."

Parts of this speech reminded Elizabeth of the Jane who was embarrassed and frustrated by her family's behaviour, but parts of it vexed and insulted her.

Elizabeth stifled a retort, stood, and said, "Shall we go down?"

Darcy intended to use the party as an opportunity to spend time with Elizabeth. He wanted to be with her always, but he worried about overwhelming her. Fitzwilliam and Bramwell urged a slow and steady approach to courting Elizabeth, and they were probably right. As much as he had not wanted to consult Rebecca initially, he was beginning to wonder if he should. He was impatient to know what Elizabeth felt for him. Could she learn to love him? Might she possibly already?

Watching her from across the room, Darcy saw she kept looking at Bingley and Miss Bennet. She seemed uneasy, and he wished he had advised her to disregard Bingley's request. Nothing good could come of further association with anyone named Bennet. With a bit of manoeuvring, he managed to get Elizabeth on her own and asked what was distressing her. When she hesitated, he persisted.

"Take my silence as a kindness, Darcy. My thoughts are not particularly agreeable at the moment. I need an opinion, but I do not know who will give me an unbiased one. It is not a bad thing. You, Rebecca—all of you—are too kind to me."

"That last part is balderdash. Tell me what is bothering you. Is it Miss Bennet?"

After a sigh, she told him of a conversation she had with Jane before the party. "I do not feel as though the Bennets are my family. It will sound silly, but I truly thought I was going home when I returned to Longbourn, and they would be glad to see me. At the very least, I expected Jane and I to be friends. Now and again, it seemed possible, but more often, it did not. I sense there is a good person inside of her that wants to emerge, like a butterfly does its cocoon, but the influence of Mrs Bennet has tainted her." She shook her head. "It weighs on her that Mrs Bennet and the girls will have so little when Mr Bennet dies. Jane said, unlike her, I have no sense of responsibility to them. She is not wrong, and it makes me feel as though I have abandoned them."

"And that leaves you feeling guilty?"

She bit her lips together and nodded.

Darcy touched her arm. "I do not know how you could look upon them as family. Do you think a single one of them feels a genuine kinship towards you, with all that entails—the rights and responsibilities—the way we, your true family, do?"

Elizabeth met his eyes for a moment. In a tone no louder than a whisper, she admitted, "If I had not returned to Longbourn, I doubt I would ever have seen them again. Certainly, they would have done nothing to bring it about. In time, we would have ceased writing to each other entirely."

Her sorrow made Darcy long to gather her into his arms. He contented himself by surreptitiously taking her hand and was exhilarated when her fingers curled around his.

"It does you credit that you could feel so much for people who do not deserve your consideration. You are sympathetic and caring and loyal and have been since the day we met."

"Darcy," she said on a soft exhale.

"Have I not seen it again and again? Everyone around you benefits from your goodness. Rebecca and my aunts and uncles, Fitzwilliam, Bramwell—they are all excellent people, and they all love you." Silently, he added, *And I love you so much I can hardly bear it.*

Her eyes drifted closed, and her chin fell towards her chest. The curve of her cheek was almost too tempting. His fingers itched to caress her, his lips to kiss her.

"They would not be so attached to you if you were not such a wonderful person. Even my mother—" Elizabeth's eyes flew open, and she removed her hand from his.

"I will *never* excuse her behaviour, but she *does* care for you. You said it seems like a better person is trying to emerge in Miss Bennet. I see the same thing in my mother, perhaps because she is removed from Lady Catherine's influence. I pray it is so and, before too long, we will not have to worry she might injure you again." He *had* to believe that, because it was doubtful he and Elizabeth would have a peaceful, harmonious life until his mother fully accepted her as an equal part of the family.

"I hope for everyone's sake you are right."

She did not say it, but it was evident to him that Elizabeth had doubts. To stop her from walking away, Darcy held her elbow. Sensing her unwillingness to discuss Lady Anne, he returned to where they had begun.

"Had the Bennets been a family to you, you would be right to care for them, but from what I saw, they did nothing to deserve you. You should stop feeling you must help them." He gestured to Miss Bennet and Bingley.

She took a steadying breath. "We go to Pemberley soon. I hope by the time we return they will have settled it between them and either marry or separate."

"If they marry, you will see her."

"Jane does not want to remain at Netherfield. Perhaps as Mrs Bingley and removed from the Bennets, she will become the good person I pray she can be."

"I hope you are right, for Bingley and for you." He paused briefly before changing the subject to a happier one—the exhibit they went to and the upcoming ball.

"Will you save the first set for me?"

"You should give that honour to a more eligible lady."

"I have no interest in dancing with any simpering young women intent on securing a husband, who believe any man of good fortune and birth will do. I want to dance with you." Darcy immediately realised he probably should have said the last part first.

"What would Lady Anne—"

"I will not live my life to please my mother. When she is unreasonable, I feel free, even bound, to ignore her wishes."

Elizabeth scrutinised him for a long moment. He was not sure what she was looking for and remained silent. Soon after she accepted his request for the set, she was called to the pianoforte to entertain the guests.

⚬⁓⚬⁓⚬

The ball celebrating Rebecca and Bramwell's engagement was a great success, and they were full of joy. Elizabeth danced and laughed throughout the evening, and the hours flew by. When she was not dancing with another man, Darcy remained by her side. He asked for a second set, and she readily agreed, even though she had felt Lady Anne watching her all night.

While she did stare, there were no scowls or pinched lips, and Elizabeth was satisfied the woman was doing what she could to keep her harsh sentiments to herself, presumably to gratify her son and brother.

A few days later, they left for Pemberley. The mix of apprehension and anticipation in Elizabeth's belly grew more and more chaotic the closer they drew to the estate, making her uncommonly queasy. Stepping out of the carriage, her legs were weak as she recalled being told she was going to Rosings Park. Lady Anne vowed Elizabeth would never be allowed back at Pemberley, yet there she was, and by Darcy's invitation. Elizabeth wanted to confront her, give vent to all the rage and pain that remained buried within her. A hand clasped hers.

It was Rebecca, and beyond her, Elizabeth saw Darcy and Lady Romsley watching her. If she turned in another direction, she would see the others, ready to give her comfort and defend her.

She turned to Rebecca and nodded to indicate she was steadier. "Let us go inside. A cool drink would do me good, then perhaps there will be enough time for a walk in the gardens before dinner."

Darcy evidently overheard her. "Excellent notion. Mrs

Reynolds has refreshments ready for us in the yellow drawing room."

He gestured for Lady Anne to lead the way but waited for Elizabeth and Rebecca to approach the door to walk into the house by Elizabeth's side.

Early the next morning, Darcy hoped to secure a private interlude with Elizabeth. The journey to Pemberley had been as comfortable as it could be, but he was certain he saw signs of strain in her. His mother said nothing disagreeable to Elizabeth that he knew of, but the silence between them was its own kind of travail. He intended to do everything possible to ensure Elizabeth enjoyed her days in Derbyshire. If he knew anything about her, it was that she would already be awake and out of doors. The butler, Hudson, told him he saw Elizabeth in her riding habit, and so Darcy made his ways to the stables.

There, he stopped at the tall double doors to observe her. She stood by Nutmeg's stall, a smile on her face as she ran her hand along the mare's broad nose. Elizabeth looked radiant, and he said nothing for a moment, preferring to drink in her beauty and savour the rush of love that flowed through his body. The arrival of a groom alerted her to his presence.

She said, "Good morning. You are out early."

"As are you. I can see you are planning to ride. Do you mind if I join you?"

She agreed, and they stepped outside to wait for their horses to be saddled. Darcy watched as she took a deep breath and let her eyes take in their surroundings.

"I wish I arrived sooner last summer. I recall learning you would be here. I was glad and looked forward to seeing you, but it also meant I could avoid my mother, let you amuse her, and not feel guilty about it." She looked at him, and Darcy continued. "I thought of myself and the way she tries to direct my life. It was not fair. I should have thought more about you."

Elizabeth shook her head and looked across the meadow. "It matters not. Lady Anne is difficult to understand. I sometimes believed she appreciated my presence. She would have me sit with her, read aloud, or play the pianoforte. Upon occasion, I thought she felt some genuine affection for me. At others, she obviously did not." She met his eyes. "Did you know she sent me a birthday gift?"

He was stunned. "In December? After what she did?"

"It was a beautiful bracelet that suits my taste perfectly. There was no note, but I recognised her handwriting on the parcel. Then, when I called on her in town—oh, I wish I could describe the way she looked at me! She must have noticed the signs of how difficult the months in Hertfordshire had been. She truly seemed concerned, and she kept pressing me to eat more. In the next moment, she told me I did not belong in this family. Her behaviour is baffling."

Darcy agreed, but before he could remark on it, a groom brought out their horses. Elizabeth's attention turned to the pleasure of the ride, and he would not rob her of it.

TWENTY NINE

lizabeth readily, even eagerly, embraced being with the people she most cared for, filling their days with enlivening activity and friendly intercourse. For the most part, the weather was agreeable, and she was outside as much as possible. Pemberley was beautiful and made the most excellent setting for their amusements.

A group of them went walking every day, and somehow, no matter how many set out from the house, she found Darcy by her side, the two of them separated from the other young people. Almost every morning, she rode Nutmeg, and even when they were joined by Fitzwilliam and Bramwell, Elizabeth would find herself talking with Darcy. He asked her to visit some of the tenants with him one morning. He wanted her opinion about a dispute between them, knowing she had dealt with similar matters at Romsley Hall when the earl and countess were absent.

Their evenings were filled with games and music and laughter. At the end of each day, Elizabeth was content to climb the stairs to her chamber and fall asleep to the sounds of the fire crackling in the hearth and the calls of wildlife through her window.

At Easter, they went to church, but although they were invited to several social gatherings, they chose to remain amongst the family party. Unexpectedly, Elizabeth discovered being at Pemberley made her yearn to return to Romsley Hall.

Staring at the view from her bedroom window, she murmured, "Perhaps I shall go when Rebecca and Bramwell do and forget about spending the rest of the Season in town. I am ready to accept it as my home, regardless of where I might live in the future. My roots grew there, first at the dower house, then in the manor. I became who I am because I lived there. Longbourn could never have been my home, not in the way I imagined."

She felt the difference in herself. If she had improved in January after leaving Hertfordshire and being with Rebecca and her parents, now she was returning to herself fully. Even Lady Anne could not dampen her good spirits. Elizabeth was never alone with her, and they exchanged few words apart from commonplaces. It was awkward, and Lady Anne's manner, which sometimes moved from being cool to discourteous, occasionally irritated Elizabeth, but all in all, her interaction with Lady Anne was acceptable to her. They would never be friends, but she need not feel anxious about having to spend time in her company, at least when there were other people with them. What she would never accept was being alone with the woman. Elizabeth was unlikely to ever trust her enough for that.

◦ ⟋◦⟍ ◦

Two days before they left for town, Elizabeth went for a walk in the afternoon, wanting to visit a few favourite places. Darcy was calling on a neighbour with his steward to discuss repairs to several gates they shared, and everyone else was happily occupied in various ways. Returning to the house, she went to the stables to play with a litter of month-old kittens. Darcy found her sometime later, sitting on an old blanket, three of the little creatures crawling on her, while their mother sat next to her and observed.

They spoke about his call for a few minutes before Darcy pointed to the kittens and asked, "Which one do you want?"

Elizabeth laughed. "All of them. None of them. I cannot presently give a home to a cat, but I do adore the little things. I believe I love them more than I do dogs, if only just a little bit. Do not tell Freya."

He chuckled and tickled an orange kitten, who issued a barely audible mewl, flopped on its stomach, and went to sleep.

"Did you not once have a cat of your own?"

"I did. Bramwell and Fitzwilliam gave her to me when your grandmother died, and I went to live in the manor. I called her Dotty because she had dots all over her belly." She smiled at the memory of her little companion. "She was the dearest creature ever."

He made a noise that indicated he remembered, and they were quiet for a long moment.

"She died a month before your father did. I felt as though I had lost two friends." Elizabeth did not know why she said it. Dotty had felt like her only companion at times. Rebecca lived so far away, and Bramwell and Fitzwilliam were busy with their education and being young men. Her governess was amiable, but they had never been close.

"Why did you never get another one? Here are three who will soon need a home."

She shook her head. "You must know your aunt does not favour cats. I never supposed I would be allowed another one. In truth, she was not pleased her sons gave me Dotty, but she agreed when they argued she would alleviate some of my grief at the dowager's death." She shrugged. "It does not matter."

"I disagree, but I shall not debate the matter with you."

She offered him a quick smile. "When circumstances allow, I shall have one again—or likely a dozen!"

Darcy asked if she would take a stroll with him. After kissing each of the cats on their heads and returning them to the safety of their gated corner, she joined him. They got no farther than the banks of the stream, where they sat on an iron bench. The day was warm, and the new spring vegetation made the air smell sweet. Elizabeth listened to the gentle trickle of water as it splashed over rocks and watched the wind rustle through the still mostly bare tree branches. Being with him was peaceful.

"You are happy here," Darcy said.

"How could I not be on such a glorious day with all this around me?"

There was silence between them for quite some time.

"Would you like to call Pemberley your home?"

Elizabeth shook her head, confused by his words. Perhaps Darcy thought she still felt adrift. They had not spoken about her newly emerging understanding of herself and her place in the world.

"I shall go to Romsley Hall, perhaps with Rebecca and Bramwell, but if not, with the earl and countess."

Darcy did not speak again for a while, then said, "I meant as Pemberley's mistress?"

Elizabeth's body jerked, and she stared at him, her eyes round and heart beating wildly. "What?"

He swallowed. "I am asking you to marry me, Elizabeth." He rushed on. "I love you. I do. Ardently, completely. I once accepted the view that I must marry a lady of fortune and connexions, but now I realise affection is more important. That sounds terrible, as though I am implying you are lacking in some way, but you are not. You are *everything* any sensible man could want. I would do anything to make you happy, Elizabeth."

She did not know what to say, and when she tried to force words out of her mouth, only a strangled sound escaped.

Darcy continued. "You must know I admire you and value nothing more than your company. You would never want for anything. Your friendship has been so important to me these last few years—so much so I mistook my growing attachment for only that, and I did not realise I was falling in love with you. Last summer, returning to Pemberley, what made me happiest was that I would soon see you again. I thought I would go mad those weeks when no one knew where you were, and I had no notion how you were or what you were doing. We know each other so well, and you know we are well suited."

"But your mother—"

"I do not need her approval, Elizabeth."

"Your father would not have wanted this."

He took her hand in his and leant closer. "I do not agree. Father adored you. If he knew us now, he would champion our union. I can only be happy with you as my wife, and I hope— oh, how I pray—you feel the same way.

"I shall not attempt to say my mother will be happy—or Lady Catherine, whose opinion means less than nothing to me. We will never see her or Anne. My aunts and uncles will not object, and my cousins will be delighted."

Elizabeth's head swam, and she could not seem to catch her breath.

"Could you love me," he asked, "as a husband?"

Of course she could. She *did*.

Had she really been foolish enough to believe she no longer loved him? Everything he said about them being perfectly suited was a truth her heart had recognised three years prior, and despite what she had been telling herself these last six months, her heart had not forgotten. She wanted to fall into his arms and shout that yes, she would marry him until all the world heard her.

But it was utterly unthinkable. Love him or not, she could not accept him. Lady Anne would never approve of their marriage, and beyond the misery it would cause her and Darcy, there was a risk to the harmony of the entire family. Lord and Lady Romsley and the Darcys were at best civil to Lady Anne, and Bramwell could barely disguise his disdain of her. Elizabeth had no doubt that either by her actions or by her words, Lady Anne would express her disgust of the union, and it would tear the family apart.

It would cost the earl his only sister, since he refused to acknowledge Lady Catherine any longer. Far worse, Darcy would either regret his choice or he, too, would have to sever his connexion to his mother or risk seeing Elizabeth miserable. She refused to play a role in such a disaster.

Elizabeth knew what it was to lose one's family, and she would not bring such misery to people she loved. She had promised herself she would find a home in which she was wanted. She could not accept anything less, and that meant spending as little time as possible with people like Lady Anne, who viewed her as an inferior.

Her heart shattered into pieces. "It is too late. We can be nothing but friends to each other."

Clutching her hands, Darcy said, "I beg of you, do not say no. If it is because of my mother, then give me time. I-I spoke too soon. I will talk to her and make her accept our marriage. Please, Elizabeth, I pray you want a life with me.

"Set aside my mother, even my failures and stupidity in the past, just for a minute. In your heart, what do you want? If it is me, I will find a way to make it possible for you to be happy at Pemberley. Unless you tell me there is no hope, I will not accept your refusal."

Staring into his eyes, feeling the pressure of his hands encircling hers, Elizabeth could not say the words that would end his hopes forever. She could not say anything at all, and so she stood, pulled her hands from his, and walked back to the house as quickly as she could.

Once inside, she asked the first footman she saw to send Rebecca to her and ran up the stairs to her bedchamber.

* * *

Over the next two days leading to their departure, Elizabeth did not speak to Darcy. She tried to act as she usually did, but he could see her spirits were affected, as were his. Darcy overheard a snippet of conversation between her and Lady Romsley. The countess asked if there was anything troubling her.

Elizabeth said, "I am perfectly well, I promise. Perhaps I am a little more tired than usual, but it will pass soon enough."

Despite her words, Darcy knew he had added to her pain. Some natural impatience had prompted his unplanned proposal. Darcy's distress would not lessen until the day she agreed to marry him. The way she looked, the tears shining in her lovely, dark eyes, convinced him that she loved him as he did her.

There was only one reason for her to refuse him: his mother. While Lady Anne was not overtly hostile, it was not enough for Elizabeth. He ought not to blame his mother, but a part of him did, possibly because he had no notion what to do about it.

Darcy told Fitzwilliam and Bramwell what happened. Fitzwilliam abused him for stupidity, saying it was too soon to propose, but Bramwell was of another opinion.

"It was precipitous to be sure, but you should not despair."
To his brother, he added, "Do you know, I am quite hopeful."

Fitzwilliam nodded. "You are correct. Elizabeth would
have told him to go to the ████ if she had no romantic feelings
for him."

Darcy walked out of the room, rather than listen to them
discuss the matter further.

After the second day of travel when they stopped at the inn
they would stay at that night, Rebecca quietly asked him to
take her for a walk. It was an unusual request, and Darcy
assumed she had something to say about Elizabeth. He was
proved correct.

His face heated. "She told you about my proposal?"

"Of course she did! You told Bramwell and Fitzwilliam."
Rebecca shook her head as though he were a halfwit, which
was how he felt at the moment. "Elizabeth cried, Darcy. *She
cried!*" Her tone was accusatory, and his chin dropped to his
chest.

"You have to understand that regardless of what Elizabeth
may feel for you, she vowed only to live where she is confident she is fully accepted and embraced. Why should she
expect or tolerate anything less? She deserves to be
surrounded by people who love her, who are kind to her and
treat her with respect. Everything that has happened to her left
her in such a state that she was even prepared to live on her
own just so she would not feel unwanted again."

Darcy recalled Elizabeth saying something similar to him
in Hertfordshire, but he had not considered it in relation to
them marrying. Of course, at the time, he had not realised the
depths of his affection for her. How could he ask her to put
herself in a situation where she might never feel as though she
belonged?

They stopped by a lone oak tree. Darcy felt chastened, but

he could not be angry with his cousin, who had Elizabeth's best interests at heart. Neither could he give up the hope of winning Elizabeth, knowing being together would bring them so much joy.

"Do you think I would not do everything in my power to ensure she is happy?"

Rebecca gave his arm a gentle squeeze. "Of course you would, but you want her to accept Lady Anne as her mother-in-law! Even if my aunt removed to the dower house, it would not materially alter the situation or resolve the underlying problem. Your mother may not have said anything horrible to her while we were at Pemberley, but you must have seen the way she constantly studied her.

"Elizabeth feels the weight of your mother's disapproval. The only reason it was tolerable was because there were so many of us present. But every time they were together, for so long as they both lived, Elizabeth would be waiting for a disagreeable look or word, certain it would come. Why would she place herself in such a precarious position? Marriage would rob her of the independence she needs to remove herself from untenable situations. That would not be an issue, if…"

Darcy closed his eyes and kept his head bowed. "If there was not an ogre of a mother-in-law awaiting her at the other side of the altar. What do I do?"

"Honestly, I think it is about what Lady Anne needs to do, not you. *She* needs to show Elizabeth she will not interfere in your marriage or, through her behaviour, cause more strife in our family, which is an outcome Elizabeth fears." Rebecca squeezed his arm again. "You are my cousin, and I love you. I love Elizabeth too. She is the sister of my heart. I would be thrilled to see the two of you find happiness together, but I shall never advise her to put herself in a situation where she cannot have the same joy I shall as Bramwell's wife."

With that, Rebecca began to walk back to the inn. Darcy watched her, and after a long interval, pushed himself away from the tree, and followed.

THIRTY

The next weeks were a flurry of activity as they prepared for Rebecca and Bramwell's wedding. Elizabeth allowed herself a few moments of sorrow when she was alone at night and sleep eluded her. At times, she wondered if she did the right thing by refusing Darcy, but she had made promises to herself that she had to keep.

Without knowing how it started, she had waking dreams of being Mrs Darcy, Lady Anne showing the world her disgust with the situation, and the resulting tumult. In Elizabeth's imaginings, Darcy, his aunts and uncles and cousins all disavowed Lady Anne. Their friends and neighbours gossiped about them relentlessly. If only Elizabeth could convince herself that such a future would never come to pass! But she could not, and she would *never* allow it to happen.

When she was with Rebecca and her other friends, it was easy to be cheerful, and Elizabeth ensured Rebecca saw no sign of her inner distress. It was not so difficult to hide. Helping Rebecca choose her wedding clothes and make arrangements for the ceremony and breakfast was great fun. If she could not be happy for herself, seeing Rebecca so elated was just as good.

Rebecca and Bramwell decided to spend several weeks in Brighton, after which they would go to Romsley Hall, following a brief stay in London. Rebecca asked Elizabeth to accompany them, saying she might like to be away from everyone for a time, but Elizabeth declined.

The couple should have time alone, and she did not want their honeymoon spoilt. She promised to strongly consider going with them into Worcestershire, even if the earl and countess intended to travel there soon after.

A week after their return to town, Elizabeth received a note from Jane, requesting she call at Gracechurch Street.

I do not know how much longer I can remain in town, but how can I return to Longbourn without being engaged? For myself, I could wait until Mr Bingley is as certain as I am that we would do well together, but I cannot bear the thought of what my mother and sisters will say.

I need your advice, Elizabeth. Why does he hesitate? Is it the influence of his sisters? Does he doubt my sentiments? I promise you, they are very real and just what they should be.

Elizabeth showed the note to Rebecca, who scowled.

"Do you want to go? I cannot forget what it was like when you last saw Jane. Is there anything more you can or ought to do for her? What would happen if your advice was not to her liking? Would she slight you again?"

Elizabeth stared at the note. "I suppose I feel as though, if Jane asks, I must go see her."

"That is generous, but does she appreciate it? Would Jane do the same for you? And, truly, what could you say to her? You are not privy to Mr Bingley's thoughts and feelings. You must let go of the notion that you can erase the influence of her upbringing and make Jane how you imagined she could be."

Slowly, Elizabeth nodded. "I know you are right. I have been telling myself the same, especially that I doubt she would extend a hand to help me if it did not happen to be convenient. Where is the affinity in that? I wanted to find a sister in her, because of my memories from before I was sent away, but I have given up on that dream.

"Fortunately, I happen to have a most excellent sister." She smiled at Rebecca, and they embraced before Elizabeth tossed aside the note and said, "I shall tell her I have not seen Mr Bingley recently and am too much occupied at the moment, which is not a lie. I cannot think of a free morning for at least the next week."

By chance, they happened upon the gentleman at a concert several days later. Elizabeth refrained from mentioning Jane, but Mr Bingley did not. He said he still called at Gracechurch Street.

"Darcy once told me not to be in a rush, and I am following his advice. My sisters do not think Miss Bennet is a suitable match, but I care little for their objections. I know the Bennets would always be part of my life if, well—"

Elizabeth would listen to no more. She had problems enough of her own demanding her attention, and as far as she could tell, Jane and Mr Bingley could resolve theirs by simply speaking with each other more openly. She would be very happy if a little conversation was all that stood between her and Darcy coming to an understanding.

"Mr Bingley, did you know Jane would prefer to leave Hertfordshire?"

"She would? She would not want to settle near her family?"

Elizabeth resisted the urge to let out a melodramatic sigh. "You must talk to her."

Fortunately, Darcy, who was one of their party, joined them and engaged Mr Bingley in a discussion of a different topic. Elizabeth slipped away and found Fitzwilliam and the earl. While she listened to them discuss the merits of a bill Parliament was debating, her eyes remained on Darcy.

How could Elizabeth be expected to have patience for Jane and Mr Bingley's romantic difficulties when everything was so unsettled between her and Darcy? She wished she could see a way to accept his offer, but wishes were worthless things. If one wants something, one must either work to obtain it or admit it is simply not meant to be.

For his happiness, as well as my own, I should make it clear I will never be Mrs Darcy.

She resolved to talk to Lady Romsley about them travelling in the autumn. That would take her mind off him and, if she were very fortunate, cure her of her love for him once and for all.

⚬⚬⚬

One Sunday in mid-May, Darcy wandered around his townhouse, not sure what to do with himself. He tried reading, but nothing could hold his attention. He could not write letters. He drafted one to his steward but tossed it into the fire because it had become belligerent, and the man did not deserve such treatment. He could not go out. All day long, a heavy, steady rain had fallen. Picking up an iron, he jabbed at the embers in the drawing room, sending sparks flying.

Since their return from Pemberley, Elizabeth was polite, but she avoided him. Just the day before, they met at a ball, and she refused to dance with him.

"I know Rebecca spoke to you. I am sorry, but…I cannot. It is time for you to give up the notion."

Darcy knew she was speaking about more than accepting his company for the length of a set. He had no further opportunity to speak to her. She spent the evening by his aunt's side, and when he approached them after supper, his aunt said, "Not now."

The door opened, and his mother entered. He glimpsed at her before returning his attention to the fire.

"I can see you are despondent," she said. "I know you wish to stay in town for Bramwell's wedding, but we should return to Pemberley afterwards. I shall make arrangements for our departure."

"You cannot believe I wish to be alone with you in the country."

"Darcy—"

"No. While Elizabeth remains in town, I remain in town. When she goes to Romsley Hall this summer, I go to Romsley Hall."

She let out an exasperated breath, and he turned to face her.

"You have cost me my happiness," he said through clenched teeth. "What is worse, you have done the same to Elizabeth."

Lady Anne averted her eyes, but before she could walk away, he continued, his tone almost pleading. "Why? How do you justify your feelings for her and how you have acted towards her?" When his mother remained silent, he turned back to the fire. "Reconcile yourself to it, madam. I love Elizabeth, and I believe she returns my affection. I *will* marry her. I will not stop until I find a way to convince her, to prove to her I will not allow you to prevent us from having the joyful future I know awaits us as husband and wife. She will be the mistress of Pemberley and mother to your grandchildren."

"You cannot! I know you will not marry Anne, but there are other ladies who would be more suitable. One of the Chaplin girls. We have known the family for years, and they—"

"No!" He faced her and as calmly but firmly as possible, said, "I love you, Mother, but I will not choose a wife based on rank and fortune. I want something different in the lady who will share my life, the lady who will be my partner and companion during the long years ahead of us."

His mother's countenance was flushed, almost as though she had a fever. Her distress was far more than the conversation called for, and he did not comprehend it.

"You *cannot* marry her. I do not care how many times your aunts and uncles try to convince me it is a good idea, it would be a disaster. You are young and do not see it, but such unequal unions, ones between people of different spheres, *cannot* work."

Within a week of his proposal, his three cousins told their parents about it and their belief the only impediment to Darcy and Elizabeth's union was Lady Anne.

Darcy closed his eyes and rubbed his forehead. "I do not understand you. How many *equal* marriages are miserable? Equality in wealth and connexions means nothing. And we are talking about *Elizabeth*—to whom you are horrible one minute, then show every sign of caring for the next. I saw it myself this winter. What you said to her in January was terrible, yet when I told you about Wickham, you were so upset, you could not remain in the room."

Tears filled her eyes. "I do not trust her! Do you not think Elizabeth longs to make a good marriage, one far above what she should expect, so she can provide for her mother and sisters? I know their circumstances will be desperate when Mr Bennet dies. Elizabeth will not care for you as you deserve, and I will not see you so deceived."

"How can you suggest Elizabeth is not trustworthy? She would never act in such a way."

"Her family—"

"*We* are her family—my aunts and uncles and cousins, me, *and you*. The Bennets have not been her family in over fifteen years, and they never will be again. It is *us* she knows and loves and who know and love her, not them."

When she opened her mouth to respond, he held up a hand to forestall her. "You have one month to come to terms with your feelings for Elizabeth. I urge you to be honest with yourself about what they are and why you disdain her. If you cannot find a way to reconcile with her, I will have no choice."

"What do you mean?" Alarm flashed in his mother's eyes.

"You will leave Pemberley and this house forever and live your life separate from me. Whether or not Elizabeth ever agrees to be my wife, I will no longer tolerate you causing her even a moment of discomfort, to say nothing of the strife your behaviour is creating within the family."

With quick, long strides, he brushed past her, out of the room, and up the stairs to his apartment. He could not bear to hear any more of her nonsense.

⁂

In the last week of May, Rebecca and Bramwell married. Elizabeth looked lovely in an elegantly trimmed yellow gown which befitted the bride's lone attendant, but she was nothing to Rebecca, who was beautiful in beaded white silk and smiles. Darcy's eyes were on Elizabeth throughout the ceremony and later at the wedding breakfast. He was not the only one watching her. Lady Anne did, too, and her expression seemed more contemplative than usual, though Elizabeth suspected she was being fanciful for thinking so. In the end, she chose to ignore them both, lest they destroy her pleasure in the day.

By noon, the newly married couple departed for Brighton,

and Elizabeth made her final preparations to remove to Grosvenor Square, where the earl and countess celebrated her return home. In the following days, Lady Romsley kept Elizabeth busy. There were parties, calls, and excursions to attend. When he was at liberty, the earl accompanied them. The countess took Elizabeth shopping for new summer gowns and accoutrements and solicited her opinion on how they would spend their days and evenings, assuring her she should feel free to mention anything she would like to do. The countess wanted only what would make Elizabeth as content as possible.

Mrs Darcy delivered a note from Jane when she called one morning. Lady Romsley said she could spare Elizabeth if she wished to call on her, but Elizabeth insisted she did not. Jane's letter was long and full of pleas, asking her to discover what she could about Mr Bingley's intentions. She was leaving for Longbourn in a week, and she worried if she went without being engaged to him, it would be the end of all her hopes. Elizabeth did nothing. She had advised them to speak openly to each other, and if they had not or their conversations had not led to the outcome Jane wanted, it was not Elizabeth's affair.

She saw Darcy a number of times but did her best to avoid private conversations with him, knowing he would attempt to cajole her into retracting her rejection of his suit. She questioned her resolve, overlooking the sensible part of her which knew it would be a mistake.

Ten days after the wedding, Lady Romsley said, "You are not as cheerful as I would wish you to be, darling. It is the situation with my nephew, is it not?"

Elizabeth's cheeks drained of colour, and the countess continued. "You do not wish to talk about it, and I will not press you to open your heart to me, but you must be aware we all know. I have hesitated to talk about it, not wanting to make you uneasy, but I want to assure you that my husband and I would be so very pleased if the two of you married, *if* it was what you wanted. I only regret I did not think of it myself. We have been assured of Darcy sentiments, but Fitzwilliam and Bramwell only think they know yours, and Rebecca would not share your secrets. I am not wrong to suppose you care for him, am I?"

There was a long pause before Elizabeth gave the barest shake of her head. "But it is impossible. Lady Anne will never accept it, and I could not marry any man under such circumstances. It would be a mistake—for me, Darcy, the entire family."

Lady Romsley put an arm around Elizabeth, who rested her head against the countess's shoulder. "I understand. The earl has spoken to his sister more than once, and she must see how upset she has made Darcy. If she is wise, she will fear where his anger with her will lead." The countess tightened her clasp briefly before releasing Elizabeth. "Well, what say we forget all about her—and him—for now and talk about music instead."

Elizabeth nodded and, a moment later, managed a small smile and asked the countess about a recent recital she had attended. She was in need of new music, she decided, and half an hour later, the ladies were on their way to see what they could find.

THIRTY ONE

Darcy called at Grosvenor Square several mornings but saw Elizabeth only once and then just for a brief interval because she and Lady Romsley were on their way to a charity event. He missed her company, and his attempts to talk to his mother about Elizabeth were not progressing as he hoped. She, like Elizabeth, had taken to avoiding him. To add to his frustrations, he found himself evading Bingley since all *he* wanted to do was talk about Jane Bennet.

Nothing much changed until two weeks after Rebecca and Bramwell's wedding. Darcy was in his study reviewing a report from his steward when his mother asked to speak to him. With enough trepidation to make his throat tighten, he agreed. She perched on the edge of a wing chair, her countenance pale and stern, and began to talk.

"I have thought a great deal about what you said to me, and even though it may not seem like it, I have been doing as you demanded." Lady Anne took a deep breath before continuing. "I wish to tell you something. You are old enough to understand, though this is a secret I hoped to take to my grave. Only my mother and Catherine knew, and I tell you now because I know I will lose you if I do not find a way to accept your decision and convince you of my sincerity.

"When Elizabeth first came to live with my mother, I could not bear to look at her. After your birth, I longed for another child. I often had hopes, but it was always in vain.

Until the last time. I was certain all would be well, although the doctor cautioned me, but then my daughter died.

"Less than a year later, my mother took in a charming little girl with big, bright eyes and a desire to please, and all I could think of was that she should not be there, my daughter should. Worse was my mother saying it would do me good to spend time with Elizabeth—perhaps have her live at Pemberley— and watching your father love her as he should have loved *our* daughter." She brushed away a tear before making a gesture that suggested impatience.

"That is not the secret, and it would not explain my mistrust of her, though Catherine encouraged my rejection of Elizabeth, my anger with your grandmother for what she had done, and with your father for accepting her. I see now, after all these years, how it made me dissatisfied, and that might have hardened my feelings further."

She glanced at him before beginning again. "I was once deceived in love. By someone of…lower quality, someone like Elizabeth. I was young, not yet out, and staying with a friend. He was an attorney in the local market town. He was handsome, and charming, as all romantic heroes should be, and he convinced me that he loved me. We planned to elope. I thought we were being discreet, but my friend's mother must have seen something between us and wrote to your grandmother. Catherine intercepted the letter and insisted on accompanying Mama when she came. Mama discovered he was only interested in my dowry and connexions. I had been duped in the cruellest way. His professions of love were all lies."

Darcy was astonished. To think that his mother, who always preached about the importance of social distinctions, had almost eloped with a country attorney!

Lady Anne continued. "Mama and Catherine never told anyone, especially not my father. He would have disowned me. You remember what he was like. I see him in Catherine, and if you say you see him in me, you would not be wrong. I truly believe you cannot trust people from the lower classes. They will seek to align themselves with you for selfish and deceitful reasons."

"Mother." Darcy's voice held a warning. He was moved by her recitation and evident distress, but he would not listen to her slurs against Elizabeth.

She lifted a hand either to show she understood his objection or to dismiss it. "What I have done, I have done to keep you safe from the sort of disappointment I suffered and the misery my life would have become. I was convinced that only someone who was your equal, especially someone in the family, could be relied upon not to betray you. To keep you safe, you *needed* to make such a match. That is how I justified trying to persuade you to marry Anne, even demand that you do. Catherine encouraged this way of thinking, but I do not seek to excuse myself."

She cleared her throat and clasped her hands in her lap so tightly her knuckles were white. "I am afraid. I do not entirely understand why I cannot rid myself of this feeling, but I have not abandoned the effort. As you said to me, this is Elizabeth of whom we speak."

Fat tears slipped down her cheeks. Darcy reached across the distance between them and covered her hands with his.

She gave him a tremulous smile. "I have no reason to distrust Elizabeth. In truth, I have every reason *to* trust her. Since your father's death and the months she remained at Pemberley, I could see what good friends you were becoming and how well suited you were." She gave a rueful laugh. "I believe I saw that you were falling in love with each other before either of you did, and it terrified me. I considered sending her away as soon as I saw the first hint of her affection for you, but I could not. Your aunt Lady Romsley said she would be a comfort to me, and she was correct, even though I refused to show Elizabeth any appreciation for everything she did then or on any other occasion. I cannot pretend this is what I want for you, but I shall never mention that again.

"My fervent prayer is that in time my sentiments will change, and I promise you, I will do what I can to make it so. I give you my blessing."

Lady Anne regarded him with so much fondness that Darcy believed she was sincere.

"I have made some decisions regarding my living arrangements," Lady Anne said, "but we shall discuss them at a later time."

She stood and ran her hands over her skirt. "I ask that you let me talk to Elizabeth before you offer for her again. I owe her an apology and an explanation. I may need a day or two, but I shall not delay long. You have my word."

Darcy's instinct was to run to Grosvenor Square and demand to see Elizabeth immediately, but witnessing how difficult this was for his mother and convinced of her determination to do better, he would not refuse her request. Once he agreed, Lady Anne left him alone.

Darcy fell back into the chair and began to laugh in relief. Elizabeth may not have said she loved him, but every instinct told him she did.

"Soon, my Elizabeth. I will beg, if I must, but I will make you my wife!"

⁕ ‿◦‿ ⁕

The house was quiet with Lord Romsley at a committee hearing, Fitzwilliam attending a meeting about possible changes to his duties, and the countess at her ladies' club.

Rebecca and Bramwell were due in town in a few days, and Elizabeth had decided to go with them to Romsley Hall rather than wait for the earl and countess's departure in a fortnight. Elizabeth was at the pianoforte in the middle of a piece by Ignaz Pleyel when the housekeeper opened the door and announced Lady Anne.

Elizabeth stood and curtseyed. "I regret that Lady Romsley is not here, if you were hoping to see her."

"I came to see you, Elizabeth."

Dreading the moment Lady Anne decided to confront her about Darcy's proposal, Elizabeth longed for an excuse to flee. Instead, she gestured for her to take a seat, but Lady Anne remained standing, clasping her reticule with both hands. Elizabeth could see her body trembling, her eyes fixed on a spot to Elizabeth's right.

With as much formality as though she were speaking to the queen, Lady Anne said, "I must first apologise for sending you to Kent last summer. When I learnt you were coming to Pemberley, that you, my son, and I would be there alone, every anxiety I have ever felt overwhelmed me. I saw the two of you were growing to care for each other, and I did not like it. When I wrote to my sister of the arrangements, she proposed I send you to her. I do not know what I believed she would do, but I had no notion that Catherine planned to send you to India, of all places. Perhaps she meant to contrive to keep you away until after she and my niece came to Derbyshire. We hoped Darcy would finally do as we wished and become betrothed to Anne. It was wrong of me, and I was horrified when she told us you had left the country to be governess to people I had never heard of before. Likewise, I was…exceedingly thankful to learn you were in Hertfordshire."

She took a deep breath. "I am called upon to revise opinions I was taught as a child by my father, opinions I have held close to my heart my entire life. I do this for my son. I know I was not affectionate towards you, unlike my husband. When you went to live with my mother, it was supposed to be for a few months, just long enough for your mother to give birth to a son. I suppose I could not allow myself to become attached to you. Why would I, when you would be gone from our lives soon, and I would never see you again? That is a weak excuse, I know, but it played a part. I had...disappointments after Darcy's birth. They likely also contributed to my feelings. The larger reason is what I learnt from my father, lessons reinforced by my sister and...other experiences. You never knew him, but you have heard about him?"

"I have." Bramwell and Fitzwilliam often compared Lady Catherine to the old earl.

"Some called him harsh, but I loved him. He taught me not to trust people who were not family or, like us, of high rank and rich. They would use you, deceive you, I was told. I once ignored his advice, and it nearly resulted in my ruin. I shall say nothing more about it. I explained it to Darcy, and he may tell you. What happened showed me my father was right."

Elizabeth was curious to learn more, but of greater immediate importance was understanding Lady Anne's purpose in coming to her, so she let her continue to speak.

"I did not trust you, Elizabeth. I know it sounds ridiculous —you were only five years old—but from the day we met, I was suspicious of you. My animosity became worse as you grew older and I watched you and Darcy become friends. I never wanted my son to feel what I did when—" She waved a hand, and Elizabeth assumed she was referring to her past misstep. "That is one of the reasons I wanted him to marry Anne. I knew she was not using him for his connexions or wealth. She does not need either."

Her eyes met Elizabeth's. "I know you want to marry him, but why do you wish it? I beg you to indulge me and answer rather than be offended at the question. Do you truly love him, Elizabeth, as a woman ought to love her husband?"

"I-I do. He reminds me of his father, who was one of the best men I have ever met. To me, that is the highest compliment I can give him."

Lady Anne's head jerked in a single nod. "I, too, love him."

"I know you do and that you want only the best for him."

Lady Anne's eyes were bright with tears. When she spoke, her voice was muffled. "For that reason, I shall welcome you as a daughter-in-law. If you were just some country miss he met when visiting a friend, I do not believe I could accept you as his wife. However, as he has been reminding me daily, I know you. I watched you grow from a curious, lively child into an estimable young woman, one whom—whatever your birth—any family would be proud to admit."

Elizabeth did not know what to say. Part of her wanted to ask for clarification to be sure she had not misunderstood. She remained as still as possible as Lady Anne stepped towards her, although her instinct was to withdraw, especially when Lady Anne's hand reached out. She touched Elizabeth's hair and tucked a strand into place. It was the first time Lady Anne had caressed her in any fashion.

Lady Anne turned and took several steps away. When Elizabeth realised her mouth hung open, she closed it and forced herself to set aside her feelings until she was alone.

Lady Anne stopped midway between Elizabeth and the door and turned to face her. "You and Darcy will marry. Pemberley has been my home for thirty years, but it is best for all of us if I live elsewhere, for now at least, until I learn to think about the world differently.

"I have decided to spend my winters in Bath. London no longer agrees with me. It is too crowded and dirty. I shall have the dower house at Pemberley renovated and use it when I wish to be in the country. We shall see each other, but there will be no difficulties. I promise."

Before Elizabeth could say a word, Lady Anne was gone. Elizabeth sank onto the sofa, covered her mouth with her hands, and began to laugh in shock, relief, and anticipated joy.

Elizabeth did not know what to do. She walked around the music room, sat, stood and examined the plants and other furnishings, and sat again. Had Lady Anne truly been there? Had she given her blessing to a marriage between her and Darcy? Had she actually hinted she cared for her, even though she had never openly shown it?

Darcy must know his mother had been there, and he was sure to follow—but when? Waiting was nearly impossible, and she wished she could go to him. She drank a cup of tea to calm her nerves and returned to her music as a way to distract herself. Once again, her playing was interrupted when the housekeeper ushered in the very person Elizabeth was longing to see most: Darcy.

Elizabeth's heart stuttered as she stood. He stepped towards her and opened his mouth to speak, but before he could, she did.

"Do you believe her? Is your mother serious?"

A grin came over his face, and he nodded. "Two days ago, she told me she accepts our union and will move into the dower house. She mentioned something about Bath too. I have no idea why she chose Bath, and frankly, it matters not. Elizabeth—"

Again, she spoke before he could continue. "You truly wish to marry me? It is not because you feel responsible for—"

"Do I truly want to marry you? Yes, a thousand times, yes, I desire nothing more than for us to spend our lives together," he insisted. "You are more important to me than anyone else. I have dreamt about our future, the two of us at Pemberley, the family and home we shall have. I have imagined the elation of being your husband and a father to our children. I love you, Elizabeth Bennet, completely, utterly, irrevocably."

Elizabeth did not know whether to laugh or cry, so she did both. "Then yes, oh yes, I will marry you, Fitzwilliam Darcy. My one and only love."

In an instant, she was in his arms, and no longer able to contain the overwhelming joy he clearly felt, he kissed her.

THIRTY TWO

Darcy and Elizabeth were sitting together on the sofa, their hands joined, when Lady Romsley found them. Darcy had never known such happiness, and as much as he wanted to shout it out to the world, he was also not pleased to have his time alone with his dearest Elizabeth interrupted.

The countess stood at the doorway and gaped at them. "Oh. Oh! Have you any news? Are you—?"

They both stood, and Elizabeth nodded, her cheeks dusted pink. Darcy longed to hold her in his arms and kiss her again until they turned crimson.

His aunt was effusive in her congratulations, hugging first Elizabeth, then Darcy before doing it all over again.

"I am so pleased for both of you," Lady Romsley said. "And Anne, although I doubt she will understand why. She gave her blessing?" Darcy said she had. "I must send for my husband, and send a note to Curzon Street, I think, unless you would like to tell them yourselves. The Darcys will be delighted. You will want to write to Rebecca, Elizabeth, and we shall send it express. She will hate any delay in receiving the news. This has all worked out perfectly!"

While she sent her messages, Elizabeth wrote to Rebecca, and Darcy added a few words to Bramwell. Within two hours, the house was loud with people talking about the happy news, and Darcy was filled with gratitude to see his family embrace their engagement. Although his aunt invited his mother to join them for dinner, Lady Anne declined. Darcy suspected she would find it too much, especially if anyone pressed her to explain why she had relented and given her blessing to his and Elizabeth's union.

Lady Anne sent Elizabeth a bouquet of flowers and a five-stone diamond and gold ring that Darcy recognised at once. The note accompanying it was short.

This ring belonged to my mother-in-law. Mr Darcy gave it to me upon our engagement. He would be very pleased to know you are the next Mrs Darcy to wear it.

"I agree," Darcy told Elizabeth. "I am absolutely convinced of it. He adored you and would have rejoiced to claim you as his daughter."

They stood apart from the others, but it was not enough privacy to kiss her until she agreed with him, so he settled for kissing her hand and slipping the ring onto her finger.

"Everything will be as it ought to be. Look at the excitement of everyone here." He used his chin to indicate their family. "You know how Rebecca will react. My aunts will have our wedding planned before dinner is over, and Lord Romsley already requested my presence for a private conversation."

"He has?"

"We do not need his permission to marry, but there are settlement papers to draw up, and who better to represent you?"

She looked embarrassed and chuckled to cover it. "I did not consider such a practicality."

"Speaking of paternal figures, I should write to Mr Bennet."

Elizabeth's hand flew to her mouth, and she managed to

muffle a bark of laughter. "You cannot think he would bother himself about the news one way or the other. I have hardly thought about it, but I could tell Mrs Gardiner when I call on her. She can inform the Bennets."

"I care not for Mr Bennet's opinion. Nevertheless, I should be the one to tell him. Perhaps I shall go so far as to ask for his blessing."

He said the last in a teasing tone, and it had the desired effect. Elizabeth laughed.

"That *is* going very far indeed," she said.

His aunts called for their attention. Darcy took Elizabeth's hand, and they went to join them.

<hr />

The wedding was not planned in its entirety that evening, but Elizabeth and Darcy decided they wished to marry in Worcestershire. It was her particular request, and he immediately agreed.

Rebecca and Bramwell returned to town as planned, and early the morning after their arrival, Rebecca insisted on hearing every detail about Elizabeth's interview with Lady Anne and Darcy's proposal.

Once satisfied, she said, "I am elated. My cousin knows you will not tolerate any disrespect, and that is a good lesson for any man to learn."

Elizabeth smiled and nodded. She was putting her trust in Darcy to do just that. "Perhaps now that Lady Anne has admitted why she was always so reticent, and once she sees Darcy is happy, she will actually allow herself to like me. If she does, so much the better. If she does not, I will still have Darcy. What more could I want?"

After breakfast, Darcy called, and along with Fitzwilliam

and Bramwell, they sat in the drawing room together. Lady Anne had departed for Pemberley that morning, anxious to begin renovations to the dower house, so it was ready for her to occupy in the autumn.

"Has anyone heard from Lady Catherine?" Bramwell asked.

Darcy made a noise that showed his disgust. "Yes. Her letter to me was abusive, and I can only imagine the one to my mother was worse. Mother refused to talk about it."

Elizabeth expected nothing other than condemnation from Lady Catherine. "Was Lady Anne in good spirits when she left? She and her sister were very close. Her cruelty must have affected your mother greatly."

"Frankly, I hope she and Lady Catherine never see each other again. Lady Anne will be the better for it," Fitzwilliam said.

Darcy agreed. "Beyond that, I hope they cease all correspondence." In answer to Elizabeth's question, he added, "She seemed glad to be going into Derbyshire and full of plans for the dower house. I believe she intends to ask Lord and Lady Romsley about staying with them after the wedding."

They spoke about Brighton and Bath for a while before Elizabeth and Darcy went to sit in another corner of the room to speak privately. He held her hand and played with her ring. It felt soothing and captivating at the same time, and Elizabeth wished his fingers would slip up her arm, which she knew from recent experience would send delicious shivers throughout her body.

"What else have you to tell me, Mr Darcy? You did not lure me to this dark corner simply to hold my hand."

He pointedly looked around him, silently suggesting he would do more than that if they were alone. "My mother promised to make whatever arrangements she can to prepare the house for its new mistress."

That meant refreshing the mistress's apartment. It would be odd to make the transition from friends to married couple, though Elizabeth found the steps they had taken thus far felt remarkably natural.

"Anything else? Rebecca squeezed every last detail of the momentous day out of me." Elizabeth laughed. "Well, perhaps not every detail. Did my brothers demand such a recount?"

He smiled at her in a way that made her light-headed. So much had changed between them since they became engaged, and Elizabeth was determined to savour every minute of it.

"They did, and they both called me stupid for writing to Mr Bennet, but I still believe it was the right thing to do."

"I hardly know what to expect. It would not surprise me if it took weeks to receive a reply, *if* one ever arrives."

"If he chooses to wish us well, good. If he is too lazy to do so, it does not matter. Agreed?"

Elizabeth nodded and meant it. "I should write to Jane. I meant to do it yesterday. She will be hurt to hear the news from her father."

"My love, why do you care what she thinks?"

He spoke gently, but his question nevertheless stung.

"I do not know what to say. I told you weeks ago I glimpse a good person inside of Jane, and I hope it will gain the upper hand. If she marries Mr Bingley, we shall see her, and it would be better to be on good terms."

Darcy laced his fingers with hers. "I want you to always remember that *you* are my priority. I would regret losing Bingley's friendship, but if he marries Miss Bennet and seeing them is disagreeable…" He lifted one shoulder. "We have other friends." He indicated the group on the other side of the room. "My cousins and others in Derbyshire, Worcestershire, and London. We would not have to tolerate Miss Bingley or the Hursts any longer."

"Oh well, with that incentive, perhaps you ought to throw Mr Bingley aside this minute." She poked his chest. "Do not make any hasty decisions out of some belief you must protect me from the world."

"Come along, you two," Bramwell called, as he waved them over. "We need to discuss the summer."

Elizabeth wrote to Jane the next morning. By coincidence, that afternoon brought a letter from Longbourn. In it, Jane announced her engagement to Mr Bingley. She expressed all the joy to be expected at such a time and said that she was glad that he had only proposed once she was in love with him. While she would have accepted him the previous autumn, it would have been for mercenary reasons, which Jane believed she would have grown to regret.

Elizabeth was not surprised to learn that Mr Bingley had decided to seek an estate in a county other than Hertfordshire or that Mrs Hurst and Miss Bingley were not pleased with their brother's intention to marry Jane. What did astonish Elizabeth was that Jane asked her to be a bridesmaid.

Elizabeth read the letter through twice before setting it aside. She wished the couple well but had no desire to attend Jane's nuptials or to act as her attendant.

She did not mention the letter to Darcy until the following day. By that time, she had a second one to show him. Mr Bennet had written to her.

Dear Elizabeth,
I was alarmed to receive a letter from Mr Darcy. I

feared you had suffered some misfortune, and he thought I should know of it. Instead, I find it contained very good news. I congratulate you and wish you every joy. I know of no one who deserves it more. Mr Darcy did not ask my permission, and were I another sort of man, I would take offence. But you are of age, and even were you not, I have little right to give or withhold consent. For what little it is worth, I offer you my blessing.

As you know, you are not the only lady celebrating the successful capture of a young man. From what I discern amongst the gibberish spoken around the house, Jane wants you here for her wedding. I believe she and Mrs Bennet argued about it. You should be flattered. I have rarely heard Jane contradict her mother, which is a shame. She is much more interesting when she does.

Do not come. Mrs Bennet and the younger girls would do everything possible to ensure the experience is horrendous. The news you are to wed such a wealthy gentleman will bring out their jealousy, and when they are not envious that you have such a grand future to look forward to, after having such a grand past to look back on, they will seek to use your prosperity to their own advantage. I have failed you in many ways, but I can at least attempt to shield you from such a fate.

I ought to have told you this long ago. It was not easy for me to send you away. My mother made a convincing argument, but I need not have agreed, and certainly not given in as easily as I did, for in truth, I put up little resistance. I should have done more to check Mrs Bennet. At the time, I felt I had little choice—to protect you and to do what I could to enable my wife to deliver a healthy heir. I was not successful at the last, though I console myself by knowing I achieved the former. I lost a daughter the day my mother took you away from Longbourn. I have only myself to blame.

You will stay in touch, I hope. Perhaps one day I shall make a long overdue visit to you. I promise that if I do, I will come alone.

    RB

"Two letters? You are popular," Darcy said when they met again in the drawing room.

"Very amusing. Let us see if you are laughing after you read them." Elizabeth gave them to him.

After finishing the letter from Jane, his eyebrows quirked up his forehead, but he said nothing. After reading the one from Mr Bennet, he tossed both letters aside.

"I am loath to agree with anything Mr Bennet says, but I concur about Miss Bennet's wedding. You cannot want to go."

"I have no desire ever to go to Longbourn again. What about Mr Bingley?"

"If he invites me, I shall decline. I cannot think he made a wise decision."

"But if they truly love each other…"

Darcy kissed her hand. "Do you believe love can conquer everything? Had my mother not said she would welcome you as my wife, would you have accepted me, even though, from what you lead me to believe, you love me?"

She pinched his arm. "Are you calling me a liar, sir?"

In a moment, she was laughing at him as he feigned injury and unsuccessfully attempted to extract a kiss from her to make him feel better.

"You are outrageous! Am I to kiss you when your aunt sits across the room?"

"If you were quick about it, she would not notice," he whispered.

"But is a quick kiss worth the risk of being caught in such an indecorous position?"

Darcy threw up his hands in defeat. "I hated seeing you at Longbourn. You were so dispirited. I dreamt about throwing you into the carriage and driving away as rapidly as possible."

"Tossing me around to get your way? What a charming image you create!"

He thanked her then sobered. "Should it ever become necessary for Mrs Bennet to rely on Bingley's support, I shall assist him, but only through him. I would not want her or any of the Miss Bennets to know, lest they attempt to make you feel you should be doing more for them."

It was Elizabeth's turn to thank him. She knew she could leave it to him to do what was right. She need not harbour any guilt about not feeling responsible to people who were, in a tenuous fashion, her family or resentment if she found herself offering them assistance, knowing they were unlikely to be grateful.

"Let us have done with the Bennets. The only one of that name I am interested in is you." He kissed her hand. "How much longer do you need to remain in town? I would like to leave for Romsley once you, my aunt, and uncle are prepared to travel."

Elizabeth said she was not certain. Their original arrangements had been altered, given the need to shop for wedding clothes and attend to other business such as the marriage contracts. They asked the countess for her opinion and decided to depart in a fortnight. They would remain in Worcestershire until the wedding. Then, by the end of August, a year after her unexpected hasty departure from Pemberley, Elizabeth would return to the estate as its new mistress.

Elizabeth wrote to congratulate Jane and decline the invitation to her wedding. That afternoon, she and Darcy promenaded in the park with a group of friends on what was the perfect early summer day. They were far from the only party walking at that hour, and the sound of voices talking and laughing, and of horse hooves clopping and carriage wheels on the gravel pathways, made it impossible to listen for birds or enjoy the peace that came with being surrounded by nature. It made Elizabeth anticipate being in the country even more.

She told Darcy that she intended to call on the Gardiners before leaving town, and he expressed a desire to meet them.

"Since you like them so much, I would be glad to know them. You say they do not resemble the Bennets."

"They do not."

"And I want to make sure you are correct."

"Doubting my intelligence? How ungallant of you!"

"I simply want to make sure they treat you as they ought."

The anxiety in his voice stopped her from teasing him further. Her arm was linked with his, and she tightened her hold for a moment.

"I had to go to Longbourn, Darcy. I shall not deny it was disagreeable, but now I know. I had long thought of it as my proper home and the Bennets as my true family. Being there allowed me to accept they are not."

"Your home is with me. We already share a family, and

one day, we will have another family, one centred around the two of us."

She sought to lighten the mood. "Are you not worried any daughter of mine might be like me? You will spend the first ten years of her life being pestered by every question that pops into her head, whether they are sensical or not. Do you remember when I was obsessed with understanding why trees were never blue?"

He smiled, and it made his eyes sparkle. "I would be elated to have such a child. You know, it was your never-ending quest for knowledge that first made my father notice you. It is a great thing to be curious and want to understand the world around you. The evil lies in denying people answers because of their sex or birth."

Elizabeth returned his smile. "How liberal-minded of you! Just like your father. He would be very proud of you."

"Stop saying such things in public, if you please, madam. It makes me want to kiss you."

She laughed loudly enough to draw the notice of a passing trio. Their censorious expressions only made both Elizabeth and Darcy laugh again.

＊ ✧✦✧ ＊

When they went to Gracechurch Street a few days later, Mr Gardiner awaited them with his wife. Darcy was surprised and pleased by the couple. Their position in life was not what he liked, but he was prepared to make an exception for them because everything he saw told him they were estimable people who, despite their short acquaintance with Elizabeth, cared for her and saw her as an important part of their family. They parted with promises to meet again at Pemberley.

THIRTY THREE

During the first few weeks in Worcestershire, the couple's chief occupations were to amuse themselves and finish preparations for the wedding and Elizabeth's removal to Derbyshire. Darcy delighted in seeing her happier than ever and flattered himself he had something to do with it. No doubt, her improved connexions with Lord and Lady Romsley contributed to her mood as well. She was easier with them and they with her than he recalled seeing before.

His uncle spoke to him about his regret for not having taken more time with Elizabeth sooner. Darcy reassured him he had it now, even though she would soon be his wife and not the earl's ward. After all, Pemberley and Romsley Hall were separated by a mere fifty miles of good road, and their family would always be welcomed to visit—as long as it was not too soon after he finally made her Mrs Darcy.

The morning of his mother's arrival, a week before the wedding, he asked Elizabeth if she was nervous about seeing her again.

"Perhaps a little, but I choose to be hopeful. Lady Anne said everything will be well, and since I know she made that promise because of her love for you, I trust she will keep it."

His feelings must have shown because she said, "You have to stop being so angry with her. From what she told us, she had reasons for how she acted. I do not say they were good ones—far from it—but they were important to her. She appears determined to set them aside. The least we can do for familial harmony, if nothing else, is do the same. Let us judge her by how she acts now, not how she acted in the past."

Darcy promised to try, but only after she kissed him.

⁂

It was just after four o'clock when Lady Anne arrived. Everyone was in the drawing room, awaiting her. The tall windows were opened, and a light breeze carried in the scent of flowers from the garden. Lady Romsley had ordered refreshments, which Bramwell and Fitzwilliam particularly were enjoying.

When Lady Anne entered the drawing room, Elizabeth would be lying if she said she was not anxious. Lady Anne's antipathy for her was well-established and might require a longer period to correct.

"Mother, I trust you are well." Darcy dutifully kissed her proffered cheek.

"I am, thank you."

The air in the room thickened as everyone watched to see how she and Lady Anne would interact. Elizabeth curtseyed, and Lady Anne managed a small smile.

Lady Romsley said, "Anne, pray sit down. You will want something to drink after your journey. There is lemonade, or I could send for tea, if you prefer."

"I would enjoy a glass of lemonade," Lady Anne said.

To Elizabeth's surprise—and that of their companions, if their expressions could be believed—Lady Anne took a place beside Elizabeth, rather than the one the countess indicated. They and Darcy spoke about her drive to Romsley Hall and other commonplaces for a few minutes. Her manner was stilted, but it was apparent she was trying her best to be agreeable.

Elizabeth appreciated it and wished she knew how to tell Lady Anne without causing awkwardness. She wanted to make everything easier for her but knew that, too, was impossible. While she would always wish for more than a civil relationship with Lady Anne, she was mature enough to know she could not make it happen on her own, any more than she could repair her connexion with the Bennets without their willing participation. Knowing she had the unequivocal support of Darcy, to say nothing of her other loved ones, gave her added confidence.

Lady Anne turned to Elizabeth. "You must tell me about the preparations for your wedding. If I can assist in any way, I would like to offer my help."

"I have hardly had to do more than agree to whatever Lady Romsley suggests. It will not be an elaborate affair, as you know."

"We did not wish it," Darcy said, "especially so soon after Rebecca and Bramwell's wedding."

Lady Anne's eyes lingered on him. "Naturally, whatever makes you happy is enough for me." She turned to Elizabeth again. "I would like to go to my chamber in a few minutes, but perhaps after dinner, you will tell me about the arrangements. I would like to explain what I have done to make Pemberley ready for your arrival. It is not all that much, but I made some changes to the mistress's apartment, and I had the lilac sitting room prepared for your use. The view of the park is superior to the room I used, which I believe you will appreciate. Until you are prepared to make alterations of your own, I trust you will be comfortable."

"I am sure I shall. Pemberley has always been lovely, inside and out. Thank you, Lady Anne."

Elizabeth tried to imbue her words with extra meaning and hoped Lady Anne understood. When her expression seemed to soften, Elizabeth thought she had. Unless she imagined it, there was longing in her eyes, the same as Elizabeth saw the fateful day Lady Anne told her she gave her blessing to her and Darcy's union.

Our marriage, she thought, as Lady Anne exchanged a few words with the earl and countess. How strange it sounded. She remembered meeting Darcy for the first time. She was frightened, confused, and exhausted after the long journey north from Hertfordshire, and he stood by his father and offered her a brief smile. It had made her feel a little less alone.

Darcy is everything I could ever want in a gentleman. In just a week, he will be my husband. I love him, he loves me, and it is settled between us already that we are to be the happiest couple in the world.

⁓⁓⁓

When she awoke the morning of her wedding, Elizabeth threw open the window to breathe in the fresh air, the faint scent of grass and morning mist filling her nostrils, as she took in the serenity of the world around her. It would be a glorious day, and she could hardly wait to get on with it. Sometime later, she sat at the mirror in her bedchamber and dismissed Herriot, who had just finished dressing her hair. The other women, save Lady Anne, were there to help her prepare for the special occasion.

"Your gown is gorgeous," Rebecca said. "Perfect for a summer wedding."

It hung on a stand, and she ran her hand over the soft lace that covered a silk underdress. The lace had been a surprise gift from the Gardiners, who sent it soon after Elizabeth told them of her betrothal. She knew at once she would use it in her wedding dress. When the garment was finished, she sketched it and sent the picture to them. They were possibly the only people related to her by blood she would ever want to know.

Mrs Darcy said, "I can hardly believe both of you will be married ladies and within three months of each other!"

Lady Romsley smiled broadly and took in the young women. "It is hard not to remember them as little girls, running around Pemberley, giggling, and exploring everything there was to see. I could not be prouder to call them my daughters."

Elizabeth and Rebecca exchanged a look of fond amusement.

There was a knock at the door, and more than one person was surprised to discover it was Lady Anne. Since her arrival, her manner had been restrained, but free of even a hint of disapproval or imperiousness, and Elizabeth was satisfied.

"I came to see how you are progressing," she said. "Darcy went for a short walk before he and the gentlemen leave for the church. My brother awaits you downstairs."

"Please, join us," Elizabeth said. "I shall be ready presently."

Lady Anne nodded and sat on the edge of the bed, clasping a flat box in her hands.

"Elizabeth," Rebecca called to draw her attention. She held the gown in her hands, prepared to slip it over Elizabeth's head. Soon, it was on, the long buttons that ran down the back fastened, and a delicate blue ribbon tied around her ribs.

Lady Romsley said, "Oh, how beautiful you look!" while Mrs Darcy sighed.

Anxious for her response, Elizabeth watched Lady Anne and was gratified by the unmistakable approval in her eyes.

"I should have given you this before," Lady Anne said, handing the box that contained a pearl necklace to Elizabeth. "You need not wear it today if you would rather not. My father gave it to me at my wedding."

The countess said, "I remember. It is very generous of you, Anne."

Elizabeth had intended to wear the necklace the earl and countess gave her for her last birthday, but she decided to wear this one instead. She took it from the box, which she passed to Rebecca, and to Lady Anne she asked, "Will you help me?"

Lady Anne nodded. Elizabeth stepped towards her and turned around to allow her to attach the gold clasp. There was a gentle caress on her shoulders as Lady Anne said, "You are everything a bride should be, and my son will be very pleased when he sees you."

Elizabeth faced her and offered a smile. After she donned her bonnet, decorated with a veil and fresh flowers, they went to find the earl.

⁕ ⳺⳺ ⁕

Darcy stood at the front of the church waiting for Elizabeth's arrival. His mother, aunts, and Rebecca had just entered, signalling that she and Lord Romsley could not be far behind. The heat of the morning and his nerves made beads of sweat drip down his back. The prospect of soon being a husband, possibly a father within the year, was daunting, but he did not doubt his desire to marry Elizabeth. Fitzwilliam and the vicar stood at either side of him. Darcy's eyes drifted over the many people from the parish who had come to witness the ceremony, most especially his family. His mother gave him a reassuring smile.

Elizabeth entered on Lord Romsley's arm. She looked beautiful and joyful, with a broad grin on her face and a bouquet full of purple, yellow, and white flowers in her hands.

My Elizabeth. Forevermore mine to love, to protect, to treasure.

Before he knew it, and with just a dream-like memory of hearing her say the fateful words that bound them together, they were married and receiving congratulations as they walked out of the church into the sunlight and to the waiting open carriage.

As he helped her step up, Elizabeth said, "I wish we could walk."

He chuckled as the carriage began to move. "I knew you would say that, but it is not a very romantic thing to say to your new husband."

Her laughter tickled his ears. "My apologies, Mr Darcy. Shall I instead tell you how handsome you are, and I adore and love you and wanted to throw my arms into the air and jump up and down with glee when the vicar announced we are man and wife?"

He leant down, and placed a quick kiss on her lips. If they were not in an open carriage, he would have done the job properly. "Much better, Mrs Darcy."

She sighed contentedly and rested her head against him, and he wrapped his arm across her shoulders. "I believe I shall very quickly grow accustomed to being called Mrs Darcy. It has a certain quality to it, does it not?"

"A most excellent one," he agreed.

They passed most of the short drive in silence. For his part, Darcy was glad to have her to himself for once. The past days had been very busy, and everyone seemed to required Elizabeth's assistance or simply wanted to spend time with her, telling him he would have his turn after the wedding. They still had the breakfast to get through, and although he was looking forward to it—their wedding deserved to be celebrated—he anticipated the delight of being able to take Elizabeth home.

~ ⌇₀⌇ ~

All day Elizabeth felt as though there were a hot air balloon inside her belly making her float several inches above the ground. How much had changed since last summer! The dreadful months at Longbourn had done her good, she reflected as she walked around the drawing room greeting people. Having experienced life amongst the Bennets, it was easy to acknowledge the Darcys and Fitzwilliams loved her and saw her as part of their family, even before her wedding day. She also had the Gardiners, who would be her dear friends if not more, and she did not deny the possibility of a relationship of sorts with Jane or Mr Bennet in the future.

Elizabeth had yet to hear from Jane since declining the invitation to her wedding, but a letter from Mr Bennet arrived the day before again wishing her joy. She was pleased he remembered the date and took the time to write.

Romsley Hall was full of people. It seemed everyone in the neighbourhood was invited to celebrate the occasion, and she could not fault Lord and Lady Romsley's desire to display their pleasure at the union of their ward and nephew. The French doors to the terrace were open, making it easy for people to wander outside and explore the gardens. Games were set up on the lawn to keep the children amused, and Fitzwilliam and Bramwell appeared content amongst them.

Servants passed trays of cool drinks, and a breakfast was laid out inside.

Lady Anne gave every appearance of being content with the day and accepted congratulations on her son's marriage with grace. Elizabeth was proud of her and very grateful. It added to her pleasure of the day, but more importantly, it allowed Darcy to fully enjoy himself.

Before she knew it, it was time to depart if they wished to reach Pemberley before nightfall. Rebecca helped her change into her travelling costume, Herriot and Darcy's valet having gone ahead.

Elizabeth's eyes filled with tears as she said fond farewells to her family, even though she would see them in October when they would be her and Darcy's first guests at Pemberley as a married couple.

⁓

As their coach approached Pemberley, Elizabeth asked, "Can we walk from the knoll where the road turns down, the one before the bridge? We made good time, and the sun will not set for a while still."

"If you wish it, my love."

When they reached the spot, Darcy had the carriage stopped so they could climb down.

The estate looked particularly magnificent as they crossed the footbridge over the stream, its banks full of wildflowers. The trees were lush, the lawn deep green, and the gardens awash in colour. There was a certain quality in the air he could never name, but Darcy was certain he would be able to recognise Pemberley by scent alone.

They were greeted at the door by the butler and housekeeper, who offered their congratulations. Darcy dismissed them and said to Elizabeth, "Let us go to the sitting room my mother mentioned—the one she thought you would like to use as your own."

Elizabeth's brow creased. "*That* is the first thing you wish to do after arriving home?"

He tried to appear nonchalant and shrugged. "Her description made me curious, that is all. Come along, Mrs Darcy." He took her hand to lead her to the staircase.

No sooner had they entered the room than he heard an unmistakable squeaking sound. Elizabeth's eyes widened, and her gaze flew around the space, to him, and then to Freya, who lay beside the empty fireplace on a cushion designed for her large body.

"What is making that noise?"

"I cannot imagine." He directed her to a settee. "Stay there, and I shall investigate."

"Darcy..."

Her tone suggested she knew he was up to mischief, but he was confident she would approve once she understood. He retrieved a covered basket from beside the desk. It shook as he lifted it, and he murmured soothing words as he carried it to her.

"What have you done?" Once the basket was on her lap, she opened it to find a pair of kittens, one silvery grey and the other pure white. Elizabeth exclaimed in delight.

"I promised I would do anything to make you happy, and it is a vow I intend to keep—even though it means sharing you with a cat or two."

Elizabeth lifted the small, furry creatures out of the basket, which he removed and set on the floor before sitting beside her. As much as he preferred dogs, the way the kittens squirmed and mewled as they crawled over her chest was enchanting. His darling Elizabeth giggled and kissed their little heads, which made *her* enchanting and a great deal more.

Freya climbed off her cushion. She sniffed the kittens just as one let out a particularly shrill miaow. The Great Dane recoiled as though afraid, and Darcy reassured her until, with a little encouragement, she agreed to meet the first additions to his and Elizabeth's new family.

Soon enough, the kittens grew tired, and Elizabeth returned them to their basket. "What do I do with them? I did not intend to spend this evening occupied with kittens, as adorable as they are."

"Herriot will care for them. I talked to her about it yesterday. She was so excited, I am shocked she did not tell you."

Elizabeth caressed his cheek. "Have I thanked you yet?" He shook his head. "It was a very sweet gesture, and it only proves I made the right decision by falling madly in love with you. Not all men would know I would value a pair of kittens more than a pair of earrings as a wedding gift."

Darcy kissed her, pulling her body close to his. Her lips were soft and warm, and he never wanted to let her go. She apparently had other ideas and, to his disappointment, pulled away from him.

Her eyes locked on his. "Now that I have seen this room, I believe you want to show me my bedchamber next."

A broad grin covered his face. "I do. I very, very much do."

Her cheeks rosy, Elizabeth kissed him. "And I very, *very* much want you to."

EPILOGUE

Two years later

I t was late August, and the family was gathered at Pemberley. Since the day was fair, with a few clouds and a breeze to keep the heat moderate, they decided to have a picnic by the lake. Elizabeth and Darcy sat on blankets with their nine-month-old son, Hugh James. Rebecca and Bramwell were across from them, watching their year-old twins, Frederick William and Philip Thomas. All five grandparents sat on chairs around them and spoke in quiet tones. Fitzwilliam and his wife of three months, Anna Maria, returned from a walk in the grove and joined in the delight of watching the next generation of cousins playing and no doubt fast on their way to being best friends and allies.

Fitzwilliam's wife was the former Miss Genova. The couple had become reacquainted two winters prior, and although it took them quite a while to realise it, they were deeply in love and perfectly matched. Anna Maria was lovely, and Elizabeth could not imagine a better sister-in-law—apart from Rebecca, naturally. Elizabeth remembered once seeing Darcy dance with Anna Maria and him speaking warmly of her afterwards. How terribly jealous Elizabeth had been!

"How do you find your first family party at Pemberley, Anna Maria?" Elizabeth asked.

"It is wonderful. Even better than Fitzwilliam said it would be. Perhaps before too long, we shall add our own little one and make this time all together even more special."

Lady Anne said, "I hope one of you has a girl. I seem to recall the presence of a girl or two amongst them did those three a world of good." Her finger drew a line from Darcy to Bramwell to Fitzwilliam.

Lord Romsley laughed. "So it did, dear sister, so it did."

Over the previous two years, Elizabeth's relationship with Lady Anne had improved, especially once Elizabeth was shrewd enough to present Darcy with an heir. Lady Anne continued to spend part of the year in Bath, where she had made many friends. She visited her childhood home for several months each spring and had grown closer to her brother and sister-in-law. She never visited Rosings Park, and as far as Elizabeth knew, no longer wrote to Lady Catherine. Every summer, Lady Anne spent three or four months at Pemberley. If she was still afraid for her son, it did not show, and Elizabeth hoped such sentiments were a thing of the past.

The Gardiners had visited Pemberley earlier that summer, bringing their children with them. It was an agreeable visit, and one she and Darcy hoped to repeat in the future. Jane and Mr Bingley were settled in Surrey and showed every evidence of being content. Elizabeth was relieved to find Jane improved now that she was removed from Mrs Bennet's influence. Even so, they had not become particular friends, and she did not believe they ever would.

Elizabeth and Mr Bennet kept a frequent correspondence, and he talked about coming to see her. He went so far as to name a date in October by which they could expect him. He claimed he wished to meet his grandson and see the place his second daughter called home and, if it could be arranged, go to Romsley Hall, where he had sent her so long ago. He wanted to thank the earl and countess in person for being the family she had needed. Elizabeth refused to believe he would come until he was actually there. Through their letters, she had begun to recognise the father she remembered from before she went to live with the dowager Lady Romsley, though she did not know what it would be like when—*if*—they were together. Whatever happened, whether he made the effort to visit or not, she would not let it injure her. He was a distant relation, someone it was pleasant to hear from now and again, but one not missed when apart. The people who truly mattered were gathered around her.

Hugh, in a sure sign he was ready for a nap, began to rub his eyes and cry a little. Before Elizabeth could pick him up, little Frederick toddled over to him, patted his back, and said, "Baby," while little Philip held out a doll to him. As one, the adults laughed, and Rebecca told her boys how wonderful they were to their younger cousin.

Elizabeth reflected, as she so often did, that there was nothing better than to be surrounded by one's beloved family and know you belonged.

GET A FREE BOOK!

Receive a free ebook when you sign up for the publisher's newsletter! *For the Enjoyment of Reading* contains short stories by Jan Ashton, Julie Cooper, Amy D'Orazio, Linda Gonschior, Lucy Marin, and Mary Smythe. Its yours, free, for signing up for the Quills & Quartos Newsletter HERE.

ACKNOWLEDGMENTS

In addition to my family, the online Jane Austen community gave me the inspiration I needed to keep writing during the difficult months of 2020 and 2021; thank you. The wonderful people at Quills & Quartos have my eternal gratitude for allowing me to attain my goal of calling myself a writer.

My thanks to Cyndy Henry and Anna Maria Genova—who appear in cameo form in *The Truth About Family*—for their generous donations to the JAFF for Ukraine Fundraiser held in March 2022.

ABOUT THE AUTHOR

Lucy Marin developed a love for reading at a young age and whiled away many hours imagining how stories might continue or what would happen if there was a change in the circumstances faced by the protagonists. After reading her first Austen novel, a lifelong ardent admiration was born. Lucy was introduced to the world of Austen variations after stumbling across one at a used bookstore while on holiday in London. This led to the discovery of the online world of Jane Austen Fan Fiction and, soon after, she picked up her pen and began to transfer the stories in her head to paper.

Lucy lives in Toronto, Canada, surrounded by hundreds of books and a loving family. She teaches environmental studies, loves animals and trees and exploring the world around her.

facebook.com/lucy.marin.355744

bookbub.com/authors/lucy-marin

amazon.com/Lucy-Marin/e/B085PX4VKJ

ALSO BY LUCY MARIN

Being Mrs Darcy

Christmas at Blackthorn Manor

Her Sisterly Love

The Marriage Bargain

Mr Darcy: A Man with a Plan

The Recovery of Fitzwilliam Darcy

COLLABORATIONS AND ANTHOLOGIES

Happily Ever After with Mr Darcy

'Tis the Season

Made in the USA
Monee, IL
08 January 2023